Only
on the
Radio

D1711777

Only
on the
Radio

by

Jean Ann Geist

Eli Kenoah Enterprises
Bowling Green, Ohio

This is a work of fiction. Names, characters, places, and incidents are products of the author's imagination or are used fictitiously.

Copyright 2013 by Jean Ann Geist

ISBN: 978-0-9891720-0-4

Cover watercolor by Sascha Instone

Book Design by Laura Tolkow

Printed in the United States of America
by Lightning Source Inc.

Dedicated to

Theresa and Louis Wannemacher

Mom and Dad

Still a farm girl at heart

What Could Be ...

The girl sat, legs dangling
Off the oak plank bridge
Hair trailing her shoulders

As the sun's afterglow
Silhouetted silos
On the neighbor's farm

She drifted from the now
Past the farm, over the horizon
Into possibility.

PROLOGUE

The script neon sign flickered *Tia's Taverna* above the heavy entrance door Liz McAlister tugged open against gusts of wind from an early spring storm. The door slammed at her back as her eyes adjusted to the bar's dim interior. All movement within the tavern seemed to stop, as one patron after another looked toward the newcomer.

With her chin up and gaze forward, Liz made her way to the rear of the room, sliding into an empty booth near the pool table. Her skirt caught on the cracked red vinyl of the seat as she scooted across it.

She knew she stood out among the bar's customers—not only *was* she a woman alone, she obviously was *not* Latina. It was as though she had stepped into a foreign land—a place where she could lose her identity, if but for a night.

Prior to this evening, she had never set foot in a bar. Had never drunk alcohol beyond an occasional glass of wine. Had never attempted to seduce a stranger.

But that was before the accident. Before God or fate or whoever turned her stable life upside down. She had visited the hospice where Mack lay dying, day by day, wasting away until only a whisper of his former self remained … until there was nothing left but an empty shell.

She had been the one to have the tubes removed, have the

breathing devices turned off. She had been the one to finally end the life of her first and only love, and on this, the second anniversary of that cruel twist of fate, anguish—and anger—welled within her anew. And she wanted to quell it once and for all—wanted to fill the hollow void within her with something stronger than platitudes and pity.

David Morales racked the billiard balls in their plastic triangle form. He balanced his cigarette along the chipped frame of the battered pool table and lined up the ball for the break. His gaze followed the shaft of his cue stick, catching a swish of material over nicely rounded feminine hips. He drew his head up to assess the woman sliding into the booth on the opposite side of the green felt table.

"Hey, *amigo*, you playin' or watchin'?" Hector Gonzales' taunts dragged David's attention back to the game at hand. He knew he should grab his hat and vamoose pronto, but he felt the familiar pull of the *gringa* woman. What was it about their creamy white skin he found irresistible? And this one actually had more flesh than bones. He liked his women with ample curves to knead and caress. That's what had gotten him into trouble before—and had cost him nearly two years of his life.

David rested his cue stick against the edge of the table and picked up his cigarette. He flicked the ashes into his hand and looked around for a receptacle to dump them in, settling for an empty plastic glass. As an afterthought, he snubbed the cigarette into the bottom of the cup and brushed his hands together to rid them of the ash residue, all the while eyeing the woman sitting alone in the booth.

He sauntered to her table and leaned against the back of the bench opposite where she sat. She glanced up at him with an assessing candor, before dropping her gaze to the scarred coating of polyurethane on the tabletop.

Violeta … her eyes were actually the color of the small purple flowers popping up everywhere this time of year. Short dark curly hair framed an oval face. A *gringa*—an untouchable—he reminded himself. The forbidden fruit.

But, ah, what fruit—a pleasantly rounded peach. *Nosiree, no skinny fashion-model types for him.* He figured her to be in her mid to late forties—around his age, give or take. Her breasts hung full, ripe, and heavy against the filmy material of her top. But her eyes, her eyes caught his attention and made him wonder where they had met before—those violet eyes with long, black lashes fluttering against her powder white skin.

"You want somethin' to drink, *gringa* lady?"

Liz took a deep breath. It was now or never. This was what she wanted—what she needed. She perused the man who stood before her. He was apparently Latino. Good. That made him more appealing. More taboo, especially for a McAlister. She wanted—needed to break taboos. Needed to free herself from this suffocating nothingness.

She flinched slightly at the inked snake coiled around his left bicep below the cut-off sleeve of his sweatshirt. His right arm bore a dragon's head and shoulders. She saw the creature's tail wrap around his forearm. Tattoos. Another taboo. Perfect. She looked up into piercing black eyes and swallowed. *Dangerous!* The word popped into her head and bounced around. But her more elemental instincts ignored the warning.

"Tequila sunrise?" She replied with the name of the first drink she could think of containing the potent Mexican liquor. He nodded and walked toward the bar. Liz took a deep breath and let it out with a shudder. There was no turning back now.

"David Morales, what are you doin' messin' around with a *gringa*? *¿You no comprendes? Ella es muy mala, muy mala ...*" The portly woman tending the bar chided him as he ordered the cocktail and a non-alcoholic beer for himself. Though not David's aunt by birth, "*Tía*" Juana treated him like a nephew nonetheless, reserving the right to try to rein in his reckless nature.

"It's okay. I know what I'm doing."

"Yeah, right, you are like all men—ruled by that t'ing that hangs between your legs. When you going to learn *gringas* are trouble?"

"How about Cassie? She's a *gringa*, and there's nothing you wouldn't do for her. You think the sun comes up in the morning and sets in the evening because she says so."

"You leave Cassandra and my Jaime out of this. That *gringa* woman over there, she's no Cassie Alvarez. She's bad news—*muy mal*—bery bad news. It's her kind that put you in the ..."

David dropped a ten-dollar bill on the counter and picked up their drinks, sloshing the *gringa's* cocktail onto the bar in his rush to turn his back on his *tía's* warning.

He sat the tequila sunrise in front of the lady, taking advantage of his position to scope out the ample slopes of her breasts as they disappeared under the loose curve of her low-riding neckline. He drew the rim of his O'Doul's bottle to his lips and swallowed a chilling draught of the amber liquid before sliding into the booth across from her.

Damn! He tried to remember the last time he had been with a woman ... The need to have her washed over him.

Liz took a sip of her drink, letting the fiery liquid coat her throat. She took another swallow, this time tipping the glass further, hoping the alcohol would ease her nerves. She leaned forward, allowing her top to gap slightly and was rewarded by dark eyes searing her breasts.

She licked her lips and smiled at the man across from her, "Hi, I'm ... Mary ... Mary McKenna ..." Liz wasn't sure why, at the last moment, she chose to say her given name—the one she used rarely—along with her maiden name. Anonymity, perhaps, added to the lurid mystique of the evening.

His lips curled into a half-smile, as though he knew she had lied ... knew, but didn't care. He fingered the smooth glass of his bottle, before bringing it to his mouth and taking a long draught. He sat the O'Doul's back on the table and swallowed.

Liz focused on his lips—full, strong, sensual—and wondered what it would be like to kiss them. To be kissed by them. To feel them pulling at her breast. A heat suffused throughout her body, settling on her intimate parts, and she gulped the rest of her drink to mitigate the warmth.

His knowing smile returned, and with a cat-like grace, he eased out of the booth, soon returning with another round of drinks.

If she didn't outright lie about her name, she sure enough evaded the truth, David was certain of that—her hesitancy and telltale blush said as much. *Well, two can play that game.*

"You can call me Juan. If you want a last name, Moreno or Perez or Smith will do."

She flashed a smile, "But none of those are your real name, are they?"

"No more than you're Mary McKenna. But Juan and Mary, they're good, anonymous names. Let's go with them, whaddya say, *gringa* lady?"

She let out a quiet laugh and nodded. She sipped her drink, and when she sat it back on the table, he took her hand in his. Electricity hummed between them, and he felt the jolt travel through his body.

"I see a long life line," he said as he traced a crease across her palm, "but a love line cut short …"

She yanked her hand from his and turned it palm down on the table. The hurt he saw in her eyes shamed his inadvertent cruelty.

"*Lo siento mucho*—I am very sorry."

"It's … it's okay." She turned her hand over and looked at it. "How did you know?"

"The white band and indentation around your ring finger—you've worn a wedding ring for a long time and have just recently removed it."

"You're very perceptive, Juan Moreno Perez Smith," she smiled again, "but this is not the night for remembrances. This is the night for forgetting …"

"I have much to forget as well. One cannot have lived as many years as I and not have much to forget." He raised his O'Doul's in a toast, "So here's to forgetting—together." She clinked her glass against his bottle and downed the remainder of her drink. She studied his face, his voice sounded almost familiar—it had a smooth, sandy quality, deep and mellifluous ...

Before she could place it, he asked, "Another?"

"I don't believe I've had enough to forget all I need to ..."

He nodded, gathered up their empties, and walked toward the bar.

The third drink went down as easily as the first two, and when Liz stood to walk to the Ladies Room, she felt just a little wobbly. She smiled at the men playing pool, knowing they watched her as she strolled by. She was succeeding in shedding her image as a dowdy, middle-aged farmwife ... a pain shot through her heart as she mentally corrected herself ... widow, if only for an evening.

When she returned to the booth, a fourth sunrise awaited her. She hesitated, trying to steady herself. The room blurred, like the lights on a Christmas tree through a frosted window. She smiled at the analogy—and at the man across from her.

She had memorized his face over the course of the evening—a scar had marred his fine-shaped brow above the right eye. He had an aquiline nose and a strong jaw line. A neatly sculpted mustache connected to a close-trimmed beard by a pencil-thin line. His hair was long and full, pulled back in a wavy ponytail. But, his lips ... his lips had captivated her attention for most of the evening.

"*Besame, besame mucho* ..." he sang softly along with the radio playing from an overhead speaker. She had to lean forward to hear his voice and his fingers lightly caressed her hand as the song segued into the next. They finished their drinks in silence, each contemplating the night ahead.

"Shall we find someplace a little more ... private?" He asked.

She nodded.

David knew she had drunk too much. Knew he should call his sister, Anita and her man, Windy, or Cassie and Jaime, to take care of the *gringa*. However, she had bewitched him, and under the spell of her *violeta* eyes, he was powerless to let her go.

He avoided looking at *Tía* Juana as they hurried past the bar and out into the night. A driving rain forced them back against the tavern door.

"Wait here and I'll get my truck."

He half expected her to bolt into the darkness, but she was standing where he had left her when he pulled his battered pickup to the entrance.

He jumped out, opened the door for her, and helped her step up on the running board. He shoved a tool belt aside so she could sit down on the frayed cloth seat.

"Sorry, the Mercedes is in the shop," he quipped as he reached across her to grab her seat belt and secure it at her side.

She looked around at the pickup's interior and gave a hint of a laugh. "Does it turn into a pumpkin at midnight?" Her words came out slightly slurred, causing her to giggle and clasp her hand over her mouth.

He cast her a sidelong glance as he shifted the truck into gear. "That what you think I am, *gringa* lady? Your prince?" He pulled slowly out onto the road, "Because I can be real charming, when I want to." He massaged the top of her thighs through the thin wet material of her skirt.

"Mmmm … my dark prince …" she purred.

Reason vied with hormones as David drove slowly through the Lower Eastside neighborhood. With a sigh, he asked, "Where do you live, Mary McKenna, and I'll drive you home."

"Home? No! Not there … not tonight! Please, not tonight!"

He took her hand in his and rested their clasped fingers on his leg.

"Okay, *gringa* lady, you win. But, I just hope you don't regret this in the morning." He added with resignation, "I hope we both don't …"

He pulled the truck in beside a small, rundown house trailer. "Welcome to my castle," he said. Releasing her hand, he clicked off the ignition, then reached down and unclasped their seatbelts. He put his arm around her shoulders and drew her to him.

His mouth covered hers, tasting tequila and the sweetness of her lips. He let his empty hand wander to her breast and held its fullness in his palm. She sighed and leaned into his caress as he kneaded her taut nipple between his thumb and forefinger. He pulled back, knowing he had crossed the threshold from which there was no return.

"I think I'm going to be sick!" Liz pulled away from their embrace and clasped her left hand against her mouth while searching frantically for the door handle with her right. David leaned back, gulped the air between them to settle the cadence of his heart, and pushed his door open, hurrying around the hood to get to her. He helped her out of the truck as she turned her head and retched against its side. She dropped to the ground, and with the rain pouring against her slouched back, heaved the contents of her stomach onto the stone driveway.

He grabbed an old blue jeans jacket from behind the seat of the truck and gently draped it over her shoulders. At last she stopped convulsing and wiped her hand across her mouth. She tried to hide her face in her hands as she scrambled to her feet. He grasped her shoulders and pulled her to his side, half dragging her into the trailer and out of the torrential downpour.

He sat her down on the couch, quickly retrieved a towel from the bathroom, and gently dried her face. He peeled her top up over her head, hesitating only a second as he exposed the sensible white cotton bra clinging to her breasts. She sank against him like a rag doll as he tugged her to her feet to inch her dripping skirt over her hips.

He toweled her as dry as possible, giving up and reaching behind her to undo the clasp on her brassiere, drawing the saturated fabric from her skin. He pulled a woven blanket from the back of the couch and wrapped it around her. Still she kept her eyes averted from his face.

He held her to his side and steered her to his bedroom. He

stood her at the edge of the bed and removed the blanket, but before he let her sink down onto the mattress, he nudged her one last item of clothing down her legs and onto the floor. He pulled back the coverlet and top sheet and lowered her onto the bed. He gently covered her body, not allowing himself the liberty of enjoying her nakedness.

He wet a washcloth in the bathroom and wiped her face before offering her a drink of water. She leaned up, accepted the glass, and rinsed her mouth, then dropped down onto his pillow. He tucked the coverlet under her chin and backed out of the room.

David gathered her wet clothing and hung it around the trailer to dry. If ever he needed a stiff drink, now was the time. But he had given up alcohol—at the same time he had sworn off *gringa* women. He chastised himself for getting into his current predicament. What if, when this Mary McKenna, or whoever she was, woke in the morning, she accused him of ... of ... taking advantage of her or worse? He could find himself back in the slammer! What had he done? *What had he done!*

Liz opened her eyes. Light streamed in through the window as she tried to remember where she was—and how she had gotten there. She raised her throbbing head only to let it fall back on the pillow. Her arm brushed against her bare breast and she quickly lifted the coverlet above her head. She peeked down under the sheet—*Naked!* She dropped the blankets, only to lift them again—naked as the day she was born!

Liz glanced toward the window and saw a man silhouetted against the light. His shirtless back was to her. A lean, muscled torso drew her gaze downward to Levi jeans slung low on his hips. Well-defined biceps bulged as he leaned against the sill, an unlit cigarette dangling from between his fingers.

What had she done? Details of the prior evening came swimming back to her in bits and pieces ending with her retching beside his—this Juan's, or whoever he was—pickup truck. She covered her head in abject embarrassment, only to remind herself she was still buck-naked.

She tried to remember if they had had sex. Surely she would remember such a thing! It had been over two-and-a-half years since a man had touched her in *that* way. *Surely she would remember!*

As though he sensed her watching him, he turned toward her. The fastener of his jeans lay undone, and she focused on the line of dark hair trailing down from his navel and disappearing under a white band of elastic. His naturally bronzed skin gleamed in the light as nearly black eyes bore into her. She pulled the coverlet to her chin, shielding her body from his penetrating gaze.

"Where … where are my clothes?" she asked.

"Drying."

"How … how did …"

"They were soaked … and you were a bit … under the weather …"

"Oh my good Lord!"

"Yours and mine both, *gringa* lady …" He gave her a half-grin as he leaned against the windowsill.

"Did we … um … have … Did we make …"

"Did I screw you? Not that I recall and, Mary McKenna, that is one thing I am sure I would recall." He let his eyes roam the length of her body, visually stripping the blankets from her hands.

He sighed deeply, flipped the cigarette onto the floor, and strode from the room. When he returned, he tossed her clothes onto the bed.

"Shower's in there," he angled his head toward the hallway. "I put clean towels out. Help yourself to whatever you need."

A wave of disappointment washed over her as she heard the outer door of the trailer open and slam shut, followed by the rumble of his truck engine.

By the time she emerged from the shower, used his blow dryer in an attempt to force her hair into submission, and tried to repair her make-up with what she had stashed in her purse, her car had been parked in the driveway and his truck was gone.

CHAPTER ONE

"Hey, Gregg, your old lady just pulled in."

Gregg McAlister shifted to a sitting position on the couch. "Hell, I'd forgotten Mom was going to stop by this afternoon." He glanced around the room, then back at his roommate who stood by the picture window overlooking the parking lot. Before he could clear his head sufficiently to think about gathering up the empty beer cans and full ashtrays left from last night's impromptu party, he heard the familiar rap on his door.

Ian O'Flannery opened the door and greeted his friend's mother with his legendary devil-may-care grin in a shallow attempt to deflect her attention from their trashed apartment. However, Liz McAlister had grown immune to her son's roommate's charm, giving a half-hearted smile in return before peeking around his broad shoulders to see Gregg still sitting on the worn overstuffed sofa.

"Greggory! What in heaven's name went on here?"

The object of her dismay unfolded his tall, lean form, stood and stretched.

"Sorry, 'If I knew you were coming, I'd a baked …'"

"Don't get smart with me, young man. What would your father say?" The words tripped from her mouth before she could stop them. Though her son's longish, unkempt hair stood in haphazard sleep-formed spikes, where his father had worn his clipped in a disciplined crew cut, the resemblance between the two never failed to catch her breath.

"Dad would tell me to get my lazy ass off the couch, get this place cleaned up, and grow up. Is that what you wanted to say?"

Liz wasn't sure those would be Mack's words, but they summed up her thoughts. "I suppose you skipped your English lit class this morning? And are you ready for your biochem test tomorrow?"

"Jees, Ma, how did you remember I had a biochem test tomorrow when I've been trying my best to forget it?" He flashed her his father's grin, complete with the single dimple indenting his right cheek, as he took the paper grocery sack from her arms. "What'cha got for your favorite son?"

She swallowed hard. "It's just a few cans of beef from your Uncle Bill's cannery and some early lettuce, spinach, and green onions from the spring garden. I gathered a bunch of dandelion greens, too, if you remember how to fix them. I hope the lettuce and such isn't too wilted; I stopped for lunch on the way here."

She paused and looked around the room, "I thought about calling you to join me, but ..."

"I know, I was supposed to be in class. Sorry, Mom. I'll study for the test tomorrow, I promise." She didn't see Ian O'Flannery raise his eyebrows and smirk behind her back.

Liz heaved a maternal sigh as her son shoved empty beer cans aside to put the bag of groceries on the coffee table. He stepped up beside her and slipped his arm around her shoulder, "I miss him, too, every day."

She looked up to the young man at her side. At twenty-one he towered over her by a good eight inches. "It was two years ago Friday..."

"I know, Mom, I know ..." He mentally finished her thought ... *since she had pulled the plug on his dad.*

They walked to the door together. He leaned down to kiss her cheek and receive her hug before she turned and hurried down the outdoor walkway from his second-floor apartment to the stairwell at the end of the building.

As Gregg closed the door, he caught his roommate grinning from the hallway, "Dude, unless you want me to mop the floor with that red hair of yours, you'll refrain from making faces behind my mom's back."

He turned to the window to watch her pull out of her parking space, longing for the day she could look at him and not see the ghost of his father.

Mallory Martin checked her cell phone messages as she walked to her apartment. *Mom ... Tyler ... Tyler—again ... drat, Tyler, give it up! ... Greggory McAlister?* The name sounded familiar, but she couldn't put a face with it. She punched in the number from the message with her thumb as she inserted the key in her apartment door. It swung open—obviously neither locked nor even latched, as a sexy male voice carried through her phone receiver.

"McAlister here. How's it doin'?"

"Mr. McAlister? This is Mallory Martin returning your call."

"Yeah? Hey, are you the redheaded chick who sits in front me in Sweeney's biochem class?"

"If you're the inconsiderate heathen who interrupts class by strolling in whenever he chooses to wake up in the morning, that is *when* he chooses to come to class at all, then I guess I am that ... chick." An instant photo flashed into Mallory's mind—tall, light brown hair with, unless she missed her guess, natural blonde streaks, smoky gray bedroom eyes and a dimple. She had noticed him.

"Ah, yeah, I guess that would be me." He waited just a beat, *"So, maybe this isn't a good time to ask, but I'm having a little trouble understanding the stuff Sweeney covered from the last chapter of the book ..."*

"Could that be because you haven't read the last chapter in the book?"

"Hey, that hurts! Of course, I read the book ..." or had tried to read it through blurry eyes after his mom had left a few hours ago. He knew he was being unfair calling a virtual stranger for tutoring

the day before the test, but if he bombed the exam he could end up failing the class. And there would be hell to pay at home.

"I'd like to help you, Mr. McAlister ..."

"Call me Gregg ..."

"I'd like to help, *Mister* McAlister, but I am busy studying for the test myself. Something I've been doing for the past week. I suggest you hang up and try it out ... but, be careful, it could be habit-forming." She hesitated only a moment before adding, "Nah, not likely in your case ... See you in class tomorrow. Oh, it starts at 10:30 ... that's in the a.m.!"

Mallory disconnected the call before he could respond. She laughed at her unexpected sense of exhilaration. She had actually enjoyed bantering with a guy! And, not just any guy, but the extraordinarily good-looking one who sat behind her in class! She wondered how he had gotten her name and number but put the thought aside as she called to the woman with whom she shared an apartment.

"Tiffany! Tiff are you here?"

"Quit your f'n yelling!" A man dressed only in boxers emerged from her roommate's bedroom, stretching, then simultaneously scratching his armpit and crotch.

"Is Tiffany in there?" Mallory glanced at the room behind him.

"That's her name? I was trying to remember. She had class or work or somethin'. Left at some ungodly hour of the morning. You got anything to eat around here?"

Liz stopped by the *Sentinel-Tribune* office to post an ad for her daughter's empty bedroom before leaving town. Tatiana had been nagging her to rent out the upstairs rooms of the rambling old farmhouse that had not long ago bulged at the seams with activity.

Tatiana was the first to leave home. Liz and Mack had driven their only daughter to the airport after finally acquiescing to her pleas to attend the Fashion Institute of Technology in New

York City. Now working with a designer in Paris, she had proven her talents—and had also convinced her mother she would not be returning home to live anytime soon.

Mack's accident had happened just after Gregg began his freshman year at Bowling Green State University. Though Mack had wanted their son to live at home while attending classes at the nearby college, Liz insisted he reside on campus. She then insisted he stay there after his father was moved to Heartland Hospice.

For over two years, Liz had rattled around alone in the large house that had been in her husband's family since his immigrant ancestors had helped clear Northwest Ohio's Great Black Swamp of its massive oaks and drained the wetlands into flat, fertile farmland. At first she needed the space. Needed to grieve without prying eyes. Needed time to sort through a flood of conflicting emotions. But after spending months of sleepless nights listening for footsteps on the stairs and being haunted by the silence, Liz had, at last, conceded that a boarder might not be such a bad idea.

As the spring semester at the university drew to a close, she thought she might find some students planning to attend summer classes. Although with all the apartment complexes being built near the campus, the likelihood of someone wanting to commute the distance to the farm seemed remote.

She flipped on the radio as she headed west on Route 6, touching the number for her favorite satellite channel. As she tapped the beat with her left foot to a Jimmy Buffett oldie, a sign alerted her to a flagman ahead.

Oh sugar snap! Had she remembered the bridge over Beaver Creek was under repair, she would have taken Poe Road. She pulled up to the man with the red flag, knowing, as the first vehicle in the line, she would likely be in for a long wait. As the oncoming traffic crawled slowly toward her, the flagman caught her attention.

Strong, muscular biceps flexed as he motioned for her to stop. A familiar tattoo snaked up and around his arm disappearing under the cut-off sleeve of his sweatshirt and neon yellow vest …

———

The tang of the mysterious *gringa's* lips had followed David Morales throughout the weekend. He cursed the weakness that had driven him to her table—and the strength that had planted him on his couch, tossing and turning through a sleepless night. He had spent Sunday hiking along the banks of the Maumee River, soaking in the still fresh sensations of freedom and trying to shake the lure of *violeta* eyes and lush milk-white breasts. But the *gringa* had infiltrated his essence leaving him restless at night and unsettled during his waking hours.

David waved the red flag signaling traffic to stop. He immediately recognized the classic red Mustang as it eased to within feet of where he stood. He watched the woman inside tighten her grip on the steering wheel and stiffen her back. Dark glasses hid her eyes from his as he paced the few steps to the door of her car.

She hesitated before lowering the window. He leaned against the roof of the car and bent down to look at her. She shifted her sunglasses to the tip of her nose, catching him off-guard with her stunning eyes.

"So we meet again." She took a deep breath, "I owe you a debt of gratitude, Mr. ... Smith ..."

"Not hardly, *gringa* lady, but I could think of a few ways to pay me back, if you really think so ..." he said in that satin smooth baritone. His gaze dropped to the fullness of her breasts as their contours heaved against a soft pastel sweater.

She pushed her sunglasses back into place, angled her head toward him, and laughed. "Another time ... another place, who knows what might have been."

He studied her, wanting to break through her veneer of anonymity. She licked her lips under his steady perusal, diverting his attention to her mouth.

"Can I call you?"

She gave her head a slight shake in reply.

They held each other's gaze for a moment longer before he stepped back from the car.

A late model BMW trailed the line of cars across the open

lane of the bridge as the woman directing the eastbound traffic gave the all-clear signal to David.

He tipped his hardhat to the *gringa*, laughing to himself as he waved the waiting vehicles across the open lane of the bridge. He would have to send old Lester Long a thank you note for demoting him to flagman for the day. He had crossed the arrogant foreman first thing that morning, and rather than fire David on the spot, the man had thought to "teach the *Mejicano* trash a lesson" by having him replace a flagger who had called in sick. Yes sir, he'd have to thank old Lester ...

As he motioned the traffic along, he searched the recesses of his mind, trying to remember where he had seen the woman with the violet eyes before *Tia's*—and wondering how he would be able to see her again. The crackle across his two-way radio brought his attention back to the job at hand, and he stepped forward to stop an oncoming eighteen-wheeler.

As the construction site disappeared in her rearview mirror, Liz tried to focus on the radio and the lyrics of Carole King's *Tapestry*—anything to shake the random memories that crowded her thoughts. She drove west through a blanket of fields—black patches of freshly turned earth beside bright green stretches of winter wheat. Through the years, Liz thought she had carefully stitched the pattern of her life, but now it seemed to be unraveling into the mismatched pieces of a patchwork quilt.

She crossed the county line and turned north toward town, remembering the overdue library book on her back seat she had intended to return last week. She skirted the Latino neighborhood, avoiding *Tia's Taverna* by taking the less direct river road along the Maumee.

She stopped at the grocery, mailed a bill at the post office, and filled up her gas tank before leaving town, dreading the hours ahead of her at the empty farmhouse.

The answering machine beeped as Liz carried an ancient

aluminum roasting pan filled with fresh-picked salad greens into the kitchen from the mudroom. She put the pan on the counter and walked to the phone.

"Hello, I'm calling about the ad you placed in yesterday's paper."

Liz hadn't expected to receive a response to her query quite so soon. She balanced the phone against her shoulder as she reached for a pen and notepad.

Less than an hour later, a well-used compact car pulled across the cement bridge over the drainage ditch that ran along the road in front of the McAlister property and parked behind Liz's Mustang. The door opened and a petite young woman stepped out. She flipped a mane of long auburn hair over her shoulder as she studied the house.

Liz shook off the lettuce she had been washing, laid it on a towel, and pulled the drain plug to the sink. As she dried her hands, she watched the woman through the kitchen window. She hesitated for a few minutes, wondering if she truly wanted to open her home to this stranger. Living by herself in the country had been lonely, but had also had its appeal. She considered the turmoil living with a college student might bring to her life. But the extra three hundred dollars a month would be nice.

Liz had opened the door and stepped onto the patio by the time the young woman had traversed the length of the sidewalk.

"You must be Mallory Martin." Liz extended her hand, "Liz McAlister."

Interest flickered in the gold-flecks of the student's brown eyes as Liz said her name, but the young woman only nodded in acknowledgement. As she withdrew her hand she looked toward the barn and outbuildings, all neatly painted a deep red with white trim. Bright green leaves springing forth on the large maple tree near the house contrasted against a clear blue sky.

"You have a great place here, Mrs. McAlister. My grandparents live in the country." The young woman looked away then said, "Their home isn't anything like this, though."

They passed through the solid oak exterior door, carved inside and out with rectangles resembling a labyrinth. Elaborate stained glass windows featuring elegant long-stemmed calla lilies bordered the open doorway from the foyer into a large dining room. Mallory lightly fingered the glass, "Awesome."

As they passed into the dining room, she exclaimed, "The woodwork ... it's magnificent!"

"My husband's great-great grandfather—or maybe it was three greats ago ..." Liz shrugged her shoulders with a laugh, "was a carpenter, as well as a farmer. He carved the detailed crown molding, cornices, stairwell balustrades, and all the rest by hand from trees cleared from the fields around the house."

Multi-colored hues glowed through decorative octagonal stained glass windows cut into the walls beside the archways between the dining room and the adjacent rooms to the north and south. More glass calla lilies graced the frosted panels lining the wide, high window exposing the room to the morning sun.

A round oak pedestal table dominated the center of the room, with an antique painted glass globe chandelier overhead. Crystal prisms dangled from the intricate brass-work supporting the globe and shimmered with reflected light. A finely crocheted cloth covered the table, and a polished wooden bowl formed from a large burl and filled with waxy fruit, served as a centerpiece.

An ornate oak buffet with various-sized framed photographs across the top sat under the east window and a matching hutch, laden with a delicate set of porcelain dishes, stood along the wall to the south. A rich, if somewhat worn, deep blue and gold woven area carpet, edged by gleaming hardwood flooring, brought the room together with a sense of understated elegance.

Mallory Martin let out her breath. "Wow! Totally rad!"

Liz smiled, "The furniture has been in my husband's family for ages. I take no credit for anything except keeping it all polished—and that, quite simply, helps to fill the empty evening hours." She trailed a finger along the tabletop and looked toward the photos on the buffet.

"I didn't intend for that to sound so self-pitying—there's

plenty to keep me busy around here." She hesitated just a second before she said, "I lost my husband, Mack, in an accident a few years ago and my children are both grown and, for the most part, on their own. It's a lot of house for just one person."

Mallory surveyed the room again. "I've always loved big old farmhouses."

"This one is definitely big—almost too big, at times," Liz said. "Each generation of McAlisters expanded the size of the house. Mack's great grandfather built the stairwell and the second story, and Mack's grandfather added the attic-level."

Liz pointed toward the kitchen, "The original house must have had a huge harvest kitchen and pantry area, because Mack's dad carved an office and bathroom from it, and installed the back stairs to the master bedroom. But, most importantly, he built on the laundry and mudrooms. Mack's contribution was converting the cellar to a TV and a game room for the kids."

Mallory looked toward the kitchen then accompanied Liz to the open staircase across the dining room. "The stairway is a story in itself!" Liz said. "The bottom step is five feet wide, with each successive step being slightly narrower until they reach the landing—it gives the stairwell its sweeping effect. The balustrades were turned on a handmade lathe, and the railing has been worn smooth by hoards of McAlisters."

Mallory fingered the large round knob on the top of the newel post and it wobbled beneath her touch. "My son knocked that loose when he was a teenager. It survived all those generations of boys, but couldn't withstand Greggory's rambunctiousness."

Mallory carefully tipped the heavy wooden knob back into place, and smiled at Liz, "I wondered if you were Gregg's mom."

"You know my son?"

"Not real well. We're in the same biochem class."

As Liz groaned and rolled her eyes, Mallory's smile evolved to a grin. "I didn't ask him how the test went yesterday, but he didn't look too pleased when he left the classroom."

"I don't know where Gregg got the idea that college was just one big party after another, but he's hanging on by the skin of his teeth." Liz sighed and shook her head. "If he fails biochemistry, he will be on academic probation. I can't figure him out—he's a bright boy. He didn't get all 'A's' in high school, but he got decent grades. Lettered in basketball and track. Now he doesn't seem to care about anything but a cold beer and little chickies that don't know enough to cover their midriff in the winter! *And he smokes!* If Mack had seen his son with a cigarette …"

Mallory glanced back up the stairs, "So I take it Gregg doesn't live at home?"

"No. We insisted he live on campus his first two years then he moved into an apartment—which seems to have been a big mistake. But he's twenty-one, so out of my control."

They walked through an archway into the living room. Deep red velvet drapes covered large windows on either side of a set of formal double doors, each adorned with an oval of etched glass. Once again, stained glass calla lilies graced panels on either side of the doors.

Queen Anne style chairs sat to the left and right of a polished mahogany table with cabriole legs along the near wall. A brass lamp with a fringed shade stood on a starched doily in the center of the table, while an inlay of lighter wood outlined the edge of the stand. A rectangular cobalt blue and gold Persian rug lay on the well-oiled hardwood floor between the chairs and the near window.

A davenport upholstered in the same red velvet as the curtains had been arranged perpendicular to the wall just past the double doors. It faced a fireplace with a marble slab mantle, surrounded by open bookcases covering the east end of the room. Matching high-backed chairs angled toward each other along the wall opposite the far window, with a similar small mahogany table between them. An identically patterned round Persian rug accented the floor between the sofa and the fireplace.

Liz drew open the near set of velvet drapes revealing sash windows divided into stained glass panes by wooden muntins.

Mallory stepped closer to the window to admire the panes as Liz opened the other set of drapes. She then flipped a switch, illuminating a chandelier overhead. As Mallory glanced up, light glinted through ruby red stained glass diamonds, each edged in copper and hung so as to refract rose-hued beams throughout the room.

"Incredible!" Mallory gasped.

Liz smiled, "The red velvet is a little much, but Mack's grandmother saved a lifetime to buy it, and no one since has had the heart to change it."

"But the stained glass," Mallory interrupted, "It's beautiful!"

"Thanks. It was a hobby I took up before the kids came along."

Mallory turned toward Liz, "A hobby? You did all of this?"

"Yeah, if you look carefully you can tell it's the work of an amateur." Liz demurred. She felt a bittersweet pride in her work, glancing over the panels before closing the curtains and suggesting they continue the tour upstairs.

The following Saturday, Mallory bid farewell to Tiffany and her current live-in and moved her few possessions into Liz's daughter's room. Together she and Liz boxed up the odds and ends Tatiana had left behind and carried them to the catchall room across the hall. When Liz went downstairs to start dinner, Mallory dove into the pleasant task of unpacking her clothes and settling into her country haven.

Tatiana's room was nearly double the size of any Mallory had previously occupied. Until leaving home for college, she had shared a room with one or more of her sisters. She had split a tiny residence hall cubicle with a roommate the first two years at Bowling Green, before moving off-campus. But even the bedrooms in her apartments could not compare with where she found herself now.

Full-length pale gold ruffled curtains printed with stylized lavender hydrangeas adorned the windows. Gold-trimmed white French *Provençal* furniture featured a bed with a canopy and a comforter to match the curtains, delicate vanity with a framed tilting mirror and ladder-back chair and a five-drawer dresser. A thick mauve carpet covered the floor, with a fringed oval gold throw rug beside the bed.

Mallory sank into the luxury of the down comforter and basked in her good fortune.

"Well, if it isn't Ms. Holier-than-thou Mallory Martin. Mom said she had rented out Tatiana's room—she just hadn't gotten around to mentioning any names."

Mallory eased her way up to a sitting position and crossed her legs in the middle of the bed. His tall, broad-shouldered frame nearly filled the door, and she expelled a breath she didn't realize she had been holding.

"Good to see you again, too, *Mister* McAlister." She waited a bit before adding, "I never got a chance to ask you how the bio-chem exam went last week."

"Yeah, well, don't …"

"That bad, huh?"

He slouched against the doorjamb, "Let's just say if I don't get an 'A' on the final, I'll be sitting out next semester. And the chances of my getting close to that on a biochem test are slim to none."

"Tell you what. You promise to read—actually read—the book and I'll tutor you until finals week. Your mom said you were a bright boy—I'm betting we can pull it off!"

He straightened and sauntered into the room. He rested his hand against the rail of the canopy over her head and looked down. Smoky gray eyes raked over her before he answered, a slight smile dimpling his cheek, "Might be fun trying, Mallory Martin. Yep, might be a real good time."

Mallory tried not to squirm under his scrutiny, "You want to have a good time, party boy, you can head back to town. If you want to pass biochem, be here tomorrow afternoon, two o'clock sharp—without a hangover."

He perused her for a moment longer, the smile and dimple

disappearing, then leaned away from the canopy. "It's a shame—such nice packaging, too bad the stuffin's so prickly." He turned and left the room.

Minutes later, Mallory watched out the hallway window as his black Ranger peeled out of the driveway.

Liz pulled a cherry pie from the oven and sat it on the stovetop beside a chicken and broccoli casserole, already zipped into a thermal holder to keep warm. She would stop back to pick them up after the funeral.

She changed into a lightweight black suit with a lavender silk shell under the jacket. As she hooked a delicate gold chain around her neck, she tried to muster the courage to face the drive into town to the mortuary. Each time she forced herself to go through the motions small-town etiquette dictated when someone died, she thought it would get easier. Thought the pain would dull just a little. But it was a constant, never-ebbing ache.

They buried Penelope Gibson in the old cemetery along the river. From what Liz had heard, she had lived a good life. She had survived a major stroke and been able to move back to her farm to help her niece, Cassandra Alvarez, with her small business, selling herbs and dried flower arrangements.

Liz interacted with her nearest neighbors, almost a mile to the west, only occasionally. While not exactly aloof, Cassandra Alvarez seemed aristocratic. Oh, she was friendly enough when they encountered each other in town, and they waved as they passed on the road, but they seldom went out of their way to visit with one another.

Liz and Mack had attended Cassandra's wedding to Jaime Alvarez in the back yard of her aunt's farm four years ago. Mack wasn't entirely pleased he would have "one of those Mexicans from the Lower Eastside" living "next door," even when Liz reminded him Jaime had been a lawyer in Canada since graduating from Harvard Law School and still commuted to Toronto regularly.

Cassie had offered her support after Mack's accident. However, he didn't want anyone's help—not their neighbor's, not their children's, not even that of his wife. Then, when it was too late, anger and grief prevented Liz from asking for aid as she sat vigil over her dying husband.

Liz sat her pie and casserole on a long table under a tent erected in the Alvarez's back yard on the unseasonably warm spring day. After offering her condolences to her neighbors, she wandered over to one of Cassie's formal herb gardens, hoping to remain inconspicuous until sufficient time had passed and she could take her leave without appearing rude.

The winter debris had been cleared away, and green shoots of perennials poked through the earth's crust. Liz hesitated as the path circled a bronze sundial surrounded by lavender bushes sending out tender shoots and looked toward the pond in the distance. She didn't hear the footsteps on the grass walkway behind her.

"So, let me guess. It's Mary Elizabeth McKenna McAlister, right?"

Startled, Liz turned to face the man who had haunted her dreams for the past few weeks, causing her to wake aching and lonely in the middle of the night.

She took a step backward, in an attempt to regain her composure, but brushed up against a lavender bush. She should have realized he would be here given the close-knit Latino community in town.

A crisp, long-sleeved, sky blue shirt stretched over his tightly muscled chest. He had undone the button at his throat and loosed his conservative navy blue tie. The sharp crease of trim black slacks led downward to polished dress loafers.

"Depends on who's asking…" She inched forward as she tossed the question back at him.

"Maybe we should start all over again," he said with a grin.

"Perhaps," Liz felt drawn into the depths of mysterious dark brown eyes—eyes that held secrets … but also, an invitation. "Mary Elizabeth is my given name, but I generally go by Liz, Liz

McAlister." She smiled as she extended her hand toward his.

"David Morales." He caught her hand in a gentle grasp and held it just a second longer than would have been proper between strangers.

"I knew I had met you before. You live down the road a mile or so, don't you?" He inclined his head in the direction of the McAlister homestead.

She nodded, "Cassandra and Jaime's wedding?"

"Yes, that's it—I'd never met a woman with *violeta* eyes before."

She lowered her long black lashes momentarily hiding those enigmatic eyes from him.

"May I call you sometime, Mary Elizabeth McKenna McAlister?"

Liz looked up at him and hesitated just a heartbeat before nodding.

David bench-pressed the weights above his chest and strained to hold the bar aloft, before lowering it. A bright sheen of sweat covered his body, forming dark patches on his gray tee shirt. His muscles bulged as he hefted the weights up again then slowly brought them back toward his chest. Up, then down. Up, then down. He wanted to empty his mind. Empty his body of the memories the *gringa* lady had imprinted on him, imprinted as vividly as the dragon coiled down his arm.

Like a moth to a flame, he circled her, drawn by those eyes … that face … that body. But could he trust another *gringa*? Or would those violet eyes torch his very soul?

"So how's the tutoring going?" Liz passed a soup ladle to Mallory. A steaming pot of chili sat between them at the small enamel-topped kitchen table.

"Surprisingly well." Mallory dipped chili into her stoneware bowl. "Once Gregg decided the only way he would pass the class was to read the book and study, he's become a model student." At

Liz's raised eyebrows, Mallory laughed and handed the ladle back across the table. "Well, that may be a bit of an overstatement!"

Liz smiled at the younger woman and drew a spoonful of soup to her lips. She had tried to keep busy since Nell Gibson's funeral. She met with Neil Rowland, the farmer who managed the McAlister fields, tilled the large vegetable garden and raked it smooth, inspected the barn and outbuildings for winter damage, and helped her new housemate settle into country life.

Much to her surprise, Liz found Mallory Martin to be more than pleasant company. She enjoyed the younger woman's quick wit and intelligence. They discussed politics—and found they were both moderates on opposite sides of the political fence. They talked about religion—Mallory confessed to being a lapsed Catholic while Liz regularly attended the little white wooden framed Lutheran church located in an old township schoolhouse just a few miles away. However, there was one topic the two women evaded …

While Liz sensed her houseguest had more than a passing interest in Gregg, she didn't press for details about their relationship. And Liz's need to talk to someone—anyone—about her growing obsession with David Morales nearly drove her to confide in the relative stranger with whom she shared her home, but the words caught in her throat.

"How's Roseanne doing? Do we have any babies yet?" Mallory brought Liz's attention back from tattoos and taboos. Liz had tamed a feral gray and white cat heavy with kittens who had chosen the McAlister barn as the nursery for her impending litter. Mallory had named the feline after the TV character, Roseanne, since she hissed whenever anyone but Liz came near her.

"Not yet, but her belly is stretched out so far, if it isn't soon, she's going to burst!" Liz said with a laugh.

After they washed and stacked the dishes and Mallory left for class, Liz walked to the barn to check on her ward. Halfway to the building, she stopped. A chill travelled her spine and she turned around. She looked all around, unnerved with the sense someone was watching her. She continued to the barn, though more guarded than before.

Neil Rowland's green pickup pulled into the driveway. With relief, Liz walked back toward the farm manager.

The white slut's parading herself to another unsuspecting victim. He couldn't abide the way she stuck out her chest as she strutted over to the truck. He refocused his binoculars so he could watch more closely. He saw the big clodhopper salivating over the purple-eyed bitch. She'd get her comeuppance in due time—and time was something he had a lot of. He had to make sure things weren't botched again.

CHAPTER TWO

Liz picked up the phone on the fourth ring, disengaging the answering machine as it clicked on. She put the bag of groceries she had just carried into the house on the kitchen counter.

"Hello."

"Mary Elizabeth McKenna McAlister?"

Liz let out a pent up breath and smiled, "One and the same."

His voice traveled soft and sexy across the line, *"You wouldn't happen to be free Saturday night, would you?"*

She thought about snakes and dragons. Corded muscles under dark skin. Strong lips. A musky, masculine scent. A heat washed over her as she licked her lips and swallowed, not trusting herself to speak.

"Liz?"

She took a deep breath, "Yes?"

"Is that 'Yes, I'm free Saturday,' or 'Yes, this is Liz'?"

"Ummm ... I think maybe it's both ..."

A husky chuckle rippled through the receiver, *"You think ...?"* Liz recovered, laughing, "Yes, it's Liz and, yes, I'll check my social calendar, but I think I can fit you in."

She felt his grin as he said, *"That's good—real good. I'll pick you up at seven."*

"Who was that?" Mallory gave her landlady a speculative look as Liz stood cradling the phone after the call had been disconnected.

"Um, a … a friend."

"Uh-huh, yeah, right." Mallory rolled her eyes, unconvinced.

Liz smiled as she laid the phone on the counter and began to unpack the paper sack of groceries. As she handed Mallory a gallon of milk, she said, "I have a date …"

"A *what?*"

"You don't have to sound quite so incredulous, I'm not exactly 'out to pasture' yet!"

"No, I didn't mean that … you're … you're beautiful, really! It's just, you hadn't said anything about … about …"

"… a man?" Liz finished Mallory's sentence.

"Yeah. So tell me about him! Is he tall, dark, and handsome?"

"Not so tall, but he has a few inches over me. Definitely dark," Liz hesitated, worrying her lower lip, "and handsome in sort of a dangerous-looking way." Liz turned toward her young friend. "To be honest, he's everything my mom warned me against when I was a kid."

Liz fretted her way through the remainder of the week. *Why had she said yes? What if the ladies from church saw her riding in a battered pickup truck with a man whose arms were covered in tattoos? A man from the Lower Eastside, no less!*

But then she thought about David Morales. Thought about his intense eyes, thought about his full, insistent lips, thought about an implied strength that went beyond the mere physical. Though, picturing David as he appeared in her neighbor's garden, to call his physical strength "mere" belied the well-honed muscles straining against the thin material of his dress shirt. She felt a warmth spread through her as, unbidden, the memory of him standing shirtless silhouetted against his bedroom window blazed through her mind.

"Damn hot flashes," she muttered as she tried to calm her heart by thoroughly rubbing a nonexistent spot from the gleaming dining room table. She tossed down her dust cloth, walked to the kitchen, and flipped the knob on the Cathedral style tabletop radio that sat on the window shelf. Mack had rewired the radio, a family heirloom dating back to the Great Depression, and built a sturdy window shelf above the sink on which to display it. Liz skipped from station to station before settling on National Public Radio's afternoon classics, hoping a soothing sonata would ease her heart back into submission.

Saturday found Liz changing from one outfit to the next before settling on dressy black pants and a black silk top slashed with shades of lavender. She tied a black scarf loosely around her neck and let it drape in front. At precisely 6:30p.m. she applied the finishing touches to her make-up and fastened on clustered opal earrings. She slipped on a pair of new strappy black heels and surveyed the total effect in the ornate full-length hallway mirror.

"Hey, who's that babe and what happened to my mom?" Gregg quipped as he rounded the corner from the narrow stairs to the attic loft he had converted to his bedroom years ago.

Liz did a slow pirouette and flashed her son a grateful grin.

"Mallory tells me you're going out on a date tonight."

Her heart gave a familiar lurch as he walked toward her, indecision clouding his face.

"It feels so strange, Gregg, almost like I'm cheating on your father."

"I guess it's time, Mom, but the thought of you out with another man ... it just ..." He stopped a few feet from her and looked at her with penetrating gray eyes, "I don't know, it's just weird, that's all."

Liz worried the gloss off her lower lip, wishing her son would leave before David arrived. "I suppose you'll be heading back to your apartment soon?"

"Nah, Mallory-the-slave-driver-Martin insisted we spend tonight studying, since the biochem exam is Monday morning. She doesn't want me out 'drinking and carousing' just two nights before the test. Of all the people you could have rented my sister's room to, you had to pick her!"

"You could show a little more gratitude, Greggory. After all, Mallory's giving up her Saturday night just so you can pass this class."

"If she had a life beyond studying, I might feel her pain, but when she isn't in class, all she does is hang out in Tat's room with her nose stuck in a book."

"That, and work two jobs." Liz shook her head in dismay at how shallow her son appeared to have become. Or did she just not notice when Mack had been here? Had they reinforced Gregg's self-absorption? She glanced at the numbers illuminated on her son's wristwatch: 6:50. Ten minutes until seven!

They heard the entrance door open and close then the aroma of pizza wafted up the stairs. Gregg shrugged his shoulders, "Can't study on an empty stomach! Old Mal stopped at Pisanello's on her way home from work at the library," he said as he followed Liz to the stairway.

"Pizza's on the table. Half pepperoni—" Mallory nodded toward Gregg, "*bor-ing*—and the other half Hawaiian." She responded to his raised eyebrows with a grin, "Some people are just a little more adventurous than others."

Liz looked from her son to the young woman in the kitchen doorway. Mallory Martin, Liz decided, was savvy enough to handle her wayward son. The sound of tires crunching on the gravel drive distracted her, and she turned with no small amount of trepidation toward the window.

Three sets of eyes watched a sleek, late-model white sports car roll to a stop beside the sidewalk.

"Holy crap, Mom! Is that a Jag?" Gregg's jaw dropped as a man in a dress leather jacket and trim black slacks emerged then bent back into the car to retrieve something from its interior.

Liz's breath caught in her throat. Her heart skipped a beat then thrummed rapidly.

"Wow!" Mallory echoed what Liz had been thinking.

Liz moved automatically to open the door, still in awe of the man who walked toward it.

As David Morales stepped across the threshold, he handed Liz a bouquet of violets and lilies-of-the-valley nestled in a small white porcelain vase.

Not trusting her voice, Liz lifted the flowers to her nose and inhaled their delicate fragrance.

"The violets, they match your eyes," he said in a soft tone meant only for her.

"Thank you," she held his gaze for just a moment longer with those violet eyes before leading him into the dining room.

"David, I'd like you to meet Mallory Martin, the student who rents my daughter's room," Liz said as she sat the vase of flowers on the table. The young woman stepped forward extending her hand. "Mallory, David Morales."

He took her hand in his, shifting his attention to the student, "Pleased to meet you, Mallory Martin." He loosened his grip on her hand as he studied her face. Mallory dropped her gaze then gave the man before her a questioning look. His nod of tacit recognition went unobserved by Liz as she turned toward her son.

"And this is my son, Greggory."

Gregg stood behind his mother, hands tucked in his pockets, back ramrod stiff.

"You're going out with him?" At the incredulity in her son's voice, Liz pivoted around to meet gray eyes glinting with steel. "You know how Dad felt about ... them."

"Greggory McAlister!" But he had stalked past Mallory and through the kitchen before Liz could say more. They heard him slam the back door, leaving a stark silence in his wake.

Liz sipped a cup of herbal tea. The waiter had cleared away the remnants of their dinner at a small, recently-opened restaurant tucked in amongst the weathered, yet still impressive, Victorian "painted ladies" gracing Toledo's Old West End, and they were waiting for their check.

"Ah, Mary McKenna, you've let your son cast a shadow on

the entire evening. How can I convince you not to worry about what he said? I've heard a lot worse, believe me!"

"I just hadn't realized how prejudiced Gregg had become."

David reached across the table and lightly caressed her fingers with his. "Can I ask you something?"

She cast a wary glance his way as she nodded.

"The small, slant-roofed buildings behind what looked to be a chicken coop by your barn—they housed migrant workers, didn't they?"

She dropped her gaze and again gave a hesitant nod.

"How long's it been since your husband hired 'tomato-pickers'?" He used the derogatory term common to the local *Anglos*.

"Fifteen or so years. The story goes that Mack's grandfather—or maybe his great grandfather—first hired migrant workers to pick sugar beets. When the beet factories shut down, his father started planting tomatoes—both labor-intensive crops." Liz took a sip from her half-empty water glass. "Peter, Mack's nephew, convinced him to go entirely to corn, beans, and wheat soon after moving back to help with the family farm in the 1990s."

"Mack—that's the first time you've mentioned his name. Cassandra told me about his accident. She was amazed at how you were able to care for him and still maintain the farm."

Before Liz could respond, the waiter brought their check.

As they walked toward the Jaguar, Liz sought to change the subject, "Gregg had me so distracted earlier I neglected to comment on the classy carriage your pumpkin turned into!"

David smiled, "I usually let my sister babysit this little job in exchange for storing it in her garage." He opened the door for Liz then walked around to the driver's side, "Nita's old Chevette bit the dust a few years back and the pickup serves me just fine—most times, anyway."

Liz stretched the back of her neck against the smooth leather headrest and closed her eyes, "Hmm, wish you were *my* brother!"

David laughed, "Then I'd have to wipe these incestuous thoughts right outta my mind!"

Liz shot him a sidelong glance as she sighed, "It'd probably be in both of our best interests if you did." Though in her heart, she knew that was much more easily said than done.

They caught the second feature at the multiplex. While David suggested a romantic comedy, Liz opted for an action/adventure movie to distract her from both her escort and their unsettling post-dinner conversation.

A spring rain forced David to concentrate on the dark road on the way home while Liz focused on droplets of water chasing each other down her windowpane.

A sense of disappointment settled over her as they approached the farm. She hadn't known what to expect, but hadn't anticipated being home before midnight. She tried to convince herself this is what she wanted. Tried to steel herself against her attraction to the man at her side. Told herself they were from different worlds and this was for the best. However, a deep sigh escaped her lips as David pulled into her driveway.

As he eased the car to a stop, Liz felt him turn toward her. She sighed again as she looked straight ahead—Gregg's truck was parked in its usual spot, beside Mallory's compact car.

David slipped his hand between her neck and the seat and she allowed him to use his thumb to nudge her face in his direction. He brought his lips to hers, lightly at first then at her urging, he deepened their kiss.

"Wow!" The quiet exclamation blew from her as Liz expelled her pent-up breath. She leaned back against the seat, fighting the desire that flamed within her.

"Damn," David swore softly as he looked at her then toward the lights flaring from the first story of the house. "Damn," he sighed again, then opened his door. He glanced back one last time before turning away from her.

The rain had slowed to a mist as they scurried to the house. They stopped under the shelter of the awning above the door and faced each other. David looked out into the darkness before settling his gaze on her face. He drew his hand to her chin and let his thumb feather-touch a circle on her cheek. He lightly brushed a kiss on lips that invited more and stepped back.

"Take care of yourself, Mary Elizabeth McKenna McAlister."

Liz could only stand and watch as David hurried away from her to his car.

He waited patiently with his lights off while she illuminated the second floor. He watched her walk past the window of what must be a hallway. As darkness blackened that window, a light at the back of the house came on. "Must be the slut's bedroom," he sneered to himself. He focused his binoculars, hoping to see her strip, but she lowered a shade obscuring his view. After another ten minutes, that window, too, went dark. He turned on his headlights and sped past the house.

"Liz, come quick! We have babies!"

Liz hurried to the door Mallory held open and they rushed to the barn together. Mallory led the way as they climbed the ladder to the haymow. In a nest hollowed out between two bales of straw, Roseanne nursed six kittens. The newborns squirmed against each other as they rooted blindly against their mother's swollen teats.

"Look, there's a seventh!" Liz exclaimed. They watched as the tiny creature, eyes still sealed shut, scooted from one sibling to the next, attempting to force its turn for nourishment. "I hope the poor thing makes it! It seems to be a bit smaller than the rest."

After a few moments, the two women backed away from Roseanne and her litter, stepping with caution down the rungs of the ladder.

"So how do you think you did?" Mallory had waited at the classroom door for Gregg to complete their biochemistry exam.

"I dunno. 'A's' don't come easy for me in any subject. Tat was the one who always hit the honor roll in school."

"And was that because she ... maybe ... studied?"

"You know, Martin, you could be a real smart ass if you tried!" Mallory ducked away from him as Gregg swatted his notebook toward her aforementioned behind.

"Whaddya say we go for a brewski to celebrate the end of the semester?"

Mallory wrinkled her nose as she lifted her chin to look up at him.

"Jees, you're a whole pack 'o fun! Haven't you ever gone out to the bars?"

"Once or twice, but I'm allergic to smoke and don't drink, so I gave it up for Lent one year and never looked back."

"Yep, a real smart ass. Tell ya what, I know a place downtown that will meet even *your* standards. It's small, classy, and, best of all, smoke-free!"

"I'm not that out-of-touch, Greggory McAlister. I know the bars have been smoke free for years."

He shrugged his shoulders, "Yeah, gotta admit, I was kind of glad, myself, when that law went through."

"I thought your mom said that you smoked."

"I did for a while, but quit. Couldn't stand the taste it left in my mouth. I just let Mom think I still do so she doesn't nag me so much about other things—though she seems to have multitask nagging down pat."

"Your mom's so cool. You don't know how lucky you are."

"Yeah, well, you're not her kid, and she doesn't see ... she doesn't look at you like you're an f'in' ghost ..."

They stopped at the edge of the commuter student parking lot. "Well, Mallory Martin, are you in or do I have to celebrate my escape from Sweeney's class all by myself?"

"Since you put it that way, I wouldn't want to be responsible for a man drinking alone when it's ..." She made a show of checking her watch, "barely noon!" Her stomach rumbled as if on cue. "Does this place at least serve snacks?"

"Yep, full-service gourmet menu, c'mon." He grabbed her elbow, tugging her toward his Ranger.

Gregg unlocked and opened the passenger door to his pickup. Mallory stepped on the running board and boosted her small frame up to the seat. She swallowed hard and took a deep breath to steady her rapidly beating heart.

As the engine fired and Gregg backed from his parking space, Mallory gave him a speculative glance from the corner of her eye.

"After seeing your dad's photographs, I can understand why your mom looks at you the way she does. With your hair cut short, you could be your dad's twin when he was your age. Give her a little more time, Gregg."

"Time? She's had more'n two years. I miss him, too, all the time. Every time she looks at me, she reminds me all over again that he's gone."

"Then why all the hostility when she went out with David Morales? If she starts dating, you'll both be able to get on with your lives."

He parallel parked the pickup on Main Street, pressed his foot down on the clutch, and pushed the gear into reverse with more emphasis than necessary.

"You know why...he's one of them. Dad would crap in his drawers if he knew she was dating a ... a ... Mexican—with a ponytail!"

Mallory looked out the window, not seeing the people rushing by. She turned back toward Gregg, "You say 'Mexican' like it's a dirty word. That's an awfully big country to condemn everyone who has roots there."

Gregg hesitated, "You know what I mean. We're ... well ... different from them. They should stick to their own kind and we should stick to ours."

Mallory didn't try to hide her disappointment. "Nice to know you're so broadminded."

"Who said anything about 'broads'? I just happen to prefer blondes." He flashed a grin her way, "Course uptight redheads can be sort of sexy, too."

Mallory closed her eyes, forcing her inner turmoil into a hidden pocket of her heart. "What am I doing here?" She glanced over at Gregg then hopped out of the truck before he could answer.

Gregg watched the waitress carry away the remnants of their lunch as he took a gulp of amber brew, while Mallory sucked a final sip of tea from the bottom of her glass.

"Real class there, Martin. Didn't your mom teach you not to slurp?"

"Where I come from, you do everything but eat the glass."

"Just where do you come from?"

The opening of the front door distracted Gregg from his question, as a tall, clean-cut man in a sharply pressed uniform walked into the dim interior. He removed his hat, revealing short, gelled, brown hair and the movie-star handsome face of a man in his early forties.

"Now that's a dude I'd like my mom to meet."

Mallory turned toward the newcomer then back to Gregg, "Air Force?"

"I think so. Probably a ROTC instructor."

The man nodded in their direction. Mallory had to admit he filled out the uniform nicely. He held himself with a military bearing and flashed them a winning smile as he walked toward their table.

"Mind if I pull up a chair? I'm new in the area and just checking out the town."

Gregg shrugged his shoulders and said, "Sure, why not?"

The officer scooted the sturdy Windsor chair back from the table and sat down.

"You students at the university?"

Mallory nodded, "Are you with the Air Force program on campus?"

"No, ma'am," he stood and extended his hand toward her, "Lieutenant Brandon Michaels. I'm with the Air National Guard in Toledo. 180th Fighter Wing."

"Hi, I'm Mallory Martin."

Gregg stood and stretched his arm across the table, "Gregg

McAlister."

"I just moved here from out west," the lieutenant said as he sat back down, "I'm not much of a city guy. I've always been partial to college towns, so thought I'd see what Bowling Green had to offer."

The officer interrupted himself long enough to order a draft, "It's a nice town. The university seems to be a fair size. I like the eclectic architecture across campus—everything from the old brick 'halls of ivy' buildings to the wild mural on the library tower."

Gregg lifted his glass toward the young woman behind the bar to indicate he wanted another beer and leaned back against his chair. "So do you have family in the area, Lieutenant?"

"Please, call me Brandon. My mother and father live near Detroit and are getting up in years, so I put in to be stationed a little closer to them."

He hesitated, taking a long draught from the glass the wait-ress had set in front of him, before going on, "I lost my wife a few years back. We never had children, so it's just me, mom and pop."

Gregg passed a slight smile across the table to Mallory, who rolled her eyes toward the ceiling.

They spent the next two hours talking—for the most part, Gregg and Mallory listened while the officer regaled them with tales of his exploits during his time in the service.

"It's getting late—I suppose you kids have dinner plans to get on with," he said, after taking a breath.

"Not really. In fact, if you're not doing anything for dinner tonight, Lieutenant...er...Brandon, would you like come on out to the house? My mom's one hell of a cook. I just need to take Old Mal back to campus to get her car, first."

Mallory reached across the table and gave Gregg an indig-nant cuff on the arm, "'Old Mal'? Thanks a lot, McAlister!"

Brandon laughed before protesting, "I couldn't impose on your mother. You can't just bring a stranger home for dinner these days."

Gregg tugged his cell phone from his pocket. "The wonders of modern technology," he said, as he scrolled to his home number.

"Mom? Would you mind if Mal and I brought a friend home for dinner?" ... "I figured not, thanks, Ma—I owe you!"

Gregg slipped the phone back in his pocket and turned to Brandon Michaels with a smile, "Bet she's putting another plate on the table as we speak. Mom always loves company. She 'bout went crazy after my sister left for college. Tatiana always had friends over, filling the house with squealing girls. Used to drive my dad bananas. I was more of the 'go to my buddies' houses' type—mostly to escape all of Tat's friends."

The lieutenant cocked his head sideways, but before he could ask, Gregg supplied, "My dad was in an accident nearly three years ago. Mom had to...to pull the plug on him two years ago last month."

"That's rough ... real rough," Brandon said. He hesitated for a moment before adding, "If you're sure your mom won't mind, I'd love a home-cooked meal. I usually go out to eat, even when I drive up to visit my parents."

"I don't know when I've had a better dinner, Liz. Your son's right—you are an exceptional cook!" Mallory and Gregg had gone up to their rooms, leaving Liz alone at the dining room table with their guest.

"Gregg said that?"

"Well, maybe not in those exact words ..."

That smile, Liz decided, had probably slain many a woman's heart. She wished hers would give at least the tiniest little skip. The photograph of Mack on the buffet behind the lieutenant caught her attention. But the memory of another man's kiss had blazed its way into her heart. Not that she still didn't miss the comfort of Mack's touch in the middle of the night— comfort wasn't exactly the feeling David Morales evoked when she awoke from unsettling dreams ...

"Liz?"

She drew her attention back to the man at her table.

"Sorry, I guess I was a little distracted."

He turned his head to look at the photographs on the buffet then back to Liz, "Gregg told me about your husband, though he didn't go into details about the accident. I am sorry for your loss."

"Thank you. I guess I'm still working through what they call 'the grieving process.'"

He reached across the table and covered her hand with his, "Would it be too forward of me to invite you to dinner on Saturday evening? I would very much like to see you again."

Liz smiled, trying to tamp down her disappointment that David hadn't called her after their date.

"I guess that would be okay ..." The words were out of her mouth before she had time to reconsider. She wanted to grab them back, but withdrew her hand to her lap instead.

Saturday found Liz standing, once again, in front of the hallway mirror. She had dressed in one of Mack's favorite outfits—one that had hung in her closet for over two years, untouched.

"This dating stuff is for the birds," she grimaced to the image in the mirror. She lifted her eyes toward the ceiling, "Damn you, Mack, why did you leave me?" Tears threatened as she adjusted the gold scarf accenting the lavender top. "You could've beat it, instead you just gave up. You gave up on all of us. Damn your selfish male pride!"

Putting her anger into words unleashed the flood of tears she had held at bay, and she leaned against the hall window sobbing.

"Mom, what's wrong?" Gregg hurried down the attic stairs and rushed to his mother's side. She shook her head as he drew her against his shoulder. "Will it ever get easier?" he asked as they clung to each other.

Liz hiccupped and wiped her eyes with a tissue. "Oh, drat, now I have to redo my make-up. Sorry, dear, I'm just too old for this stuff. Being married to your father wasn't always easy, but it beat the heck out of being back in the dating circuit."

"Hey, cheer up—Lieutenant Michaels seems to be an okay

guy. He's certainly a step above who you went out with last week."

"I don't know, maybe so …" But the words came from her mouth, not her heart.

"Thank you, Brandon, for a lovely evening. Dinner was wonderful, and it's been an age since I've been to the Stranahan. I'm still amazed you were able to get tickets to *Les Miserables!*"

They stood on the patio as she searched her handbag for her key. The foyer light provided a dim illumination in an otherwise darkened house.

"Ah, there it is. We used to never lock our doors, but after Mack …"

"You can never be too careful these days," Brandon Michaels cautioned. He closed the space between them, tipping her chin up to face him.

"May I kiss you?"

Liz nodded and he brought hard dry lips down to meet hers. *Nothing*, Liz thought. She didn't exactly expect bells and whistles, but a little flutter would have been nice. She pressed herself against him, hoping to stimulate at least a physical reaction to the man. He dipped his tongue into her mouth and she nearly gagged. She stepped back and pasted a smile on her face.

"I should go in. Thank you, again, Brandon." She unlocked the deadbolt, stepped across the threshold and closed the door before he could insist upon more.

She went to the kitchen, poured herself a glass of water and rinsed out her mouth.

"Damn you, Mack," she repeated her earlier epithet then added, "and damn you, David Morales!"

The whore had done it again. He'd teach her a lesson soon enough. He watched a light toward the back of the house come on, then off again. Then the same upstairs room as last week lit up. Must be a back stairway—he might be able to use that. He thought about her full breasts and became hard again, wanting more and knowing his time would come.

Liz sat cross-legged on the floor of the haymow watching Roseanne tend her kittens. Their mews pierced the air as they struggled for nourishment. The mother licked the tiny gray head of the runt kitten. Liz worried it wouldn't survive its first few weeks of life.

The notes Gregg had plugged into her cell phone toned, and she braced herself up on her knees so she could ease it from her pocket.

"Hello." ... "This afternoon?" Liz hesitated before answering, "Sure, I guess so." ... "Okay, see you in an hour."

Liz sat back on her heels, looking at her phone. *An hour!* David would be here in one short hour! She dragged her hand through her tangled curls and looked down at her dusty jeans. She had changed into her work clothes after the early church service, mucked Desert Pro's stall, and taken the purebred Arabian to the back pasture to lunge before riding him through the woods. She smelled like his lather and the wind had knotted her hair beyond hope!

"One hour!" she exclaimed at the squirming mass of kittens.

Roseanne raised her head and gave Liz a look as if to say, "You think you have problems?" and continued grooming one of the two white kittens Liz had dubbed the twins.

"Timing is everything," Liz grumbled as Gregg's pickup followed David's car into the driveway. She grabbed her windbreaker off the back of a chair and hurried out the door, hoping to stave off a confrontation between the two men.

She reached the end of the walkway just as David emerged from his car. He wore a tee-shirt emphasizing not only his bulging muscles, but also the tattoos winding around them.

Gregg gave a pointed look at the dragon and the snake and then at his mother.

"What are you doing here?" he asked David.

"Greggory, this is still my house, and I won't have you being rude to my guests."

"I thought Brandon might be stopping by today."

David's eyes darted from Liz's son back to his mother. "Brandon?"

"Greggory ..." she said, stretching out his name as a warning he was skirting the edge.

With a smug look confirming he knew he had said enough, the younger man brushed by his mother and walked to the house.

"Brandon?" David repeated.

"He's just someone Gregg brought home with him to dinner." Then wondering why she felt the need to be secretive about seeing another man, she added, "And I went out with last evening."

David arched his eyebrows, "That so?"

She nodded as they walked around opposite ends of his car to the passenger door. He only looked at her as he opened it. He said nothing as he pulled out of the drive. His silence held as he turned north at the stop sign and continued down the narrow township road toward the bridge over the Maumee River.

"I haven't been to Goll Woods in years—what a wonderful idea!" Liz exclaimed with a little too much enthusiasm when she could no longer tolerate the quiet stretching between them. David had suggested on the phone they drive to the Nature Preserve on which grew the last stand of old-growth timber in Northwest Ohio.

He cast a sideways glance toward her. "A date? You went on a date with this Brandon guy?"

"What? You expected me to sit around waiting for your call? What if it never came? Was I supposed to pine away for you until I was old and gray and ... and ... my boobs sank to the floor?"

He snapped back his head and laughed out loud. "Maybe not that long. But I would have thought a week wouldn't have been too much to ask!"

"We've gone on, what, one date?"

"Well, there was that night after you stopped by *Tía's* ..."

"A gentleman wouldn't remind a lady of *that* night ..."

"A lady? I don't remember a lady at *Tía's*. A hot *gringa*, maybe ..." He shot her a grin that took the sting off of his words.

"Besides, I thought we had a fresh start that day in Cassandra's garden!"

"Yeah, Mary McKenna, a fresh start …" he patted her knee and let his hand rest over hers before returning it to the steering wheel.

They talked about everything but Liz's date the previous evening—the winter wheat crop, whether the corn had been planted too early or too late, the cloudless azure sky overhead. Liz described Roseanne and her litter to him, and he teased her for being a "softie" when she worried about the little gray and white runt.

They passed through the small town of Archbold and finally arrived at their destination. David reached under his seat and pulled out a bottle of mosquito spray. "I know it seems early for 'skeeters, but I've never been to this woods when they weren't biting!"

They sprayed the mist over each other. He wet his hand with the liquid, and gently rubbed it on her cheeks. His palm rested at the nape of her neck, his thumb caressing its slope. He tugged her face closer, brushing her lips ever so lightly.

"So, did this Brandon guy do this?"

She pulled away and looked toward the ground.

"He did. He kissed you." Unbidden memories of her body nestled against his as he carried her to his bed the night they met seeped into his heart. "What else did he do? No, don't answer that. I don't want to know if …"

"David!" She cut him off before he could say anything more. "Do you honestly think I am the kind of woman who jumps into any man's bed?" Then, with flushed cheeks, she went on, "No, don't answer *that*! After what I did at *Tia's*, I guess I couldn't blame you if you thought I was a …"

David quieted her with another light kiss. "I know you're not a loose woman, Mary Elizabeth McKenna McAlister, but after what your son said …"

It was her turn to cut him off with a kiss that stretched on a little longer than the last one.

"Oh, *gringa* lady, you do make it hard to be good!"

They walked hand-in-hand past the kiosk outlining the trails and entered the woods on a well-worn path.

"Look at the size of that tree!" Liz exclaimed. "I'll bet it was here when the English landed at Jamestown!" Deep furrows lined the trunk of a cottonwood leading up a hundred or more feet to where leaves were sprouting from spreading branches.

"See the little white flowers along the edge of the path?" Liz stooped down to look at the blooms David had spotted.

She laughed up at him, "They look like old-fashioned ladies bloomers!"

He bent down beside her, "Close. They're called Dutchman's britches. One of my favorite spring wildflowers."

Liz cocked her head toward him, "Well, aren't you full of surprises! I wouldn't have taken you for a botanist!"

"Just an amateur naturalist, at best. I spend a lot of time outdoors now."

"Now? That implies there was a time before that you weren't such an outdoorsman."

"Ah, Mary McKenna, there is much you do not know about me." Then nearly under his breath, David added, "Much you do not want to know."

She gave him a curious glance, but let the comment drop.

They continued along the path without saying anything. The songs of migrating warblers trilled overhead, while a woodpecker added its percussive rat-a-tat to the melody. A hawk soared low above the canopy formed by interlocking branches of ancient trees searching for prey.

David took her hand in his again. He stopped to point out the furled fronds of young ferns springing forth from a mat of dry rotting leaves, "Those are called fiddleheads. The books say they're edible."

"It'd take quite a few to make a salad!" Liz said. "I prefer dandelions in the spring, myself."

"And here I thought I was the nature boy on this tour!"

"I'm a farm girl, remember?"

"So, have you always lived in Ohio?"

"No, my dad was a preacher. We moved around quite a bit, as he shifted from one parish to another. I met Mack when Dad took over the Presbyterian Church in town. I was a junior in high school and Mack was a big football hero. When he lavished his attention on the new girl, I was hooked. From that time on, I never dated anyone else."

Liz went on, "My mom was from the east and my dad was a history buff, so when a position in Williamsburg, Virginia, opened up after Mack and I got married, Dad took it. I was hoping they would stay in Ohio to be near the kids, but it worked out well. We've had lots of great vacations in what they call the Historic Triangle." At his quizzical look, she explained, "Yorktown, Jamestown, and Colonial Williamsburg—where our country was born!"

"Guess I'm not much into history—all those old white men makin' sure their power filtered down through the ages. Even now, it's the rich old white men who tower over the rest of us," he raised his free arm upward, "just like these trees!"

"I'm not sure the founding fathers were all that old when they wrote the Constitution … but trying to run the farm since losing Mack—it does sometimes feel like I'm a woman in a man's world. I'd be lost without Neil."

David again raised his eyebrows and Liz explained, "Our farm manager."

As they neared the end of the Burr Oak Trail, they heard a whinny. Two teenagers—a boy and girl—on horseback crossed the road and reined in their animals in the parking lot. They were teasing back and forth, unaware that they were being watched. They drew their horses close together and he leaned toward her. She met him midway, but before they could kiss, her horse raised its head drawing her attention back to her mount.

David put his arm around Liz's shoulders, unwitting spectators of another of nature's spring rituals. They stood in companionable silence in the shadows of the big trees as the riders turned their horses back toward the road.

"C'mon, I'll show you the cemetery where the original owners of all of this are buried."

They spent the next half-hour reading old gravestones before returning to the car for their drive home.

David turned north at the highway rather than south toward Archbold. "I hate to go back the same way I came. Different scenery, you know."

After a few minutes, David turned right on Route 20A and headed east. As Liz glanced back over her shoulder, a faded mural caught her attention. "Yes, but even if you take the same road, you see the opposite view. Case in point, the barn we just passed must be the Ohio Bicentennial Barn for this county. If we were driving west, we would have seen painting on its side right away. Driving east we could easily miss the mural."

"You are a wise woman, *güerita*. Maybe I just want to prolong our afternoon, driving north to go south." He rested his hand on the gearshift on the console that separated them. She smiled, turned toward him in her seat and let her hand lightly cover his.

"*Güerita*? No more '*gringa* lady'?"

He slipped his hand over hers. She felt its warmth, its weight, sending ripples through her.

"*Gringa* has a … How can I explain it? A harder edge to it." He hesitated then said, "I've met some real *gringas* in my time."

He checked the rearview mirror, then pulled into the left-hand lane to pass a bright green John Deere tractor, the yellow inset of the wheels still gleaming.

"Must be brand new," he mused before glancing to the woman at his side. "I thought calling you a *gringa* might keep me from falling under the spell of your *violeta* eyes—but I was oh so wrong."

David smiled, "*güerita* is softer, like you." He looked toward her and was caught off guard by the intensity in those violet eyes. "You are *mi güerita*," he said then returned her intensity with a twinkle, "loosely translated, 'my pale-faced lady.'"

Liz giggled, "I think I liked it better before the translation, but it's better than *gringa*. '*Güerita*,'" Liz repeated, trying to soften the "g" almost to a "w" the way David pronounced it.

"*Mi güerita,*" he said with tenderness instead of a twinkle.

David pulled into a parking lot beside a large neon ice cream cone and they walked up to the window of a small roadside stand. Liz ordered raspberry sherbet twist in a cone while David asked for plain vanilla. They traded bites of sherbet for ice cream as they walked back to the car. David opened the door, and as Liz turned to slip by him, he caught her lips in his. The sticky sweet residue stayed with them as they drew apart. Liz lifted her cone to her lips, and David licked a drip from the side toward him before stepping back with a slight shake of his head.

"Oh, *mi güerita*, what you do to me. You are dangerous, so very dangerous."

Liz recalled she thought the same about him when they first met. *Perhaps they should listen to their instincts ...* She worried her lower lip, still tasting of ice cream and David.

They meandered along the back roads crossing the Maumee near the little village of Texas. "I think Ohio has the most towns named after other states than any other in the Union," David observed. "There's Florida, just down the road, Wyoming, Idaho, Nevada, Kansas, Delaware…"

"…and Oregon by Toledo," Liz interjected, then asked, "How do you know so many small towns around the state?"

"I did some short haul trucking. One of my many career moves," he said with a half-hearted laugh.

His comment reminded her again of just how little she knew about the man at her side.

When they arrived back at the farm late in the afternoon, Brandon Michaels' gleaming black Miata was parked beside her son's pickup and Mallory's little red Chevy.

CHAPTER THREE

As David added his Jaguar to the line-up, three figures emerged from the barn and walked toward them. By the time Gregg, Mallory, and Brandon approached them, David and Liz were waiting beside his car.

"Talk about awkward," Liz let out a barely audible sigh, just before the others came within earshot. "Greggory is in for it ..."

Brandon Michaels, in his dress blues with his hat low over his forehead, stood back, as though sizing up the competition before extending his hand in a smooth, well-practiced gesture, "Brandon Michaels ... and you're ...?"

Whether intentional or not, the officer's introduction, height, and uniform, put David at a distinct disadvantage. He hesitated before returning the handshake, "David Morales."

The men assessed each other for a minute or so longer before Mallory broke the tension, "We were just introducing Brandon to Roseanne and her kittens. The little one is growing but not at the same rate as the others. Brandon thinks we should feed it with a dropper."

"They're not even two weeks old yet. Let's just keep an eye on them for now," Liz said, relieved at Mallory's distraction. Liz looked from David to the taller man standing beside her son.

"I was about to leave," Brandon said. "I just stopped by to see if ..." then stopped midsentence and gave Liz a boyish smile.

"Well, I suppose this is a little far out to have 'just stopped by.'" He shifted his gaze to David then back to Liz.

"I'll call you," he said as a statement, not a request.

After a second's hesitation, David said, "I'd better go, too. Thanks for a lovely afternoon, Liz McKenna McAlister."

"But …" Liz interjected.

David's smile reflected both his amusement at her predicament and disappointment at his. He nodded at the others and then to Liz he said, "Better keep that phone close by, 'cause the soldier-boy's not the only one who'll be using the number …"

"Greggory McAlister!" Liz seethed through clenched teeth as David's Jaguar followed Brandon's Miata out of the drive.

"What? What are you doing going out with one of them, Ma? You know how Dad felt! And those tattoos … and a ponytail! Hell, Dad made me cut my hair if it hit my collar! He made Tat remove that little heart tattoo she got just above her boob. He was furious the day he saw it above her bikini top."

He looked at his mom, then added, "You knew about it before then, though, didn't you?"

"I did," Liz said evenly. "In fact, I gave her the money for it for her 18th birthday. And do you know what else, Greggory McAlister? She still has it. She was just real careful not to let your dad see it again. Or you, either, I guess."

Mallory watched, her discomfort apparent, as mother and son faced off against one another. But Liz turned abruptly and stormed toward the house before the disagreement could erupt further. Gregg watched his mother's retreating back then looked toward Mallory.

"So that was pleasant." He glanced back at the house as the door slammed shut. "I don't see why she can't dump that guy for Brandon. He has so much more to offer her."

Mallory just shook her head and followed her landlady to the house.

Liz stood at the kitchen sink looking out the window toward her son. She took a long drink from the glass of water she held in her hand. When Mallory approached her she turned toward the younger woman.

"Maybe I *am* just rebelling against the control Mack had over me all those years. I was thinking of all the little ways besides Tatiana's tattoo that I tried to exert myself while we were married—volunteering at the food pantry and the hospital guild when he wanted me to be at home to help with the farm. Maybe my dating David is just another way to prove my independence."

She gave a slight shake of her head before going on, "Gregg's right—David is everything Mack would hate. So stupid of me now that Mack is gone. I'm so mad at him for leaving me!"

Liz brushed away a tear that slipped down her cheek, "But I know he would be here if … if it weren't for that blasted accident. It's so mixed up, so messed up. Everything was going so well before …"

Liz turned toward Mallory, "… when Mack was here."

When another tear followed the first, Mallory wrapped her arms around the older woman, offering what little comfort she could.

Gregg walked quietly to the kitchen door before retreating to his attic hideaway.

When Brandon Michaels called Liz that week, she told him with relief she "guessed she really wasn't ready to start dating again." When David Morales called later the same day, she conveyed the same message, only that time her words were tinged with regret.

Two weeks passed, then a third. Gregg kept a distance from his mother, staying mostly at his Bowling Green apartment.

Mallory found a part-time job at the public library in town, which in addition to picking up extra shifts at the university library, allowed her to quit her weekend waitressing job in Bowling Green. Between work and classes, she was away from the farm more than she was there.

Liz busied herself in the garden. She planted enough vegetables to feed the county and edged the plot with annual flowers. She raked away dried leaves and other debris from the bushes around the house. When the grass was barely high enough for the blades to cut, she mowed the lawn in a diagonal pattern just the way Mack liked it.

He insisted the farm looked well kept—except for the mulberry trees, elderberry bushes and goldenrod that grew up around the migrant housing. Liz wondered why he hadn't had the decrepit buildings removed ... which reminded her of David's remark that night at the restaurant ... which made her upset with Mack ... which left her feeling guilty and working extra hard at what would have pleased him ...

Roseanne's kittens had developed from mewling newborns to tumbling bits of fur. The twins chased each other around then flopped on their backs and batted their little paws at their sisters. Liz had been dismayed to discover all of the kittens were female and hoped that the vet would give a volume discount on spaying. As often as not, Liz found the littlest kitten in the haymow, hiding in the nest where it was born. How the tiny thing got up and down, Liz didn't know. Perhaps Roseanne fed her separately from the others, knowing she needed more nourishment than her siblings.

Gregg had gone to his favorite retreat, Put-in-Bay on Lake Erie, with his friends for Memorial Day weekend. The libraries had closed for the holiday, and Liz and Mallory enjoyed a morning cup of tea at the kitchen table. Liz had been to the cemetery earlier in the week to clean the remnants of winter from the McAlister graves. She had planned to attend the Memorial Day program there after the parade that morning, but without Gregg or Tatiana, she wondered if she would have the courage to go alone. When she said as much to Mallory, she offered to go with Liz to the cemetery.

They stood together as various veterans' organizations read tributes to their fallen comrades. Mack's oldest brother, Michael, was killed in Vietnam, and Liz always felt a sorrow at the loss of such a young life in a war that seemed so … controversial, at best. Liz searched the crowd for the face of the son Mike had never met. She didn't know the full story behind Peter's birth, only that he had moved here with his wife to take up farming after his grandfather's heart attack. She found him standing with his family near the high school marching band. Peter looked up at that moment and exchanged a smile and nod with Liz. *That smile … those eyes*, Liz thought, *so like Gregg's … so like their fathers'*.

As the ceremony drew to a close, Liz felt a tap on her shoulder and turned to find Mack's middle brother, Bill, standing behind her, along with his wife, Marian, two of their married children, spouses, and grandchildren. She introduced Mallory to the group before Marian pulled her aside.

"Liz, dear, people have been talking …" Liz waited through her sister-in-law's pregnant pause, "Just the other day Dolores Tyler approached me at the grocery store and said she had been told that you were seeing one of those boys from the Lower Eastside. I told her it couldn't be, knowing how Mack felt and all—and especially after you showed no interest in Frank Blakesly when I introduced him to you—but I just thought I would let you know. I can't imagine what would have triggered such a rumor!" Marian's uplifted eyebrows invited Liz to confide a possible answer.

Liz knew she should admit to seeing David Morales but did not feel up to a confrontation. Besides, she had called the whole thing off, so it would be much ado about nothing. Instead she simply said, "Well, you know how Dolores likes to gossip. The older that woman gets, the more her tongue wags. I wouldn't worry about what she says, no one listens to her anymore." Liz then turned her attention back to Mallory and Bill, excusing herself and Mallory at the first opportunity.

"I heard what your sister-in-law said," Mallory observed as they walked amidst the gravestones back to Liz's Mustang. "I hope I don't offend you, but are all of the McAlisters as prejudiced as she and Gregg?"

Liz shrugged her shoulders, "Some people have a harder time than others accepting the fact that times have changed. I'm afraid I have to share the blame for Gregg's views. I should have stepped in long ago when his dad made comments at the dinner table about the migrant workers. I did my best to ensure that their living conditions were as good as we could make them ... but they were still pretty awful."

"Yeah, I'm sure they were ..." Mallory said, with an uncharacteristic edge to her voice. She walked to the car ahead of Liz and they rode to the farm in silence, each seemingly lost in her own thoughts.

"Sometimes I feel so hemmed in by this place," Liz said as she pulled into the driveway. "It's such a stronghold of the McAlister's, I feel that somewhere along the line I lost track of who I was. Where's Mary Elizabeth McKenna in all of this?"

Mallory let the question dangle, unanswered. She glanced toward the migrant shacks as she followed Liz up the sidewalk and into the house.

Mallory hesitated in the foyer, "What am I doing here?" she said under her breath.

"Did you say something?" Liz asked.

Mallory shook her head and reached out to touch the decorative window beside the door. "What about all of your stained glass? You've made the entire downstairs a work of art!"

"That?" Liz looked around as though she hadn't noticed it again since the day of Mallory's arrival. "It kept me busy before the kids came along. I took some classes then set up shop in the old cob shed behind the house."

Liz drew water into the teakettle and set it on a stove burner to heat. "Would you like a cup of tea?" she asked, and when Mallory answered, took two mugs from the cupboard and placed them on the table.

"Mack and I got married right after I graduated from high school," Liz said, measuring loose tea into muslin bags. "He wanted to start a family right away, but I wasn't ready. I liked working with glass and aspired to be a great artist." Liz gave a self-conscious laugh. "I wanted to do something before I settled down to being a mother."

Liz withdrew a package of lemon bars from the old-fashioned breadbox on the counter and set them on the table.

"Then I miscarried—three times. They didn't think I would be able to have any children so I used my hobby to take my mind off of … babies. I spent a lot time in that shed. It was a rough stage in our marriage—we almost didn't make it."

Liz walked to the sink and traced the glass lily beside the kitchen window above the basin, "I loved surrounding us with callas."

She took two saucers from the cupboard and put them on the table.

"Then I became pregnant with Tatiana. They couldn't figure out why I had miscarried before. The McAlister family doctor, an old guy set in his ways, suggested that my work with glass might have been the cause—because of the lead and all."

She carried her favorite porcelain teapot and the bags of tea to the stove. "So I gave it up. I couldn't take any chances that anything would happen to Tat…and then three years later, Gregg came along, and I was so busy raising them and being a farmwife…I didn't have time to miss my hobby."

The teakettle whistled and she poured the steaming water over the teabags. She carried the pot to the table and put it beside the lemon cookies. "I don't know if Mack ever forgave me for the miscarriages. I think he believed what the doctor said about my working with lead…I guess I believed it, too, deep in my heart." For the first time since beginning her story, Liz looked at Mallory. "I still don't know if I am responsible for the deaths of my babies …"

Liz poured their tea and they sat in silence as they sipped the hot liquid. After a few minutes, Mallory asked, "Would you show me your studio? Is it still there?"

"No … I mean, no, it isn't still there. Mack threw everything away. He wouldn't even let me give my equipment to my teacher.

He broke the unused glass and threw it in a pile behind the barn. It's a wonder he didn't replace all of this with plain glass."

"That would have been awful!" Mallory interjected.

"Yeah, I think he knew that would have been the last straw. I guess he thought keeping me was worth the trade of putting up with … all of this for the rest of his life."

Liz bit into a cookie then brushed crumbs from her face with a napkin.

"Wow! Where did all of that come from? I didn't mean to burden you with my past history, Mallory. Please don't say anything to Gregg. He doesn't even know about the miscarriages, much less the part my glasswork may have played in … in them."

"Sure, I promise," Mallory agreed, picking up her cookie. *How could Gregg have gone through his entire lifetime without learning of his mother's past?* she wondered to herself.

Liz watched the sunrise over the cornfield that stretched from the edge of the garden to the woodlot a half-mile to the east. As the fireball nudged upward over the horizon, she tried to imagine the bright orange-pink set in stained glass. Without conscious thought, she carried her coffee cup through the mudroom and out the back door.

Mack had maintained the cob shed as meticulously as the other outbuildings—the small milk house to the east in which Liz stored her gardening tools, the chicken coop out by the barn that housed the riding mower, weed whacker and other lawn care equipment, the pig house beside the garden and even the small outhouse beside the chicken coop, with the crescent moon on its door—all painted the traditional barn red with white trim. After emptying the cob shed of all signs of Liz's detested hobby, Mack had used it to store lumber, hardware, and other odd and end carpentry supplies.

As Liz creaked open the shed door, memories flooded back. Memories of escaping for hours into her solitude—just her and the deejays of Detroit's notorious CKLW, with their doo-wop and

Motown tunes and lurid tales of spectacular news events. Memories of working late into the night on one design or another—she wondered at the effort it took Mack to help her install her creations into this window or that. Happy memories of how at first he had enjoyed her enterprise, joking with her as he cut holes into the walls for the small windows between the lower level rooms.

But as time passed and she lost one child after another, she became more immersed in her work, and he became less of a willing partner and more resentful of each new project. Perhaps if she had listened to him ... if the doctor had said something earlier ...

Liz closed the door on her memories and returned to the house. She sat her cup of untouched coffee on the counter and turned the knob on the antique radio that sat on the window shelf. Not in the mood for national news, she changed the channel to the local station. As the smooth baritone of the deejay's voice floated from the airwaves, she leaned closer to the receiver.

"Sweet sugar snap!" she exclaimed, "No wonder his voice sounded familiar!"

The woman being interviewed answered a question David had asked, but Liz was too nonplussed to listen to what she was saying. David asked another question, and Liz became aware that the interviewee must be a local author. The woman bantered easily as David spoon fed her questions. The conversation seemed so intimate, Liz felt as though she was eavesdropping—or perhaps she was coating the voices with her own emotions.

She sat mesmerized through the local news and weather. She noticed the melodic fluctuations in David's voice as he announced area birthdays and anniversaries, giving a personal touch to each name read. She listened through his eclectic selection of songs until the program ended almost two hours later. Her heart thrummed long after she silenced the radio. Still unnerved, she gathered her gardening tools and was walking around the old milk house when Neil Rowland drove in followed by another pickup truck. She waited while the two drivers made their way toward her.

"Mornin' Liz," her farm manager greeted her. "I'd like you to meet Aaron Caine, the new man I said we had hired."

Liz assessed their latest employee as she extended her hand. Aaron Caine appeared to be anything but a farmer as he removed his nondescript black ball cap and briefly took her hand in his. Tall, lean, with a white-blonde crew cut, he looked more like an albino tiger tensed and ready to spring. Eyes the hue of ice in winter seemed to take her measure. *Chilling* ... Liz thought as he put his cap back on, shading his face.

"Pleased to meet you, Mr. Caine. If you need anything, I'm sure Neil will be able to assist you." Instinct told Liz she wanted little to do with the new farmhand. He touched his fingers to the bill of his ball cap and gave a slight nod.

Liz watched the two men walk away—Neil in his baggy overhauls and worn tee-shirt and Caine in new snug-fitting jeans and a chambray shirt that almost looked ironed. No ... she didn't have a good feeling about Aaron Caine at all.

David Morales chalked the tip of his cue stick and sized up the table before him. "Three ball in the side pocket, then eight ball in the end over there."

"Man, you gonna beat me again, *compadre.*" Hector Gonzales complained as his opponent executed the called moves with precision.

"Yeah, well, put up or shut up," David replied as he put a quarter on the edge of the table, retrieved the balls from the shelf below and racked them in the black triangle.

"You know, *amigo*, you're not so much fun to play with anymore. It's that *gringa's* turned you bitter. *Tia's* right, she was no good for you from the start. Let it go, bro, or she's gonna eat you up!"

"You being my shrink now, Hector? 'Cause if you are we'd better find a couch and set a price. It'll take more than a quarter's wager to dig out what's messed up in here." David pointed to his head.

"Don't think that's where the problem is. I think your head has it all figured out, it's *el corazon* that's all twisted." He poked at his friend's chest with the end of his pool stick. "If I could wipe that lady out of your heart, I would. But I don't think it's all that easy."

David held the filter of an unlit cigarette between his teeth. "Good that *Tia's* finally on the right side of the law, but I sure could use a smoke about now." He shifted the cigarette to his left hand and took a swig of his 'near-beer,' "… and a drink of something stronger than this piss water."

"Man, you got it bad," Hector commiserated.

"I've had enough of this pity party. I'm gonna find me some fun." David jammed his cue into the rack on the wall with a bit more force than necessary and made a beeline for the backdoor as his friend called after him, "You take care of yourself, Morales—don' do anything stupid!"

David drove to a fishing pull-off along the Maumee. He parked the truck, and as he opened the door he eased a cigarette pack from his shirt pocket. He stood, tipped the pack upside down, and tapped it against his hand.

"I don't need these damn things," he said as he crumpled the nearly full pack in a clenched fist. He glanced around for a trashcan then tossed the pack back onto the seat of his pickup. He tipped his head, looked toward the sky, and sighed, "What I need is just as deadly. Hector's so right, you've got it bad, Morales."

He made his way down to the river's edge where he found a dry rock to use as a bench. The water washed over pebbles and lapped at the toes of his sneakers as he scanned the shoreline of a small island to the northwest. A great blue heron bobbed its head underwater. After a few tries the bird caught a small bass. It stretched its long neck upward and swallowed its captive whole, leaving just the tail for one final gulp.

I know just how that little fish feels, David thought.

Herring gulls flew low over the water, cavorting and calling to one another, while turkey vultures soared overhead. David eyed the large black birds as they seemed to circle ever lower above him.

"Not dead yet …" he tossed the words upward, but they fell

to earth with a thud around him.

He searched the ground for a small flat stone. Finding a likely candidate, he tried to skip it across the water but it sank after just one hop. He found another then tossed it away before rising to his feet with resignation. Even Mother Nature couldn't give him solace from what tugged at his heart. He climbed into his truck and headed back toward town.

"Roseanne, where are you?" Liz poked around the haymow looking for her ward and her new family of kittens. She heard a soft mewling from behind a stack of straw bales and walked toward the sound. The little gray and white runt, the only longhaired kitten of the litter, sat shivering on the hard floor.

"Where's your mama?" Liz asked as she picked up the little bundle of fur and held it in front of her face. She nuzzled the kitten against her neck and cuddled it to her breast as she continued her search.

"Meoooowww…" This time the sound was distinctively louder and came from the main floor of the barn. Liz peered over the edge of the mow to see Roseanne looking up at her with the kittens scurrying in after their mother from the lean-to behind the main bay of the barn. They batted at each other and ran circles around the older cat. Desert Pro munched oats from the feed box in his stall then neighed as if adding his commentary to the commotion caused by Roseanne and her litter.

Liz carried the littlest kitten down to where the others tumbled about, but it clung to her with tiny razor sharp claws, raised its head and looked up, wide-eyed.

"You poor little 'fraidy cat! You're scared of your own siblings!" Liz took the kitten back to the mow where she had found her. As she put her back in the nest, Roseanne was approaching to feed her little runt.

He sat watching the farmhouse as he had so often over the past several weeks, biding his time until the right opportunity presented it-

self. The purple-eyed witch came and went as he imagined what he could do to her. He'd watched her go into the barn … Maybe he'd take her in the haymow. He pictured her lying naked against the hard floorboards. He'd make her beg … all in due time …

Liz listened to David's morning show, *Davy Jones' Locker*, every day for the next week, marveling at his interviewing skills. No matter if his guest was the president of the local woman's club or an opponent of factory farms, he put them at ease. His apparent research gave him the knowledge to elicit their best responses. He interspersed the second half of his show with selections from local singer songwriters and invited artists into the studio to perform.

He also took questions for his guests as well as song requests from his audience. Liz counted the rings as she held the phone to her ear. *C'mon, pick it up before I chicken out!*

David answered, *"Davy Jones' Locker."*

Liz hesitated a few seconds before asking, "Mr. Jones, I have a request for a very special song. It's called *Besame Mucho* …"

A full minute seemed to pass before the familiar voice came back over the phone lines, *"I could sing that for you, mi güerita, but it would have to be an in-person performance."*

"I think that could be arranged …"

"I have missed you …"

"Call me …"

They disconnected from each other as the last few notes of the Eagles' *Desperado* played out.

David's voice filtered into Liz's kitchen, "This *desperado* just got a request from a lovely *señora* so let's listen to a station ID and we'll be right back with *Besame Mucho*."

"Give me a little time, Brandon. Mom will come around." Brandon Michaels was in full uniform as he and Gregg shared a tall table in one of Bowling Green's newer pubs. He laid his hat on the table and rested his hand on its brim as he smiled at the younger man across from him.

"I would like to see your mother again. She is one fine lady," the Lieutenant responded as Gregg's cell phone intoned an incoming call. He fished it from his pocket and checked the number.

"Mom?" He raised his eyebrows at the man across the table, "Yeah, I know I haven't been home in a while. I thought we needed some space." ... He nodded, "Sure, you can stop by tomorrow. I'll be home from class by two."

Mallory passed by the phone just as it rang. "Hi David. I think Liz is around somewhere ..." She laughed as she handed the receiver to Liz, who was lifting a plate from the dishwasher.

Liz put the plate on the counter as she said into the phone, "David, I finally figured out why your voice sounded so familiar. Why didn't you tell me you were Davy Jones?" ... "Right now? Not much of anything." ... "Sure, stop on over."

Mallory grinned, waiting until Liz disconnected the call before heading toward the door, "I'm off to the library. Be back tonight!"

Liz had just enough time to wash up and change out of her gardening clothes before David pulled into the driveway. She watched him walk to the house and ring the bell before she opened the door.

They stood inches apart, not moving, before he stepped past her and into the foyer. He looked at her with anticipation when she closed the door and led him into the dining room. He stopped just inside the doorjamb and glanced around the room.

"Wow! Who did all the stained glass?"

Liz glanced around then looked down to the floor as a flush crept up her cheeks.

"You did all this?"

Liz nodded her head.

"This is amazing stuff! I have to have you on my show— you can describe how it's done! I could have you talk about doing glasswork at home and Mel ..."

"No, I couldn't ..." Liz interrupted, "it was so long ago. I haven't touched glass since before Tatiana was born."

"But you're an artist! Have you thought about taking it up again? I know someone who ..."

"Mallory said the same thing." Liz shook her head then shrugged her shoulders, "I don't know. I've looked at my old workshop. So many memories ... so much stuff piled in there."

"I could help you clear it out and get a studio set up!"

"Thanks. I'll think about it ..."

She led him through the archway into the living room, giving him almost the same spiel as she had to Mallory and receiving almost the same reaction.

"You amazed me before, *mi güerita*, but now I'm blown away. You shouldn't let such talent go to waste!"

As they walked back through the archway and by the stairs to the upper level, he cocked his head in the direction of the steps.

She shook her head, "I don't think it would be a good idea to show you the bedrooms. Who knows when Mallory might return."

He took her hands in his and pulled her toward him. "You afraid of me?" he asked as he took possession of her lips. His hands roamed from her back to caressing the sides of her breasts. Their lips parted and she rested her forehead on his chin while their breathing slowed to an acceptable rate. They kissed again and broke apart.

"Afraid of you? I don't know—maybe of my reaction to you. I don't know why you make me feel the way you do ..." She looked up into those unfathomable dark eyes before going on, "... and I'm not sure I'm ready for it ... not sure at all."

"We'll take things slow, Liz McKenna. You set the pace and I'll follow."

"Sweet sugar snap," she expelled a breath. "What my body is saying right now scares the heck out of me."

As they drew together again, his hands found and claimed her breasts. Her hips thrust forward in their need. He tugged her top free from her skirt, but she stayed his hand before he could go further.

"David, David," she sighed, "If we go through with this now ... and there's nothing I would rather do ... we'll burn out the passion ... and I'm not sure there would be anything more." She took a deep breath, "When I walked into that bar that night ..."

"*Tia Juana's*," he supplied.

"Yeah, there. I wanted to get ... well ... laid. There's no other way to say it."

"Not in polite company, anyway," he laughed, "but you were pretty much a walking advertisement."

"Was I that obvious?"

"Maybe only to the horny toads in the room, like yours truly."

They both chuckled, then Liz said, "We've come a long way if we can laugh at that night. Thank you, David Morales, for being such a nice guy and letting me get to know you."

"I'm not really all that nice. There are things you don't know ... things you should know before you let me get any closer to you." He hesitated, "And what I did that night had nothing to do with being nice. I wanted you so bad ... But taking you then would have been tantamount to rape." He looked past her then pulled her close. "So much you do not know ..." His words were muffled against her hair.

As they passed through the kitchen Liz pointed to the antique radio on the shelf above the counter. "So how is it, Davy Jones, that you can deejay and work on the road crew?"

"I don't seem to be able to, as it turns out," David said. "I had the radio gig first, but it didn't pay the bills. I had experience in heavy equipment and was on the call list with the union. They needed someone to operate the asphalt truck with the Beaver Creek project and I was able to work my schedule out for that. But I think my boss there put the skids on my road-building career. I'm still technically on the call list, but my phone hasn't been ringing off the hook. Meanwhile, I've got some savings that I'm living off of until something else comes up. I'm pretty versatile so I'm sure I'll catch a break before too long.

"And as long as I have my radio gig, I'm okay." He patted

the side of the 1930's radio case. "So this is what you listen to *Davy Jones' Locker* on? I'll keep that in mind during my shows." His smile was intimate as he reached for Liz's hand, tugging her toward him. Their hands broke apart as their arms encircled each other. He leaned against the counter and she, against him. Their lips met, again drawing them near to a space they dared not enter.

Liz drew back, placed her hands against his shoulders and stole one last kiss, before stepping backward toward the mud-room door. He remained where he was, hands pressed against the counter top, for just a moment longer, before following her through the door.

She showed off her garden. Squash, cucumber, and melon vines trailed down their hills in their quest for domination over the pole bean tripods and sweet corn that edged their section of the plot. Neat rows of carrots, red beets, onions, lettuce, and radishes grew in long straight lines. Tomato, pepper, and eggplants, each spaced a few feet from one another, had been recently weeded.

"You are one ambitious lady. You surely can't eat all of this!" David stood by four small okra plants, looking over what he calculated to be an acre of vegetables.

"I used to can and freeze a lot of it, but not anymore. I've taken boxes of produce into the food pantry, but last year I couldn't even give it all away. To be honest, it's more a habit now … and a time-filler … than anything. I guess I'll cut down on the garden size eventually, what with Mack, Tat, and now Gregg gone …"

"I could ask Cassandra if she might want to sell a few things in her herb shop," David ventured.

"That thought had crossed my mind, too. I don't really know her well. Her aunt, Penelope Gibson, lived at the farm with that … handyman … or whatever he was for as long as I can remember. They had the strangest relationship—she came here from California, they say, and he followed her. They were nice enough, but never quite fit in, and Mack's family never approved of their living arrangement. Then there was a legendary summer where Penelope Gibson took in one of Mack's dad's migrant families. That didn't set too well with the McAlisters *at all.*

"When Cassandra moved here after her aunt's stroke there was all that business about the embezzlement from O'Shay's. She was exonerated, of course—it was all her ex-husband's doing. He'll be in prison until he's an old man along with that creepy sheriff … I can't remember his name now …"

"Crenshaw—Billy Joe Crenshaw," David supplied.

"Yeah, that's right. Of course, you would know all about that, given you're related to Cassandra's husband …"

David gave Liz an assessing look. "Just *amigos.* My sister Anita is Cassie's best friend." He was used to *Anglos* thinking that every *Latino* in town was related but hearing Liz make the assumption only emphasized the differences between them.

Liz stepped away from him and looked down at the ground. As she raised her head the migrant housing caught her attention. She sighed and looked at David across the chasm that had opened between them.

You can't miss Mom's red Mustang, Gregg thought as he watched his mother pull into a parking space in front of his apartment complex. The car was an anniversary gift from his dad a few years before the accident. His mom had talked about a Mustang convertible all during Gregg's childhood, then when she got it, she chastised his dad for spending so much money on a car. *Women!* It's like last week when he called Old Mal for help with his economics test. She got all hot with him just because he hadn't finished the chapter. It wasn't like he hadn't picked up the book all summer! He was still annoyed as his mom rang the bell. When he opened the door, she was gripping two large canvas bags of groceries in her hands. He reached over, took one from her, and peeked inside.

"Great! More of Uncle Bill's canned beef!"

"I haven't been here for so long, I didn't know what you might need," she said as he bent down to get his customary motherly peck on the cheek.

"Thanks, Mom, but you don't have to worry about me going hungry—I do get to the store once in a while!"

"I just thought I'd help out a little," she said as she glanced around the room. Freshly vacuumed, no beer cans, no ash trays … "Is this the right apartment? I thought my son, Gregg, lived here."

"Can't a guy clean up for a visit from his mom?" Gregg asked as they carried the groceries to the kitchen. Liz sorted out the perishables and handed them to her son to put in the refrigerator.

"A sirloin? Yes!" Gregg said, with a slight pump to the hand holding the steak before he put it in the meat drawer.

They had emptied the sacks and Liz had poured a diet cola over ice while Gregg popped the tab on a beer, when the doorbell rang. Gregg sat his beer on the near-empty coffee table and walked to the door. When he opened it, Lt. Brandon Michaels stood on the other side dressed in his crisp blue uniform, hat in hand.

As he stepped across the threshold, Liz looked with suspicion from one man to the other.

"Greggory, did you tell Brandon I would be here today?"

"Nope," he answered. "Didn't say a word. Guess it's just a lucky coincidence."

Liz had to admit that Lt. Michaels presented a dashing picture in his dress blues flashing her a boyish grin that was anything but innocent.

"I must confess, Liz, I've been bugging Gregg to see you again. We were together yesterday when you called."

Disarmed by his honesty, Liz allowed herself to be beguiled by his smile. Gregg retrieved a beer for the lieutenant and surprised his mother with a plate of homemade cookies.

"Okay, I didn't make them—but somebody did!" he said.

Brandon laughed, saying they were almost as good as his mother's. "My mom's chocolate tortes were so well-known, she sold them to wineries throughout Napa Valley."

"Napa Valley? I thought your parents lived in Detroit." Liz said.

Brandon raised his eyebrows but his smile never slipped,

"They moved east to take care of my grandparents when I was accepted into the academy at Colorado Springs. "

When Liz left for the farm a few hours later, Brandon had inveigled a date with her for the following Saturday.

Just as well, she thought as she eased the Mustang onto Route 6 for the drive home. She needed something to distract her from thoughts of David. He didn't mention seeing her again when he left yesterday. *They were just too different*, she tried her best to convince herself.

Their lives were just too far apart.

Liz and Mallory sat at the patio table under a red striped umbrella drinking iced tea. The slate gray pavers soaked up the afternoon sun on this hotter-than-usual mid-June day, and they both had their feet propped up on empty chairs to escape the heat.

They watched Neil Rowland and Aaron Caine working with the grain bins across the road and a short distance to the west. A pickup pulled into the drive, and Peter climbed out and walked toward the other men.

"Why is that called 'the Other Place?" Mallory asked.

"There used to be a house similar to this on that property—I think it belonged to Mack's great uncle—but it burned down long before I joined the family. They never rebuilt and in the 1960s or 70s, Mack's dad and uncle tore down the old barn and built a large pole building to hold bigger machinery. Since this was the home site, they called that 'the Other Place.'"

Liz took a sip of tea. "Mack and Peter put up the second pole barn ten or so years ago to hold the new combine with its headers as well as the grain truck."

"Headers?" Mallory questioned.

Liz explained, "That's what they attach to the front of the combine to take off the various types of grain. There's a header for soybeans and wheat—the one with the long rotating slats and tines that most people think of when they see a combine. Then the corn header is the one with the long points across the front."

The persistent chirp of a robin drew their attention to the maple tree branch overhead. "Look, there's a nest in the fork of that limb. That mom's agitated about something!"

They watched the bird for a few minutes before Mallory looked back toward the Other Place. "What are the big steel bins for?"

"Grain drying and storage," Liz said. "Mack's dad and uncle put up the older ones. Peter and Mack updated and expanded the operation a few years after they built the pole barn. When the grain's harvested, it needs to be dried to get the moisture content down to a certain percentage so it doesn't spoil when it's stored. If we can dry it and store it ourselves, we don't have to pay to have the grain kept for us in an elevator."

Mallory looked from the Other Place back to Liz. "I never realized what all went into farming."

Liz nodded. "Mack was known around the county as a smart farmer." She lifted her glass and smiled at the memory, "He seemed to be able to read the weather and the markets. He had a real head for math—knew how much seed to buy and how to make the most of the land."

Mallory spread her hands and asked, "How much of this do the McAlisters own?"

"A lot. Mack's ancestors settled in this area back in the days when it was still a swamp. They either claimed or bought up most of the land in this quadrant of the county. Mack's grandfather talked about cutting trees and using the trunks to build roads—corduroy roads, they called them because they were so rough. They hauled their grain to the Maumee and sent it upriver on canal boats. Grandpa McAlister was full of stories handed down from his grandfather."

Liz smiled, "But, to answer your question, Mack's father and uncle farmed something like twenty-five hundred acres—mostly corn, soybeans, and wheat, but also tomatoes in the fields around our house."

Mallory shifted in her chair to glance back at the migrant

housing that had all but disappeared in a thicket of shrubs and fast-growing trees. "So people lived back there until ...?"

"I think it was 1996. Peter wanted to stop using migrant labor when he moved back, but it wasn't until after his grandfather's heart attack that they stopped planting tomatoes altogether. It was economics that finally won out. Mack's mom had turned the accounting books over to us, and Peter convinced Mack it would be more profitable to plant all grain and eliminate the need for seasonal workers. I think it was a moral issue for Peter, but we never really talked about it."

"Wow, that's big." Mallory said.

"What do you mean?" Liz asked.

"Nothing." Mallory said. She traced her fingers down the side of her glass, making trails in the condensation that had collected there. A dragonfly landed in the circle of water left on the edge of the table by her glass. It flicked the tail of its long iridescent green body before flying off on diaphanous wings. "So do you still do the paperwork for the farm?"

"I tried to for a few years, but I'm as bad at math as Mack was good. After they hired Neil, his wife, Linda, took over the accounts for the farm. Everything's done on the computer now." Liz gave a quick laugh and said, "The combine even has a computer in it that measures the dryness of the grain when it's harvested! It's all way beyond me. I've tried to keep up since we lost Mack, but I just don't have the aptitude for farming like he did. And I'm not a natural with computers like Linda." Liz gave a slight shrug to her shoulders, "I look over the weekly reports that she sends me, but more and more, I trust Neil and Peter to take care of it all.

"Linda even tried to get me involved in a farmwives group on Facebook—they have a website and everything—but I just don't have any interest in it." Liz raised her eyebrows and shook her head. "I guess I really wasn't cut out to be a farmwife. I helped haul grain to the elevators in town until I dumped a wagonload of soybeans in the ditch. That was pretty scary! After that, I was relegated to taking lunches and dinners to the field. Some days during planting and harvesting they worked nearly round-the-clock. Mack could never rest if the time was right to be in the fields."

"Yeah, but I've seen all the 'Best of Show' rosettes that you won hanging in the office off the kitchen," Mallory said.

"I was more interested in vegetable gardening, my berry patches, and little fruit orchard. Mack was always proud that my produce and canned goods won blue ribbons at the county fair. He's the one who hung all of my ribbons above the computer."

They watched the men working for a few minutes before Mallory asked, "Does Gregg's grandfather still help with the farm?"

"No, after his two bypass surgeries, he turned over control of the farm to Mack and Peter, and bought a retirement home in Arizona. He still farmed some when they came back to Ohio in the summers, until…" Liz glanced toward the field across the road, "Mack's accident—his dad hasn't come out here since. After losing Peter's dad in Vietnam, Mack's death was too much for him to take. When Mack's parents come back, which isn't that often anymore, they stay at Bill's—the middle brother. You met him and his wife Memorial Day at the cemetery. He has the cannery southwest of town."

Mallory nodded.

"Mack had hoped Gregg would take over our share of the farm. He had wanted him to study agriculture at Ohio State, but Gregg had no interest in going anywhere but Bowling Green. He always enjoyed helping his dad with the farm, but hasn't shown much interest in it since the accident." Liz looked back toward the field before adding, "Maybe that's just as well."

Mallory lowered her feet to the tiles and leaned in toward Liz, "Can I ask what happened to his dad…or would you rather not talk about it?"

Liz watched the robin flit to a branch higher in the tree. She listened as it trilled a warning to its unseen mate. She thought about the small blue eggs that might be tucked away in the nest. *Mack*—she hadn't told anyone the details of the accident. All of her friends and family had known what had happened. She glanced back at the young woman who, in such a brief span of time, had evolved from boarder to friend. Liz sensed in Mallory a kinship and compassion beyond her years.

"It's okay." Liz said as she swirled the ice cubes in her glass and took a sip of tea. She looked toward the Other Place. "It was in October—a beautiful Northwest Ohio fall day, with the maple trees blazing reds and oranges. I can picture it as though it were yesterday. Mack was plowing the back field of the section across the road. He said later that the plow kicked up a rock that lodged between the blades. When he stood to see what had happened the tractor lurched forward and he lost his balance."

Liz held tightly to her iced tea glass, looking beyond the woman across from her. "The plow ran over him. It severed one leg and mangled the other so badly it had to be amputated. He had lost a lot of blood by the time a neighbor found him." She closed her eyes and bit the inside of her lower lip, concentrating on the pain.

"He could have died there in the field, but by some miracle, he lived. But he couldn't face life without his legs. Rather than fighting to survive, he languished, first in the hospital, then in hospice. His body shut down little by little, and then it was over. Just over …" Liz looked back at Mallory, "… for him, anyway."

They sat in silence, letting Liz's words settle around them.

Mallory spoke first, "That's a lot for you—and Gregg—to deal with."

"And Tatiana, too, though she seems to have been able to get on with her life.

"But Gregg … I'm not sure how he's coping. He appears to use his father's death as an excuse to avoid growing up. He's floundered from one major to another—I wonder if he will ever graduate! I'm glad he, at least, has you to help him focus on his classes."

Mallory sighed and rubbed her cold glass against her hot cheek, "Problem is, Gregg sees me as a conduit to a passing grade and … nothing more. He has me pegged as a brainiac—it doesn't help that I work two library jobs."

Liz nodded as she watched Neil Rowland and Aaron Caine negotiate the drive from the Other Place to the home site with a sprayer the width of the road and tractor pulling a cultivator. Peter followed them out of the drive in his pickup, waving to Liz and Mallory as he passed by the house.

"Give him time. He'll come around. He's not as shallow as he seems ... I hope ..." Liz finished with a half-smile. "And, I hate to say it, but until he matures a little, you may be better off looking elsewhere."

"Yeah, tell me how that works ..." Mallory said to the older woman, "... on Saturday night. You did say you were going out with Lt. Michaels and not David, didn't you?"

Liz took a drink from her glass and chose not to respond as the two men approached their table.

Neil spoke as Caine stood slightly aside, hands on his hips.

"Aaron has suggested that we sell the corn we have in storage. The price per bushel is higher than I've ever seen it, and he's thinking it will be dropping in the next few weeks."

"What do you and Peter think?" she asked her farm manager, still uneasy about their new hired hand.

"Could be. Aaron says he's messed around with the commodities market some, and the indicators he's noticed point to a downturn in corn. The regulators are letting more in from foreign markets."

Liz looked from one man to the other. *If this Aaron Caine has any inside track or instinct or whatever on the market*, she thought, *we may as well take advantage of it. Lord knows, I haven't been able to figure out when to hold and when to sell.*

Aloud, she said, "I'll follow your lead, Neil. If you think Mr. Caine knows what he's talking about, go ahead and sell."

She gave an unsmiling nod to the new man and was rewarded with an icy glare.

Caine followed Neil up the sidewalk, hesitating as he stepped onto the gravel driveway to glance back toward the patio. Mallory shivered in spite of the heat. "There's something about that new guy that gives me the heebie-jeebies."

"I know what you mean," Liz said, as Aaron Caine climbed into the sprayer cab in his too-new jeans and too-crisp chambray shirt. He just did not fit the farmer mold—not at all.

CHAPTER FOUR

When the strawberries came on, they ripened with a vengeance. Liz stood and stretched her back as the early morning dew settled on her ankles. She had already picked eight quarts and was only halfway through the patch. The berries were larger than usual—the rains had come at just the right time, along with warm sunny days and cool nights, to produce a bumper crop, far more than Liz could use.

By late morning she had changed from her work clothes, packed several quarts of berries into a cooler in the trunk of her Mustang, and headed down the road to the old Gibson farmstead, hoping she would find Cassandra Alvarez in her herb shop. When Liz pulled into the drive, Cassie was walking to the house from the direction of the flower fields behind the barn with her arms full of fresh picked blooms.

Liz stepped out of the car as Cassie approached.

"Can I help you with those?" Liz asked.

"If you would just get the door to the shop, that would be great!"

Liz helped Cassie put the flowers into water, as she explained, "I'm taking these into Ela's Herbary in town. They need centerpieces for a tea this afternoon."

"Is there anything I can do?" Liz offered, marveling at her neighbor's ability to look fresh even after coming in from the flower fields. Her ash blonde hair was twisted into a knot at the nape of her neck, with only a few tendrils framing her face. Cassandra Alvarez was definitely a classy lady—almost intimidatingly so. Liz ran her hand through her barely controlled black curls before adding, "Or would you rather I came back another time?"

"I'd be glad for the help and the company. Jaime's in Alaska with Tina and Ben's at basketball camp all week."

Liz began sorting the flowers, while Cassie trimmed and arranged them for a half a dozen bouquets.

As she separated a snapdragon and a coreopsis whose leaves had become entangled, Liz said, "Would you be interested in expanding your shop to include produce? I have several quarts of fresh-picked strawberries in the car …"

"Let's get them in the shop before the sun turns your trunk into an oven," Cassie said, "and we can talk about it."

They sat the cooler along the wall and each sampled a juicy berry. Cassie handed Liz a section from a paper towel roll as she said, "Just by coincidence, Meredith Murphy and Emily Anderson stopped in last week with a similar idea."

"Meredith Murphy and Emily Anderson? Aren't they the…"

Liz hesitated as Cassie gave her a questioning look.

"…new neighbors who moved into the Carver place the next mile over?"

Cassie nodded, "They've kept the farm as it was and expanded the garden, hoping to sell at the farmer's market in town. But they are also considering bringing produce here to the shop.

"I've been thinking about it. After Aunt Nell could no longer help with the shop, I limited my hours to Tuesday and Thursday afternoons and Saturday nine to one," Cassie said. "If Meredith and Emily, and now you, covered Monday, Wednesday, and Friday afternoons, we could add fruits and veggies to the inventory to bring in more customers."

Cassie smiled, "I'd even thought about renaming the shop 'Country Ladies: Herbs, Flowers, and Produce.'"

Emily used her experience as a graphic designer to create fliers for the Country Ladies, and Meredith, a marketing instructor at the university, laid out their advertising strategy.

After the shop closed on Saturday, Liz and Cassie delivered fliers throughout the area, finishing late afternoon in Bowling Green. They celebrated with lattes at Grounds for Thought, the local coffee shop, bookstore, and arts venue.

As they shared a table beside a shelving range filled with cookbooks, Liz took a sip from her glass mug. She sat it on the table, saying, "You're so lucky you have Jaime. I hate being in the dating circuit."

Cassie watched her neighbor as she stirred her drink. She could understand David's attraction to the woman across the table. Her heart-shaped face was framed in black curls with the lightest peppering of silver. With her striking violet eyes, Liz McAlister presented a very beguiling picture.

"Take tonight," Liz said, "I'm going out with this Air Force guy that Gregg is hot on my dating. He's okay, but there's just nothing there, if you know what I mean."

Cassie thought she understood what Liz was saying and nodded her head, "What about David Morales? I heard you were also seeing him?" Cassie didn't say that David had been by to see Jaime, but stayed to talk with her when he found out her husband was gone.

"David? We're just too … too different. How do you do it, being married to Jaime? How do you fit into his culture? I don't think I could adjust."

"Jaime's family was so accepting of me, it was easy. David's sister, Anita, was my closest friend throughout school, so I guess I learned Latino ways from her—even though my dad was dead set against my seeing Jaime."

Liz fiddled with her drink, "Beyond my limited contact with migrant workers years ago, I've never had much to do with … other cultures. I know it works well for you being married to Jaime, but I just think I should stick to … how can I say it … my own kind."

Cassie sighed, "If that's really the way you feel, you're probably right. It's hard to overcome such an inbred…" She stopped, not wanting to offend her new partner, but Liz supplied, "… prejudice."

Liz's date with Brandon went a little better than the last. He took her to the Hollywood Casino near Toledo. Brandon tried to introduce Liz to the blackjack table, but after watching him play a few hands, the intensity of the game unnerved her.

She slipped away, finding a nearby slot machine featuring one of her favorite old-time crooners, Dean Martin. The machine inhaled her five-dollar bill, and she selected the buttons on the console to place her wager. Bells clanged and within seconds her five dollars had nearly doubled. She wagered again, and it tripled. When her winnings registered twenty-five dollars, she punched the button to receive a voucher for her prize money.

She walked back to the blackjack table, where Brandon was just cashing in his chips. They strolled around the large room, trying this machine or that. Liz stopped at a "one-armed bandit" that actually had a long lever on its side to pull. However, after trying the game a few times, she realized the bar was only for show, as she watched her money increase even before she released the lever.

They sipped cocktails at the raised lounge in the center of the casino. After attempting conversation, only to be drowned out by the clamor of the slot machines surrounding them, they quietly observed the other gamblers, now and again pointing to an obvious winner … or loser.

When they added up their winnings on their way home, they had accrued over $300. Brandon suggested they spend their stash the next day on a trip to Lake Erie.

They stood on the patio soaking in the warmth of the June night. "I haven't been to the islands in years," Liz said. "Gregg goes to Put-in-Bay all the time, but I can never remember whether it's on South Bass or Middle Bass Island."

"Just leave the driving to me …" he said as he closed the distance between them.

She looked up at his boyishly handsome face, his perfectly styled hair, gray eyes filled with anticipation, the charming smile, and willed herself to feel something ... anything. She thought she may have felt a stirring deep within her as she stepped into the circle of his arms. His kiss was deep and thorough and should have curled her toes ... should have ...

"Maybe we could save the island trip for another day. I'm pretty tired tonight ..." Liz said as she took a step backward.

"I'm not giving up that easy," he said looking down at her, his face shadowed. "How about a quiet stroll through the art museum. Toledo has one of the best in the world, I'm told, but I haven't had a chance to get there yet."

Liz nodded her acquiescence as Brandon bent down for a brief taste of her lips. "I'll be here at one o'clock," he said.

He watched again as lights went on and off, learning the lay of the house by her movement. As her bedroom light came on and she lowered the shade, he thought about her peeling her clothes from one layer to the next until she stood naked before him. The light went out as he let his imagination explore the places he would one day go....

David pulled into the driveway Sunday soon after Liz and Brandon had left for the Art Museum. Mallory had a rare day off and was relaxing on the patio with a book.

"Hi David," Mallory shifted in her chair. "You just missed Liz."

"I suppose that's for the good. I doubt she'd want to see me anyway. I just wanted to tell her that," he looked at Mallory as though considering his words, "a ... ah ... friend of my sister does stained glass work and she offered to help Liz get back into it."

Mallory lowered her eyes against his scrutiny before saying, "Yeah, I can't believe her talent! It would be too bad if she gave it up for good."

"Maybe you could mention that I stopped by. If she's interested, she can give me a call."

Mallory nodded. David had taken a few steps toward the driveway when she called to him. He turned toward her, but she just said, "Never mind ... I'll let Liz know."

Gregg's Ranger passed David's Jaguar in front of the house. Gregg kicked up stones as he skidded to a stop by the walkway.

"What's he doin' here?" he asked Mallory as he covered the walk in long strides.

"Hello, Gregg, nice to see you, too." Mallory said without looking up from her book.

He poured his lanky form onto the patio chair opposite where Mallory sat.

"So how's it going, Mal? They let you off from the library and all you have to do is read?"

"It's the only time I have to read what I want," she explained, *unless you have a better offer,* she added to herself.

"I was looking for Mom, but since her Latin lover boy just left, I don't suppose she's around."

"It should please you to know that she left with Brandon fifteen or so minutes before David arrived."

"Yeah? That rocks!"

He went on, "It's a beautiful day. What's say you and I head to Lake Erie? We could catch a few rays at the beach at East Harbor. You could even bring your book along for company if you get bored with me."

Mallory hesitated for just a second before closing her paperback, "Sure, why not?"

She hurried to her room and stuffed her bathing suit, beach towel, and a change of clothes in a canvas tote. At the last minute, she tossed her book in the bag, as well.

They stopped at Gregg's apartment so he could grab his swim trunks. Mallory stepped gingerly across the threshold as Gregg held the door for her. The place was disheveled, but not the total disaster described in Liz's stories.

Ian O'Flannery lay sprawled across the davenport wearing only a pair of plaid shorts, but straightened to a sitting position when he saw Mallory. He gave her a onceover as he pulled his tee-shirt over his head while rising from the couch.

Mallory returned the tall redhead's perusal, obviously amused at his quick movement. Before Gregg could introduce them, she extended her hand, "Hi, I'm Mallory Martin."

"You're the tutor this slug's been whining about? Man, I think I'd learn real quick with you by my side!"

"Keep it zipped up, O'Flannery. Old Mal and I are off to Lake Erie."

"Old Mal?" Ian and Mallory said in unison.

"Listen, Mallory, honey," Ian said. "If this loser doesn't treat you right, you just come to Ian. I'll take good care of you."

Gregg glared from one to the other before stalking off to retrieve his bathing trunks.

"C'mon, *Mallory*," he said, "if you're going with me. Or you could stay here with this creeper."

Mallory gave a slight shrug to her shoulders and smiled at Ian as she left, "See ya around."

"You can count on it," he replied as he leaned against the doorjamb watching the unaffected sway of Mallory's hips as she walked to his roommate's truck. Gregg looked up and caught Ian's smirk and then opened the door for Mallory, closing it again with a bit more force than was necessary.

Gregg slathered suntan lotion on Mallory's back, appreciating the slope of her shoulders as they curved under the strap of her modest two-piece bathing suit. *Nope, no bikini for Old Mal*, he thought. He rubbed the white cream on her back to where it disappeared under her suit bottom. He appreciated the natural tan of her skin, wanting to see more, before reminding himself that this was Old Mal, the stickler for books.

Mallory returned the favor, rubbing the lotion gently onto Gregg's back.

"Oops, guess I used a bit too much," she said, as it took her a little longer to rub the white streaks into his skin.

"No problem." Gregg found he wasn't minding the warmth of her touch or her nearness.

She spread out her towel a short distance from the lapping waves and pulled her book from within her canvas bag. Gregg shook out his towel and laid it close—but not too close—to hers and dropped down to catch a nap.

"You're no fun to play with anymore," Hector Gonzalez complained as he racked the balls after winning yet another pool game against David. "Forget the *gringa*. She's bad news."

"Just keep your nose in your own business and break." David Morales leaned on his cue stick. He had to admit he'd been in a bad way since meeting Mary Elizabeth McKenna McAlister. She had bewitched him with her violet eyes and left him thinking about little else.

"If I could wipe that woman out of your mind, I'd do it. We just got you back—and it was a *gringa* like that one who put you behind bars. Leave her alone, *amigo!*" Though David didn't react, Hector's plea did not fall on deaf ears. David resolved to stay within his own realm and away from the McAlister farm.

One day fell into another, as a week passed and then a second. Mallory had told Liz about David's visit. She roamed the house tracing the outlines of her stained glass creations, but did not call him, nor had he made a return stop. She took him with her to the garden in the morning on a portable radio, telling herself she just wanted to listen to the music on *Davy Jones' Locker*.

Cassie, Meredith, Emily, and Liz alternated afternoons at The Country Ladies. Liz had met Meredith Murphy, a tall, striking redhead with gorgeous hair, bright green eyes, a smattering of freckles, and a ready smile, and her partner, Emily Anderson, the week after delivering the fliers. In contrast to Meredith, Emily was five-foot-two at best—or as she put it, "vertically challenged." She was more rounded than shapely and wore her wavy brunette hair clasped in a barrette at the nape of her neck. Emily's wide brown eyes were her most striking feature—sparkling with an amusement known only to her.

Much to the delight of the partners, the number of customers making the trek from area towns seemed to increase daily. A women's club even came from Toledo, stopping in the quaint little canal town of Grand Rapids for lunch before driving on to the Country Ladies.

Gregg had begun to come home with more regularity, helping Liz with the garden and various chores. She smiled as she noticed he and Mallory had taken up their early roles as student and tutor.

Liz had gone to dinner with Brandon once, and at Gregg's invitation, he had joined her, Mallory, and Gregg for a barbeque. Liz was concerned he was making more of the relationship than she—if what they had could be called a relationship.

One morning Liz was pulling weeds from the hills of melons, squash, and cucumbers when she heard Mallory scream from the direction of the barn.

"OH MY GOD! LIZ! LIZ! COME QUICK!"

Gregg vaulted toward the barn from where he had been washing his truck, reaching Mallory several steps ahead of his mother.

He grabbed his mom and pulled her to his side before she could see the carnage that lay strewn before them. Mallory stepped back into the circle of his other arm, her hands clasped over her mouth.

Roseanne's kittens had been strangled and placed in macabre positions around the cement slab of the barn's floor.

"This isn't the work of a tomcat or coyote," Gregg said when he could find his voice.

Roseanne poked out from behind a straw bale, mewling as she nudged the still form of each of her babies. She looked up at the people standing just within the barn door, as though pleading for their help. She leaped onto the ladder to the haymow and scampered up the rungs, peering down over the edge when she reached the top.

They heard a mewing, but this time the sound did not come from the mother cat. Gregg climbed the ladder taking two steps at a time, disappeared, then reappeared with a small gray and white furball in his hands.

"Look, Mom, Mal! The little 'fraidy cat survived!"

He climbed back down to the barn floor and handed the shivering little creature to Liz. Roseanne followed him down and rubbed her fur in and out of Liz's legs. She bent down and placed the tiny survivor next to its mother who thoroughly cleansed her baby with her tongue.

They stayed a little longer in the barn before walking slowly back to the house.

"Who could have done such a thing? What kind of monster do we have around here?" Liz said, looking from Gregg to Mallory then back to her son.

As they sat around the kitchen table, Gregg asked his mother, "How well do you know that guy from the Lower Eastside that's been hanging around here?"

Liz started to respond, then sat back in her chair. *It couldn't be David, it just couldn't!* she thought, but aloud she said, "Not very well, I guess."

They sat in silence, feeling both apprehensive and helpless. Finally, Gregg scooted his chair back from the table and stood, "I'm going out to clean up the barn."

After a few minutes, he popped his head back through the kitchen archway, "Mom, I think Roseanne has something for you …"

Liz and Mallory joined Gregg by the open foyer door. Roseanne was sitting on the patio step holding her surviving baby in her mouth by the scruff of its neck. Liz reached down and took the kitten in her hands, bringing it up to her face to nuzzle. Roseanne meowed, rubbed Liz's legs, then walked off toward the road. Midway, she hesitated and glanced back toward the woman holding her kitten then continued to the ditch and disappeared down its bank.

The morning after finding the kittens, Liz didn't turn on the radio. Instead she busied herself with her new ward.

"You poor little thing," Liz said as she held the kitten close. She shut her eyes, in an attempt to block out the intrusion of the previous day's gruesome scene. She opened them again as the little creature wriggled from her grasp and dropped to the floor. The kitten skittered to a small opening between the table leg and the wall and cowered out of Liz's reach.

Liz poured milk in a shallow bowl and sweetened it with tuna broth. She placed it under the table a short distance from a chair and sat down. After nearly half an hour, the kitten crept toward the bowl and sniffed the liquid. She gave it a few tentative laps before planting her paws on the edge of the bowl and sticking her face into it. She then lifted her head and with a quick shake splattered tuna-flavored milk onto Liz's legs.

Liz smiled down at the little gray and while ball of fur. "Guess the first thing we need for you is a name." As she reached over to pet the cat, it jumped backward, nearly tipping the bowl, and braced itself, wide-eyed, on the linoleum with four splayed legs.

"I know, how about 'Fraidy Cat?" Liz asked with a bitter-sweet grin.

She leaned over to pick up the kitten and it mewed and scampered sideways. "You're such a shy little princess," Liz said as she lifted the tiny bundle of fur up to her face and looked into its eyes. "Maybe we should call you Princess 'Fraidy Cat, what do you think of that?"

Liz brought the kitten to her chest where it squirmed from her hands and skittered up her shirt to her shoulder. It seemed to give its approval as it rubbed the fuzzy flat of its forehead against Liz's neck.

Princess 'Fraidy Cat tagged Liz as she picked strawberries for the Country Ladies. Liz faced the barn as she plucked the red berries, but kept her eyes averted from its gaping center doors.

Dew saturated the kitten's long fur and she left a wet trail around Liz's ankles. When the Princess stopped to lick her white ruff dry, a small yellow butterfly flitted past. The kitten jumped between the strawberry plants then peeked out from under their broad leaves. She crouched further back, batting at Liz's hand when her new mistress bent down to pick her up.

"You truly are a 'fraidy cat," Liz laughed as she held the Princess against her and was greeted with both trembling and an exceptionally loud purr.

Liz packed the quart boxes of strawberries into her car along with bags of fresh-picked salad greens, peas in their pods, radishes, and green onions. Last, she got down on her knees and pulled the little kitten out from where it was hiding behind the Mustang's rear tire. She tucked the Princess on her lap as she drove the short distance to Cassie's.

Liz introduced Princess 'Fraidy Cat to Cassie, who in turn suggested they let her tawny tomcat, Slack-Eyed Joe, babysit. When Liz sat the kitten down beside the older cat, he looked up at her with his one good eye, as if to ask, "What am I supposed to do with this?" For once, the little Princess did not seem at all afraid. She clambered over Joe's back and rooted against the fur on his far side. He glanced up at Liz again then settled his head onto his paws to continue his nap. The activities of the morning had evidently worn out the kitten, as well, since she curled up in a little ball, nestled against Slack-Eyed Joe, and promptly fell asleep.

As they unloaded the produce from the Mustang, Liz described the events of the previous day to Cassie. Cassie backed her head out of the trunk and looked toward her neighbor with alarm, her immediate thoughts going to her ex-husband. She shook her head to dispel the notion. Paul was in prison. She would know if he had been released. Jaime would know …

Aloud, she asked, "Who would do such a thing?"

"I've been thinking about it all morning. Neil hired a new guy, Aaron Caine, to help in the fields. He … well he just doesn't seem the field hand type. He seems to know farming, but he makes me ... I don't know ... uneasy."

"Have you said anything to Neil about this Caine fellow?"

"No, but after what happened, I will. Then there's Brandon Michaels ..."

"That Air Force guy that Gregg introduced you to?"

"Yeah, he's a little full of himself, but I couldn't see him hurting anyone—or anything." Liz stood, a brown grocery bag filled with salad greens in either arm. She hesitated then looked at Cassie.

"What are you thinking?" Cassie asked.

"Gregg said something about David. He asked me how well I knew him, and I had to admit, not well. He's so mysterious about his past. He's mentioned his dark side a few times, but never explained what he meant ... You know David—could he do this?"

Cassie's response was curt and immediate. "If you think he could, then you're not the woman I thought you were. As to David's past, that's for him to tell you, not me." She turned her back on her neighbor and carried a flat of strawberries into the shop.

They packed the greens into coolers in a strained silence. As they arranged the peas, onions, and strawberries onto the display tables Meredith and Emily had gleaned for next to nothing at a going-out-of-business sale, the shop door opened and Jaime Alvarez stepped into the room.

Cassie dropped the onions she had been holding and greeted her husband with a warm smile. "I thought you would be in Toronto for the rest of the week!"

He only had eyes for one woman, Liz observed with a tinge of envy. Jaime took Cassie in his arms and kissed her thoroughly, as though Liz weren't in the room.

"Guess not," he said in a voice meant only for his wife.

Though he had put on a few pounds since his marriage to Cassie, most likely due to his hectic schedule, Liz thought Jaime Alvarez was still one of the most attractive men she had ever met. She was rescued from tumbling into melancholy by soft fur against her ankles. She stooped to pick up her little ward—her movement breaking the spell that had encompassed the room since Jaime's arrival.

"Hello, Liz," he smiled the easy smile of a contented man. "Who's this little guy?"

As Liz filled Jaime in on how Princess 'Fraidy Cat came to be there, contentment turned to concern.

"Paul's still in prison, isn't he?" Cassie asked. Her husband nodded, but assured the women he would verify the fact. "It's something Paul Alexander would be capable of doing, but even if he were around ... which he isn't ... why would he pick on Liz and the McAlister farm? It's not logical ... but, then, there's nothing logical about brutalizing kittens."

They talked a little longer. Though it was Cassie's afternoon to watch the shop, Liz offered to cover for her, given Jaime's unexpected return. Few customers stopped by. An acquaintance of Liz's picked up arrangements Cassie had made for an awards banquet that night. She was delighted with Liz's fresh greens and strawberries, saying they were better than what she could get at the grocery store. Another lady wanted raspberries, but when Liz told her they wouldn't be ripe for a week or so, she took the last of the strawberries. As Liz was about to close the shop, a car pulled into the drive and Ben, Jaime's son climbed out of the back seat. He waved to the passenger in the car as it disappeared around the curve of the horseshoe drive.

"Hi Ben," Liz called as he walked toward the shop.

"Hey, Mrs. McAlister, I thought Mom was in the shop this afternoon."

The boy brightened when Liz said that his father had returned home earlier than expected. "Cool, he promised to teach me how to drive!"

Cassie had told Liz that Jaime and Ben had had a tug-of-war about her stepson's driving. Liz smiled at the boy, remembering a similar battle between Mack and Gregg when he turned sixteen. But Gregg had been driving farm machinery for a few years, so he had more of a sense of the road than, perhaps, Ben might.

"It's hard to believe that you're sixteen already," Liz said.

"My sixteenth birthday isn't until next month, but I can get my temps now, if Dad'd only let me. He wants to wait until I get back from Alaska." The boy sounded less than excited about the trip to stay with his mother's family. Jaime's children, Ben, and his twelve-year-old sister, Christina, had an Inuit mother who had died birthing Tina. Cassie had explained that the children both spent time with their mother's family over the summer—time that Tina loved, as she more resembled her native Alaskan family. But Ben, who took after his father, was more focused on activities with his high school friends.

"Maybe if you had gone to wrestling camp instead of basketball …" Liz teased the boy.

"Yeah, but I've been playing basketball since middle school. Dad should be over it by now." The boy's impish grin let Liz know he enjoyed being his own person, as his dad had been a state-wrestling champion in high school. Cassie had told Liz that Ben was doing well at the North County Consolidated School, without the harassment that his father endured at the old Tecumseh High. "Different generations," Cassie and Liz had agreed. Though, given Gregg's attitude toward David, Liz had wondered …

Ben opened one cooler lid then the next. "Do you have any of those strawberries left, Mrs. McAlister?"

"Sorry, I sold them all, and the patch is about spent. We'll have raspberries and blackberries in a week or so, though"

"Guess I'll have to wait," he said as he spied Princess 'Fraidy Cat curled up against Slack-Eyed Joe. "Does Joe have a friend?" he asked.

Though it was the third time Liz explained the kitten's presence, she found herself tearing up when she described finding the rest of Roseanne's litter in the barn.

Wide-eyed, Ben bent down to pet the feline friends. "Looks like she thinks Joe is her papa," Ben said. "Do you have any idea who might have done it?"

Liz shook her head, not wanting to worry the boy with any of her conjectures. She wanted to ask him about his "Uncle" David, but knew that would be unfair to the child.

"Your mom and dad should be home soon. They took a picnic to the park along the Maumee. Something about a special path or place where they liked to go." Liz thought about Cassie's ex-husband, wondering if she should stay with Ben until Cassie and Jaime returned.

"You should probably keep the door locked and be on the look-out for anything unusual," Liz said as Ben helped her pack up her produce containers. As they closed the trunk, Ben's parents pulled into the drive. Liz waved as she climbed into her car and left for home.

Liz sat alone in her kitchen with only Princess 'Fraidy Cat for company the Sunday before Independence Day. Mallory had left Friday on an unexpected trip to visit her family. Finding the kittens earlier in the week had rattled her more than Liz had realized, and the younger woman needed time away from the farm. Gregg and Ian had gone to Put-in-Bay with friends for the week and weren't due back until the fifth.

The phone rang, startling Liz out of a mild depression.

"Tatiana?" At the sound of her daughter's voice, Liz sat up and smiled. "What time is it there? Shouldn't you be in bed?" … "Yes, no matter how far away you are, I am still your mother!" Liz laughed into the phone. … "Gregg told you about the kittens?" Liz knew her son and daughter talked to each other, even though Tat was in France.

"You needn't worry about things here. We'll figure this out." Liz waited as Tatiana started to say something then stopped. Her sigh was audible but she just cautioned her mother to be careful. "Yes, of course I will!" Liz replied, "Now, tell me everything that's going on with you!"

Liz talked with her daughter for another half-an-hour. She was still smiling when she hung up the phone. Princess 'Fraidy Cat had been skittering around the kitchen and became fascinated with the sunbeam that shone through the window onto the hardwood planks. When the kitten peeked over the edge of the bright rectangle of sunshine, she saw her shadow and scampered back across the room before turning around and approaching the sunbeam again. She meowed and pawed at the silhouetted cat then crouched around the perimeter of the patch of light.

Liz had told Tatiana about the possibility of taking up stained glass again and, as Liz knew she would, her daughter gave her enthusiastic support. Liz left her ward chasing her shadow and meandered out the back door to the shed that had been her studio. She began shifting boards covered in dust and cobwebs, hoping to find a remnant of her earlier life. But Mack had been thorough when he cleaned out the shed decades before. As she stood in the doorway staring at the jumbled mess, unbidden tears began to fall. She wiped her eyes with her forearm and searched her pocket for a tissue.

"Liz?" She turned toward the unexpected but oh so familiar voice behind her.

"David? What are you doing here?" She rubbed her eye with the heel of her hand as he pulled a clean white handkerchief from his back pocket and offered it to her.

"Thanks. You do have a way of catching me at my best," Liz said after wiping her face and blowing her nose. "I'll wash this and get it back to you."

"If it means I'll see you again, it's a deal." He gave her a questioning look. "Jaime told me about the kittens. He and Cassie are both concerned about you."

"Did Jaime find out whether Cassie's ex-husband is still in jail?"

"All tucked away in a cell in Marion," he said. "But they did suggest he might hire someone in the area to harass Cassie. She mentioned a new farmhand working here?"

"Yes, Neil hired a fellow named Aaron Caine to help with the fields. He seems a bit strange, but Neil assured me that his credentials checked out. He worked in Illinois before coming here and is staying with his sister in Bowling Green for the summer."

"Maybe he got tired of hassling with the kittens while working in the barn." David conjectured.

Liz had been looking toward the barn through the shed window, but now turned her head to the man at her side.

He locked eyes with her, "Do you really think I could do something like that, Mary Elizabeth McKenna McAlister?"

"No ... no. I just didn't know what to think. You seem so mysterious about your past—you hinted at a dark side. I mean, think of Ted Bundy, he was supposedly such a nice guy, but he killed all those people."

"Is that what you think I am, a Ted Bundy?"

"No, of course not, but ..."

He stood with his arms crossed, glanced at Liz and back at the barn without further contradiction ... or explanation of his secretive past.

He retained the stance for a few minutes longer while Liz fidgeted with her hands. Finally he asked, "Did Mallory tell you about ... ah ... my sister's friend who works with stained glass? She said she'd help you set up shop, if you were interested."

Liz nodded that she had been told. She knew she should have at least called to acknowledge his offer. She worried her lower lip, realizing she was not coming off well. She looked down at the dusty pile of boards and debris in front of her, and sighed, "I was just thinking about trying to clean this shed out. Unless I find something hidden down under all of this, Mack got rid of all of my equipment."

At David's quizzical look, she just shook her head and said, "It's a long story ..."

David shifted a board lying on the top of a pile and dust motes exploded upward. He tugged the board toward the door and moved to grab it in the middle.

"You don't have to help, especially after ..." Liz protested, but David interrupted her, "You take this end and I'll get the other."

They worked together moving remnants of plywood sheets, various lengths and widths of boards, and boxes of scrap lumber out of the shed. As they carried the first load to the barn, Liz stopped just outside the door—she had to force herself to walk through each time after the discovery of Roseanne's kittens. True to his word, Gregg had cleaned up all trace of the carnage, but the sight was burned in her memory.

The stall next to Desert Pro's was nearly empty. They moved an old galvanized tin washtub and a few plastic fertilizer buckets then stacked the lumber neatly inside the rough-cut cobwebbed interior.

As they stepped out of the barn, David paused and looked toward the ramshackle migrant housing. "Could I look around over there?"

Liz hesitated before nodding. They walked the fifty or so yards to the sheds and made their way through the overgrowth of mulberry trees and elderberry bushes. The door to the first building hung partially ajar on one hinge. David kicked it open and stepped inside.

"I hadn't remembered it being this small," Liz said. Scraps of clothing lay about. An old mattress, home now to families of mice, covered most of the floor. The musty smell of animal droppings sent them back outside for fresh air.

"Just fifteen years ago?" David asked, not needing an answer.

"More like twenty," Liz said, knowing it made no difference.

David contrasted his life to those who may have lived in this shed. Henry Morales had worked hard to give his children all he could provide, including a stable home and, for David, the opportunity to attend the University of Toledo. His engineering degree had opened some doors for him, but others, he found closed. His move to Las Vegas, though, had been his undoing. *Oh well*, he thought, *it's water over the dam now.*

They worked together for the remainder of the afternoon, moving and sorting lumber as they stacked it in the stall.

"Thanks for helping me, David. I'll get the rest of the little stuff carried out, if you'll say something to your sister's friend."

"So am I back in your good graces, *mi güerita?*"

Liz looked down then lifted her eyes to meet his, "Am I in yours?"

He folded his arms over his chest, let his glance graze by her then brought his unfathomable deep brown eyes back to hers. He let a long breath escape.

"You are a temptress, you know that, don't you, my beautiful *violeta* eyes." He put a hand on either side of her waist, brought his lips down to hers, and suckled sustenance from her willing mouth. He broke the kiss abruptly, leaving both of them wanting. "Such a temptress," he said, more as an expelled breath than actual words. He bent down, lightly pressed his lips to hers, let them linger for a few seconds, then stepped back out of the spell of those eyes.

"I'll be in touch," he said then turned and sprinted back to his car.

CHAPTER FIVE

Liz arranged the pint boxes of blackberries and raspberries on the display table. Her hands itched from picking the fruit all morning, and she hoped someone would come in to make her labors worthwhile before the berries lost their initial sweetness. She had given a pint of black raspberries to Ben when she first arrived and laughed as the boy sported purple fingers and a ring around his mouth before leaving the shop.

Princess 'Fraidy Cat was teasing Slack-Eyed Joe, who humored her by rolling over and batting at her as she practiced her pouncing on him.

The bell above the door tinkled announcing her first customer of the day. She turned to see an attractive Latina woman perhaps a few years older than herself.

"May I help you?"

Rather than returning Liz's smile, the woman looked at her evenly, as though taking her measure.

"Could be. Or maybe I can help you." Liz waited patiently for an explanation. "I'm Anita Windmiller." Liz tried to recall where she might have heard the name before. "David Morales' sister." Recognition dawned—Cassie's best friend!

"David said you were interested in setting up a stained glass studio. I know someone who might be willing to help you."

"I worked with stained glass years ago. David and Mallory,

the young woman who rents a room from me, are both encouraging me to take it up again."

"I could bring my friend by your place later in the week, if you're going to be around."

They made arrangements to meet Friday morning. As David's sister turned to leave, Liz called her back. "Would you like to take a few pints of berries home with you? They're just picked—that's when they're the sweetest!"

The offer earned Liz her first smile from Cassie's friend, "Thank you. Windy—that's my other half—loves black raspberry pie." She took two pints of raspberries and one of blackberries, insisting on paying for the latter.

A deep golden sun added glowing yellow striations to the predawn pinks and lavenders of Independence Day. The early morning chill all too soon gave way to the heat and humidity of midsummer in Ohio. Liz had canvassed the farmyard in a restless need to escape the solitude of the house. The Country Ladies was closed for the holiday, so there was no need to gather any produce. Liz was relieved when *Davy Jones' Locker* had been supplanted by special patriotic programming—hearing David on the radio would only exacerbate her loneliness.

Brandon had asked her to watch the fireworks with him, but she had declined. She was debating calling him to say she changed her mind, just to avoid being alone on this day of family togetherness, when Neil Rowland pulled into the driveway. He emerged from the driver's side door of his pickup—and Aaron Caine, from the passenger's.

Liz met them on the patio. "Aaron and his sister are coming to our place for a barbeque later this afternoon, and we thought you might want to join us." Neil said. Liz knew Neil's wife, Linda, but not well. Caine stood motionless. Liz tried to imagine a smile cracking his sharply chiseled face, but was cut short by those glacier cold eyes. She shivered in spite of the heat.

"Thank you, Neil! And do thank Linda for the offer, but I

have plans for later this afternoon." She hoped the lie tripped off her tongue in a convincing manner.

She hadn't noticed until then that Aaron Caine had removed his black cap and was holding it in his hands as Neil spoke. He placed it squarely back on his white-blonde crew cut and returned to the pickup without so much as a nod.

"Another time, perhaps," Neil offered. "We'll be checking the wheat on the back field this morning. We'll most likely start taking it off tomorrow if we can get the header working. She's getting a bit touchy in her old age. But Aaron's a whiz with mechanics and technology. If anyone can get her going, he can."

Liz hoped Neil could nurse the combine, along with the wheat header, through another season. A new one would cost more than her house was worth! She could never get used to the high price of farm machinery. "Just do your best, Neil, and send me my share of the bill."

Liz puttered around the house, flipped the radio on then off again, poured another cup of coffee, all the while second-guessing her decision to turn down both Neil and Brandon. Maybe she shouldn't be so hard on Caine, but spending the afternoon with him at a cook-out? *No, thank you,* she answered her unvoiced question.

She grilled a cheese sandwich for lunch and as she sat the plate in the sink, she heard a loud motor from the road in front of the house. As she looked out the window past the old radio, a gleaming black motorcycle pulled up beside her Mustang. When the cyclist dismounted and removed his helmet, recognition dawned. She was out the door and halfway down the sidewalk before he had secured his helmet on the bike.

"You are, David Morales, a man of many surprises!"

"You don't know the half of it, *mi güerita!*"

They stopped a few steps short of one another, their pleasure obvious to the one beholding it.

"Thought you might like to take a ride?"

"Me? On one of those things? Not hardly!"

"Aw, c'mon, where's your sense of adventure?"

"There's being adventurous, then there's being foolhardy. You will *not* find me on the back of one of those death machines!"

"That's a little harsh—I've been riding *el Diablo* since I was a kid, and I'm still here."

"*El Diablo?* You named your bike after the Devil and you expect me to just hop on?"

"I was hoping ... I bought the best helmet I could find for you and paid a pretty penny for this protective jacket. It's made with Kevlar—the latest thing in bike wear!"

Liz took the red jacket emblazoned with white slashes. "Sport mesh? That's supposed to protect me from pavement at 60 miles-an-hour?"

"Nope. What's going to protect you from that pavement is an experienced rider at the controls. Time to step out of your comfort zone, Mary Elizabeth McKenna McAlister!"

The grin he gave her was both disarming and challenging, and Liz vied with her common sense. She had never allowed her children to ride motorcycles, and now she was actually considering David's offer!

"Just how far would we be going on this ... this ...?"

"If you aren't careful you're going to hurt *El Diablo's* feelings. That would not be a good thing."

"A bike with feelings? Now I've heard it all!"

"And to answer your question, to Anita and Windy's for a barbeque. They always have a big to-do on the Fourth, invite lots of family and friends over. They do a quarter of a beef over an open pit using combine grates. It's quite an operation!"

"No, nope, not ready for the family thing. I'll just stay here with my skin intact, thank you!"

"It's that comfort zone again. Sliding right back into it ..." He took a step closer, teasing her with his eyes and a slight upturn of those ever so tempting lips. He touched his forehead to hers and she caught the mint scent of his breath as he finished, "You'd rather sit home watching fireworks on TV than cuddle up on a blanket and see the real things burst over the Maumee with *me?*" As he said the last word, his lips grazed hers. When she pressed her mouth against his, asking for more, they both knew he had won the debate.

"I am crazy. This is absolute lunacy!" Liz mumbled. Helmeted and jacketed, she tried to pay attention to David's lesson on elementary bike safety. He promised to not go fast and stick to the side roads and she promised to hang on as tight as she could. As Liz climbed on behind David and he eased the bike out of the driveway, she felt her misgivings whisked away with the July breezes.

Twenty minutes later, they were hugging the curves of a narrow country road along the Maumee River. David slowed in front of an expansive farmstead with rows of cars and pickups parked in a newly mown hayfield. Two large red barns neatly trimmed in white and joined to form an "L" dominated the grounds, with twin concrete silos towering above them. A smattering of outbuildings, similarly painted, provided a backdrop for various activities from volleyball to croquet.

A family of life-sized cement cows stood in the front yard of a white two-story bungalow. The cows were adorned with patriotic clothing, including a sunbonnet on the mother. Liz attempted to take it all in as David maneuvered his bike around the drive and parked it by the hayfield.

Liz held back as David started toward the scattered clusters of partiers. She didn't know what to expect—didn't know how she would fit in with David's family—didn't know if she wanted to go any further. Squeals from a little girl running toward them, followed at a short distance by a chubby-legged toddler, caused Liz to stop where she stood.

"Granpa! Granpa, you came! Mom said you weren't going to. Do you know what? 'Lissa pushed me down and I hit my tooth and now it's loose! And do you know what else? Mom's making a tooth pillow so the tooth fairy can leave me money when it comes out! Isn't that 'mazing?"

The girl took a breath and for the first time, noticed Liz. She twisted a braid and looked at David, "Who's that lady, Granpa?"

By this time the toddler had traversed the distance to David and threw his little arms around David's leg. David lifted the child above his head and was rewarded with a cascade of giggles.

"Again, Gampa, pease?"

A younger version of Anita hurried across the grass toward them.

"Hey, Dad! I thought you said you were going hiking today! You needed to get away from it all!"

David gave Liz a sheepish look and shrugged his shoulders—no easy feat, as he held a squirming toddler in his arms with a little girl hugging his legs from behind.

"Liz, I'd like you to meet my daughter, Melody, my little princess, Anacita, and this little bundle of energy is my grandson, Joshua James."

Regardless of how Liz may have imagined the day unfolding, nothing prepared her for learning that David was a grandfather! She was sure that after this introduction, she could handle anything else that happened.

David went on, "And this lady is my very good friend, Liz McAlister."

The children shyly took her measure, but David's daughter gave her an unexpected hug and said, "So glad to meet you, Liz McAlister!" in a way that led Liz to believe the young woman was not unaware of Liz's relationship with her father.

Anita strode across the lawn with a redheaded man in tow. "Hello, Bro! You made it!"

David smiled, hugged his sister with his free arm, juggling his grandson to his other then shook hands with the man.

"You've met Anita, Liz. This is Sam Windmiller, the unfortunate man she snagged when he wasn't looking a few years ago."

Liz shook hands with David's brother-in-law, as he said, "You can call me Windy, everyone else does."

"'Cept me," Anacita interjected, "I call him 'Uncle Windy,'

'cause that's what he is!" Windy grinned down at the child, gently tugged her brown braids, then picked her up so she would be at eye-level with the adults.

They all laughed with the girl, whose thin face lit up at being the center of attention.

"I understand you want to set up a stained glass studio?" Melody said as Joshua James lunged from his grandfather to his mother with a giggle. She caught her son with a "Whoof!"

Liz glanced at David and his sister with suspicion, before turning back to his daughter, "Don't tell me you're Anita's *friend* who does stained glass?"

Melody looked questioningly from Liz to her aunt to her father, who chuckled, "'Nita, here, wanted an excuse to meet you, Liz. She had heard a few things through the grapevine and thought she needed to give you her stamp of approval before letting you get further entangled in our family."

Liz laughed, "I guess it's a good thing for me you like black raspberry pie, Windy!"

"We can talk about what you need to get started on Friday morning," Melody said as the group walked toward the others at the gathering.

Liz spent the rest of the afternoon being whisked from one group to another. She made a valiant attempt to remember names early on, but relied on whomever her escort happened to be at the time for assistance with who was who and to whom they belonged.

She had worried that, as she knew no Spanish, she would feel uncomfortable. However, she noticed only the older generation spoke the language to any degree. The Latinos her own age used an occasional Spanish idiom or exclamation, but the younger generations were of blended cultures and had completely adopted the ways of their peers.

She eventually discerned the various groupings of guests— the Morales and Windmiller families of course, the teens and twenty-somethings that belonged to both families, and unrelated friends and neighbors.

A large deck, shaded by mature maple trees, extended out from behind the house and overlooked a pond with a sandy beach that covered a half an acre or so. A gaggle of children were lined up to jump off the high and low diving boards, playing chicken on a huge brightly colored inner tube, and swimming out to a wooden raft floating on empty oil drums in the middle of the water. Toddlers played with sand toys on the beach or splashed in the shallow water just beyond its edge, carefully guarded by parents and older siblings.

Liz and David joined Cassie and Jaime at an umbrella table on the deck. Liz was introduced to Cassie's mother and her husband, Theo. Though Liz had met them at their double wedding with Cassie and Jaime and had seen the couple here or there about town, she hadn't had an occasion to talk with them. She knew—thanks to Dolores Tyler and her ilk—about their secret courtship and, rather than disgraceful, as Dolores would have her think, found it to be a delightful reassurance that one is never too old to find love.

Liz smiled at David and rested her hand on his under the table. He looked at her with a pleased question in his eyes but only gave her a satisfied grin in return.

Late in the afternoon, David and Jaime helped Windy and the other men turn the grates with the quarter of beef lodged between them one last time. Falling into the traditional roles, the women brought bowls of potato salad, baked beans, guacamole, corn, and black bean salad outside to long tables covered in checkered cloths. Liz carried out a plate of cut cheeses and small chorizo sausages.

Anita brought out a platter of triangular shaped turnovers, "*Empanadillas,*" she explained. "Jaime's mom makes them and they are out of this world. It's one of the recipes that she won't share with anyone. Jaime jokes that his brothers and sister are going to have a lottery to get her recipe book when she passes!" Anita held the platter out to Liz, "Here, try one before they're all gone. I'll have one with you, just so you don't feel uncomfortable."

"Yum," Liz said as she swallowed a bite of the savory turnover. "I've never tasted anything this good!"

"That's her over there with Jaime's dad and aunt. Would you like to meet them?" Liz looked in the direction that Anita pointed. She couldn't miss Jaime's father—the resemblance was striking. And she immediately recognized *Tía* Juana beside a woman that could be her double.

"Ah … later … perhaps." *Tía* Juana was the last person Liz wanted to meet. She was sure the tavern owner would remember her from that infamous first night with David.

They were distracted by Jaime and Windy, who carried two huge pans filled with beef and placed them on either end of a long table. Jars of barbecue sauce were lined up between the pans, each numbered in order. An older Latino man wearing a wild Hawaiian shirt and a straw hat with—of all things—a pig with wings fastened to the top brought out a large crockpot and placed it on the table by one of the pans of meat.

David came to Liz's rescue as Windy banged on the lid of one of the pans with a large metal spoon. "Okay, here are the rules, same as always. Each person can vote for one and only one barbeque sauce—that means you, Anthony," Windy pointed toward a tall, balding man who laughed and tipped his cap, "Write the number of the sauce you think is best on a slip of paper and drop it in the jar at the end of the table.

"Uncle Walter's pork is, as usual, in the crockpot. If that gets low, let him know. He's got more in the house."

The older man interrupted Windy, "Yeah, you bet! The day Walter Carlos Morales don't bring pork to a barbeque is the day pigs fly!"

David explained the barbeque sauce competition was a time-honored tradition in the Morales family. Windy had embraced it wholeheartedly, combining it with his family ritual of cooking a beef quarter over an open pit to create an Independence Day event.

"However, Uncle Walter insists that his sauce is best over pork. He used to roast a pig all night in a pit, and we would pull it in the morning. But, as he got older—and we got lazier—he started buying pork loins and slow cooking them in the oven.

"And just so you don't feel like a freeloader, I provide the loins as my contribution to the table. Walt and I have an agreement—I'll buy 'em if he'll bake 'em.' "

Liz tried to eat just a little of this and a bite of that, but was still too full to approach the dessert table.

"But there's every kind of pie under the sun!" David coerced, "You've got to try *Tía's* famous chocolate flan cake! And my mom's *sopapilla* cheesecake is incredible!"

Liz glanced at the crowd gathering around the tables. "Are your parents here?"

David lost his smile as he looked away from her toward the distant horizon. His ready smile reappeared as he said, "We lost Dad last April. He'd had emphysema for several years, and it finally got him. Mom went downhill after that—she's at Pleasant Valley now."

"I'm so sorry!" The trite words came out automatically.

"That's okay," David said, resting his arm on her shoulder and pulling her to his side, "Anita made the cheesecake this year using Mom's recipe."

Liz looked up at David then back at the gathering. Her expression changed from concern to apprehension at *Tía* Juana's approach.

"Ah, David, so I see you fell into the *violeta*-eyed *gringa's* trap!"

David suppressed a laugh as he said, "*Tía* Juana, I'd like you to meet Liz McAlister."

"*Sí, yo recuerdo esta gringa.*"

Though Liz knew no Spanish, she had no doubt *Tía* remembered this *gringa.* "May I apologize for that night? I was ... not myself. For one, I don't drink more than an occasional glass of wine and I've never set foot in ..." she stopped, not wanting to further offend the tavern owner.

Tía nodded, and Liz went on, "I guess I did look like a … brazen hussy."

David laughed out loud.

The corners of *Tía* Juana's eyes crinkled as a grin split her round face. She looked up at David, "Hokay, you're old enough to take care of yourself, David Morales. Jes watch out—those *violeta* eyes …" she switched her gaze to Liz, "… can be bery dangerous." The twinkle in her eye belied her words.

"Don't I know it!" he said. Then softly to the woman in his arm, he repeated, "Don't I know it."

The sun set as it rose—with golden striations amidst lavenders and pinks—reflecting over the still waters of the Maumee, as the partiers spread blankets and lawn chairs across the yard facing the river.

Anita had told Liz earlier that Windy and his brothers had a "fetish," as she called it, for pyrotechnics. Fortunately, a sister-in-law was an RN and a nephew, an EMT, and, she assured Liz, "The guys are super-careful, especially with all the kids around."

David had borrowed a thick brown plaid wool blanket from his sister, and they spread it near the patriotic cows in the front yard. David motioned toward the statues, "Talk about a 'fetish'— ask my sister about her love affair with cows! These guys were here when she and Windy bought the farm, and she dresses them for all occasions. Santa and Mrs. Claus at Christmas, the Easter bunnies, red heart blankets on Valentines …"

"Do they raise cows?" Liz looked back toward the pasture area behind the barn.

David shook his head, "The 'factory farms' put the original owner out of business. Windy tried raising a few heifers for meat, but 'Nita had a hard time eating the beef she had gotten to know personally."

He chuckled, "Windy even named them Whopper Jr. and Double-Cheese! The last one, Arb-e-que, hated him. She hissed at him when he fed her and kept finding ways to escape. The last time the cow escaped, 'Nita had to round it up by herself, and she put her foot down. After that, the only cows she would allow on the farm were the kind she collected!"

"I noticed a *few* around the kitchen—not to mention the curtains, and hand towels, and that doorstop is definitely unique!" Liz said.

They laughed as they turned to each other. The dusk was settling toward darkness as the sliver of a moon rose above the barn. His lips brushed the top of her head as he scanned those around him to see who might be watching them.

Anacita ran up to their blanket, sparkler in hand. "Can I watch the fireworks with you and this lady, Granpa?"

"First of all, be careful with that sparkler! It's pretty but can burn anyone you touch with it!"

Melody came hurrying toward them, holding Joshua James with a smoking sparkler rod.

"I'm watching the fireworks with Granpa and this lady," Anacita declared.

Melody grinned at her father, "Hmmm … this could be worth something in exchange …"

"Little Merry Melody …" David called his daughter by his pet name for her.

"Okay, Daddy … but you owe me!" Melody lifted an eyebrow and smiled at Liz. "C'mon kids, give me your sparkler wires and we'll get some more from Uncle Walter." To Liz she said, "Walt's just a kid in an old man's body!"

As Melody and the children disappeared into the dusk, a dazzling fountain of silver drew David and Liz's attention to the grassy area across the road. Several Roman candles shooting circles of colored stars into the sky soon followed. Bright eruptions from what David called "mines" burst from the ground to above the tree line. White-hot comets trailing glittering tails shot over the river, their reflections on the rippling waters doubling their effect.

The audience gave a collective "Oooh!" as green and red aerial rockets burst into a strobe effect followed immediately by an oval of blue stars with flickering cascades of multicolored confetti.

Liz snuggled against David's shoulder as the show continued for nearly half an hour. A grand finale crackled and boomed, echoing down the river channel, while red, white, and blue rockets filled the sky overhead.

They rode back to Liz's farm under a canopy of stars. Liz rested her helmeted head against David's back, absorbing the sensations of the night—the coolness of the wind against her skin, the sound of the motor as they cut through the darkness, the taste of the man in front of her as she pressed her lips to his shirt.

They held hands as they walked toward the doorway. There was no other vehicle in the driveway and Liz knew they would have the night uninterrupted. David curled his arms around her as they approached the door, drawing her close. His lips caressed … massaged … coaxed … and lips that needed no coaxing returned his kiss. His hands roamed her back, cupping the soft curve of her bottom before edging the fullness of her breasts. She forced herself against his length, wanting to fill every crevice between them, before pulling back, sucking in deep breaths.

"No one's in the house," he whispered as his lips again found hers.

"Oh David, David … I want to so badly, but I know I'm just not … not ready. I don't think I can give myself fully to you. There's just too much … I have to deal with yet."

"Does that include that stuffed shirt in uniform that your son keeps bringing around?"

Liz took a step back, "Brandon? No … I'm pretty sure not. I'm so messed up! When I'm with you, my body takes over. What I feel … in places that haven't felt anything in such a long time. My head … my mind … turns to mush. I just can't trust myself to do what's right."

David took her hands in his but maintained the distance Liz had created. "It has to be right for you, *mi güerita*. I won't push."

He kissed the palms of each of her hands then brought his

lips to hers once more.

"Goodnight Mary Elizabeth McKenna McAlister. Sweet dreams."

Liz unlocked the door and stepped inside. She turned the deadbolt and flickered the patio light to let David know she was secure. She walked to the kitchen window and watched the taillight from David's bike as it turned from her driveway toward town.

As Liz switched on the kitchen light and walked to the cupboard to get a glass, she noticed a saucer lying on the tile floor. *Odd, how did that get there ...* she wondered to herself.

The cross stitch above the counter caught her eye as she pulled the faucet handle forward. Its frame had been tilted to a nearly forty-five-degree angle. She turned slowly, surveying the kitchen for anything else that might be out-of-place, but found nothing. She took her rolling pin from a drawer and carefully went into the mudroom to check the back door—locked with the deadbolt.

She flipped on the laundry room light. Nothing out of the ordinary. She edged back into the kitchen glancing at each closed door ... the bathroom ... the office ... the back stairway ... the basement stairs door. She gingerly checked behind each, flicking lights on and off. The basement door had a lock they seldom used, but Liz pushed the button on the doorknob in then wedged a chair against it.

She grabbed the phone as she passed into the dining room and pressed the "talk" button. Silence! She punched the button again, but still no dial tone. *Where's my cell phone?* She quickly retraced her steps to the kitchen to retrieve her purse from the counter. She searched its interior as she walked back to the dining room, but could not feel the hard phone case. She dumped the contents onto the oak table, but her phone was not among them. As she scattered keys, wallet, tissues, a brush, and cosmetics across the crocheted cloth, she saw Mack's photo had been moved from the buffet to near the burl bowl. She looked at the man in the displaced picture and thought ... *It's upstairs in my big purse, isn't it? Dammit, Mack, I need you!*

Rolling pin in hand, she turned the switch to the chandelier in the living room. "Noooo!" she cried out as she saw colored glass shattered under the left velvet drape. Rather than open the curtain to find the extent of the damage, she glanced at the panels on either side of the door to ensure they were intact. She quickly crossed the room to check that deadbolt then retreated to the dining room.

She hesitated at the sweeping stairway debating whether or not to attempt to run to her Mustang. Was her invader still inside the house or waiting in the blackness beyond the foyer door? Or was he just trying to scare her as with the kittens ...

The kittens! Princess 'Fraidy Cat! Where was her little ward! *Please, Dear God, don't let anything have happened to her Princess!*

Instinct kept her in the house as she sank to the bottom step. If anyone were still in the house, they would most likely be waiting upstairs. She glanced over her shoulder to the landing, slowly getting to her feet and turning around. Empty ... The house was so quiet she could almost hear the percussive beating of her heart.

She went from room to room turning on each light hoping that her little kitten would emerge from her hiding place, while searching for the most secure room in which to barricade herself. So many doors in the kitchen! She crossed over to the bathroom choosing it as her safest bunker.

CHAPTER SIX

Men's voices calling to each other over sounds of farm machinery roused Liz from where she lay curled up in the bathtub, rolling pin still clutched to her breast. As she sat upright she saw little gray and white paws reaching under the bathroom door.

Liz shifted the chair she had wedged under the doorknob and was greeted by the frantic mews of Princess 'Fraidy Cat. Early morning sunlight streamed past the radio through the kitchen window. She quickly lifted the kitten to her face and held it tightly to her cheek and neck.

"I thought I had lost you, little girl," she whispered as her tears dampened the kitten's fur.

Liz turned on the radio and David's voice flowed into the kitchen, comforting her as he interviewed his guest. The kitten jumped from Liz's shoulder to the counter and then to the shelf, transfixed by the disembodied voice. She pawed at the radio case then gave Liz an inquisitive look as though asking where the other people were. She peeked around the back of the radio, then took a sideways jump before plopping down in front of the vintage case looking up at the ornate façade from which the voices seemed to come.

Hearing David's interview, watching the kitten's antics, and sipping a hot cup of coffee combined to take the chill off of the previous night's terror. Liz walked to the kitchen window—who should she call? What should she do? She saw Neil working on the combine header and thought about saying something to him. But then Aaron Caine climbed down from the tractor and looked directly at the house. Liz quickly stepped back from the window as the chill returned.

Cassie! Cassie would know what to do! Liz picked up the telephone receiver—still no dial tone. *Do I dare go upstairs for my cell phone?* She grabbed her rolling pin and slipped up the back stairs to her bedroom. Her large quilted purse lay in the middle of her bed. She edged along the wall to her closet, threw open the door and hit the light. No sign of anything amiss. She hurried to the bathroom peeking her head around the door. She pulled open the shower curtain. With a sigh of relief she crossed the room to her bed.

She quickly emptied her bag—without finding her cell phone. Just when panic threatened again, she spotted the little lavender rectangle poking out from under a decorative pillow. *It must have fallen out when I switched purses before going to the barbeque with David ... Was it only yesterday?*

She hit Cassie's cell number on the speed dial. After two rings, her friend's voice carried through the phone. Liz sank to the bed as she told Cassie of the events of the night before. She wondered aloud if, perhaps, she wasn't just imagining things ...

"My dresser top!" Liz cried as she quickly stood up. "Everything's moved around!" As she crossed the room, Liz heard a crunch under her feet. Shards of glass from a hand mirror lay on the carpet. "He's ... he's been in my room!"

Within minutes, a dark sedan pulled into the driveway. Cassie emerged from the passenger door while Jaime stepped from the driver's side.

A detailed inspection of the house revealed nothing missing, with just enough disturbed to let Liz know that someone had had access to her home.

They checked the lower level and basement windows to ensure that they were all shut and locked. "The deadbolts were all on

..." Liz chewed her lower lip as the full impact of the incursion settled upon her.

"At least whoever did it only broke three of your window panels in the living room," Cassie said.

Liz nodded, "And they spared my favorite one with the rose."

"We have to call the sheriff's office to file a report." Jaime said.

As Liz protested, Cassie shook her head, "No, trust me on this, Jaime is right!" Liz looked from one to the other as Jaime shot a half-grin toward his wife.

Within an hour, the familiar black and white sheriff's car pulled into the driveway. Liz, Cassie and Jaime met the officer halfway down the sidewalk.

Cassie smiled as she extended her hand toward the man in uniform, "Deputy Moran ... or rather, Sheriff Moran—I voted for you in the last election."

The officer tipped his hat to Cassie, "Thank you, Mrs. Alvarez. It's good to see you again. We don't have any coat boxes filled with money in that barn, do we?"

Cassie laughed, "I surely hope not!"

Liz looked to Jaime for an explanation, but the officer turned toward her, "Mrs. McAlister?" Liz nodded as she shook his hand. "Please excuse us. The Alvarez's and I have ... ah ... history."

"I'll never forget the feeling of those handcuffs," Cassie said. "It's not even been five years ... but it seems like a lifetime!" She leaned back as Jaime placed his hands on her shoulders.

"Mr. Alvarez, glad you called. Let's get this report going."

They toured the house with the officer taking notes and photographs as Liz talked. Princess 'Fraidy Cat emerged from the kitchen and Liz stooped to pick her up. Liz petted the scruff of the kitten's neck as she related the fate of Roseanne's litter.

"Do you have any idea who the perpetrator might be?" The officer asked as they stood on the patio nearly an hour later. Liz hesitated as Neil Rowland came up the walkway.

"I don't know," she glanced at Aaron Caine's back as he busied himself with the combine. She had no more than a feeling to go on ... not enough to accuse her hired man of any wrongdoing. "Not really, I guess."

Moran gave her a quizzical look but said no more, as she introduced the patrolman to her farm manager. She gave a brief summary of the previous night's events to Neil.

"You should have said something earlier this morning!"

"By the time I had pulled myself together enough to talk to anyone, you and Caine had gone on back to the wheat field. All I could think to do was to find my cell and call Cassie."

"Speaking of phones," Moran said, "Your landline should be working. The lines hadn't been cut, just pulled from their jacks. All I had to do was figure out which line went in which slot and reconnect them."

"By the way, Mr. and Mrs. Alvarez, you may be interested to know that the former sheriff was paroled last month for, of all things, good behavior!"

"Crenshaw?" Jaime asked, "Paroled? Why weren't we notified?"

"Don't know. Seems you should have been." The officer turned back toward the house as he said, "Think he could have had anything to do with all of this?"

Cassie and Jaime looked at each other then shifted their gaze to Liz. She gave a slight shrug to her shoulders and said, "All I remember is he was that weasely-looking guy who was in cahoots with your ex, Cassie—and was responsible for your nearly going to prison. The few times I saw him, he made my skin crawl—but I don't think he knows me from Eve. Why would he want to frighten me?"

"It doesn't make sense, unless maybe some of the money stolen from O'Shay's did end up in your barn. ... Naw, that's too far-fetched," the sheriff countered his own theory. "Anyway, I should be able to track down his whereabouts through his parole officer. Maybe we can ask him a few questions."

As the sheriff left, Jaime said, "They didn't say anything

about paroling Crenshaw when I checked on Paul. I'll follow up with Moran to find out more about Billy Joe."

"Thanks, Jaime. It's a comfort having you and Cassie just down the road."

"Not if we're the ones who have brought this down on you," Jaime replied.

"Oh snap! Of all the days for Gregg to get home early!" Liz said as her son parked his pickup beside the sheriff's car. "I'm not looking forward to this."

Gregg rushed up the walk as the officer backed up his car to turn around.

"What's going on, Mom? What are the cops doing here?"

"Since Gregg's here, we'll leave you two to talk," Jaime said.

"Call us if you need *anything*!" Cassie added.

"I can't thank you enough!" Liz said giving her neighbors a quick hug.

She nodded toward her farm manager who stood to the side, arms folded across his chest.

"Neil, I'd appreciate it if you'd let me know if you notice anything out of the ordinary."

"Sure thing."

To her son, Liz said, "I need another cup of coffee before I go through all of this again."

Liz carried her mug with her from room to room as she told Gregg about the strange occurrences the day before. She left out that she had spent Independence Day with David on the back of his motorcycle.

"That settles it, I'm moving home. Don't try to talk me out of it!" Gregg said. "I'd been thinking I should be here helping Neil and Peter and that new guy with the farm. The first summer term at the university is over—and, though you didn't ask, I pulled a high 'B' in econ—and I'm not signed up for second term. Ian's buddy came up unexpectedly a week ago for classes and has been sleeping on our couch, so it's perfect. He can have my room. We'll see what happens in the fall."

If Gregg expected an argument from his mother, he was disappointed. "It would be great to have you here. I'm sure Neil could use the help and I'd like to get your opinion of Aaron Caine. I'm going to suggest to Mallory that it might be best if she finds another place to live—I would hate for her to get hurt by whomever is doing this."

"You might suggest it, but I'm betting Old Mal will stay right where she is!"

"'Old Mal'? Honestly, Gregg—why she puts up with you is beyond me!" Liz shook her head at her son.

"Maybe because I'm cute?" He replied with a dimpled grin, causing his mother to lift her head upward as though imploring his father for help with their wayward son, before drawing him to her side with her free arm.

"You are your father's son, Greggory McAlister—in so many ways!"

Liz intended to call David as soon as Gregg was out of earshot. She punched David's number into her cell phone, while her son was talking to Neil, but hung up as Gregg turned back toward the house after pulling a suitcase from within his Ranger. She helped him move his luggage and boxes from his pickup bed into his attic hideaway. As the day wore away, it became easier to procrastinate making the call to David. As much as she wanted to talk to him, she dreaded the confrontation that would ensue with her son.

On Friday morning, Liz hung a load of wash on the line, barely filling one of the four plastic-coated ropes strung between poles that had supported at least three generations of McAlister laundry. She thought about times past when there wasn't enough space to hold Mack's work shirts, Gregg's tee-shirts, and Tatiana's designer jeans, along with Liz's own clothes. It would be comforting to add Gregg's wash to hers again.

David's white Jaguar pulled into the driveway giving Liz a

start, as his voice had followed her from the house on the radio. But, instead of David, Anita emerged from the driver's door and Melody, from the passenger's.

Liz left her empty wicker basket under the clothesline and walked toward David's sister and daughter. She offered to brew another pot of coffee as she gave the women a tour of the downstairs level of her home.

"This was just stuff I did as a hobby. I'm sure your glasswork is much more professional, Melody," Liz deferred to the younger woman.

Melody and Anita exchanged looks then turned in unison.

"Dad said you were good, but he didn't tell the half of it! You have a fabulous eye for detail and color combinations! Your leading is so clean—thin lines, you can hardly tell where it's soldered!" Melody walked over to where cardboards covered the stained glass panels that had been knocked out of the window behind the velvet curtain. "What happened here?"

Liz debated as to whether or not to mention the break-in, but knew they—and David—would find out about it eventually, so she gave her guests the capsulized version of what had occurred while they were celebrating the Fourth of July together.

"Holy Toledo, does Dad know about this?" Melody exclaimed, then answered her own question, "No, of course not, or he would have told us! Why didn't you call him?"

Liz blew out a deep breath, "I was going to last night, but then I was up talking with my son until late. Gregg's moving home from Bowling Green, so it won't be just Mallory, my tenant, and me here. Unless Mallory decides to move because of all this ..."

"Yeah, Cassie told me about the kittens," Anita said. "That took some real sick dude to do that!"

As if on cue, Princess 'Fraidy Cat scampered into the room and pawed at Liz's ankles. Liz picked up the kitten and rubbed foreheads with her, before telling Melody the story of her littermates.

"I appreciate your offer to help me get back into the art glass world, Melody, but maybe it would be better if you didn't involve yourself in my life until we find out who's behind all of this. If you would get hurt … or Mallory … or anyone … because of me, I wouldn't know how to forgive myself!"

Melody thought for a few seconds, then replied, "Considering we are all adults, I'd say the responsibility for what happens to us is ours, not yours. You've been straight with us, so we can decide whether to go or to stay. I, for one, would like to see what you have available for a studio!"

"Thank you, Melody Morales!" Liz said with relief.

"Actually, it's Melody O'Hanoran."

"O'Hanoran? Like the lawyers on the back of the phone book?"

"Yep, exactly. The younger one with the wavy strawberry-blond hair is Derek, the father of my children—my ex. What a jerk! Let's go on to more pleasant topics—just where is this studio?"

"Former studio," Liz said as she guided Anita and Melody through the kitchen and mudroom to the cob shed behind the house.

They stood inside the shed, studying its possibilities. "David helped me move the bigger pieces of scrap lumber to the barn. I am hoping I can use some of it to make a work table."

Melody sized up the room. "I'd guess it to be twelve feet by fifteen plus this little space to the side of the door. What do you call this? A cob shed?"

Liz nodded, "I understand years and years ago they used to heat the house with corn cobs, which were stored in this shed. The little inset by the door was the smokehouse. How they kept from burning the shed down when they were smoking hams and such is beyond me!"

"Or the house!" Melody exclaimed. "Can you imagine heating with corn cobs?" After a moment, she said, "The room should be large enough for two work tables, a light table, and storage units for your glass. You could build a counter for your grinder along the back. Or maybe that's where you'd build the shelves to store your glass.

"We could take a field trip to Columbus—they have a great art glass studio in the German Village. I'm like a kid in a candy store when I go there!"

"Do you have your own studio?" Liz asked the younger woman, thinking about David's grandchildren.

"No. Joshua James and glass would spell disaster! Besides, I'd worry about the lead. Not that it isn't safe for me. I have my blood levels tested at least once a year and wash my hands a lot, but it's different for little kids."

Liz glanced out the window, thinking about her own miscarriages. "Is it dangerous for a pregnant woman?"

"I don't know. I suppose it could be if she were around it all the time …" Melody laughed, "but since there's no chance I'm pregnant, I don't worry about it!"

Relieved that David's daughter had misread Liz's intent, she asked her the next logical question, "Where's your workshop, if not at home?"

"I'm the art glass person at a glassworks place. They do everything from glass for commercial buildings and storefronts to mirrors and windows and storm doors for houses. I do their stained glass—both new and restoration work.

"If you'd like, I'll ask if I can give you a tour. You can hang out and watch—I'm sure the guys won't mind!"

Impressed, Liz replied, "I'd love it—as long as it's okay with your boss!"

While Liz and Melody discussed what would be needed to set up a studio, Anita poked around the back of the shed.

"Wow! What's this?" she asked, holding up a smooth black-handled knife with a curved blade.

"It's my Don Carlos knife!" Liz exclaimed as she carefully took the handle from Anita. "Bet the blade is still razor sharp, once I get the dirt off of it! I thought this was gone forever! Where'd you find it?"

"In the corner under that box of wood scraps. It's a good thing I saw the handle first!"

"This is truly a treasure! My teacher gave it to me. It's a genuine Don Carlos from Germany—check out this ebony handle!" Liz said as she examined the knife in her hand. "It was like part of my hand when I worked with the leading."

"That cinches it—Aunt 'Nita's finding your knife is a sign that it's time for you to set up your studio again!"

They made plans to drive to Columbus on Melody's next day off. "My Aunt Susan watches the kids while I work—she loves the little ones! She has a sort of an unofficial daycare—Anacita and Joshua James have a ball with the other kids and she doesn't mind if I leave them whenever I need some time away. She's pretty incredible—beautiful, smart, and can she bang out a ragtime tune on the piano!"

"…And the voice of an angel," Anita added.

"Sounds like you've got a wonderful family!" Liz said, as she walked with David's sister and daughter toward his Jaguar.

"Thank you both so much for coming!" Liz said then glanced at her watch, "I didn't realize how late it was! I've got to get to the garden before Country Ladies opens at one."

"Have you thought about selling your stained glass in Cassie's shop once you get set up?" Anita asked as an afterthought. "Bet she would love to have your stuff there!"

"Maybe … I guess I'll have to see if I still have the knack for it …"

When Liz delivered her load of cucumbers, green beans, summer squash and other vegetables to the Country Ladies, Emily and Meredith were just opening the store.

"Cassie had some deliveries to make, so we told her we'd cover the shop," Emily said. "Let me help you bring in your produce."

A little girl of four or five ran out of the building toward Emily. "Mommy, can I help, too?" Her blonde curls kinked in the humidity, springing out-of-control from the confines of a red headband.

"Sure, sweetie. Liz, I'd like you to meet our daughter, Abigail."

The little girl thrust her arm out to shake hands with Liz, saying, "You can call me Abby, 'cause Abigail is just too much of a mouthful for a kid like me!"

Liz laughed as she shook the precocious child's hand. "Tell you what, would you like to carry Princess 'Fraidy Cat into the shop? She and Joe are good buddies," she said as the girl reached out to take the kitten.

"Cool!" She held the kitten tightly as she skipped back to the shop.

"I didn't know you had a daughter," Liz said to Emily while carrying the produce into the shop.

"She's Meredith's ... but she's ours ..." Emily let her sentence drop as the three women began arranging the vegetables on the display shelves. The conversation soon evolved to Liz's break-in while Princess 'Fraidy Cat entertained Abby by pouncing on Slack-Eyed Joe.

Gregg was standing by Neil Rowland's pickup talking to the farm manager when Liz returned from town that afternoon. Aaron Caine hopped down from the truck bed and joined them as Liz lifted a bag of groceries from the car. She sat it back on the seat and walked toward the men as a familiar black Miata crossed the bridge.

They all paused as Lt. Brandon Michaels stepped out of the car in his dress blue uniform. Liz glanced toward her son, intercepting Aaron Caine's icy glare directed toward the newcomer. Caine's face turned impassive when he caught Liz watching him. He hesitated, looked from Liz to Brandon then to Liz again. "I'll be back in the morning," he said to Neil and strode to his truck.

Liz introduced Brandon to the farm manager. After shaking hands, Neil turned toward Gregg. "We'll meet at the Other Place around 7:00 tomorrow. You can help me finish the back field here and Aaron can go with Peter to work the section behind the Alvarez' farm."

As Neil took his leave, Gregg shook his head, "Whoa! 7:00 in the morning? I haven't been up that early since I pulled my last all-nighter! I'm going to catch a shower and finish putting my stuff away. Good to see you again, Lieutenant."

He took a few steps, stopped abruptly and backtracked to his mom's car. "Might as well take a bag or two of groceries while I'm going."

Liz popped the trunk as she and Brandon walked to the car. "Let me help you with those," he said.

Gregg pulled two full canvas bags from the trunk and Brandon retrieved a gallon of milk and sack of potatoes. Liz closed the lid and picked up the sack she had put down on the seat earlier.

"I tried to call you, Liz," Brandon said following her up the sidewalk, "but didn't get an answer. Then I stopped by Gregg's apartment, but his roommate said he'd moved home because there'd been some sort of break-in at the farm." As Liz pushed the door open ahead of him, he asked, "You okay? What happened?"

"It wasn't anything, really. Just a few things out of place, nothing missing that we can tell."

Brandon followed her into the kitchen, trailing her with boxes and cans as she unloaded the groceries. When she stretched to reach a high shelf with a jar of olives, he took it from her hand and easily fit it into the cupboard. He cautioned her to keep the doors locked and said he was glad Gregg was home, then chatted idly about a robbery that had occurred when he was at the Academy in Colorado Springs while Liz carried a bottle of detergent to the laundry room.

When she returned Lt. Michaels had shifted his attention to Gregg, who had emerged in search of a snack.

"I was just about to put a pot roast on with vegetables from the garden. It should be ready in an hour or so," Liz told her son. After a moment's hesitation, she added, "Would you like to join us, Brandon?"

"Oh no," he replied, "I couldn't impose …"

"I told you before, Lieutenant, Mom loves company—don't you, Mom?"

Both men seemed not to notice Liz's failure to respond as, much to her surprise, Gregg challenged their guest to a chess game before dinner. Mack's mother had given her son a chess set she had made in ceramics class for Christmas one year, and Mack and Gregg had played ongoing games throughout Gregg's high school years. The game had been stored in a buffet drawer since before Mack's accident, but Liz heard Gregg rifling through the buffet in search of the set.

When Liz was at last alone in the kitchen, she noticed Princess 'Fraidy Cat peeking at her from behind the bathroom door. She bent to pick up the little kitten, who was meowing at her mistress with wide green eyes. Liz finger-combed what was fast becoming the kitten's most striking feature, her long white ruff, before returning her to the floor. As the men's voices filtered in from the dining room, Princess 'Fraidy Cat skittered from the bathroom to the mudroom and disappeared.

"That was excellent, Liz," Brandon declared as he leaned back in his chair and patted his stomach. "Topped off with apple pie a la mode—what more could a man ask for?"

"It was just one I had left from last fall. It's a wonder it didn't have freezer burn," Liz said dryly as she gathered the dessert plates from in front of the men.

She was rinsing the plates in the sink when she heard a familiar rumble and looked up to see David crossing the bridge on his cycle.

Oh snap, this is all I need! Liz swore to herself.

She looked toward the dining room table where Gregg and Brandon had resumed their chess game. *Maybe I can slip out the back door,* she thought as she ran her fingers through her hair.

David had his helmet off by the time he met Liz halfway up the walk. He bent to give her a quick kiss before nodding back toward the black Miata in her driveway.

"The officer dude here again?" he asked needlessly.

Liz nodded, her frustration apparent in the way she crossed her arms below her breasts—drawing David's attention away from her face.

"Stop leering at me, David Morales ... and I didn't invite him here, if that's what you're thinking."

"Never sure what to think where you're concerned, Mary Elizabeth McKenna McAlister," he said softly, wetting his lips with his tongue.

They stood for a moment longer before the foyer door opened and closed. Liz turned to face the two men who emerged from the house. Lt. Michaels hung back as Gregg strode toward his mother.

"A motorcycle? Please don't tell me you've ridden on that with him, Mom!"

At Liz's silence, her son went on, "What the hell? You wouldn't allow me to have one because they were too dangerous! You even overrode Dad on that one!"

"Don't swear in my presence, Greggory," his mother stated defiantly.

Gregg was about to respond when Brandon called to him, "Come on back inside, son. We have a chess game to finish." The bill of his hat shaded his face as he spared David a brief glance before smiling at Liz, "It was a fine dinner, we just need a little more time to work off that pie."

Liz turned back to David hoping the unwarranted guilt she felt did not show on her face.

"I came as soon as I could after I heard about the break-in on the Fourth. Why didn't you call me?" David asked, the tenor of his voice betraying his hurt.

"I don't know," Liz glanced over his shoulder at the lavenders and pinks that harbingered a sunset much as the one they had shared just days before. "Things have happened so fast. Gregg moved home and Anita and Melody came out this morning ...

"They told you, didn't they?" Liz asked, knowing the answer.

"I wish it had been me, David. I wanted to call, it's just …" Liz knew whatever she said would sound lame and inadequate. Instead, hoping that Gregg and Brandon had, indeed, resumed their game, she stepped toward him and standing on her toes, kissed the lips that invited so much more.

"Gregg's home for the summer?" David asked into their mingled breath.

Liz nodded, knowing her son's return further complicated any relationship she might have with David.

He brushed her lips again, momentarily deepening his kiss, before breaking away. He placed two fingers against his lips then to hers.

"What you do to me, *mi güerita!*" he sighed as he widened the gap between them.

She watched as his motorcycle roared from the drive before returning to the house.

Lt. Michaels had draped his blue uniform jacket over the back of an empty dining room chair and sat with his shirtsleeves rolled up and tie loosened, intent on the game before him.

Liz quietly joined them, as her son moved his silver rook and Brandon positioned his gold bishop. It was obvious by the pieces remaining on the board Gregg had been outplayed. Brandon studied the game before sliding his queen diagonally toward the younger man's king.

"Check and mate," the airman said with a smile.

"Man, you're good!" Gregg said as he carefully wrapped each ceramic piece in tissue and placed it into the tin where his father had stored them. "Maybe you can teach me some of those moves."

"Be glad to, son. You're pretty good yourself—just a little rusty is all."

They shook hands as Gregg excused himself, saying he had an early morning ahead of him.

Brandon followed Liz to the kitchen, "Let me help you with those dishes."

"It's not necessary, really," Liz replied, then added, "But

thank you … for taking Gregg back into the house … you know … earlier tonight …"

"No problem. I'm used to defusing tense situations." He took the plate that she had rinsed and put it in the dishwasher.

"You know, Liz McAlister, you deserve some fun after all that you've been through and we still have our winnings from the casino to spend. Why don't we take the Jet Express to Put-in-Bay for the weekend?"

Liz turned so abruptly she nearly dropped the plate she was holding. "What? The weekend?"

"Well, maybe not for the weekend, but for the day, anyway. We could catch the ferry at Port Clinton Sunday morning and return that evening. I'll pick you up at 10:00—we'll catch the noon boat."

"Brandon, no …" Liz said.

He flashed her his boyish grin, "I'm not taking 'no' for an answer."

He slipped into the dining room and retrieved his uniform hat and jacket leaving Liz, arms akimbo, in the kitchen. "See you Sunday," he said, "Ten o'clock sharp," then closed the door behind him.

Liz ran to the door and pushed it open. "Brandon, *no!*" she called but he stepped into his car as though he hadn't heard.

That's the second time that man has talked me into doing something I didn't want to do, Liz fumed at herself as she latched the deadbolt behind her, *and it's not happening again!*

Liz wanted to call David on Saturday but how could she avoid telling him about her date with Brandon on Sunday? She wanted to call Brandon to cancel their date but she didn't have his phone number. She wanted to ask Gregg for Brandon's number but didn't want to explain why. Her mind circled from one thought to another tying her into knots of indecision.

She fluttered from one task to the next, first dusting the dining room but leaving the cloth lying on the middle of the table, then weeding the garden but stopping before she'd even finished hoeing between the bean rows. She rested the long handle of the hoe beside the cob shed door and opened it. She planned the layout of her shop then walked to the barn to survey the available lumber. Desert Pro whinnied from his stall, reminding Liz she hadn't lunged or ridden him for too long of a time. She worked the Arabian from a walk to a trot to a canter. However, the heat of the day soon had them both in a lather so they returned to the shelter of the barn.

By late afternoon, Liz was at wit's end. She tried to relax in a soaking bath scented with a calming lavender oil but whenever she closed her eyes she felt the shadowy presence of the man who had intruded into her private space. *Had he searched through her drawers, fingering her underwear?* The thought chilled her more than the cooling water.

She toweled dry, hesitantly opening the door into her bedroom. She visually searched the room, top to bottom, corner to corner. The closet door was slightly ajar. *Had she left it that way? Would she ever feel safe again?*

The sound of footsteps on the main stairwell echoed through the silence and Liz froze in a self-induced panic.

"Liz? Liz are you up here?"

Liz sank down on her bed as Mallory's voice broke through her terror. She took a deep breath before answering, "I'm in my room. Just give me a minute, I'll be right out!"

Liz flipped on the closet light and threw open the door. *Nothing out of the ordinary*, she reassured herself. She grabbed her long plush purple bathrobe from a hook behind the door, and drawing the sash around her waist, she hurried across the room.

"Is everything okay?" Mallory asked after exchanging hugs with Liz. "I saw Gregg's truck out there, but the place seemed deserted."

"Not exactly, but we'll talk about that later. First of all, how was your trip home?"

"Fine … good. I got to see everyone … except my dad" Mallory sighed, "But that's okay. Maybe next time …" She touched her finger to the corner of her eye and wiped away a tear. "Right now I need to get my stuff moved in and get back to life as normal."

"Why don't you just relax while I dress and fix dinner. We have lots to talk about. Gregg's moved back home—he can help you with your luggage after we eat."

"Gregg's moved home? Maybe I will rest and touch up the make-up a bit … if you don't mind. Then I'll help with dinner."

"Not to worry," Liz said. "We're having leftovers, so take your time."

"Hot damn! Is that Old Mal come home?"

"You mean like 'Lassie Come Home' or 'Homeward Bound'?" Mallory turned her head to see Gregg standing in the doorway as she lifted three dinner plates down from the cupboard.

"Not hardly … Lassie, old girl, never wore anything like that!"

Mallory shifted her head back toward the cupboard to close the door … and to hide her blush from Liz's son. Gregg let his gaze wander from her thick mane of auburn hair that left just a hint of bare shoulders uncovered, down to where a slinky hot pink material clung to her shapely hips and thighs before giving way to toned calves and matching pink sandals.

"Damn," he repeated under his breath.

Liz watched the two young people with amusement. "Gregory, would you please take the dinner plates from Mallory and set the dining room table? And, Mallory, can you reach the salad plates on the second shelf? Or, maybe you could get them, Gregg." Her son was a step ahead of her, as he reached around Mallory to get the smaller plates. As he brushed against her he looked down into deep brown eyes.

"Daaamn…." The word took on almost a reverent tone as their fingers touched when he handed the dishes to her.

"Maybe … maybe I should clean up before dinner. Neil had me combining all day—I feel like I showered in wheat dust!" He stepped back from Mallory and crossed to the safety of the other side of the room.

"Might be a good idea," Liz said, admiring her handsome, nearly six-foot three-inch son as he moved toward her. She closed her eyes, remembering another well-muscled young man in a dirty white tee-shirt, hungry after a hard day's work.

"You're thinking about him again, aren't you, Mom?"

Liz nodded her head, "But it's okay. It doesn't hurt quite as much. I'll always love your dad and always miss him … but I am so glad I have you!" Greggory McAlister wrapped his mother in a dirty, sweaty hug. She laughed and gave him a quick squeeze, before pulling away, "But, phew, you could use a shower … with water, this time!"

They talked about the break-in over dinner, and as Gregg had predicted, Mallory had no intentions of moving.

"Where would I go? Back into a crummy apartment with strangers after living out here in the country? No way! The farm has become like a second home to me."

"Speaking of home, where do you live, Mal? Was it a long drive?"

Mallory hesitated before answering Gregg. "Yeah, you could say it is. My family's from Texas. Near San Antonio. I'm lucky my car made it there and back."

Liz listened quietly. Any questions that she had asked Mallory about her past had been answered with vague responses.

"San Antonio? Bet it was hot down there!" Gregg said.

"Hot and dry. We have fields of prickly pear cactus like you have…I don't know…what kind of weeds grow in fields around here?"

"Oh, my sweet innocent," Gregg laughed. "I'm sure mom can introduce you to a few!"

Princess 'Fraidy Cat had been underfoot all during the dinner preparations but had disappeared when they moved into the dining room. Her frantic meows brought all conversation to a stop.

"Sweet sugar snap, what now?" Liz asked as she looked from her son to Mallory.

"Stay here," Gregg ordered, "I'll be right back …"

"Greggory, no, wait!" Liz jumped from her chair to follow him into the kitchen with Mallory at her heels.

The kitten's cries seemed to come from the mudroom. Gregg was the first to burst through the open door—only to stop short, with Liz and Mallory nearly colliding into his back.

"What is it?" Mallory asked, "I can't see anything!"

Gregg stooped, picked up the kitten, then bent down again and turned around.

"AAAAHHHHHHHHHHHHHH! Get that thing out of my face!"

"Aw, Mom, you're not afraid of a little garter snake are you?" Gregg shifted the hapless snake toward Mallory, who reached out to gently take the wriggling reptile from him, "It's just a baby!"

"Look at that! The woman's a snake handler!" Gregg said, his astonishment obvious.

He held the back door open as Mallory carried the snake toward the yard, shrouded in darkness. "Wait, I'll come with you!"

They walked toward the garden where Mallory crouched down and released the harmless snake. It slipped between two bean plants and disappeared into the night.

Gregg helped Mallory to her feet. They stood facing each other as fireflies flickered their mating signals across the landscape.

Gregg lowered his head. Mallory rose to her toes. His arms came around her, nearly lifting her off the ground in his haste to taste her lips. Just as their mouths met, Gregg noticed lights flash on as a car sped down the road from in front of the house.

"What the hell … who was that?" He asked as Mallory slid back onto the heels of her sandals. "Let's get back inside."

Liz stood at the mudroom door petting the Princess. "Such a brave little girl, you are!" she cooed into the kitten's soft white ruff. She stepped aside as Gregg and Mallory rushed through the backdoor pulling it tight and locking the deadbolt.

"What happened? What did you see?"

Gregg and Mallory exchanged glances before rushing to tell Liz about the car, both at once.

She looked at the two of them and quietly asked, "How do you suppose that snake got into the mudroom?"

CHAPTER SEVEN

Liz groaned as the alarm woke her the next morning. She, Mallory, and Gregg had sat around the dining room table sharing a bottle of wine trying to settle their nerves after the snake incident. Liz lay awake for hours afterward, listening to every noise. She worried that she was putting Mallory and Gregg in danger but was relieved they were in the house with her. Pre-dawn light was peeking through the east window before she finally fell into a deep sleep.

"Do I really have to go to Put-in-Bay with Brandon today?" She peeked at the clock then pulled her pillow back over her head. The alarm had roused at least one member of the household, as Princess 'Fraidy Cat jumped up on the bed, pounced up her mistress's back and pawed at the hair sticking out from under the pillow.

"Ouch! At least keep your claws in, little lady," Liz laughed as she rolled over and hoisted herself up from under the covers, kitten in hand.

The black Miata hugged the curves as they sped up Route 105 toward Port Clinton. Liz involuntarily braced her arm on the dashboard as Brandon barely slowed the car when they passed another yellow arrow and a speed limit sign.

"That's just a suggestion," Brandon laughed. "This baby will take the corners better than any other car on the road."

If I make it through this day, I promise I will be in church next Sunday morning, Liz prayed silently. Aloud she said, "I'm just a little jittery after last night."

"I was thinking about what happened," Brandon said as he geared the Miata down and eased to a stop sign. He crossed the intersection before continuing, "If someone really wanted to hurt you, they would have done something more than put a harmless snake inside the door. How would they even know the cat would find it?"

"That's true ..." Liz said.

"I'll bet the car that the kids saw had its lights on all along ... they were just too interested in each other to notice. I think, by the way, Mallory has finally gotten your son's attention."

The explanation sounded logical. Liz had to admit she was so on edge that the least little thing out of the ordinary set her on high alert.

"Thanks, Brandon, you're probably right ..."

Liz and Brandon arrived at the Jet Express to Middle Bass Island and Put-in-Bay just as passengers began to board the triple-deck ferry. When it was finally their turn to get on the boat, Brandon insisted they take the stairs to the upper level to get the best view of the Lake Erie shoreline. As the ferry motored away from the dock and up the channel to open waters a stiff breeze picked up.

Liz ran her hand through her hair as her curls tangled one into another. Her lightweight jacket proved no match for the wind that blustered across the upper deck once they left the shelter of land behind. Brandon pulled her against his shoulder as she tried to shield herself from the gale that had other more prepared passengers scrambling into windbreakers.

It seemed longer than the advertised eighteen minutes until they finally rounded the north side of Middle Bass Island and docked at the resort town of Put-in-Bay.

Liz could understand how the island would appeal to her son as they made their way through the crowd of tourists strolling along the lakefront. Musicians in Hawaiian shirts sang island songs from gazebos in outdoor bars along the streets that skirted a long rectangular park.

"That must be the Perry monument I've heard Gregg talk about. He said taking the elevator up to the top was a must!" Liz said as she pointed toward a tall stone obelisk that dominated the shore east of town.

"As long as we don't have to take the stairs. That's got to be over three-hundred feet tall!" Brandon said as he lightly placed his hand on the small of Liz's back.

He really is quite attractive, Liz told herself, trying not to be annoyed. She had noticed several women giving Brandon second looks as they passed by.

They waited in line for the elevator inside the monument between a young couple dressed in black, with more piercings than Liz's pincushion, and a family with two young children. Liz guessed the older boy, a slight blond with mischievous blue eyes, to be around seven, and his younger brother, a stout little redhead, at, perhaps, three. The ranger at the entrance relished sharing his knowledge of the Battle of Lake Erie in 1813, during which Admiral Oliver Hazard Perry captured the British fleet and uttered his famous quote, "We have met the enemy and they are ours."

"This monument," the young man said in a voice that carried throughout the base of the obelisk, "is an International Peace Memorial to honor the treaties between the warring factions of the United States, Great Britain, and Canada."

With that, the elevator arrived and Liz and Brandon stepped on board with the others. When the doors opened a few minutes later, the vast expanse of Lake Erie lay before them. The two boys scurried out ahead of their parents who were in quick pursuit, while the young man pulled the hood of his black sweatshirt tight and backed against the cement tower wall holding on with both hands.

Liz walked from corner to corner of the square observation

deck. Each right angle supported a bronze map showing the islands surrounding Middle Bass. Kelleys Island to the east was by far the largest.

"If you look carefully," Brandon said, "you can see the faint outlines of the roller coasters at Cedar Point. We'll have to go there with Gregg and Mallory."

I don't think so, Liz said to herself. To Brandon, she averred, "The last time Mack forced me to ride a coaster with him, he ended up with teeth marks on his arm. I don't do well with heights! In fact, this is getting to me just a little. Would it be okay if we headed back down to solid ground?"

They rented a golf cart and toured the island, stopping at a winery and a butterfly house along the way. He told her about his past, growing up surfing the California coast, his time at the Air Force Academy in Colorado Springs, white water rafting through the Grand Canyon, serving as a state senator and setting up a local food pantry, before reenlisting in the Air National Guard … He talked about fishing in Lake Erie for perch and walleye during dinner at a restaurant on the boardwalk overlooking the shoreline. By the time they caught the Jet Express to the mainland, the sun was dipping low behind the horizon, reflecting its colors across the ripples of Lake Erie.

Liz closed her eyes, falling in and out of a restless sleep on the ride home. Spending the day in the sun had left her exhausted—but not nearly so much as spending the day with Brandon Michaels. She enumerated the reasons she should be attracted to him. But she wasn't—not in the least. How could she disentangle herself from his attentions when he and Gregg had developed such a close relationship? Especially with Gregg living at home? She stared out the window as trees whizzed by in the gathering darkness.

The drone of cicadas followed them up the walk as Brandon lightly rested his arm on Liz's shoulders. He stopped on the patio and drew her to him. She thought she would give one last try to summon at least some response to his kiss. As she tilted her head back, she reminded herself that he was nearly perfect for her—

handsome, caring, giving, and seemed to have an understanding of her son. His lips claimed hers as he pulled her against him. Dry … hard … tongue to tonsils … Liz tried not to gag as she carefully extricated herself from his embrace, sliding her hands down his arms until her fingers clasped his. She brought their hands up between them, holding his between her palms.

"Thank you, Brandon, for a lovely day. But … I just don't think …" Liz started again, "You are Gregg's friend. I think he may even look to you as a father figure, which is what makes this so hard." Liz knew she had to finish what she had started before she lost her nerve. "I want to be honest with you. You are a good man and far more than I could hope for …"

He smiled down at her, "There's a 'but' coming, isn't there?"

She nodded, looked away, then back at the man before her. "… But could we just be friends?"

He touched his fingers to her cheek, traveling her jaw line to her chin, then brought his lips lightly down to hers.

He stepped back then replied, "We'll do it your way … for now. But I won't say I'll give up on you, Liz McAlister. Besides, I still owe your son some chess lessons …"

Liz stretched her back and looked toward the house. She had already picked a half-bushel of beans. Morning dew had left dark, wet splotches on her jeans and cotton shirt as she stooped from plant to plant. She brushed her hands on her pants legs then wiped the sweat from her forehead with her arm.

"Whew! It's gonna be a scorcher!" she said to the gray and white kitten frolicking after a grasshopper then rolling on her back to catch a bean leaf that had attacked her.

Liz thought she saw Aaron Caine look her direction before Gregg drew his attention away by pointing toward something at the Other Place.

Gregg had left the house early, but not before informing his mother, "That other guy—you know, the one with the motorcycle—stopped by yesterday. I told him you'd gone to the Island with

Lt. Michaels."

Liz stooped down between the bean rows, lifting the leaves to find the pods hiding beneath. *Just as well*, she thought. *I need to keep my distance from David Morales.*

The week passed without incident. Mallory returned to work at the libraries and, though she and Gregg seemed to be more aware of each other's coming and going, they, too, appeared to keep their distance from one another. On Wednesday, Anita called to say that Anacita was carrying a fever, so the buying trip to Columbus for the studio would have to be postponed. Traffic at the Country Ladies was as sluggish as the hot July days, and on Thursday, the four partners discussed alternatives to drum up business while Abby played in a corner with Princess and Joe. Jaime popped into the shop long enough to report that Billy Joe Crenshaw had been confined to the county and was living in the McGruder Park apartments downtown.

On Friday morning, lethargy left Liz sipping a second cup of coffee. As had become her custom, Princess 'Fraidy Cat had plopped herself in front of the radio and was listening to *Davy Jones' Locker*. The kitten had developed a fascination for the sound coming from inside the cathedral case and seemed to be especially mesmerized by the same voice that had captivated her mistress.

"Liz?" Mallory wandered into the kitchen in her bathrobe, "I thought I heard David's voice!"

Liz nodded toward the counter where the kitten sat, her head cocked to the side as though wanting to hear every word.

"Only on the radio …"

"What? David's a deejay? How did I not know that?"

"I only listen to his show when I'm alone. One of my guilty pleasures—or torture, depending on the day." Liz gave a wan smile toward Mallory, "Today I think it's the latter."

"Still haven't heard from him?"

"No, nor do I expect to after last weekend."

"Why don't you call him?" Mallory asked, poking her head

in the refrigerator and pulling out a yogurt.

"I don't know. That wouldn't be fair—I don't want to lead him on. I just can't figure out how I feel about him … or anyone."

David's voice cut through the kitchen, introducing the next song. "Here's a rarely played Beatle's cover of a classic favorite, 'Besame Mucho.'"

Liz splashed coffee onto the table. "Oh, David Morales, you don't play fair!" she said, much to the younger woman's bewilderment.

Gregg came bounding down the stairs on Saturday morning, "Neil's going to the lake for the weekend and Ian and the guys are heading up to the Island. Do you think you'll be okay here without me?"

Liz looked up from running the dust mop under the buffet. "I'm sure we'll be fine. You go and have a good time!"

Mallory called down from the stairs landing, "This is the weekend I'm babysitting for Jessica, the new librarian at the university. They're going to a Cincinnati Reds game and may not make it back until late, so I was going to spend the night. But I can come home if you need me to!"

"No, there's no need for you to be driving all hours of the night," Liz protested. "Tell you what, Jaime left for Toronto yesterday morning. I'm sure I can stay the night with Cassie and the kids, if that will make the two of you more comfortable."

Alone in the house, Liz wandered from room to room tagged by the little gray and white kitten. She stooped to gather up the longhaired furball and was rewarded by a tiny sandpaper tongue licking her chin. She carried the kitten over to Mack's photo on the buffet. She searched the face in the frame, trying to remember his touch … the sparkle in his eyes … the feel of his lips on hers … She lifted the picture to eye level then sat it down on the oak table in front of her.

"Mack … Mack … Mack … What am I to do? Life wasn't

always easy with you, but it's a real bear without you!" Princess 'Fraidy Cat rubbed her head against Liz's neck as tears trailed down dampening the kitten's fur. "Forgive me … forgive me for going on without you … forgive me most for what I am about to do …"

Liz looked up at the flickering neon sign before tugging open the heavy entrance door to *Tia's Taverna*. Stars studded the black sky overhead as she held the door ajar while her eyes adjusted to the bar's dim interior. As before, all movement within the tavern paused, as one customer after another sized-up the newcomer.

With her chin up and gaze forward, she made her way to the rear of the room, sliding into the same empty booth near the pool table. She lifted her skirt before scooting across the cracked red vinyl seat.

She glanced toward the nearby pool table …

David Morales racked the billiard balls in their plastic triangle form. As he lined up the white ball for the break, his gaze followed the shaft of his cue stick and was caught by the swish of material over nicely rounded feminine hips. He drew his head up to assess the woman sliding into the booth on the opposite side of the green felt table.

"Oh no, *amigo*, not again!" Hector Gonzales groaned as he slowly shook his head.

David rested his stick against the edge of the table and eyed the woman sitting alone in the booth. He shot a grin back at his friend as he sauntered to her. He leaned against the back of the bench opposite where she sat. She glanced up at him with an assessing candor, before dropping her gaze to the scarred coating of polyurethane on the tabletop.

"You want somethin' to drink, *gringa*?"

Liz took a deep breath. It *was* now or never. This *was* what she wanted—*what she needed*. She studied the man who stood before her … tattoos traveling up well-defined biceps … full, tempting lips … his long hair pulled back in a ponytail … bet he even rides a motorcycle … definitely a man to break all taboos …

"Red wine?" She asked, her *violeta* eyes teasing. He tipped his head back and laughed.

"David Morales," *Tía Juana* raised her knowing eyes to meet those of the man who had always been like a nephew to her. "I guess you are old enough to know what you are doin'," she shook her head, a smile curving the corners of her mouth.

He sat the sangría in front of the lady, taking advantage of his position to scope out the ample slopes of her breasts as they disappeared under the loose curve of her low-riding neckline. He drew the rim of his O'Doul's bottle to his lips, and swallowed a chilling draught of the amber liquid before sliding into the booth across from her. There was a time when he needed a woman … but now he needed *this* woman.

Liz took a sip of her drink, letting the cooling liquid coat her throat … then another swallow, this time tipping the glass further, letting the alcohol ease her nerves. She leaned forward, allowing her top to gap slightly and was rewarded by dark eyes searing her breasts.

She licked her lips and smiled at the man across from her, "Hi, I'm … Mary … Mary McKenna …"

He fingered the smooth glass of his bottle, before bringing it to his mouth and taking a long draught. He sat the O'Doul's back on the table and swallowed.

Liz focused on his lips—full, sensual—she knew their tenderness and their strength … and wanted to know the feel of them pulling at her breast. A heat suffused her body, settling on her intimate parts, and she gulped the rest of her drink to mitigate the warmth.

He tried to keep his lips from curling into a smile, but his eyes danced with anticipation. "You can call me Juan. If you want a last name, Moreno or Perez or Smith will do."

Her tongue wet her bottom lip, "But none of those are your real name, are they?"

"No more than you're Mary McKenna. But Juan and Mary,

they're good, anonymous names. Let's go with them, whaddya say, *gringa* lady?"

She let out a quiet laugh and nodded. She sipped her drink and when she sat the glass back on the table, he took her hand in his. Electricity hummed between them, and he felt the jolt throughout his body.

Her fingers traveled to his face and she traced the nearly imperceptible scar above his right eyebrow. "Where did you get that?"

He shifted his head, catching the palm of her hand with his lips. "Some forgotten escapade of a misspent youth," he said, his words muffled as he spoke them against her fingers.

"But let's toast to the future and let the past lie where it may … for now." He raised his O'Doul's and she chinked her glass against his bottle.

"Another?" he asked.

She shook her head, her violet eyes dark with invitation.

"*Besame, besame mucho …*" he sang softly without regard to what was emanating from the speaker above their table. They finished their drinks in silence, each contemplating the night ahead.

"Shall we find someplace a little more…private?" He asked. She nodded.

They paused momentarily at the bar to pay their tab and say goodbye to *Tía* Juana. They heard the older woman chuckle, "Brazen hussy," as they walked out into the night.

They strolled together to his battered pickup under a canopy of stars. He opened the door for her and helped her step up on the running board before shoving his tool belt aside so she could sit down on the frayed cloth seat. He crossed in front of the truck and hopped in beside her.

"Sorry, the Jag's out at 'Nita's," he said as he reached across her to grab her seat belt. He allowed his lips to graze the rise of her tantalizingly close breasts as he secured the belt at her side.

"I think this is where I say something about this," she patted the dash as he climbed into the cab beside her, "turning into a pumpkin at midnight."

"… And I say I can be a real prince charming when I want to."
His hand again massaged the top of her thighs only this time he
edged the thin material upward until his fingers touched bare skin.

"Mmmm … my dark prince …" she purred her response.

There was no reasoning as David drove slowly through the
Lower Eastside neighborhood … only desire.

She took his hand in hers and rested their clasped fingers on
his leg, while shifting her skirt back over her knee.

He pulled the truck in beside the same small, rundown
house trailer as before and killed the engine. Releasing her hand,
he reached down and unclasped their seatbelts. He put his arm
around her shoulders and drew her to him.

His mouth covered hers, tasting sangria and the sweetness
of her lips. He let his empty hand wander to her breast and held
its fullness in his palm. She sighed and leaned into his caress as
he kneaded her taut nipple between his thumb and forefinger. He
pulled back, knowing he had—this time for sure—crossed the
threshold from which there was no return.

"You feeling okay, *mi güerita?*"

"I am feeling so fine, David Morales." She found his mouth
again as she repeated, "… so fine."

"The windows are steaming up and, though it's not much—
there's a bed in that trailer over there …" He whispered in her ear
as his tongue traced its outline. They broke apart, each needing
what the other offered.

Once inside, David closed the louvers of the cheap metal
Venetian blinds against the prying eyes of the night.

He placed a hand on either side of her face and tilted her
head up toward him looking deep into her purple eyes. "If I am
dreaming, I never want to wake up."

"This is no dream. There is only now. Only us …" she said as
she lifted her lips to meet his.

Liz opened her eyes. Light streamed in through the window
as she recalled where she was—and exactly how she had gotten

there. As she raised her head to check the pillow beside her, her arm brushed against her bare breast. She stretched, reveling in her nakedness.

Liz glanced over toward the window and saw a man silhouetted against the light. His shirtless back was to her. A lean, muscled torso drew her gaze downward to Levi jeans slung low on his hips. Well-toned biceps bulged as he leaned against the sill.

As though he sensed her watching him, he turned toward her. The fastener of his jeans lay undone, and she focused on the line of dark hair that trailed down from his navel and disappeared under a white band of elastic. His naturally bronzed skin gleamed in the light as nearly black eyes bore into her. She lowered the coverlet just enough to reveal the tops of her breasts.

His lips curved into a smile as he walked toward the bed and stood beside her. "Again? You are insatiable, woman!" But he didn't stay her hands as she lowered the zipper to his jeans and drew them toward the floor. Instead, he pulled them the rest of the way off. She tugged on the elastic waistband of his white briefs and as they, too, gave way to gravity. He pulled back the coverlet revealing the soft curves of her body.

She tried to pull the blanket back over her nakedness but he replaced it with his skin. He buried his face in the fullness of her breasts, caressing them in every way he had imagined. He retrieved his last condom from the bedside stand and warmed her waiting body with an oil he thought he might never use. Their lovemaking was slow and thorough, leaving them both gasping and sated.

"How can you want me?" she asked. "Look at you—you're … I don't know, so strong, so … in shape … so young!" She sat up, tugging the sheet to her chin. "I … I don't even know how old you are!"

"Ahhh … it's a little late for modesty, Mary Elizabeth McKenna McAlister…" he smiled as he traced the curve of her hips through the thin cotton. "I'm old enough to be a grandpa, so I guess that makes me old enough to make love to a sexy lady who isn't a grandma yet."

"But I … I have … belly fat!"

He slowly lowered the sheet from her body, exposing her midriff to his exploration. He bent over and gently blew on her stomach, letting his tongue explore her navel. She felt a now familiar warming coursing through her as he kissed his way up to her lips.

"You are everything I want in a woman … everything," he said, as he lay heavy on top of her letting his body massage her doubts away.

"Ummm, Cassie," Liz unloaded vegetables onto the display shelves Monday afternoon as Cassie sorted wildflowers for arrangements to be picked up later in the day. She hesitated a moment holding purple coneflowers and looked toward her neighbor questioningly.

"If Gregg or Mallory ask—not that they will—but if they do, would you say that I spent the night here Saturday?" Liz blushed under her friend's scrutiny.

"Sure … I thought you had that little extra glow about you this morning … but … well … do I get more of an explanation? I mean, not details … except … just tell me it wasn't that Air Force guy …"

Liz gave Cassie a shy smile and shook her head.

"David? Sweet heaven, you did *it* with David!" Cassie grinned, "So when's the …"

"It's a little early to ring the wedding bells, if that's what you're getting at." Liz interrupted. "There's still so much we need to know about each other. Like, anytime I mention the past, he dodges faster than … Ali in his prime!"

Cassie laughed and pressed her lips together, then said, "Well, girlfriend, you're not getting anything from me. Whatever you find out has to come from the mouth of David himself. Don't believe anything anyone else tells you.

"Now you've got to tell me how you pulled this off with two twenty-somethings living under the same roof with you!"

Wednesday morning found Liz zipping down Interstate-75 toward Columbus, Anita and Melody in tow. Her excitement was contagious as the three women chatted about the field day ahead.

"Dad said that your son flipped out when he found him helping you build your work table Monday evening. Guess your boy needs his horizons expanded a bit," Melody laughed from the back seat. "Just wait until I meet him—I'll lay it on real thick, then watch him run!"

"So you and my brother have been getting a little ... cozier ..." Anita asked, giving the driver beside her a sly look.

"I was taught by my preacher pappy to never kiss and tell," Liz rejoined then said, "Well, maybe that wasn't what Dad said, but you're not getting anything from me."

"Yeah, that's pretty much what David said, too. So I figure it must be true." She turned to Melody, "I think this *gringa's* getting it on with your papa ..."

"Just so long as she doesn't break his heart, I think it's pretty cool!"

They parked by a medium-sized red brick building that blended so well into the quaint German Village neighborhood Liz would have missed it had Melody not been with her. The shop's plate glass windows were filled with suncatchers of various sizes, colors, and techniques, while elaborate stained glass windows adorned the entry doors.

"Sweet sugar snap! Look at the price tag on that window!" Liz exclaimed as she clutched her shoulder bag to her side to ensure she wouldn't accidentally come in contact with the freestanding wood-framed creation.

She stood just inside the inner door, in awe of all that she saw—rows of stained glass sheets in a myriad of colors, art glass equipment, supplies and racks of pattern books for all levels of artisans.

"I still can't believe I'm doing this!"

With Melody's help, Liz selected a grinder, soldering iron, lead vise, glasscutter, grozing pliers, and various other tools.

"Is this how the lead comes?" Anita asked as she fingered long metal rods.

"Yep," her niece responded as she picked up two different shaped lengths. "It's actually called 'came.' See, this one looks like an 'H' from the end. It's used to connect two pieces of glass together." She turned the section of lead on its side. "You fit a piece of glass in each groove." She laid that came down and held the second in her hand, "This is 'U' shaped. It's used to finish the outside of a design that won't be framed."

They ordered six-foot lengths of the lead came and a variety of solid-color cathedral glass sheets, as well as streaked, and milky opalescent glass with waves of color.

Melody had tried to talk Liz out of buying a light table, but in the end, the older woman persisted. Liz arranged to have the grinder, glass sheets, and came delivered, but had the light table and smaller supplies put in the trunk of her Mustang.

"Lunch at Schmidt's—my treat," Liz insisted.

They spent an enjoyable afternoon exploring the neighborhood and taking advantage of other shopping opportunities the capitol city offered, not heading northward until late in the day.

"So where did Mom take off to?" Gregg asked Mallory as he dropped down on a chaise longue beside where she relaxed, reading a paperback. He popped the top on a Coke and slowly poured it over a glass of ice. He had showered and changed from his work clothes to a tee-shirt he had modified by cutting off the sleeves and ripping the sides to a few inches above the ribbing.

Mallory tried not to notice the rippled abdomen barely concealed by the loose-fitting shirt as she replied, "I think she was going on a buying trip for her studio."

"So, looks like we're on our own for dinner, Old Mal."

"Ah, no...*you're* on your own for dinner, *Mister McAlister.*"

As a familiar silver Ford Focus pulled across the bridge,

Mallory gracefully extracted herself from the chaise. Gregg noticed her sundress clinging to the curve of her hips. She bent to smooth the skirt drawing his attention to cleavage that she hadn't intended to reveal. He dropped his hand to his lap as he straightened to a sitting position.

"What's O'Flannery doing here?" he asked, suspicion dawning as the sparkle of rhinestones on the straps of Mallory's flip-flops caught his eye. "Don't tell me you're going out to dinner with that loser?"

"I am going to dinner *and a movie* with Ian," Mallory said, suppressing a smile.

Ian waved to his former roommate then gave a low whistle as Mallory walked toward him, with perhaps a slightly exaggerated sway to her hips.

The Focus had to wait in the driveway for Liz to pull her Mustang across the bridge.

"That ought to shake my son up a little," Liz smiled, as she waved to Ian and Mallory.

"Who was that?" Melody asked. "The girl looked like someone I should know."

"That's Mallory Martin, the young woman who is renting a room from me."

"Mallory Martin?" Anita questioned as she looked back at Melody. "Couldn't be ..."

Anita left her comment dangling as Liz parked the car. Gregg rose from the chaise and walked toward them.

"Your son?" Melody asked.

"Yes, that's Gregg," Liz confirmed.

"*Verrry* nice ..." Melody assessed.

Liz just shook her head and laughed.

"Mom, where have you been? You didn't tell me you were going someplace!" Gregg charged, opening Liz's door.

"I didn't realize I needed to check in with you," Liz raised her eyebrows at her companions as she climbed out of the front seat.

Melody and then Anita caught his attention and he stepped

back from the car, looking from his mom to the Latinas with her then back to his mom again.

When Melody and Anita had joined Liz, she introduced them to her son as David's sister and daughter.

Melody lowered her lashes and gave Gregg a soft smile while extending her hand. He hesitated for just a second before taking it in his.

Liz almost snickered as she watched her son's reaction to the extremely attractive Latina in front of him ... and at the way Melody played the scene.

Melody drew her hand slowly from Gregg's while maintaining her hold on him with enigmatic brown eyes.

"Could you help me carry my new light table to my workshop?" Liz asked, taking mercy on her son. He glanced back at Melody as he followed his mother to the trunk of the car.

Liz had Gregg place the large rectangular box on the counter David had built just inside the cob shed doorway where the smokehouse had once been. She carefully unboxed the plexiglass-covered metal enclosure that she would use to backlight her designs.

"Dad could have made you a bigger light table using plate glass and fluorescent tubes for a whole lot cheaper," Melody stated, arms akimbo.

"I could do it, just let me know what you need," Gregg protested.

Liz exchanged an amused look with Anita.

"I didn't think you were interested in my little hobby—isn't that what you called it when I asked if you could help David and me Monday night?"

"Yeah, but you were with ..." Gregg gave his mother an accusatory glare as all three women waited for him to finish his sentence.

Gregg shifted his gaze to Melody then to Anita.

"What can I do to help?" he asked at last with exasperation.

"I need to have vertical storage shelves built to hold the glass sheets that are being delivered next week, as well as two fair-sized sturdy tables in the middle of the room."

"If you can give me the dimensions, I guess I could work on them this weekend," he acquiesced, earning him a nod of approval from his mother and subtle grins from the two Latina women.

Princess 'Fraidy Cat pawed at the radio dial then meowed at her mistress the next morning.

"Okay, give me just a second," Liz said as she ground coffee beans before turning on the radio. The kitten seemed to need her daily fix of *Davy Jones' Locker* the way Liz needed her steaming cup of coffee. The little feline poked her head around the back of the machine as a woman described her desire to provide a venue for local artists in her new shop downtown. When David's voice came on, asking his guest to describe how her career as an art teacher influenced her decision, Princess jumped to the front of the radio and appeared to listen intently.

"Yeah, I know, his voice does that to me, too," Liz smiled as she lightly ran her fingers down the backbone of her companion.

"What's so interesting on the radio?" Gregg asked coming through the kitchen door, then without waiting for an answer, "Any more of that coffee that smells so good?"

"Sure, it's in the pot," Liz said, caught off-guard by her son's first question. David responded to a comment from his guest, with no reaction from Gregg. Sighing, Liz wondered how her son could be so antagonistic to a man whom he didn't know enough to recognize his voice when he heard it.

Gregg appeared to relegate the program to background noise as he told his mother about his discussion with Neil to perhaps diversify their crops from corn, wheat, and soybeans.

"Caine suggested we try canola. The Canadians seem to be having considerable success with it, but Peter thinks we should stick with what we know works. I'm going into Bowling Green to use the university library. They can get all kinds of information from Ohio State."

He took a sip from his mug then looked toward his mother,

"I'm meeting Brandon for lunch, if you'd like to come with me."

Liz laughed and shook her head, "You just don't give up, do you?"

"What I can't give up on is that you would choose to see that other guy over Lt. Michaels."

David's voice gently wove its way between mother and son as they each finished their coffee in silence.

When Liz delivered her produce to the Country Ladies that afternoon three cars were lined up in the driveway. Emily had designed large signs to post on the highways that ran a few miles to the north and to the south of the shop and Meredith had written informational articles for several local newspapers. She had even gotten a brief article with a photo of the four partners in the Sunday Peach section of the *Blade*. Business was again steady, if not booming.

"Sorry I'm late," Liz said to Cassie. "Tatiana called out of the blue. She's coming home in August!"

"Moving home? You must be thrilled!" Cassie exclaimed as she helped bag produce for two women.

"Not moving, but at least she will be back for a visit. I was running behind already as I had decided to pick a bushel of low-hanging early Cortlands. There's a ton up on the trees—should keep us in apples for a while!"

"Cortland apples?" one customer asked. "I'd love to have enough for a pie—and some to eat, if they're crisp and tart."

"These are more tart than sweet as they won't be fully ripe for a while yet. You're welcome to try one as soon as I get them unloaded."

Ben helped Liz carry the apples, zucchini and yellow squash, tomatoes, sweet corn, peppers, new potatoes, and eggplants into the shop and arrange the produce on the display shelves, baskets, and bins.

When the last customer had left the shop, Liz turned to Cassie, "I'd stay to help this afternoon, but I'm meeting Anita at the glass shop where Melody works. I can't tell you how excited I am to set up my studio again!"

"I'm looking forward to having your suncatchers for sale here at the shop. We could have an opening with tea and crumpets and the like—that would be fun and great publicity!"

"First we have to see if I can still do it! My glass and lead should be delivered next week. I am so anxious—what if I don't have it in me anymore? All that money—wasted!"

"You'll do fine!" Cassie assured Liz. "Have fun this afternoon and give my hellos to 'Nita and Melody."

Liz and Anita arrived at the glassworks at the same time. They opened the door labeled "Entrance" in bold black letters and were met inside by Melody. She led them into her studio, a large room set off from the rest of the shop. Two sizeable tables dominated the center of the area, with smaller counters and storage units around the perimeter.

A computer sat off to the side on a desk between two windows. "I'm about to start the jungle scene that's on the screen. It's fairly big, so I had some trouble printing off the cartoon—that's what we call the pattern," Melody explained to her aunt.

"It will have several shades of green, so I'll need to be careful to keep the pieces marked."

Melody walked to the vertical shelving units along the wall, explaining that each shelf was four inches wide by forty-four inches high and held different colors of glass sheets, most solid cathedral but some with flowing opalescent patterns. A row of twenty-inch high shelves held smaller glass sheets above the larger shelves, with a third row of shelves half that height at the top of the unit. She pulled out a sheet of pink opalescent glass from a shelf in the middle unit and carried it to a large counter beneath the window by the computer.

Melody flipped a switch, turning on two fluorescent light tubes beneath the surface illuminating a four-foot square of ¼-inch thick plate glass set into the countertop.

"That *is* a pretty incredible light table—wish I'd had that when I was making my calla lily designs!" Liz said.

Melody placed a twelve by sixteen inch pattern of a rose on the glass surface, "This is a cartoon for a smaller window that I'm working on. I saved the last few cuts to show you the process."

Melody put the pink glass over the cartoon. The light beneath the plate glass surface allowed the dark lines of the pattern to show through, enabling Melody to draw the outline of the petals she needed on the opalescent glass.

She took the glass sheet to the smaller worktable, and using a glasscutter that she kept in a mug with an oil-soaked sponge, she carefully scored the opalescent glass along the lines she had drawn.

"Let's hope this baby runs the break," she said as she grasped the glass sheet in one hand and used a pair of flat-edged pliers to snap the glass petal from the sheet.

"Yay! It worked! Sometimes, especially with textured glass, it jumps the run, and I have to start all over again." She successfully cut two more petals. "Some glass is like cutting butter and some is just what I call angry—it's brittle and there's no working with it."

Melody carried the petals to the larger table that had two boards nailed in the upper left-hand corner at right angles to each other. Two-thirds of the glass pieces for the rose window had been laid out on top of a duplicate cartoon of the design that fit snugly against the boards, with sections of lead came separating each segment of glass.

"This little guy doesn't quite fit." She lifted one of the newly cut petals from where she had placed it on the cartoon and took it to the counter along the wall opposite of the shelving units holding the glass sheets. A small grinder sat on a foot-square plastic grid in a larger tub.

"There's a reservoir of water just below the grid and a sponge behind the grinder that wicks the moisture up from the reservoir. As I grind the glass the sponge wets the silica—essentially powdered glass. The wet silica sticks to the tub walls, keeping it from flying all over. If you breathe in too much of the silica you could get silicosis, a lung disease that can kill you. " Melody explained as she donned safety glasses before shaving off a small fraction of glass from the petal's edge.

"How do you keep from cutting your fingers?" The question earned Anita a laugh from her niece.

"You don't. After a while your fingers become somewhat calloused. I was definitely glad when Joshua James became potty trained—I felt every little nick when I changed his diapers!"

When Melody had laid the altered piece back on the table, she pulled on a pair of close-fitting mechanics' gloves. "I probably should have had a pair of these by the changing table at home," she laughed.

She selected a length of lead. "The came has slight kinks and bends in it when it's delivered. I stretch each piece to strengthen and straighten it before I use it on a design."

Melody measured a piece of "H" came against the glass piece already secured into the window beside which the new petal would be fitted. She marked the came with her Don Carlos knife, nodding toward Liz, "I know how you felt when Aunt 'Nita found your Don Carlos—I'd be lost without this guy."

She took a pair of lead nippers from an old coffee can filled with pens, pencils, and various tools, and cut the came to connect the new glass to the pieces on the table.

"Amazing!" Anita said softly.

Melody swept the glass with a soft brush to clear away any lead particles.

"The last step is to solder the sections of came together, but it's generally not a good idea to do that until the entire picture is done. As you can tell by looking at the cartoon underneath, the leaves are just a little off. The bigger the window and the more pieces in the design, the more problematic it becomes.

"I'll solder the came here in the corner just to show you how it's done. The iron is heated to around 700 degrees. I'll brush the joint with flux first. While I feed the solder over the came with one hand, I touch the iron to it with the other."

After Melody had soldered a few joints, she laid the iron in its cradle.

"I don't like the way that joint fits together. See how it's wavy?"

"My niece, the perfectionist," Anita quipped.

"That's one way I knew you were really good." Melody looked toward Liz, "Your joints were so smooth I could hardly see them. And some of the smaller window panes had to have a hundred pieces of glass or more in them!"

Liz gave a slight shrug to her shoulders, "I couldn't do a lot with the larger windows, but I did have fun designing the smaller ones."

The co-owner of the glassworks poked his head in the door and Melody introduced Liz and her aunt.

"Glad to have you here. I understand one of you ladies is a pretty talented glass artist yourself. If you ever need a job, we have enough orders to keep two of you busy!

"We just got a restoration project in to fix thirty leaded glass windows in the local armory. It's used as a reception hall now so they want to take it back to the way it looked when the windows were new." He invited the women to tour the rest of the facility before disappearing through a door into the shop.

"Don't worry, Melody," Liz laughed, "I understand that a woman's studio is her domain. An artist needs her space! Besides, we're not even sure I can make a suncatcher, much less an entire window, anymore."

Liz extended the tape measure from the crossbeam supporting the roof of the cob shed to the floor then jotted down the dimensions for the vertical shelving in a notebook. The largest sheet glass she had ordered only measured sixteen by sixteen inches, so the majority of her bottom shelving only needed to be twenty inches high. The second level would be fourteen inches and the top level, eight. *The shelving,* she mused, *could be built on a base cupboard, to store supplies. And I could have a few taller shelves at the end to hold larger sheets later on …*

"Whatever you're planning must be pretty intense!"

The notebook clattered to the floor as Liz wheeled about to see David standing in the door watching her.

"How long have you been there?" she asked, her smile lighting up her eyes.

"Oh, maybe five minutes or so …"

"You could have helped me hold the tape measure, at least!"

"Ah, but it was more fun to see you bend over then stretch up. Have you ever thought of being a waitress?"

He walked toward her and she met him in the middle of the room. Their lips touched, as each delighted in their newfound intimacy.

"So is that what you do when young women wait on your table? Leer at their backsides like a dirty old man?"

"Nope … I much prefer women with a little experience and a calculated sway. Why don't you walk to the back wall and let me reassess …"

Instead she let her hands wander down his back and tucked them into the rear pockets of his jeans, drawing him closer to her. Their lips continued their exploration as their bodies strained to become one.

When they at last broke apart, they inhaled deeply to regain their breath.

"Well isn't this cozy. You could have at least closed the door!" Gregg's accusation fell as ice water between his mother and her lover.

"Your secret's out, you son of a bitch!" Gregg glared at David. Photocopies of a newspaper article fell at Liz and David's feet as Gregg retreated, running back to his pickup.

Liz bent to pick up the papers. The copies were of a Nevada newspaper, not quite three years old.

"Ohio Man Convicted of Rape and Murder," the headline blared.

She glanced up at David, then read on, "David Henry Morales, an Ohio native currently living in Las Vegas, was found guilty of the rape of Brittanie Marie Adamson and the murder of Tiffany Crystal in their rooms at the Enchanted Castle motel."

"David, please tell me this isn't you!"

"Would you believe me if I did?"

"I don't know what to believe. All I know is you've been damn mysterious about your past. *Rape and murder?* Oh my God!"

David let out a pent-up sigh. "I should've known this was too good to last," he said as he turned from her and walked out the door.

CHAPTER EIGHT

Liz had read the article a half dozen times. She had memorized the details of how the raped woman had accused David, *her David*, of assault and that his semen had been found on her. *At the very least, he had had sex with this Brittanie*, Liz thought. She and Mack had taken a short vacation to Las Vegas several years back. Liz remembered the scantily clad women who served drinks—the kind of women who had more than a little experience and more than a calculated sway.

The murdered woman had last been seen leaving a backroom card game with David. His wallet had been found in her room, and he had been arrested, apparently still drunk, in his apartment the next day.

Where to go? What to do? Liz felt at a loss. Gregg returned home, but she refused to talk to him. She sat at the kitchen table staring at the radio. Princess 'Fraidy Cat wound herself in and out of Liz's ankles, and she picked the kitten up, nuzzling her face into its fur.

Tears evolved into sobs as Liz held the kitten close. Mallory walked to the kitchen door, but Liz only shook her head and motioned the younger woman away. The kitten licked Liz's neck, the touch of its rough tongue calming its mistress.

"Oh, sweet princess, what am I to do?"

Dinnertime had come and gone without notice. Liz put

some fresh food in the kitten's bowl, grabbed her purse, and left through the mudroom door. She closed and latched her studio door as she walked by, not letting herself think about how happy she had been to see David just a few short hours ago.

She drove past Cassie's house. The Country Ladies had closed for the night. Jaime's car sat in the driveway. Seeing the two lovebirds together was definitely not what she needed on this night.

The sun sank lower in the sky as she headed north across the Maumee River. She meandered the back roads and barely noticed as she passed through Archbold. Within minutes, she had pulled her Mustang into the parking lot at Goll Woods.

Had Liz been less distracted, she might have noticed the vehicle that had pulled out from behind the bins at the Other Place and followed her at a distance.

"So I suppose you're the one who's responsible for this?" Mallory tossed the photocopied pages back on the table as she glared at Gregg coming in through the mudroom door.

"I was at the library today doing some research ... Don't look so shocked—I do know where the library is! Anyway, I just thought I'd check out your *friend* and that's what I found."

"And you just couldn't wait to show your mom. Ian's right, you are a real jerk!"

"What? What was I supposed to do, just pretend I hadn't seen it? He's a convicted rapist and murderer and you think I should just sit on it because my mom's hot for him?"

"Did you try to look a little further? They don't usually let murderers out after only two years."

"Yeah, well ... maybe he escaped! Maybe he's the one that's been creeping us out! Maybe he's stalking my mom. He could be after her right now!"

They both looked at each other, then at the clock, and the darkening sky outside the window.

"How long ago did she leave?" Gregg asked.

Mallory shrugged her shoulders. "I met Ian in town for pizza and just got home a little while ago."

Gregg rested his hands on his hips and glanced back at the clock. "She was so pissed, she wouldn't even look at me. I figured I should lay low for a while. She was still here when I left a couple of hours ago."

"Maybe she went down to Cassie's," Mallory offered. But, when she called, neither Cassie nor Jaime had seen Liz. Mallory asked Cassie for David's cell number as Gregg shook his head.

"She's my mom and you're not calling him!" he said as she ended her call.

"You have any better ideas, Sherlock?"

"No," he admitted. "She's put all her energy into the Country Ladies and her studio. I can't think of anyone else she's spent time with recently. I'm sure she wouldn't go to Uncle Bill's or Peter's."

"Let me call David. He may have an idea as to where she might have gone."

Liz cut down the path she and David had walked on that early spring day seemingly so long ago. Daylight faded into dusk as she let herself be swallowed up by the mammoth trees forming a canopy overhead. She sank to a bench while darkness blanketed the woods.

She shook her head, clasping it between her hands, in an attempt to empty it of the conflicting thoughts that wove webs of discord in her mind. She sat until the night chills seeped under her skin. She listened to the sounds that surrounded her—insects and tree frogs. The distant howl of a coyote and an answering wail alerted her senses.

The coyotes were most likely down by the river she tried to assure herself. As she remembered the cemetery nearby, she felt the hairs on the nape of her neck stand on end. Shadows skittered across the path when a light breeze rustled through the leaves above.

She heard the snap of a twig close by. Now fully aware, she rose to her feet and started back the direction that she came. But the rustle she heard was more than leaves. She pivoted, quickening her step as she sensed something large looming behind her. She ran, tripped over a root, picked herself up, and ran on. The rustle took on the cadence of footsteps—rhythmic, even paced, and drawing ever closer.

The moonless night shrouded the path ahead as Liz lost all sense of direction. The trails were short, she told herself—she should be closing in on the parking lot. The path turned and she followed her instincts. She stumbled, swore, rushed onward.

"Oh God! I'm back at the bench!" she cried out loud. She panted, leaning on a tree, listening. The footsteps seemed to have stopped. She held her breath—only the drone of insects and the shrill chirping of tree frogs broke through the night. She dropped to the bench, her legs shaking, her heart thumping against her breastbone. After a few minutes she heard an engine turn over and tires spit stones from the road just beyond the woods.

He could have had her. It would have been so easy. But the timing wasn't right. Not yet. He gave a smirk—sure scared the crap out of her though. She'll be looking behind her for a while to come. His laugh held a sinister edge as he sped off into the night.

"Liz! Liz where are you? Are you okay?" David sprinted from his pickup around the back of the Mustang and into the woods. He illuminated the path with a broad-beamed flashlight. A night creature skittered across the trail just beyond the circle of light.

As he rounded a curve, he saw her sitting on the bench. She watched him come toward her, neither moving nor speaking.

He killed the light as he knelt before her, taking her arms gently in his hands.

"Good God," he was breathing heavily, "I was so scared. So damned scared, Liz. What in the hell are you doing out here?"

She drew back from him, crossing her arms over her breasts.

"Someone followed me here. Chased me," she said into the night. Then she looked down at the man in front of her. "How—

did—you—know—where to find me, David? *How did you know?*"

He leaned back on his heels, and tipped his head toward the black sky before again finding those violet eyes in the night.

"Is that how it's going to be? Tried and convicted without so much as a hearing? I don't know why I expected more."

He rose to his feet and extended his hand toward her, "I thought you might be different from the others. Not the first time I guessed wrong."

He flicked on the light and led the way back to the parking lot.

Liz listened to the news on National Public Radio the next morning. It was Friday—her afternoon to work at Country Ladies. Though, for the first time, she dreaded going to the shop. She drank an extra cup of coffee before dragging herself to the garden.

Dew clung to the grass as a low-hanging gray sky seemed to lock in the smothering humidity. Not even Princess 'Fraidy Cat wanted to venture forth on this oppressive late July day.

She dug new potatoes, picked green beans, and pulled red beets.

"Oh snap!" she exclaimed as she noticed a tomato plant partially stripped of its leaves. She stooped down to find a long green hornworm busily eating its way up the stem. She retrieved an old coffee can from the milk house, plucked the worm, and dropped him inside. She investigated each tomato vine, finding three more of the fat creatures and disposing of them in like fashion.

"I'll let Gregg take care of you guys," she said as she fit the plastic lid on the can.

She filled her garden cart with her morning's gleanings and pulled it under the shade of the maple tree, before retreating to the house for a shower.

The air conditioning unit whirred as Liz unloaded and arranged her produce for sale. By the time she was ready to open the shop, she felt as wilted as yesterday's salad greens, but she was relieved that Cassie hadn't been there to help.

Liz had relived the nightmare of the previous evening over and over in her mind while she harvested her vegetables that morning. She thought about David—she knew him intimately but, yet again, not at all. She remembered what Cassie had told her about David's past—not to believe what others' said. But she had read the newspaper articles! Sweet heaven, could he possibly have been guilty of those heinous crimes? And how did he know where to find her last night if he hadn't followed her?

The bell above the entrance door clanged as two women entered the shop. Liz welcomed the distraction from the disturbing maze in which her thoughts had become entangled.

As Liz bagged the produce and sleeved a bouquet of zinnias and snapdragons for the customers, the door opened again. As the women left, a man entered—slight, thinning hair, vaguely recognizable, with an almost comical swagger.

He looked at Liz with a familiarity that made her skin crawl. "Cassie happen to be around?"

"She's off for the afternoon. Could I help you?" His eyes traveled from her face to her breasts and back to meet her steady gaze.

"Might be able to, doll …" He stepped closer, lifting his hand toward her face. Liz instinctively brought her arm down against his, knocking his wrist against the counter's edge.

"Aaayyyy," he grabbed his arm with his other hand, as he glared at Liz, "You may live to regret that …" He started toward her, but the bell rang again. This time, Abby burst through the door with Emily and Meredith close behind.

The man turned toward the child then to her parents. Abby retreated, hiding behind Emily.

"Well if it isn't the dykes from down the road—this neighborhood's gone to hell in a handbag," he said looking at the trio, then back to Liz, "Tell Cassie an old friend stopped by to say 'hello.'"

As he brushed by Emily, he reached down to take Abby's face in his hand. "Cute kid," he said.

Meredith stepped between the man and her daughter. "Keep

your filthy hands to yourself."

The man glowered at Meri then turned back toward Liz with a smirk, "I'll be seeing you, dollface." He let the door slam behind him.

"Who was that creep?" Emily asked, still holding Abby against her.

"I can't place him, but I'm sure I've seen him before," Liz said. "I don't know what brought you guys here, but your timing couldn't have been better!"

"Believe it or not, we were on our way home from town and hoping you had some ripe tomatoes. We sold out yesterday and wanted a few for a salad tonight."

They all turned toward the door as it, again, opened and Cassie walked through.

The moment their eyes met, Liz could tell Cassie had talked to David, but she turned toward the child, "Hey, little miss Abigail, how are you?"

"There was a real creepy guy here. He tried to grab my face! I think he was going to do something bad to Liz before we got here."

"What's this?" Cassie asked, looking from one woman to the next.

"I told Em and Meredith he looked familiar. He had a slight build, thinning hair—reminded me of Barney Fife gone to the dark side!"

"Billy Joe Crenshaw!"

"The sheriff," Liz nodded.

"Former sheriff," Cassie corrected.

To Meredith and Emily, relative newcomers to the area, she explained, "Billy Joe Crenshaw was the county sheriff five years ago. He and my ex, Paul Alexander, were buddies since high school. The less I say about Paul, the better. He was the kind of vermin that gives sewer rats a bad name. Paul's locked away without hope of parole until Abby here is old enough to be a grandma, but somehow Billy Joe was released this spring for …" she rolled her eyes upward, "… good behavior."

After Meredith and Emily left with Abby, Cassie began to rearrange her cut flowers in the stand-up glass-front cooler, culling those with faded or wilting blooms, while Liz sorted through the vegetables. Several minutes passed in strained silence before Cassie pushed the refrigerator door shut with extra force. She did an about face and strode halfway across the room, stopping by a bin filled with new potatoes, arms crossed at her chest.

Liz stood facing the display table under the window, her back to Cassie. She paused and rested the palms of her hands against the table's edge. She took a deep breath then turned toward her friend and colleague.

"I blew it. I totally blew it, I know. I read the articles Gregg gave me and just lost it. *Rape and murder*, Cassie! Why didn't you tell me?"

"You still believe David's guilty, don't you?" Cassie accused. "If you want to see someone who was found guilty of a crime they didn't commit, just look at me! Courts make mistakes!"

"I know, I know, but …"

"Did you give David a chance to defend himself?"

Liz's downcast eyes answered Cassie's question.

"I told you not to believe anything about David's past without asking him." Cassie dropped her arms to her side with balled fists and walked to the door. As she opened it, she bent her head toward Liz, "David's been through hell. He's the last person I would call vulnerable…unless it involves you." The accusation in her tone could not be missed.

"Dammit, Cassie. Someone is trying to terrorize me. Maybe … assault … maybe even *murder*! How did David know I would be at Goll Woods last night unless he followed me? *How could he know?*"

"Do you think, maybe, he could love you enough to search heaven and earth until he found you?" Cassie closed the door, then opened it again, "His words, not mine."

Aaron Caine pulled his pickup out from the Other Place, followed Liz into her driveway, parked beside her and waited until she emerged from her Mustang before opening his door. Liz tried to avoid noticing as she busied herself lifting empty crates from her trunk. However, when he reached for the bushel basket she was holding, she was forced to look up into those unnaturally clear, unfathomable eyes. The sharp angles of his face and white-blonde crew cut reminded Liz of a character from one of those militaristic comic books she used to find under Gregg's bed. Liz could picture this man in camouflage fatigues much easier than the chambray shirt and blue jeans he now wore.

As his fingers brushed hers over the wire handles of the basket, Liz released her grip and edged backward along the bumper of the car until the rear fender separated her from her hired man.

A hint of a smile touched his face as he noticed her reaction. "I'll help you carry these to the shed."

His voice was even and steely. *Clint Eastwood. The Good, the Bad and the Ugly.* Her mind projected the thought before he finished speaking.

The patio door slammed, startling Liz. As Gregg walked toward them, she regained her composure, "Thanks, anyway, Mr. Caine, but my son can help me.

"Greggory, would you please give me a hand ..." she called toward the house.

The man sat the basket back in the trunk, nodded and said, "Another time, perhaps." He tipped his hat to Gregg and slid back into his truck.

They watched him back up and pull over the bridge, before Gregg spoke, "So you're talking to me again, Mom?"

"Better you than him. But don't flatter yourself too much," she said as they retrieved the baskets and crates and carried them toward the milk house.

After they stacked the containers in the shed, Gregg said, "I'm sorry. Maybe I was out-of-line. But with all the stuff happening around here, I couldn't not tell you!"

"No, no … I guess not." Liz tilted her head back so Gregg could see her face, "I know you don't like David … don't trust him. And after reading those articles, I questioned whether I was just being thickheaded and letting my emotions take control of my life. I can't expect you to agree or to understand, but I know David could never have hurt those women any more than he would hurt me … I just know it."

"Okay, Mom, but just be careful, please?" He looked away, clearing his throat. "I couldn't take it if I lost you, too. I couldn't!" As he blinked his eyes to hold back tears, Liz saw the face of a boy who was still coping with the death of his father. She wrapped her arms around him. He returned her hug then stepped back.

"I've got something to show you. I hope it's okay." He opened the door to her studio. Two sturdy tables stood in the middle of the room. "I hope they're the right size. They're both three by six feet. The plywood tops are an inch thick and I built a brace under the center of each one. They're heavier 'n heck! I had to get Neil and Aaron to help me move them."

"Aaron Caine was in my studio?"

"I don't see what you have against the guy, Mom. He's a little stand-offish, but he's okay."

"Yeah, well, let's just say we have a difference of opinion when it comes to the men in my life …" She patted the top of the nearer table, "But these are great! Just the right height, too!"

She stood on tiptoe and kissed her son's cheek. "Thank you, sweetie."

As they left the shed, Liz smiled back at him, "But this doesn't absolve you from your promise to help me build the shelves in the back of the room this weekend!" Gregg responded with a mock groan as he rested his arm on his mother's shoulders.

When Gregg saw his old roommate's car cross over the bridge and come to a stop behind the Mustang, his groan turned more audible and authentic.

"Women! What's Mallory see in him, anyway?"

"Maybe you should ask her," Liz said with a shake of her head.

"I hardly see her anymore. Besides, she was as ticked at me as you were last night. And I'm not her son, so she probably isn't as inclined to play nice."

They watched as Mallory walked out of the house. She wore a spaghetti strapped lime green sundress with a matching rosette clip that set off her flowing auburn hair. She glanced back at Gregg and Liz and waved, before tucking her hand into Ian's.

"Think I'm going into town or maybe I'll drive over to BG and catch a band at one of the bars," Gregg said.

It was Liz's turn to caution her son, "Just be careful. If you drink, don't you dare drive home. Because if you think losing me would be hard, if anything happened to either of my children …"

"Don't worry, Mom, I will." He bent down and pecked her cheek. "Love you," he said as he bounded toward his Ranger.

Liz poked her head in the refrigerator in search of a quick dinner, pulled out a container of cottage cheese and sat it on the table. Little Princess 'Fraidy Cat was lying on the window shelf, head resting on her front paws, staring at the radio.

Liz walked over, picked up the kitten, and nuzzled her as they both watched the sun dip lower in the western sky. "I miss him too, baby. But I think I've stepped over the line this time. I'm not sure he'll be able to forgive me. I hate being afraid of my shadow!" Liz gave a quick laugh as she held the kitten close, "Guess I shouldn't make fun of you, little furball!"

Liz dolloped the cottage cheese on top of a cut-up tomato and ate mechanically. She rinsed the plate in the sink. The Princess had returned to her perch by the radio, her eyes closed as she exhaled gentle kitten snores.

"I can't stay here looking at the walls and listening for strange sounds all night," she said to her sleeping companion.

For the third time, Liz tugged open the door of *Tia's Taverna*. With a determined stride she walked past the row of barstools. Though several people milled about the room, their—hers and David's—booth appeared to be empty.

What if he isn't here? She didn't allow herself a glance toward the pool table until she sat down. When she did, she recognized David's opponent from the previous games, but not the man shooting the balls with his cue stick.

She sat on the cracked red vinyl bench for several minutes, trying to collect her thoughts. The man who finally sat down across from her was not David Morales, but his friend.

"Listen, *gringa,* don' you think you've done enough? Why don' you leave *mi amigo* alone? He's jus' beginning to get over all that stuff that happened when he went west. He doesn't need you addin' to his troubles."

Liz looked toward the bar and saw *Tía* Juana behind the counter staring at her with a frown. She felt as though the entire room was holding its collective breath, waiting for her to leave. She nodded her head and slid off the seat. She retraced her steps to the front of the tavern. A man by the door opened it for her and she nodded her thanks, unwilling to trust her voice. The door closed against the clamor of the bar as she faced the silence of the settling dusk. A few stars twinkled in the distant sky.

"Star light, star bright, first star ..." she began then paused as she saw a familiar battered pickup ease its way toward her.

The pickup stopped beside her and the driver rolled down his window. "You comin' or goin'?" he asked.

"That depends ..." she said.

"Hop in." He leaned over the seat to open the passenger door.

She nodded as she headed around the front of the truck.

He looked at her but said nothing more as he drove out of the parking lot. He followed the same roads as before, pulling up beside the same small trailer.

She didn't wait for him to open her door, but met him as he came around the hood. She led the way to the mobile home. He fit the key into the lock and pushed the door open.

They faced each other in the dim interior, searching for answers to unvoiced questions. She moved first, lifting her lips to his. He stood hands at his side as her mouth spoke her apology in a way words could not.

They broke apart, "David ... David ..."

"Shhh, don't say anything." He pulled her toward him as their bodies continued their conversation in a language without limits.

He tugged at the hem of her silk blouse while she worked the buttons free. His tee-shirt fell to the floor next to her top. She worked the snap to his jeans and he unfastened the hooks to her black satin bra.

Their lips met again, their bodies relishing the feel of skin on skin. They drew apart just far enough for her to ease the waist of her skirt over her rounded hips. She kicked off her low-heeled pumps and he sank to the couch to remove his sneakers. She stooped in front of him, nudging his jeans down over his hips until they were freed from his legs, and tossed the pants aside.

He rested his hands on either side of her breasts and drew her on top of him. He took each brown nipple into his mouth. Their bodies strained to couple against cotton and satin as she rocked in a slow pace over him.

They shifted in unison making their way to the bedroom. Cotton and satin mingled on the floor as their bodies reclaimed the intimacy both thought they had lost.

They satisfied hungers with a sustenance only they could provide, moving with a rhythm fed by familiarity.

"I have to go home tonight," she said, laying on her back, clothed only in a soft sheen.

He shifted his head toward her and nodded, his arm resting across his forehead. He leaned up on his elbow then gently eased himself over on top of her, bracing his upper body on his forearms.

"Save next weekend for me. Tell the kids whatever you want, but you're going with me ... I promise you'll come back alive," he said straight-faced as his lips found hers. "We have much to talk about, *güerita mía*."

CHAPTER NINE

"Ya know, Mom, you could've left a little wood at Lucky's," Gregg said as they pulled out of the local lumberyard. They had loaded the bed of his Ranger with the boards needed to build the shelving for the glass sheets Liz had ordered.

Mallory followed them into the driveway at the farm in her little Chevy.

As she joined Liz and Gregg at the tailgate of the pickup, he asked, "What? You're not out with O'Flannery?"

"We have a date for a movie tonight." Mallory said, as she accepted the small stack of shelf sides he piled on her upturned forearms.

"That so?" he said as he picked up another stack of wood and followed her up the walk. He stayed a few feet back so he could appreciate the snug fit of her modest shorts revealing legs that were second to none.

He thought about Ian O'Flannery running his hands down those legs in the back seat of his car and nearly dropped the boards he was carrying.

When the wood had been neatly stacked on the worktables, Liz brought out glasses of iced tea and sat them on the patio table.

"Time for a break before we put this all together," she said.

"I can help for a while longer," Mallory offered as they relaxed on the patio. "It's the first Saturday I haven't been scheduled at either library in a month. It'll be a change to work on shelves that aren't already loaded with books!"

"That would be great!" Liz said, casting a knowing look toward her son.

Gregg measured, sawed, and nailed the shelves while Mallory sorted the precut sizes and held boards in place. Liz stayed clear of her studio except to poke her head in now and again for a supervisorial comment.

For the first hour Gregg and Mallory worked in silence, only exchanging words when necessary. They finished the base cupboard with its drawer for storage. The drop-down front had been especially challenging.

"You're pretty handy with a drill," Mallory allowed.

"Thanks, my dad was an incredible carpenter—he taught me well."

"Not every boy would take the time to learn."

Gregg laid down the drill he had been using. "I'm not as much of a dumb ass as I pretend to be." He looked at her then affixed the drill bit into a screw head and joined two parts of the shelving unit together. He inserted two more screws into the shelves before putting the drill down to retrieve another board.

"You're better off with Ian, even if he is a loser." Gregg gave Mallory a half grin. "I just thought we had something going. Guess I was wrong."

Mallory wanted to say something, needed to respond, but the words remained a jumble in her head. She watched the muscles in his shoulders cord together as he worked. She wanted so badly to reach out to him. But she had developed an affection for Ian, too—he was fun to be with, appreciated her in a way that she wasn't sure Gregg could, and most of all, he was safe.

"Looks like you have things under control here." Not the words she wanted to say.

He turned to face her. "Guess I blew my chances. Thanks for getting me through biochem and helping me with econ earlier this summer, Mallory Martin."

She hesitated, searching for a way to avoid the inevitable outcome. "No problem," she said lamely. They stood looking at each other separated by much more than the worktables Gregg had built for his mother, before Mallory turned and walked out the door.

Gregg worked the remainder of the afternoon, accepting an iced tea when his mom brought it to the cob shed turned art glass studio. She helped him with a heavier board, but didn't ask about Mallory, who had come in the mudroom door earlier, walked silently past Liz in the kitchen, through the dining room, and up the stairs to her room.

A quiet Sunday slid into a rainy Monday. As usual, Liz and the little Princess listened to *Davy Jones' Locker*. David had called on Saturday evening, but they agreed not to see each other until the coming weekend.

Mud covered Liz's hands and feet Tuesday morning as she harvested vegetables barefoot after an overnight downpour. She stood to wipe her face, leaving a mud streak across her forehead when she noticed a brown delivery truck pull across the bridge and park at the end of the sidewalk.

They weren't supposed to come until tomorrow! Liz grabbed the garden hose and sprayed off her hands and feet as best as she could. She met the driver as he was about to knock on the foyer door and signed for the delivery. Just as he placed the last box on the worktable, Neil Rowland and Aaron Caine came up the walk.

"Need help, Liz?" Neil asked while Caine cocked an eyebrow and let a vestige of a smile break through his customary impassivity as he checked out her mud-splattered appearance.

"Thanks. I think it's all in the studio now," Liz said then glanced toward Aaron Caine. For a fleeting moment, she caught a glimpse of the man behind the mask ... and it left her more unsettled than did their usual encounters.

"We were looking for Gregg. We thought he might like to ride up to Michigan—there's a big Ag Expo at East Lansing."

Liz grabbed the opportunity to retreat into the house. "I'll send him right out," she called over her shoulder as she disappeared through the door.

It was mid-afternoon before Liz was able to get back to her studio. A pungent odor had greeted her when she dropped her produce at the Country Ladies, and she joined Meredith and Emily in their search for its source. They rearranged the fruits and vegetables, culling those that were past their prime until Emily discovered a potato that had fallen behind its bin.

"Ewww! Gross!" Abby had pinched her nose shut with her fingers while insisting upon seeing the rotten tuber.

Liz laughed to herself at the memory as she finally unwrapped the glass sheets she purchased in Columbus. She sorted them, filing each in its own slot in the shelving unit Gregg and Mallory had constructed over the weekend.

When everything had been stored away, she took out a book of patterns she had bought featuring vegetables and fruits. She searched from cover to cover for a design that wouldn't be too challenging, deciding on a trio of peppers with only nineteen pieces of glass and three colors that she had available.

"Liz?" When Mallory poked her head into the shop, Liz realized that night had fallen while she worked.

"I can still do it!" Liz stood back from her worktable as Mallory stepped into the room. Green, red, and yellow glass pieces lay on the table arranged to form three peppers. "I only broke two pieces in the process!"

"Cool!" Mallory said as she lifted a green section.

"I haven't soldered the lead yet. I think I'll wait for that 'til morning." Liz brushed her hands against her jeans then asked, "Have you had dinner yet? Wish they delivered pizza this far out."

"This must be your lucky day, because I picked up a veggie deluxe at Pisanello's on my way home and was hoping someone would share it with me!"

Between the Country Ladies and her studio, Liz had little time to spare the rest of the week.

On Friday morning she fed Desert Pro, cleaned his hoofs and brushed his mane.

"Sorry, guy, you've been a bit neglected the past few weeks. Maybe we'll get a ride in this evening.

"I won't be around this weekend. David's kidnapping me to some undisclosed location. Talk about total trust!" She leaned her forehead against his withers, feeling his sleekness, absorbing his warmth. "Just like you trust me, right, boy? Well, I'll do better by you in the future ..." She straightened, reaching up to rub his shoulder.

"... and I'll do better by David. I just need to hear his side of the story."

A scurrying noise from the center bay of the barn caused Liz to turn around abruptly. The picture of Roseanne's kittens as they lay strewn about the cement floor slid through her mind, and she wrapped her arm around Desert Pro's neck for reassurance.

"Probably just a raccoon or groundhog, right Pro? I'm so damn tired of being afraid of my shadow. Who was it, boy? Did you see who did it?"

The horse whiffed and blew air through his nostrils carefully shifting his head toward his mistress.

"If only I could understand what you're trying to tell me," Liz said as she pulled a fresh-picked carrot from her pocket and fed it to her friend.

The gray clouds reached their saturation level just before Liz arrived at the Country Ladies. She carried a box of tomatoes, two bushels of sweet corn, peppers, squash, carrots, red beets, okra and other gleanings from her garden into the shop through a drizzling rain. Cassie had come and gone, leaving the lights on and the store ready for Liz to open, but the damp chill outside carried into the building.

Bet there won't be many customers out today Liz thought as she recounted the cash in the drawer under the counter before unlocking the door. Much to her surprise an SUV pulled into the drive as she hung the new OPEN sign that Emily had designed and painted.

Two young women emerged from the front seat, while two … three … four children hopped out from the back.

Liz held the door open as they hurried in through the rain.

"We've been wanting to stop all summer!" the tall brunette said. "We're friends with Meri and Em and love the idea of the Country Ladies." She glanced around the room before going on, "We were wondering if you had thought about expanding into local arts and crafts, but you don't have a lot of extra space."

"As a matter of fact, I hope to sell some of my smaller stained glass pieces here as soon as I can build an inventory," Liz said. "What were you thinking about?"

"Nicholas, put that apple down!" the woman directed as she caught her son reaching into one of the bins with her peripheral vision.

"It's okay," Liz smiled, "it's pesticide free and the rain washed it before I picked it yesterday! We'll call that a free sample."

"Thanks!" the woman said, then to her son, "Go ahead, but thank the nice lady first," and back to Liz, "I do ceramics and thought you might be interested in carrying a line of garden art— you know, the butterflies and frogs and such on copper stakes— and other smallish items that I created. Mags makes really cool garden markers using wooden paint stirrers."

Her friend, an equally tall woman with a long blond ponytail, joined them. "I have a few in the car, if you'd like to see them."

"That would be great! I can show them to Cassie—it's really her shop — and Meredith and Emily, but then you said they're friends, so they've probably seen your work already. Anyway, we can get back to you next week. Just leave your names and phone numbers."

The women filled two shopping baskets with produce. While

she waited, Liz read the names they had written on the notepad on the counter—Chelsea Clark and Maggie May Stuart—and chuckled to herself.

After Liz tallied their total and they paid their bill, she turned to the blond with a smile, "Forgive my asking but given your name and approximate age …"

"My dad was a huge Rod Stewart fan … with what I call a warped sense of humor. But I've gotten used to it. It's my mom I haven't forgiven—she had control of the birth certificate!" Maggie May laughed. "Besides, his second choice was 'Lovely.' My brother's named Jude—he won't work a job where he has to wear a nametag, for fear of being serenaded! Dad's whole family has a case of Beatlemania!

"Of course, the Stuart part of my name is my fault—I could have married a man with the name of Jones or Smith. At least Adam spells his name different from Rod!

"But that's more than you wanted to know, I'm sure!"

Liz shook her head, "Not at all." The conversation led to other interesting names they knew. They would have talked longer but the children were getting restless.

"We'll be in touch," Liz assured the women as they trailed their children out the door.

The next hour passed quietly. Liz was studying a book of flower patterns she had bought at the glass studio in Columbus, trying to mentally reconstruct her inventory of glass sheets, when the door burst open and Emily came rushing in.

"God, Liz! I just got a call from the police. Someone tried to kidnap Abby! Meredith had taken her to Toledo shopping, and Meri was in trying on something when she heard Abby scream. By the time she got dressed I guess the man had made it to the parking lot with our little girl. No one even tried to stop him! Somehow Abby jerked away from the guy and ran toward Meri right in front of a motorcycle. The cyclist swerved, missing Abby but he hit Meredith. She's in the hospital now and I don't have enough gas to make it there. Can I borrow your car, please?"

"You're in no shape to drive. Let me jot a note for Cassie. I'll close the shop and take you there."

A female EMT sat with Abby in the waiting room of the large hospital. As Emily scooped her daughter into her arms, the EMT said, "Your friend's in ICU. They think she'll be okay, but she got a nasty concussion and is skinned up pretty badly—maybe a cracked rib or two."

"Can I go up to see her?"

The woman shook her head, "Only family can be in ICU. I'm so sorry—I'll check on her condition and let her know you are here with Abigail before I leave."

When the elevator doors closed taking the EMT up to her partner, Emily let her tears fall onto her child's blond curls as she held her close.

"It's not fair! Meredith is as much my spouse as Cassie is Jaime's, but I can't be with her when she needs me most!"

At a loss for words, Liz thought about the hours she had spent at Mack's side after the accident. What if she hadn't been allowed in ICU with him? She just assumed it was her right. But sitting next to her friend, understanding her pain and her fears, questions poured through her mind.

"I want so badly to marry Meredith. I love her more than life itself," Emily said through her tears. "Would you believe it? We can't even have a civil union in Ohio. We actually thought about not moving here, but Meri was offered a tenure-track position at Bowling Green, and those are hard to come by these days." She blew her nose before adding, "We should have moved to Toledo. If we lived there we could have registered as domestic partners— that's something, at least."

Emily rested her head against Abby's soft hair for a few minutes, then took a deep breath. "I'm so sorry. I shouldn't have gotten on my soapbox with you. It's not your fault life's the way it is. Besides, we have Abby and Meri's going to be okay. That's what's really important."

When, after several hours under observation out of ICU, Meredith was released from the hospital, a torrential rain splattered into puddles already filled with water. The black pavement blended into a darkness barely illuminated with overhead lights. Emily waited at the curb with Meredith in a wheel chair holding their sleeping daughter, while Liz dashed to her car. She drove her friends to the shopping center where Meredith had parked so many hours ago, then followed them home to help get Meri situated, before calling Cassie.

"The motorcycle rider was the real hero," Liz said to Jaime and Cassie, who had joined Gregg and Mallory around the McAlister dining room table after Liz's call. "He dodged Abby then dumped his bike to avoid hitting Meredith. If he had caught her square on rather than grazing her side ..." Liz looked away as she dabbed the corner of her eye with a crumpled tissue. She picked up the wine glass in front of her and took a sip, "He broke an arm and lost considerable skin on his right side, but thank God he was wearing a good helmet. They kept him overnight. Abby insisted on thanking him before she left the hospital. She's quite an incredible little girl!"

"What about the scumbutt that tried to take her?" Jaime asked, his face taut with a smoldering anger. "Anyone who would hurt a little kid should be locked away."

"Abby tried to describe him and they interviewed witnesses in the store, but one person said he was medium height with blond hair and another, that he was tall with dark brown hair. He wore a dark red or brown or black windbreaker with the collar turned up and his face was pretty much covered by a hat. The police put out an APB but don't have much hope of finding him. Everyone was so distracted by the accident, not one person saw the vehicle he drove."

The phone in the kitchen rang and Mallory jumped up to get it. "It's for you, Liz."

Liz took the phone as she stood up from the table, "David?

Hi! I'm sorry about our weekend!" Liz caught the look on her son's face as she walked toward the kitchen. "Yeah, I guess everything conspired against us—the weather is horrible! There are tornado warnings north of us!" ... "I agree. Having Abby and Meredith safe is the most important thing. If I were you, I'd drive to Melody's and hug those grandchildren of yours." ... "That's where you are? Well, hug them for me, too!" ... "I know, I was looking forward to our time together." ... "Bye ..."

Liz cradled the phone and walked to the back of the dining room, pulling a second bottle of wine from a side compartment of the buffet. "Anyone up for a refill?"

With Mallory at work and Gregg off to Bowling Green, Liz was anticipating a long afternoon in her studio—she wanted to replace the broken panels of glass in the living room before Tatiana came home as well as replenish her inventory at the shop. She had just turned on the radio when she heard a car in the driveway. She glanced out the window above the light table, to see Brandon's Miata stop by the walk. She clicked off the radio, locked the studio door, and picked up Princess 'Fraidy Cat to keep her from mewing.

She pulled the curtains closed and stepped back from the window as Brandon gave up ringing the doorbell and turned toward the cob shed. Liz heard him try the door and after a few seconds of silence, the echo of his footsteps against the concrete sidewalk. She waited for the expected sound of his tires on the gravel drive. She peeked out the corner of the window but Brandon didn't appear to be in the Miata.

As she pulled the curtain shut, she regretted covering the back window with the shelving. She had decided to go in search of Brandon and just cracked the door open when she heard a second set of tires cross the bridge. She peered through the slit in the door as Aaron Caine's pickup coasted to a stop within inches of the Miata. Caine climbed down from the cab and stood next to the truck as Brandon walked into Liz's view. He stood beside his car, his arms crossed.

Caine stepped away from the door, spread his legs slightly, and rested his hands on his hips. There was a tautness to his stance—like a cat ready to spring. Or a gunslinger ready to fire.

Brandon shifted his stance, so he directly faced Caine. They stared at one another for several seconds then Brandon glanced toward the house. Liz held her breath, hoping he wouldn't notice the door ajar.

"Something tells me there's no love lost between those two," Liz whispered to her kitten.

Brandon looked back at Caine then opened the car door and sank into the interior out of Liz's sight. He eased the Miata forward, pulled around the truck, and sped out of the drive, kicking up stones with his tires.

Aaron Caine shifted his gaze to the house. With a slight curl to his lips, he tipped his hat before climbing back into the truck and heading toward the barn.

Liz expelled her breath, "Wonder what that was all about?" Then to the Princess, she said, "We dodged one that time. The last thing I want to do is waste an afternoon kibitzing with Brandon Michaels when I need to get those windows done." She shook her head with a laugh, "I never thought the day would come when I'd be glad to see Aaron Caine!"

The four Country Ladies' partners met on Monday afternoon to discuss the expansion of their business. Emily and Meredith were still shaken, with Meri sporting bruises and scrapes up and down her left side. A subdued little Abigail sat in a corner petting Joe and the Princess. Every once in a while they would hear her talking to the animals.

"Shhh, listen," Emily said to the others as Abby told her friends in a soft voice, "... and the bad man tried to take me away but I was saved by a superhero on a ... on a ... motorbicycle. He saved my life!" With that, she looked over at the adults in the room. "He did, didn't he, Mommy?" Both Meri and Em nodded in unison.

The group readily agreed that adding Chelsea and Maggie May's crafts to Liz's stained glass pieces would greatly enhance the appeal of the Country Ladies. They eagerly rearranged shelving units and bins, while Meredith directed from her chair. Jaime had bought them an industrial-sized display cooler from a grocery store in a neighboring town, which, along with Cassie's floral display cases, put constraints on their options, but with four creative minds at work, they soon developed a floor plan.

"It just makes sense to have Liz's suncatchers and the other crafts displayed in and under the front bay window. With it's southern exposure and the produce under it, we had to keep the shades pulled most of the day," Cassie said.

"Definitely!" Meredith agreed. "I'll bet we can find an old tri-fold dressing screen at one of the antique stores to block the sun from the produce and give wall space for display shelves."

"It's already the first of August. Any chance we could manage an open house this weekend with wine and cheese on Friday evening and, maybe, lemonade and snacks on Saturday?" Cassie asked.

"Wow! It'd be a lot of work!" Liz said, "But I have enough suncatchers and small windows done. Think we could find a dressing screen and work out display shelves for Chelsea and Maggie May?"

"I think we could do it! I'll start working on a marketing campaign right away," Meri offered. "It will keep my mind off last Friday."

"And I'll work up graphics for an advertising flyer," Emily added. "I can run off paper copies as well as send it out over the Internet. We've collected a fairly extensive list of e-mail addresses and we can make it the home page on our website."

"We have several hundred 'likes' on our Facebook page, too," Meri added. "We can post a notice there."

"Don't you just love having a tech-savvy marketing prof. and a graphic designer for partners?" Liz asked Cassie before adding, "Hey, I'll bet I can get us some radio air time. Anyone game for doing an interview on *Davy Jones' Locker*?

"David?" Liz said into the phone when he answered her call.

"I really, really don't want to ask this, but can we postpone our weekend one more time?" Liz went on to explain the expansion plans for Country Ladies and for the open house the weekend ahead.

"We know it's short notice, but we had hoped you would have some time to promote the open house on your show." ... "I think you should interview Cassie, but she's got a phobia about public speaking." ... "Okay, I'll do it, as long as it's just a short interview and you promise to be gentle with me!"

After Liz hung up the phone she poured herself a cup of coffee and sat down at the kitchen table. Princess 'Fraidy Cat rubbed against her ankle and she picked up the kitten. They both stared at the silent radio on the window shelf.

Liz sipped her coffee as she absentmindedly pet the cat on her lap, "Tomorrow morning! I'm going to be on *Davy Jones' Locker* tomorrow morning!"

"We have a special guest today on *Davy Jones' Locker*, a renowned local gardener and up-and-coming stained glass artist, Ms. Elizabeth McKenna McAlister." David grinned at Liz as she rolled her eyes. His introduction had caught her off-guard, but had also relaxed her just a bit.

"Liz is a partner in a thriving new enterprise just south of town, the Country Ladies. Can you tell us a little about the history of the Country Ladies and how you came to be involved in the shop earlier this summer?"

Liz told of Cassie's herb and flower business and her offer to expand to include produce from Meredith and Emily and Liz's gardens. She credited Meri and Em with their marketing and graphics expertise, reading the Country Ladies' web site address from a slip of paper and inviting the listeners to visit their facebook page, while playing down her own role in the shop.

David's smile set her heart pulsing as he said, "I've seen examples of your stained glass art. Could you tell our listeners when and how you became interested in working with glass?"

Liz took a deep breath, "I've always been fascinated with the way light played through church windows. My father was a Presbyterian minister, so I spent a considerable amount of time in churches of various denominations as we traveled from parish to parish and Dad acquainted himself with other ministers in the towns where he served." Liz found her nerves calming as she talked about the colors and textures of the windows in the old Gothic-style Roman Catholic churches.

Liz told about meeting Melody, observing her at work, and Melody's help setting up Liz's studio. With considerable coaxing, she described some of the pieces she had crafted for the Country Ladies but quickly segued into detailing Chelsea's ceramics and Maggie May's garden stakes.

Liz concluded by saying, "We invite people from all area communities to our open house this weekend."

David reminded his listeners, "All of the growers and artists involved with Country Ladies are local women, so let's go out and support their efforts this weekend and throughout the rest of the summer and fall.

"I'd like to thank Ms. Elizabeth McKenna McAlister for telling us all about the Country Ladies. And now a word from our sponsor before we announce today's birthdays and turn on the tunes during the second hour of *Davy Jones' Locker*."

David plugged in the station promo segment then turned to Liz, "You were a natural! I wish every interview could be so easy!" He checked the time, then motioned for Liz to wait. At the end of the station break, David introduced Helen Reddy's "I am Woman," then arose from his chair and motioned for Liz to follow him out of the sound booth.

The room was empty except for the technician who was intent on checking her smartphone. David pulled Liz close, "I've missed you, *güerita mía!*"

"Yeah, me, too." Liz said as she leaned into him, tilting her head to meet his lips. Their kiss lengthened until the technician tapped on the window of the booth and motioned toward David's chair.

"Guess I have to get back to the show," David said as he gave her a quick kiss, then slipped back into his booth.

When Liz flipped on the radio in her car, *Besame Mucho* filtered across the sound waves.

The remainder of the week was spent picking produce, arranging and rearranging the Country Ladies' shop, and taking care of their rapidly increasing line of customers, leaving time for little else. Chelsea had found the perfect dressing screen at one of the antique malls. She had to talk the dealer into taking her displays down from the tri-fold screen, but the woman readily agreed when Chelsea told her it was for the Country Ladies.

"The dealer heard Liz on the radio and plans to attend the open house!" Chelsea told the others as she carried the screen into the shop.

Jaime arrived from Toronto Thursday evening with cases of Lake Erie wines as well as a selection of cheeses. The women had stayed up until the wee hours of the night preparing trays of their favorite hors d'oeuvres. A tent had been erected in the yard in front of the Country Ladies, with tables and chairs for the anticipated guests.

The rain that threatened Friday morning moved off to the north and by mid-afternoon the sun broke through the clouds. The sweltering August heat failed to materialize, and a gentle breeze served as a natural fan.

By six o'clock a few cars began to trickle in. Ben directed them to the mown hayfield across the road. The partners took turns staffing the register, replenishing the hors d'oeuvres trays, and assisting customers in the shop.

Jaime made a dashing sommelier, with women finding reasons to stay at the makeshift bar even after their wine glasses had been filled. Mallory carried trays of food to the guests, while Gregg took charge of the soft drinks.

Chelsea and Maggie May's husbands, Marcus and Adam, had set up a cornhole game and other entertainments for the children under the far end of the tent, before retrieving sound equipment, a keyboard, and saxophone from a van. They formed two thirds of a well-known local jazz trio, with their percussionist arriving soon after to help with the set up.

By seven o'clock, people were milling under the tent, in the shop, and throughout Cassie's cottage garden. The partners restocked the shelves as they rang up sale after sale. Liz was working the register when she stopped mid-transaction as David walked through the door. He wore a short-sleeved lavender shirt with black jeans, momentarily mesmerizing her.

She finished ringing up the purchases and chatted with the customer, but had no recollection of doing so.

Cassie walked over from where she was rearranging produce, gave David a sisterly hug then said to Liz, "You haven't been out of the shop for a while. Why don't I take over here and you check to see if they need anything under the tent?"

"Thanks, Cas," Liz and David said in unison.

Once outside, though, they walked toward the barn rather than the tent. As soon as they could, they disappeared into the shadows behind the shop.

"I feel like a kid again," David laughed softly as he found Liz's waiting lips. When they broke apart she kissed her way down the corded muscles of his neck then rested her head against his chest before looking up at him.

"I know. Sneaking off like this. You, David Morales, make me act like a giddy teenager!"

"Yeah," he whispered and nodded toward the barn, "want to take a roll in the hay?"

Liz giggled, "Yes!"

David laughed out loud, wrapping Liz in a hug, then letting his hand wander down to her bottom before covering her lips with his once again. When she finally drew her head back, she said with a twinkle, "However, since I'm nearly fifty and not fifteen, I'd better check on what's happening under the bigtop, as Cassie asked."

David pulled back reluctantly, stole another kiss then, taking her hand, walked toward the shop as a delivery truck stopped beside the balloon bouquet at the end of the walk.

"Is there an Elizabeth McAlister around?" the uniformed woman asked.

Liz glanced at David then identified herself.

"I have two boxes of perishables for you," the woman said as she stepped into her truck. "They're from New York City."

"Bubbies Homemade Ice Cream? What in the world?" Liz said as David placed the cartons on a table. She read the label as David opened the first box, "It's something called Mochi Premium Ice Cream."

Liz lifted the inner carton out from dry ice and opened it, "Look, there's a gift tag!" She read the note, then looked up, "It's from Tatiana! She says, 'Wish I could be there! See you in a few weeks!'"

Liz caught a tear from the corner of her eye with her free hand as she laid the note on the table. She picked up one of the packets and read, "Chocolate Espresso," then unwrapped it to find eight rounded mounds of chocolate. She lifted one to her mouth and took a bite. "Mmmm ... frozen, but incredible!"

She held the half-eaten confection up to David, who took it between his lips. After a moment, he nodded, "I'm not big on chocolate, but that's good—very good!"

Others clustered about to investigate the special delivery boxes and Liz invited them to sample Tatiana's offering to the party. "Tiramisu!" Emily read from one of the packages. Meredith opened a packet of light green balls, then glanced back at the wrapper and said, "Yum! Pistachio!"

David smiled at Liz as he opened another box with pale orange treats. "This one's for you." As she took a bite, he gave a lift to his eyebrows and grinned, "It's passion fruit!"

As the evening progressed, the crowd grew larger. More people arrived, but few left. Gregg made a run into town to buy more snacks, soft drinks, and supplies.

Liz was gratified that many of her McAlister relations had come to the open house. They were clustered around a few tables toward the children's area. David had gone to help Jaime with the wine when he and Liz had returned to the tent earlier in the evening, but she knew Mack's family would find out soon enough about her relationship with David.

Deciding to control the situation rather than hide from it, Liz waited for David to uncork a wine bottle and hand it to Jaime before drawing him away.

"I have some people I'd like to introduce you to," she said, adding, "Mack's family."

David searched her face, "Are you sure you want to do this?"

Liz nodded as she took his hand and walked toward the McAlister tables. Conversation stopped as one after another of Mack's relatives noticed her approach.

Liz stood at the end of the table, "Hi everyone! I'd like to thank you all for coming tonight. It means a lot to me and I know it would to Mack, as well."

She almost lost her nerve as Bill McAlister leaned back in his chair, his face shaded by his John Deere cap, while Marian openly glared at her.

Liz gripped David's hand for support as she turned to him, "And I'd like you to meet David Morales.

"I loved Mack with all my heart and I miss him every day. But, I guess time wears the edges off of even the sharpest pains." She let her eyes wander to each of the McAlisters assembled before her.

"David came into my life," she laughed quietly and looked at David, "or I guess it would be more accurate to say that I came into his, this spring. Circumstances brought us together several times throughout the summer and though I tried to fight my feelings," Liz glanced again at those around the table then back at David, "I've grown quite fond of him.

"I don't expect your blessings but I want to be honest with

you. You were my family for nearly thirty years—you will always be family to me, but ..."

"There's no need for 'buts' Aunt Liz," Peter scooted his chair back and walked to where Liz and David stood. He put his arm around her. "You will always be a part of our family."

He extended his hand to David, "Pleased to meet you, David. I'm Peter. My dad was Mack's oldest brother."

"The Vietnam soldier," David said as he shook Peter's hand. "And you farm the land now."

"I do, so I expect I'll be seeing you around." Peter gave them both the McAlister smile before returning to his seat.

Neil Rowland sat next to Peter, and his wife Linda gushed, "I listen to *Davy Jones' Locker* all the time. I love your interviews! You did a great job talking up the Country Ladies and the open house this weekend, Liz!"

When others asked, Linda turned to tell everyone about David's program. Conversation soon resumed its normal pace, and after a few minutes, Liz and David excused themselves, having been welcomed by all but Bill and Marian.

As they made their way to the bar, David put his hand in the small of her back and leaned close to her, "You are one brave lady. Thank you."

Liz looked toward Gregg, whose expression was unreadable. "I just wish I could convince my son that I'm not betraying his father."

With the arrival of Anita and Windy along with Melody, Anacita and Joshua James, their attention shifted to the front of the tent. The children had spotted their grandfather, and Anacita began wending through the maze of adult legs in his direction before David and Liz could get to them. David swept his granddaughter up into his arms, carrying her to where his grandson tried to squirm his way out of his mother's grasp. When he saw Liz, however, Joshua James wrapped his chubby little arms around his mother's neck and peeked with suspicion at the woman with his grandpa.

"You remember my friend, Liz, don't you, little buddy?" David asked as he lowered Anacita to the ground to take his grandson into his arms. After the adults exchanged greetings, Liz and David walked Anacita to the children's area where Jaime's daughter, Tina, and a friend were keeping the young ones entertained, under the watchful eyes of a few parents.

"Anacita, this is Abby," Liz said as they led David's granddaughter to meet Meredith and Emily's daughter.

It only took a few minutes for the two gregarious five-year-olds to clasp hands and run toward a circle of chanting children tossing a ball from one to another.

"Don't worry, Uncle David, we'll take care of Anacita," Tina assured them. "Do you want me to take Joshua James, too?"

"Looks like you have your hands full without this guy. I'll take care of him."

Liz resumed her duties inside the shop as David went in search of his daughter and sister.

Dusk settled in as the sun sank lower in the sky. Occasional squeals from the children rose above the mellow tones of the saxophone. Guests wandered in and out of the shop, most carrying purchases to their cars before returning to the tent area.

"I cannot believe the turnout!" Cassie said to Liz and the others, as all but Chelsea and Emily gathered around the counter. "Think we'll have enough for tomorrow's open house?"

"Chelsea and I have some…" Maggie said, but was interrupted by a loud male voice and sounds of a scuffle from outside. They all rushed through the door in time to see a prone Billy Joe Crenshaw lying in Cassie's cottage garden, while Jaime stood over him rubbing his knuckles.

"Jaime! What in heaven's name?" Cassie began as David and another man helped Billy Joe to a standing position.

"Caught this scumbucket hanging around the kids area. Anacita and Abby were hiding from the others when they thought they saw someone behind a tree. By the time they took us to where they were playing, we found Billy Joe staggering across the yard—he almost knocked Tina down."

The former sheriff spat on the ground at Jaime's feet then yanked his arm from David's grasp.

"You'll regret this … all of you." He glared toward Cassie then to Liz. He reached down and picked up his suede cowboy hat, shoved it on his head, and stalked from the tent, everyone giving him wide berth as someone said, "What a piece of work!"

"Yeah, that guy's a real joke," another agreed.

Jaime eyed the ex-lawman as he disappeared into the night, "Maybe … but give a clown a gun and he gets the last laugh."

"I can't believe it's nearly midnight!" Cassie said stretching against her chair, "I'm beat!"

"I'm so sorry about your hibiscus, *amoracita*," Jaime said to his wife, referring to the small bush with the large pink flowers that had suffered the brunt of Billy Joe's fall.

"I'm sure it will recover. How's your hand?" She gently rubbed his knuckles with her fingertips.

"It's fine. I shouldn't have let him goad me like that, but the thought of him with Abby and Anacita … It's obvious he'd been drinking and was looking for a fight. The things he said about …"

"If you hadn't decked him, I would have," David interjected before Jaime could finish. "And with all the McAlister's gathered round, that would not have been a good thing." Liz nodded her head in agreement as she nestled her hand in his.

"Thanks for picking up the tempo with the music," Jaime said to Marcus and Adam. "You guys saved the night."

With the money counted, the four partners, along with Chelsea and Maggie May, agreed that even Billy Joe Crenshaw couldn't ruin this day.

A pair of high-powered binoculars shifted focus from one person to the next as those gathered under the tent rose to share hugs and handshakes. The glass circles settled on Liz … shifted to Cassie … moved slightly to the left where Jaime stood … next the focus fell on David … and then centered back on Liz, as David walked her to her car.

CHAPTER TEN

With the success of the Country Ladies' open house, Liz spent every waking hour the next week either harvesting produce or crafting suncatchers and other smaller stained glass creations to keep up with the demand of new and returning customers. She hardly noticed the comings and goings at the farm as she went from bed to her garden to the Country Ladies to her studio and back to bed.

She barely had time to think about her upcoming weekend with David. After being delayed by Meredith and Abby's accident and then by the open house, she found it difficult to convince herself their trip would actually happen. Though she hadn't seen him since Saturday, she listened to *Davy Jones' Locker* faithfully, and they talked on the phone daily.

David caught her speechless when he asked her if she liked to camp—*as in a tent!* Liz had at first laughed, but then realized he was serious.

"Didn't you take your daughter camping with the Girl Scouts?" David had asked then chuckled as Liz confessed, "Roughing it for our girls was shopping at a discount store rather than a mall!"

What do I pack to tent camp? Liz wondered, as she opened one drawer after another Friday afternoon, tossing Capri pants and coordinating tops onto the bed. She carefully folded more than enough clothes and laid them in her suitcase.

"What have I left undone?" Liz asked Princess 'Fraidy Cat, as she picked the kitten up from her favorite perch on the kitchen shelf. Her bags were stashed inside the foyer door and David wasn't due to arrive for another half an hour. She had told Mallory and Gregg she would be gone for the weekend and nothing more.

She walked with the kitten to the buffet and looked down at Mack's picture. Her husband's charismatic smile with the McAlister dimple had been captured in the photograph as his gray eyes locked with hers.

"Oh Mack, I hope you understand, wherever you are. I hope someday your son will understand. I can't live my life in the past. I love our children, but they have their own lives and I need mine." She tucked her head in her kitten's furry ruff before reaffirming to the man in the photo, her voice barely a whisper, "I loved you so much—I still do. You will always be a part of me. But I have to go on …"

Liz watched for Windy's blue Silverado pickup—David had told her he would be swapping trucks with his brother-in-law for the weekend. "Not enough room in the Jag and not enough class in my old heap," he had said.

As she saw the truck approach the bridge, she called up the stairs, "I'm leaving. Have a good weekend!" and grabbed her bags. She was almost to the end of the sidewalk by the time he stopped the pickup. He laughed as he popped open the rear door to the cap, giving Liz a quick kiss as he took her luggage and tucked it safely into a corner of the truck bed. He opened the cab door for her. As she stepped on the running board, she glanced back at the house to see her son standing in the hallway window. She thought about waving, but slipped down onto the smooth leather seat instead.

"I can't believe I am actually doing this!" Liz exclaimed as they sped down the road away from the farm.

"I turned my cell off so that you couldn't call me this afternoon," David confessed.

"Camping?" Liz asked, "We're actually going camping? I've never been in a tent in my life—unless you count the kind we had at the open house!"

"Yep, camping. The weather's supposed to be perfect once this front passes through tonight. But first, I'm going to expand your horizons a little. Experience a different culture … if you're game …"

"I'm in your hands!"

He glanced at her, "It means a lot to me—your trust."

He covered her hand with his, letting it rest there as the pickup hugged the curves along the Maumee River following its course northeast toward Toledo. He moved his hand to downshift as he turned onto an eastbound side road. After a few miles, he eased onto the highway then took a quick right-hand turn into a neighborhood of modest homes with bicycles and children's toys scattered about on small, well-kept lawns.

"Welcome to the Heights," David said. "It's a Latino community that sponsors an annual 'South of the Border' festival. I like to support their efforts when I can."

David pulled Windy's pickup onto a grass-covered lot and stopped beside a minivan at the end of a row of vehicles.

"Hope the rain holds off," he said to a petite young Latina woman as he handed her a five-dollar bill for parking.

As David and Liz walked toward the entrance to the festival, he pointed to an impressive white building behind a large striped tent. "That's the Community Center's gymnasium they built a half-dozen or so years ago using festival proceeds. Now they fund staffing and activities for kids."

David paid their admission fee, and they meandered past one stand to the next. One vendor sold CDs featuring Latino musicians and another, brightly colored tee-shirts with catchy slogans. But mostly, they offered food—tamales, enchiladas, burritos, beans and rice, and the traditional Mexican soup, *menudo*.

"Look! There's even elephant ears and funnel cakes!" Liz said as the aroma of fried dough wafted their direction.

Liz chose enchiladas while David opted for tamales. After helping themselves to homemade green salsa, they found seats under the main tent, just as raindrops began to fall.

The folding chairs around the long tables soon began to fill, as others ducked in out of the rain. Liz noticed the diversity in the crowd—at first she attempted to codify people by their skin tones, but soon recognized her folly. It would be impossible to identify Latinos from those with lighter or darker skin, and as everyone mixed together, she realized how little it mattered. She could be here with David and not stand out.

A man on the stage played a lively tune on an accordion, and a few accomplished dancers made their way around the floor, their moves sultry while at the same time energetic.

Several giggling teenage girls gathered in the chairs behind Liz and David. Liz thought she saw one point toward David and say something to her friends. Liz assumed the girl either recognized David from his show or just thought he was a hot older guy. She felt a surge of pride at being seen with him and rested her hand on his thigh in an acknowledgement of their intimacy. He drew his attention from the dancers, laid his hand on hers, and gave her a look that made her flush with the thought of the weekend ahead.

The main event for the evening was the Latino Idol contest and several entrants lined up along the side of the tent toward the gymnasium. As they milled about waiting their turn on the stage, David leaned toward Liz.

"Tomorrow's the big day," he said. "That's when you'd see the real dancers. Their costumes are incredible! I don't know who's performing this year, but in the past they've had dance groups from all around.

"Melody and … a few other girls … took lessons together and danced at the festival several years back. They held their embroidered skirts in their hands, swooping back and forth—moving their arms so that the bright colors swirled around them like a kaleidoscope," he smiled as though picturing his daughter sweeping around the tented area. "All the while they clicked their black heels to the music—they had rhythm, those girls did."

The emcee, a local deejay, introduced the first Idol contestant. They listened for a few minutes before David went on, "The last time I came—a few years before …" he looked away, "… before I went to Vegas, Melody had worked up a dance routine with one of my nephews. She'd hold her full white skirt in her hands with her hair twisted up around bright red roses. She looked like a butterfly as she twirled around the room while little Ricky in his starched white shirt and black pants clicked his heels dancing around a sombrero in the center, his red sash flying … He must have been twelve or thirteen back then, and Melody had just graduated from high school. I was so proud of those kids!"

"Does Melody still dance?"

"Nah, not with the kids and work. I haven't seen her dance since that day at the festival … Guess I should've paid more attention. I wasn't the best of dads back then. Come to think of it, I was a pretty lousy excuse for a dad while she was growing up—it's a wonder she's turned out so well!"

Liz took his hand in hers, trying to come up with placating words, all the while realizing she had no idea what David Morales had been like before he went west—which left her more than a little apprehensive about what she might learn of his time in Vegas.

Liz watched the crowd as the contestants each took a turn on the stage. They were amazed as a young girl belted out a song with a grownup voice. They cheered an obvious local favorite and encouraged a hesitant performer.

At the end of the first round of competition, the featured band took the stage. The lead vocalist played an accordion, accompanied by a guitarist, bass player and drummer. The upbeat tempo brought dancers to the floor circling the perimeter of the open area in the center of the tent. Most of the couples did a variation of a two-step, with some executing intricate, practiced maneuvers.

"It's almost like the Schottishe that … that Mack's family used to do at weddings and such. They loved their polka fests." Liz glanced around the tented area. "This reminds me of some of the events we used to go to."

"Would you like to try a go-round?"

"Me?" Liz asked. "No thanks—I have two left feet. Mack tried to teach me to square dance but gave up. He actually said at one point, 'a monkey would be easier to train!'"

David shook his head registering his disbelief, "You just 'dance to your own drummer,' *güerita mía*," he said as he lightly ran his fingers up and down her forearm.

"We should probably head up the road anyway—we have a tent to get up before dark," he finished, his smile meant for her alone.

The sun vied with rain clouds for dominance of the skies by the time they arrived in Marblehead, along the southern shore of Lake Erie.

"Kelleys Island Ferry Boat Line?" Liz read as David veered left following a designated lane to a tollbooth where he stopped to pay their boarding fee.

"Ever been to Kelleys?" David asked.

Liz shook her head, remembering only that it dominated the islands around Put-In-Bay when she looked down upon it from the Perry Monument that day with Brandon.

Liz gave a sigh of relief as David drove the pickup from the dock onto the deck of the ferry, grateful she wouldn't have to deal with the gale-force winds she encountered with Brandon.

When the vehicles had been parked as per the crew's directions, the passengers meandered toward the perimeter of the boat and to the upper deck. Liz followed David between the cars to the front of the ferry. A light breeze stirred the balmy air as the bow cut through the calm lake waters.

They leaned against the side of the boat, their arms resting on the railing.

"Look, a rainbow," David said as he pointed toward the sun

reflecting off the rain still falling to the west. He pulled Liz within the circle of his arms.

"It's a double!" she exclaimed leaning her back against the strength of his chest, contentment coating any apprehension she may have felt about the weekend ahead.

As the ferry approached the island, David called her attention to a large cupola-topped manor house dominating the shoreline.

"That's the Kelley Mansion—it was built in the 1860s. Part of the appeal of the island is its sense of history. They've maintained a lot of the old homes constructed from native limestone as well as the ruins to some of the early wineries. The residents have fought to keep franchised restaurants and motels off the island, so it's like taking a step away from all the overwhelming commercialism of the mainland. No golden arches, no Holiday Inn Express dominating the landscape."

Liz cast a curious smile toward her companion.

"What?" he responded with a grin.

"You just surprise me, that's all. First Goll Woods, now this historic island. It just doesn't seem to be ... I don't know ..."

"They're not places you would have found me before ..." he shifted toward her so he could look at her face as he said, "... before I went to Vegas. I've changed ... what I value has changed. I wanted you to get to know me ... now ... before I told you about my past.

"But there'll be time for that later," he said as the ferry maneuvered the waters toward the dock.

David slowly made his way down Division Street—the 2½-mile road that separated the west half of Kelleys from the east. With a nearly universal speed limit of 25 mph across the island, golf carts and bicycles shared the streets equally with cars and pickups.

He pulled into the state park campground at the north end of the island and eased along the drive to a designated lakefront site. By the time they unloaded the camping gear, the sun was ducking low in the west.

"Better get this tent up," David said as he carried a long box toward a grassy flat area near the front of the site. He poured out the contents of the box, sorted the pieces then studied the diagram on the instruction sheet that was included.

"I thought you said that you camped a lot," Liz observed with a note of skepticism, as she lifted a corner of the obviously unused tent.

"I do, but I have a little pup tent that I barely fit in. I bought this baby on sale at the Bass Pro Shop. Wait 'til you see the fancy blow-up mattress I found!"

"You bought all that for one camping trip?" Liz asked, arms crossed against her chest as she leaned against the sturdy picnic table by the fire ring.

David stood and laughed her direction, "Caught! I was actually hoping you'd fall in love with the island as much as I have, and this would be the first of many trips." He shrugged his shoulders, "Can't blame a guy for trying!"

It was Liz's turn to laugh as she joined him at the tent site. "Just tell me what to do, Dan'l Boone!"

The tent was up and staked in a relatively short time. True to his word, David inflated a comfortable air mattress within the structure.

"Are you sure this flimsy nylon will protect us from the rain ... or anything else?" Liz asked fingering the tent dome from the inside.

"Rain? Yes—I took extra care to waterproof all of the seams ... As to 'anything else'—there aren't any bears on Kelleys ... yet ..." David teased, "... and the most you have to worry about from the human animals is your fellow campers who've had one too many Brandy Alexanders at the Pump!"

"The Pump?"

"A legendary Kelleys' pub. We'll pop in tomorrow if we have time when we tour the island."

David pulled two canvas lawn chairs from the back of the

pickup as well as a bundle of wood and built a fire in the ring. Liz slipped on a jacket and joined him by the crackling blaze.

They sat in a companionable silence listening to the waves lap the shoreline below the ten-or-fifteen-foot drop-off at the edge of their site. A nearly full moon peeked between accumulating gray clouds.

"Looks like we might get some wet stuff after all," David said. "Maybe we should bank this fire and turn in for the night."

They weren't far from the restroom for their section of the campground, and Liz gathered her train case with her makeup and pajamas along with the flashlight and carried it to the gray cinder block building.

With a shy smile, Liz stepped within the tent walls wearing lightweight cotton pajamas with tiny lavender flowers under her windbreaker. She kicked her sandals off by the doorway and unzipped her jacket, clutching it around her.

David had changed to a black running suit with white stripes up its sides. He held his hand out toward the woman just inside the doorway, then stepped past her and zipped the door closed, securing it against the wind that buffeted the west side of the tent.

He pulled her close as she shivered from the cascading outside temperatures. "Let's get under the covers before the wind picks up any more."

David had zipped two sleeping bags together, creating a sheltering cocoon. He lowered the zipper of the bags on the nearest side of the bed, and Liz slipped between them. David switched off the small electric lantern hanging from the crossed rods at the center of the tent ceiling then ducked around to the other side of the air mattress.

Liz heard him unzip the jacket to his running suit and held her breath, waiting to see if he removed the remainder of his clothing. Instead he climbed into the sleeping bag and turned toward her. She tentatively reached out to touch the tee-shirt covering his muscular chest. He drew her toward him, brushing light kisses against her cheek before finding her lips in the darkness. He rested his hand on the curve of her breast then shifted it to her back.

"You make it difficult to keep my promise, *güerita mía*."

"Hmmm…" she said beginning to regret the clothing between them. "What promise is that?"

"To keep my fingers off of you until I've laid out my entire sordid past," he said. His actions, however, belied his words as his hands wandered down soft cotton to her rounded bottom.

"And," he continued, "to be up in time for the sunrise and be the first one in line at the bakery in town."

"Sunrise?"

"Yep, weather permitting, of course," he replied, burrowing against her softness.

They awoke in the night to the patter of raindrops against the tent and snuggled closer together.

"Mmmm … cozy," she gave a sleep-drenched purr. "I like this."

She nuzzled against his neck, finding bare skin for her lips to caress before nestling into the hollow of his shoulder as he lay on his back. He gently fingered her tangled curls, angling his head to kiss the top of hers.

The rain had moved on by morning but gray skies obscured the sun. They slept a little longer, cradled in each other's arms before facing the chilly day.

Eventually David spoke, "Did the wind keep you up?"

Liz gave a muffled laugh, her head still tucked against his tee-shirt. "Only when I thought the tent might fall in on us! I'm sorry I doubted this little scrap of nylon!"

They completed their morning ablutions, greeting other early risers as they took their turns in the showers. Liz tried to tame her curls into some semblance of submission, then gave up, slipping a rainbow colored stretch band around their mass.

"I'm ravenous—must be sleeping outdoors," Liz said as they met back at the pickup. "And I *need* a cup of coffee!"

"You're in luck. Climb in and I'll take you to the source of the best apple turnovers and double-espresso lattes on the island!"

They drove downtown, parking across from a small storefront with the logo "Rock, Baker, Sippers" above it.

"Hey, Denise, how's it goin'?" David greeted the baker, barista, and proprietor of the shop as he and Liz passed between the magnetic screen doors and up to the display case loaded with donuts, scones, turnovers, cookies and other breakfast treats.

"Haven't seen you around for a while," the trim blonde replied as she dusted her hands against a red chef's apron, giving Liz a curious onceover before raising her eyebrows toward David.

"I'd like to introduce you to my friend, Liz McAlister, who is in desperate need of a cup of java."

Denise nodded her acknowledgement, "I'd offer to shake hands but I just gave some donuts a powdered sugar bath."

She turned to a sink to wash asking over her shoulder, "What can I get you?"

Liz studied the description of coffee drinks posted on the wall, "I'd like a double espresso latte … and can that be made with skim milk … no whipped cream, please."

The corners of the proprietor's eyes crinkled as David said, "I'll have the same, except you can put her whipped cream on mine!"

They sat at a round white wrought iron table sharing a turnover and a scone as they sipped their lattes and watched the island slowly come to life. Denise joined them when she had a break in her line-up of customers.

"So, David, my man," she began, "this isn't the cute Latina woman you had with you last time you were here …"

Liz sat her latte back on the table, looking from the man on her left to the woman on her right then back to the man, who had rolled his eyes upward. Denise held a straight face for a moment longer before laughing.

"And where are those grandbabies of yours?"

It was Liz's turn to laugh and roll her eyes, "You brought Melody and the kids here?"

David nodded, "The kids loved camping … but, Melody—not so much!"

A loud backfiring drew their attention to a strange vehicle making its way past the bakery on Division Street. It looked a bit like a golf cart with a cab or a shrunken pickup, painted an almost illusionary metallic purple or green. A man with a long red flowing beard saluted as he chugged by.

Denise returned his wave, giving a wistful smile. "Kelleys attracts the most interesting characters …

"Take this guy," she nodded toward David, "the only thing his tattoos and ponytail do is make him memorable to the locals. Doesn't matter who you are, as long as you can adapt to the island pace, you're welcome here."

As two young women, one pushing a stroller and the other being towed toward the bakery by a pre-schooler, approached the door, Denise excused herself from the table. "Hope to see you again, Liz. Enjoy your stay … and if he gives you too much trouble, I have an extra bed at my place!"

By the time David and Liz returned to the campground, the sun had risen above the few remaining wisps of clouds.

At David's invitation, Liz followed him to the back of the pickup, her curiosity piqued as he opened the rear door of the cap and dropped down the tailgate. He disappeared into the bed, soon backing out with a bicycle.

As Liz stepped forward to help him lower the bike to the ground he turned to retrieve another.

"David Morales, you don't expect me to ride a bicycle, do you?"

His grin answered her question as he lifted the second bike to the ground.

"Do you know how long it's been since I've ridden one of these?" she asked, not hiding her incredulity.

"C'mon, don't tell me you've forgotten how. Can't be done ... you know the old saying, 'It's like riding a bicycle—once you learn how you never forget.'"

After a wobbly start, Liz gained her footing and followed David out of the campground.

They stopped at the Glacial Grooves, walking up the stairs and along the path above massive striations worn into the limestone bedrock by receding glaciers eons ago.

"The grooves were much longer originally, but they were quarried out in the 1800's or early last century. We're lucky these were saved," he said as they crossed a footbridge above where the grooves ended and the remnants of the old quarry began.

They returned to their bikes with David leading across a small bridge to the north end of the road. He braked and dismounted, with Liz doing the same. He locked their bicycles together, drew a bottle of water and a small bag out of a canvas carrier attached to the back of his bike, and took Liz's hand in his.

They walked up a well-defined path past a rusted out early-model truck, abandoned so long ago the cab was folding in upon itself. A tangle of shrubs and vines partially obscured the disintegrating flatbed while young trees grew in haphazard formations around—and through—the decaying metal.

"Bet there's been a lot of photos taken of that," Liz said as they moved by the picturesque vehicle. The path narrowed as they passed an old two-story limestone ruin lined by arched openings and clearly marked, "No Trespassing" in several places.

"Cool," Liz said, "wish I'd brought my camera! What was that?"

"I thought at first it was an old winery. Did you notice the one on Division Street this morning? Talk about cool! There was a thriving wine industry on the island before Prohibition.

"But Denise told me this was a crusher building used during the limestone quarrying days. Originally there were railroad tracks running under the building. The quarried stone was dumped in the crushers on top and shakers with various screen sizes filtered the crushed stone into railroad cars."

Liz studied the ruins again, "Interesting!"

David led as the path became less defined. "You aren't allergic to poison ivy, are you?"

Liz shook her head as she noticed the plant covering the ground around them.

"'Leaves of three—let it be!'" she quoted as she walked single file behind David. "I learned about poison ivy when we first moved to the Great Black Swamp. All Mack had to do was to look at it and he'd break out ... I'm sorry, I didn't mean to bring him into our weekend."

"Hey, Liz," David said turning toward her on the path. "You were married to the guy for a long time. He's the father of your children. I don't want to compete with him or try to replace him. I'd lose on either count—you have too much history together."

He took her chin loosely in his hand, lowering his lips to hers, and while their breaths mingled, he finished, "I want to help you write the next chapter of your life. That's why I need to tell you about my past. So we can build on what was, rather than pretend it didn't happen ... and maybe have a future together."

They walked on in a quiet hush, broken only by David pointing out an occasional shallow, square overgrown pit. "Footprints of the houses of the early quarry workers," he explained.

They had been following a high ridge separating the path and the lake, but finally rounded its tapered end. A short way ahead they saw a weathered sign by a path leading down to a cliff above the rocky shore.

Liz read the worn lettering on the sign aloud, "'The North Shore Alvar State Nature Preserve protects a unique habitat on Kelleys Island's north shore. An alvar is a rare, hostile environment consisting of limestone rock or pavement that is disturbed frequently by wave action and ice flows scraping and grinding along the rock ...'

"Look it says here that 'Alvars are found only on the Great Lakes and the Baltic Sea'!" Liz said, pointing to the text midway down the sign. "That's pretty wild!"

They negotiated makeshift steps formed by tree roots down to a limestone slab, then along a sketchy path leading over crevices and through thickets until they finally arrived at the beach.

"Careful," David said, as they stepped onto the loose cobbles covering the shore. They eased down to the water's edge where tiny crushed shells made walking easier.

"That's better," Liz said.

"Yes and no," David commented and he bent down to sift his hand through the shells. "These are zebra mussels. They're an invasive species and will eventually cover the stones and change the whole contour of the beach.

"The locals dig for beach glass along the shoreline here," David explained. "It was discarded in Toledo …"

"The Glass City," Liz interjected. "We have such a strong history of glassmaking in Northwest Ohio. I love being a small part of it all."

David smiled as he tossed the shells into the water then stooped to pick up something caught in the smoothed rocks under the shells.

He stood up, holding a rounded brown shard. "This is a piece of pottery," he said as Liz took the potsherd from him.

"Years ago, the glass and pottery factories along the Toledo shore dumped their broken pieces in the lake. Some eventually wash up on this beach, their edges smoothed by being rolled from there to here along the lake bottom.

"If the mussel shells continue to cover the rocks, they won't catch the beach glass in the spaces between the pebbles and it will wash back out into the lake."

Liz bent down and worked her hands through the shells and rocks just washed over by a wave. She cupped them together bringing what she had captured up so that they could examine the contents.

"Beginner's luck!" David said, holding a tiny, almost circular piece of deep red glass nearly a quarter-inch in diameter between his index finger and thumb. "Red is the hardest color to find—this is the first I've seen."

He handed the piece of glass to Liz who held it to the sun, appreciating the depth of the color in the light. She placed it with the pottery shard in the bag David had brought with him.

They found two flat elongated stones to use as shovels and dug into the pebbles and sand.

After a few minutes David paused, examined a shell, then tossed it aside. "The neatest things to find are called lucky stones. They're the size of a dime and white like ivory. Denise said they're the ear bones from drum fish. The channel on one side of the flat bone is shaped like an 'L'—that's the lucky stone. The channel on the other side looks like a 'J' and is called a Jesus stone. She was told by islanders that the Jesus stone is unlucky and should be tossed back into the lake."

They uncovered two more pottery shards and a few pieces of the more common green and clear glass before continuing on their walk along the shore. David picked up a flat flake of limestone and gave it a level toss low across the water. It skipped four hops before sinking into the lake.

"Guess this is my lucky day, too ..." He drew her to his side, "or I hope it will be after what I have to tell you ..." he said under his breath, his words muffled as he pressed his lips against her rainbow headband.

Liz watched a gull ride the waves as they washed toward the shore ... pretending not to hear.

They biked a short way down Division Street before cutting across the west lobe of Kelleys to Lakeshore Drive. By the time they rounded to the south side of the island, the sun hung directly overhead. A few more minutes of pedaling brought them to downtown Kelleys Island, which covered a few blocks at the southern tip of Division Street, where it met the perimeter road.

They locked their bikes to a rack and strolled past an eclectic mix of shops, bars, and restaurants. Liz contrasted the historic

wood-framed and brick storefronts with the newer and brasher
Tiki bars and souvenir shops along the streets of Put-in-Bay, enjoying the slower, more relaxed pace of the island—as well as the
attentions of the man currently at her side.

After lunch at a dockside restaurant, they continued their
bike ride around the east lobe of the island, pausing when one or
the other pointed to a particular house or point of interest. By late
afternoon they had visited the Kelleys Island Historical Society at
the Old Stone Church, purchased books on the island's architecture and history, and coasted down the hill on Division Street past
the old brick Estes School to the campground.

"I don't know about you, but I could use a swim before dinner," David said as he wiped his brow with his forearm after parking their bikes at their campsite.

"I was afraid it would come to this …" Liz hedged.

"It's okay if you don't swim—it's barely chest high at the
bouys."

"It's not *just* that I don't swim…I don't own a bathing suit. I
haven't put one on in years." She gave a quick laugh and shrugged
her shoulders, "I thought about buying one in case …" She swept
her arm toward the lake then went on, "but I didn't have time …
or I was too chicken to try one on."

David gave his head a slight shake, "Oh my beautiful lady, we
are going to have to do something about that …"

She gave an apprehensive lift to her eyebrows.

"… but not now," he said as he sank down into one of the
lawn chairs facing the lake.

Liz gave a sigh of relief as she joined him. They passed the
books about the island back and forth, discussing what they had
seen during their afternoon's excursion, touching hands, and reveling in the unfolding process of getting to know one another.

It was nearly seven o'clock when they took a hiatus in their
conversation to change for dinner. David wore a Hawaiian shirt
with stylized blue and silver waves splashed across it over lightweight cargo shorts. Liz emerged from the tent wearing the same

gauze print skirt and top that she had on when she first walked into *Tía's Taverna*.

At David's smile of recognition, Liz asked, "Do I pass muster?"

"Ah, *güerita mía*, what you do to me!" Then with an underlying huskiness to his usual smooth baritone, he said, "We'd better head out before I change my mind and drag you back into that tent."

They drove across the island to the West Bay Inn, an old winery that had been converted to Kelleys' only outdoor Tiki Bar, choosing seats on opposites sides of a table that faced the sun as it sank lower in the sky toward the watery horizon.

Words that had come so easily just a few hours ago seemed to be stifled by the August heat that hung heavy between them. They split a platter of Lake Erie perch while the sky turned from blue to lavender to an iridescent pink and orange as the glowing sphere silhouetted the distant Perry Monument before slipping from view.

"I loved being with you today," David began, then faltered.

Liz waited, worrying her lower lip.

"But it's time to talk about the elephant in the room. I brought you here so I could tell you about my past, except I don't know where to begin. I'm a pretty tough bird … but you—you've gotten under my skin. If I lose you now …"

She shook her head as she reached across the table. "David Morales, I placed my trust in you and you brought me to this beautiful island. Now you need to trust me."

He nodded as the waitress brought their check to the table.

CHAPTER ELEVEN

David delayed the telling of his story until they returned to the campground. He took a blanket from the back of the pickup and slipped Liz's hand into his. They meandered past sites with campers gathered by small fires, one with a guitar player singing softly while others toasted marshmallows for s'mores.

"I always played life on the edge. In school, I did just well enough to keep above water. I was accepted into the University of Toledo on probation. My dad worked his tail off so that I could get a college education. He was so proud when I graduated with an engineering degree ... but I threw it all away.

"He never held it against me—he always seemed to understand my need to go one step beyond what was acceptable. I could never stay at one job—either I'd have a run-in with my boss or I'd grow bored dealing with lines and numbers. I don't know, I was just restless ... always restless."

He looked away then said quietly, "The best thing that happened to me at UT was Melody, though you couldn't have convinced me of that then. She was such a beautiful little baby. Her mama was a kid like me. I did what I could to help her stay in school while she was pregnant, but she wanted to move back to Detroit with her family before Mel was even one-year-old. At least we didn't compound our mistake by getting married."

"What happened to her?" Liz asked.

"Life got too hard. She married another guy. He was okay, but she didn't love him, either. Eventually they got a divorce and she moved back to Toledo to get away from a bad situation. But she kept me away from my girl for all that time. She didn't want me to meddle in her life.

"I partied a lot. We sat around playing poker and more often than not, I ran the table. I'd win big and spend big.

"When Melody's mama moved back to Ohio, I was able to reconnect with my baby, but she was in school by then so I'd just tag along to her plays and recitals and whatever. Her mama really gets the credit for raising her.

"Melody got pregnant with Anacita when she was at the community college and married the younger O'Hanoran brother—who proved to be as big of a jerk as he looks on the back of the phonebook. When she showed up at her mama's door with a black eye and marks from his fingers on her arm, I was ready to sign up for a gun permit. I swear, if he'd laid a hand on my granddaughter ...

"The real kicker was when the ..." David hesitated, "... slimebag came back all loaded with apologies and fancy gifts—Mel was a sucker for the guy and when she went back to him, I knew I had to clear out or I might do something real stupid."

They had left the campground and David led them down the road toward the beach.

"That was soon after Cassie and Jaime's wedding ... I was good with cards and ... good with women." He looked toward her under the light of a full moon. "That sounds pretty egotistical, I guess, but I never had a problem with the fairer sex."

"Why don't I find that hard to believe?" Liz gave a lift to her eyebrows as she shot him an encouraging smile.

He brushed her lips with his, "Ah, you caught my attention the first time I saw you and your *violeta* eyes. I was pretty unscrupulous back then—if that big farmboy husband of yours hadn't kept you close that night at Cassie and Jaime's wedding, who knows what I might have tried ..."

He unfolded the blanket and spread it over the sand under a tree. He kicked off his deck shoes, lowered himself to the blanket then drew her down beside him. She slipped her flats off, burrowing her feet in the cool sand at the edge of the coverlet.

After a few minutes, he went on, "I had always wanted to try my hand in Vegas, so I headed west. I had deejayed at a local station when I was in college and, though that'd been a few years back, I was able to snag a job on a radio station in the suburbs. I did my radio gig during the day and found some backroom poker games at night. I did pretty well—for a year or so ...

"The smartest thing I did was to regularly send my winnings back to Anita to bank for me and, for the most part, live on my radio earnings. I knew if 'Nita had control of the money, I'd be less likely to squander it. If I lost, I'd cool down for a while, then try my hand at it again."

David leaned forward, draping his arms around his bent knees, and sighed, "Things went on like that for over a year. I made acquaintances, but few friends. I had the reputation for being a badass—mostly because of being Latino and my tattoos and all, but I played it up ... I guess it was only a matter of time until my house of cards came tumbling down. I drank some, but not when I played cards—booze and money's not a winning combination.

"One night this cocky California guy was sitting in on one of our games. I knew most of the others in the room, but I hadn't met this rooster before. He had a girl with him—blonde, built like Marilyn Monroe. The kind of girl you don't see around Vegas much—more flesh than bones."

Liz had been listening intently, while leaning back, her arms braced on her hands. Now she straightened and shifted to look at the man at her side.

He gave a dry laugh, "I've never been attracted to skinny women, and, I tell you, this woman had curves in all the right places. It was obvious to everyone in the room that the California dude kept her on a short chain. He kept flipping orders to her, 'I need a drink, babycakes,' 'get me somethin' to eat, babycakes,' 'do this, babycakes,' 'do that, babycakes.' She kept makin' faces at me behind his back when he barked out his demands, but she jumped at his every command."

David drew his hands together, pressed his palms to each other, and leaned his face against his fingers. "He was a lousy card player—easy to read. He had little facial tics that gave his hand away. They became more exaggerated the more he lost. Then the girl started hitting on me. I knew she was just trying to goad him into noticing her as more than a go-fer.

"They'd both had quite a bit to drink. It was after midnight—I had lightened his wallet to the tune of $50,000 or so. The cards were falling my way and the other guys in the game were playing pretty conservatively, but the more I won from the dude, the more he drank and the more he bet. He started getting mean with his girlfriend, so I folded and pulled my winnings."

David leaned up and sifted sand through his hands. "That proved to be a bad move on my part.

"The dude threw a royal fit, tossed his cards … and his girl across the room. She gathered herself up off the floor, stumbled over to me, wrapped her arms around my shoulders, and kissed me right on the smacker. The other guys in the room were holding her boyfriend back as she said, 'I'm going home with him.'

"I couldn't leave her there—I was afraid of what he might do … so I cashed out and helped her back to her motel room." He stopped sifting the sand, leaned back and stared at the horizon shrouded in darkness.

"She kept saying things about how she liked screwing boys with dark skin—we were such great lovers." He gave a harsh snort as he peered into the black sky. "When we got to her room, I opened the door with her key. She tried to pull me in with her, saying she'd show 'him a thing or two about how to treat a lady.' She was so drunk I helped her to the bed—that's all … that's all." He took a deep breath then exhaled.

"Honest to God, she was alive when I left her."

Liz let the anguish in his words settle before wrapping her

arms around him. She wiped the dampness off his cheek with hers. He rested his chin on her curls as he tried to regain control ...

He took a handkerchief from his back pocket and wiped his eyes and nose, "I stopped on my way home and wired my winnings back to 'Nita, as usual. When I got to my place, I fell into bed. I heard a pounding on my door in the middle of the night. When I opened it, one of the other girls who'd been watching the game— an overly-endowed brunette—was there with a bottle of Scotch. I told her to go home, but she pushed her way into the room. We'd messed around in the past and she began coming on strong. She poured me a Scotch. The whole thing was pretty surreal ..."

He turned away from Liz, again draping his arms over his knees and hanging his head. "No more ..." he said in a raspy whisper.

"David, you have to tell me—for us. I have to know what happened next."

He shook his head, but then said, "I drank the Scotch. She stripped and I guess I did, too. We f... banged. It was nothing. I don't know why I did it. Anyway, she must have slipped something into my drink because the next thing I knew, it was daylight and the cops were breaking down my door. They drug my naked ass— sorry ..." he said, turning away from her.

"They drug me out of bed and out of my place, barely giving me a chance to throw on a pair of sweatpants. I was hauled off to jail without a clue as to why ... Miranda rights? Ha! What a joke!

"The brunette that came to my room? She got beat up real good—and blamed it on me. Said I had raped her. Since she jumped my bones, the cops had proof I'd been with her.

"The blonde was found strangled in her room. Her body had been bashed almost beyond recognition. Everyone knew I had walked her home and somebody at the motel saw me go into her room when I put her to bed ... Guess they didn't hang around long enough to see me leave a few minutes later. Anyway, the bru-nette must have lifted my wallet since it was planted in the dead woman's room, so the cops figured they had all the evidence they needed.

"To make a long story short, I was given a court-appointed lawyer who could have cared less if I lived or died. A kangaroo court said I was guilty, and I was hauled off to the state pen in record time."

He took a deep breath and looked back at Liz. She shifted toward him, gently laying her fingers on his forearm.

"Didn't your family help?" she asked. "Or Jaime?"

"I wouldn't let them. It was all over the papers—you saw that. Talk about low—if I could have gotten ahold of a gun, I'd be dead.

"It was Jaime that found a group of law students led by a pretty awesome lady lawyer. I didn't know what was happening on the outside, I was totally wallowing in self-pity.

"Anyway, he convinced them that I was innocent. When they looked into the case they found all sorts of sloppy work and suppressed evidence. I guess my room had been ransacked after the police drug me away, but no one bothered to investigate who did it or why.

"But the key was finding the brunette who came to my room. Once they tracked her down in Reno, it didn't take much to talk her into revising her story to the truth.

"Turns out the California guy paid her off to set me up and get his money back. When she didn't find it, he beat the crap out of her and then must have torn my place apart looking for it. While she was in my room shaking me down, he was taking care of his 'babycakes.' She said she didn't know anything about that until afterward, when he threatened to kill her, too, if she talked."

"Did they find the monster that beat her up and murdered the other girl?" Liz asked.

"Nope. Never did. There's still a warrant out for him, but he's disappeared. Swallowed up into some black hole."

"What happened to the girl who came forward?"

"I don't know. I gave her the $50,000 in blood money I won. I hope she used it to get the hell out of Dodge."

Silence settled over them as they stared toward the moonlit waters. A light cut through the darkness followed by the faint rumble of a boat motor. They sat separated by a few inches, each seemingly absorbed in their own thoughts as the boat crossed the horizon and disappeared around the point to the North Shore. The low growl of the motor faded, leaving waves lapping at the sands' edge to fill the quietude.

"Two years," he finally said, his harsh whisper discordant to the sounds of the soothing water. "Almost two years on death row."

A chill traveled through Liz in spite of the humid night. She shivered in the darkness, huddling against her bent knees. She held a gauntlet of images of prison life at bay as her heart writhed in pain for the gentle man at her side. Nausea threatened as his words seeped through her defenses.

He swallowed hard before going on. "I was lucky," he said, looking back at her. She searched his face for understanding.

"I had family on the outside working for me. I didn't realize until I got out how tirelessly they worked. I had a place to go and money in the bank."

"Didn't the state compensate you for what it took from you?"

He shook his head. "They walked me to the door and waved good-bye."

"*What?*"

"I didn't need anything they had. No amount of money would make up for ..." He stopped again staring into the horizon.

She moved her hands tentatively toward him, needing to offer comfort, but helpless as to how. He turned toward her, his arms meeting hers, absorbing the absolution she freely dispensed.

"It's like I've been carrying this huge weight around and now it's gone." David's voice was husky as he turned away and swallowed hard, brushing his cheek with the back of his hand. A beckoning moonlight danced across the waters. In a fluid motion, he stood then reached down to assist Liz to her feet. They strolled toward the lake, hand in hand, until the tantalizing waves licked at their toes.

"Ever gone skinny dipping?" David asked.

"No, and I'm too old to start now!"

He peeled off his shirt, tossed his wallet on it, and took a few steps into the water.

"Okay …" he said, "… ever swim with your clothes on?"

Liz glanced back at the rocky ledge above the beach, knowing under the full moon, they might be visible to campers gathered around their fire circles.

She hesitated then shrugged off any remaining inhibitions from her past, following the primal pull of this enigmatic man into the unknown.

The water inched slowly upward as they walked toward the horizon, covering her ankles then sweeping her skirt around her calves. The lake rose above her knees, spreading ripples out ahead of them. After several more steps the water reached her waist. She quivered as the filmy material covering her breasts wicked the moisture upward. He stopped and shifted toward her, his smile guileless and inviting. She had known love before and thus recognized its power as it swirled through her—swirled through her as surely as the waters of this lake washed around her and this man, this David, this second chance.

David pulled on his shirt and they retrieved their shoes, wrapped themselves in their blanket and meandered toward their campsite, the silence of the night broken by their hushed voices.

In the shelter of their tent, eager fingers worked at buttons and hooks made all the more challenging by soaking wet material. Spontaneous laughter spurred by sexual tension slowed their movements.

"I got checked out," he whispered in her ear.

"What?"

"After the last time we were together, I did the blood work. I'm safe. HIV negative. No STDs."

"David, you did that? For me?"

"For you … and for me. My past has been … compromising,

at best. I knew I was at risk. I had been hiding from the truth …
been afraid to know the truth. Anyway, I'm clean," he finished as
he found her lips … her breasts … her body in the darkness.

"*Güerita*, look!"

"Mffft … what time is it" Liz mumbled searching in vain for
his naked body in the cocoon of their sleeping bags.

"Almost sunrise. You have to see this!"

She sat up, drawing the soft lining of the top bag to her chin.

He was peeking into the tent dressed in his running suit,
holding the flap open so that she could see a hint of pink lighting
up the flat horizon.

"It's like a natural cathedral out here. Our own Sunday
morning sunrise service."

She laughed, "You are a most intriguing man, David Morales! Give me a few minutes to pull myself together."

They sat on canvas chairs as a deep azure sky gave way to fiery orange, the pre-dawn silence broken only by the splash of dark
waves pushing one another toward shore. A blaze of white light
broke above the horizon, dispelling the night into the shadows.

A screech and the sound of wings breaking into flight startled them as a great blue heron rose from the sands below the
rocky ledge and silhouetted itself against the waking sun.

"Awesome," Liz said with quiet reverence.

"God's in his heaven, all's right with the world," David
agreed.

Liz's smile was tinged with a questioning look.

"Robert Browning. *Pippa Passes*." His gaze followed the silhouetted bird as it disappeared from view. "There wasn't much to
do at Ely … That's where the prison was—Ely, Nevada. The local high school collected books for the prison library." He cast a
sheepish grin at Liz. "I think I read every book of poetry they had
on their shelves."

She gave her head a slight shake and repeated her earlier
assertion, "… a most intriguing man."

A peaceful silence enveloped Liz and David as they watched the shoreline of Kelleys fade into the distance. They had stopped downtown for coffee and to bid goodbye to Denise before breaking camp. After lunch, they spent a few hours browsing souvenir shops then, with reluctance, boarded a late afternoon ferryboat.

Liz relaxed against the seat of Windy's pickup as David zigzagged west along back roads and blue highways. She drifted off to sleep, waking within a few miles of her home.

"You're beautiful when you sleep," David said, lifting her hand to his lips.

"As long as you think so, that's all that matters ..." she said with a sated smile.

Gregg came running out of the house as the Silverado rolled to a stop. Liz glanced at David, reading in his eyes the regret that she felt as her son approached the truck. He barely paused to look at David as he raced to open his mother's door.

"Where have you been?" This time he spared a moment to glare at the man at her side. "I've been trying to call you since yesterday!"

"I'm sorry, dear. The cell service on the north side of the ... where we were ... was spotty and my cell died. You know how I am with that phone. I forgot to take the charger with me."

"Damn it, Mom!"

"Greggory, what's wrong? What happened?"

"Tatiana called. She's coming home tonight!"

"Tonight? She wasn't supposed to be here until next week!"

"I know. She wouldn't tell me anything. She just said she needed to talk to you. She sounded ... I don't know ... almost scared, Mom."

"We'll find out soon enough what's happening. There's no need to borrow trouble—whatever it is, we'll deal with it together, as a family."

Liz laid her hand on her son's arm. The young man he had

become retreated, and Tatiana's little brother peered back at her with frightened eyes.

"It will be okay," Liz assured him, hoping her voice displayed more confidence than she felt.

David had climbed down from the pickup and gotten Liz's bags from the bed of the truck. Gregg helped his mom step to the running board then to the ground. As they walked to the back of the truck, Liz asked Gregg to carry her luggage to the house. After her son stalked off, bags in hand, Liz motioned for David to follow her to the far side of the pickup where they would be out of view.

"Thank you … thank you for showing me your island hideaway … and for trusting me."

His lips found hers in response. "The pleasure was definitely mine …" He broke away, "but your children need you now. Once a mother, always a mother …"

Liz gave a wistful laugh, "I'll call and let you know what's up."

She kissed him again then stepped back. As she turned to walk around the pickup bed a movement drew her attention toward the Other Place. A chill traveled down her spine when she saw Aaron Caine leaning against his truck watching them.

"You spent the weekend with *him*, Mom," Gregg accused, as Mallory joined them in the kitchen. Liz gathered Princess 'Fraidy Cat off of her shelf and pet the purring kitten's back. "Some example you set!"

Liz turned to face her son. "Greggory, I'm old enough to make my own decisions—and you're old enough to know your own mind. I have a feeling you wouldn't be nearly so concerned about my spending the weekend with a man if I had chosen Lt. Brandon Michaels. I trust one day you will learn the difference between love and expediency. It would have been very convenient for me to develop a relationship with Brandon—especially given your friendship with him." She gave an exasperated sigh, "I tried. I truly tried. But David … David is different …"

"You can say that again …"

Mallory shook her head, giving Gregg a look of disgust.

"What?" He turned on her, "You got something to say, Miss Holier-than-thou Martin? Maybe I'm a little testy because you didn't get home until noon today! You could have called to say you were shacking up with that pervert ex-roommate of mine."

Mallory and Liz looked at each other then back at Gregg, "Okay, let's set the record straight, *Mister McAlister*," the younger woman said, arms akimbo, "I am definitely *not* 'shacking up' with Ian. I enjoy his company, but there's only one man who will get past 'first base' with me, and that's the man I marry." She glanced toward Liz, "It's different for you and David … you're … you're older …"

"And Greggory's father was my first …" Liz stopped as her son shot her a warning look. "Anyway, I admire your fortitude. Not many women your age have waited for the right man."

"Thanks, Liz," Mallory said, then to Gregg, "I went with Ian to one of the parties your apartment appears to be infamous for. By the end of the evening, he'd had a few too many beers, so I decided to spend the night on the couch. He was still in bed when his roommate offered to drive me home this morning.

"And, actually, I had fun at the party, met some interesting people and learned how to play Texas Hold'Em! Must have been beginner's luck, because I ended up with enough nickels to order pizza for the house."

"Are you sure you aren't related to David?" Liz asked with a lift of her eyebrows.

Mallory cast her a questioning look, "Don't think so!"

Liz stepped to the window as she glimpsed a silver sedan crossing the bridge into the driveway. A tall, slim, well-dressed young woman emerged from the driver's side and paused surveying her surroundings. The oversized round lenses on her trendy sunglasses as well as the wide brim of a stylish sunhat momentarily hid her face. A slightly taller dark-haired man soon joined her. She gave an elegant sweep of her hand and said something to her companion.

Liz sat the kitten by the radio, calling over her shoulder as she rushed to the door. "It's Tatiana! My baby's home!"

Liz ran down the walk, throwing her arms around her cosmopolitan daughter. "We didn't expect you home until next week!"

"Got an earlier flight from Paris to New York. I ... I needed to see you—I've missed you, Mom!" Tatiana said, wiping a tear from the corner of her eye. "I've missed all of this!" She swept her hand to take in the entirety of the farm.

"We've missed you, too, sweetie," Liz said then peered beyond her daughter to the young man pulling a large suitcase and carrying a valise.

Before Tatiana could make introductions, she was caught in a bear hug from her younger brother.

"Are you still growing, little bro? I swear you're taller than you were when you and Mom came to New York last March!"

"Nah, you just don't have on a pair of those six-inch heels that you fashion-tarts insist on wearing!"

Tatiana took a playful swat at her brother before stepping back and tucking her hand around the arm of the man who, until now, was a casual observer of the unfolding family reunion.

"Mom, Gregg, this is André Lefèvre. I know I should have told you I was bringing a guest, but I wanted to surprise you ...

"André and I are engaged!"

Liz looked from one to another then wrapped her arms around her daughter again. "Engaged? My baby's getting married? You're not old enough ..."

Tatiana laughed at her mother. "I could be fifty and still not be old enough to you!"

Liz extended her hand to André then changed her mind, wrapping the stranger who might become her future son-in-law in a hug as well.

"I am very pleased to finally meet the beautiful mother of the woman who will be my wife." André spoke with a heavy accent and Liz strained to understand him—however, words were secondary as she interpreted the loving look he exchanged with her daughter.

Liz smiled, "You're from France?"

"*Oui, Maman,*" Tatiana answered, "André and I met in Paris the year I studied abroad and reconnected this summer. His family is from Alsace."

Liz smiled up at her daughter's fiancé, "My mother's ancestors came here from the Alsace-Lorraine area in the 1830s—Tatiana even went there when …" Liz hesitated and Tatiana confirmed her mother's growing suspicion. "André was my guide … we were just friends back then."

Liz found it reassuring her daughter's engagement had deeper roots than just a summer romance.

"Let's get your things into the house. I don't know what we'll do for dinner—it's too late to get anything out of the freezer."

"I've been dying for a Pisanello's pizza … just ask André!"

"I have heard of nothing else—except for your chicken pot-pie noodles and chocolate cake, Mrs. McAlister."

"A little flattery will serve you well," Liz said with a smile as they made their way up the walk.

Mallory stood just inside the foyer door waiting for the entourage. Liz introduced her to Tatiana and André.

"I'll move my stuff so you can use your room," Mallory said.

"No need to do that—I'll sleep with mom. She's got a king-sized bed, so there should be enough space!" Tatiana gave her mom a quick hug. "And, assuming the catchall room is still packed to the gills, André can sleep in the living room. We wouldn't want to scandalize my little brother by sleeping together out of wedlock!"

Liz and Mallory burst out laughing while Gregg swept all three women in an unappreciative glance.

"I'll be glad to drive into town for pizza," Mallory offered.

"As long as it's Pisanello's," Tatiana said, "Pepperoni and fresh mushrooms!"

"Demanding, as always, Big Sister. I'll go along—just to make sure Mal gets enough," Gregg added.

"Get some money from my purse," Liz instructed. "It's on

the dining room table."

After Mallory and Gregg left the house, Tatiana walked with André into the dining room and suggested he make himself at home. "Why don't you check out mom's stained glass work in the living room?" she said. André inclined his head slightly toward the kitchen and Tatiana gave a brief nod. "Take your time," she added. "You're welcome to explore upstairs, too."

Liz had taken a peach pie out of the freezer and was setting it on the counter to thaw as Tatiana walked into the room.

"Mom, there's something I need to tell you."

Liz turned toward her daughter, "You're pregnant! I'm going to be a Gramma!"

Tatiana gave a somber shake to her head, walked to the table, and sat down.

Instead of taking the chair across from her daughter, Liz pulled two glasses from the cupboard and crossed the room to the refrigerator. She filled the glasses with ice cubes and put them on the table. Then she retrieved a pitcher of tea from the fridge.

"Mom! Sit down, please!"

Princess 'Fraidy Cat poked her head in from the laundry room, and Liz picked up the cat, holding it close as she finally lowered herself onto the chair across from her daughter.

Now that Tatiana had her mother's undivided attention, she hesitated as though searching for words. "I found a lump in my breast when I was in France. The doctors there didn't think it was anything, but André insisted that I have it biopsied. That's why we came back to the States early. He can work from New York as well as Paris, so he came with me … in case the news wasn't good."

CHAPTER TWELVE

Liz sat frozen in her chair, waiting for Tatiana to go on.

"I've been diagnosed with invasive ductal carcinoma—breast cancer. The lump is 2.1 centimeters—it's stage two."

"What does that mean? I … I don't understand any of this!" Liz scooted her chair back, stood and pivoted toward the cupboards, holding her kitten tight against her chest. She swallowed hard, worrying her lower lip—after a few seconds, she turned back toward Tatiana and slumped into her chair, "Cancer! You're too young!"

Tatiana reached across the table toward her mother. "No one's too young for cancer, Mom, but we'll get through this. My oncologist says there's so many women diagnosed with breast cancer these days—one in five—it's almost routine. And the survival rate for stage two is 75 to 80%. I'll be okay!"

Tatiana gave her mother a reassuring smile, supporting one of her ample breasts in each hand, "You know, Mom, I always thought these casabas I inherited from you were a curse. I was convinced they were what stood between me and my dream of being a fashion model. But according to my oncologist, they *are* what's standing between me and a mastectomy.

"The tumor is in the fatty tissue away from the breastbone so she thinks she should get what she calls a 'clear margin' with a lumpectomy. I've … well, André and I have … done the research.

Given certain conditions, a lumpectomy is as effective as a mastectomy." Tatiana took a deep breath, "Anyway, I go under the knife a week from tomorrow."

"Oh my God, Tatiana," Liz exclaimed swallowing back tears. "I need to get a plane ticket! I need to be there with you!" Princess 'Fraidy Cat jumped to the floor as Liz leaned forward.

"No, Mom," Tatiana shook her head. "Not that I don't want you to be with me, but André will be there and I have other good friends in Brooklyn who will help me out if I need it." She hesitated, "If you come and stay at my apartment it will make things seem much worse than they are. It's a minor surgery—they actually call it outpatient, though I'll probably be in overnight. Please understand and don't be hurt!"

Liz blinked away her tears, "But … but you're my baby girl. What if you need chemo and radiation? I need to be there for you!"

"Mom, listen, you need to be *here* for me. You have your studio and the Country Ladies … I need to know that life is normal back here. I will keep in touch, I promise. If you would use your e-mail a little more, André and I could send you updates almost daily."

"E-mail. The computer's so … so impersonal. I can't hug a computer. I can't look in its eyes. If the words say you are all right—how will I know for sure without seeing your face? I am your mother—I need to see your face!"

"Listen, Mom, while we're here I'll get Skype on your computer. Oh, wait, you don't have *wifi*, do you? Well, it's about time you did. I'll get Gregg going on that tomorrow. Anyway, with Skype we can talk face to face."

Liz sighed, "I feel like I've had my head in the sand with this computer stuff since your Dad's been gone. Okay, I give. If we can get this Skype thing set up, I'll stay in Ohio," Liz conceded. "But I'm not doing any of that Facebook stuff," she added, attempting a smile.

"Afraid you'll get hooked on those games?" Tatiana teased.

"Yeah, right." Liz wiped her eye with the ball of her hand.

"Whew—you really dropped a bombshell this time, sweetheart. Let me touch up the mascara that's probably running down to my chin before your brother gets home.

"Tomorrow I'll introduce you and that handsome young man of yours to the Country Ladies. Cassie should be at the shop then—she had a lumpectomy six or seven years ago. Maybe she'll have some advice for you."

Liz was up early on Monday morning enjoying a cup of fresh-brewed coffee. She and Princess 'Fraidy Cat were listening to *Davy Jones' Locker* when Tatiana moseyed into the kitchen, looking every bit the fashion model she had hoped to be, wearing black slim-leg pants and a chartreuse boatneck crepe top, with her shoulder-length honey blonde hair swept up and held in a clasp at the back of her head.

"Mmmm that smells great ... have any more?" she said as she took a cup from the mug tree. She answered her own question as she located the coffee urn on the counter by the window.

"Look at your kitten! It's like she's listening to the deejay!" Tatiana said as the Princess sat on her shelf staring intently at the radio.

"She is. She's been fascinated by his voice since the first time she heard him ..." Liz took a sip of coffee, "... and she's not the only one."

"Say what?"

"What would you say if I told you I ... might ... be ... I'm ... ah ... sort of seeing another man."

"So this guy on the radio is the same one Gregg's been carping about?"

"He told you about David?"

"Are you sure he's a good guy, Mom? I mean what Gregg's said ..."

"Your brother's a little more closed-minded than I thought. David is ... Latino ... with a ponytail ..." Liz took another sip of coffee then gave her daughter a sheepish look over the brim of the cup, "... and tattoos ... and rides a motorcycle ..."

"Wow, are you sure you're not just having a midlife crisis? I mean ... if I'd brought a guy home who fit that description, you would have had a fit!"

"Yeah, guess I wasn't as enlightened as I might have been."

"How about the newspaper articles Gregg found?"

"He called you about those?"

Tatiana nodded. "It might have been nice to hear about them from my mom ..."

"Yes, I suppose ..." Liz glanced away from her daughter, "but David was found innocent. He told me all about it. He served almost two years for brutal crimes he didn't commit," Liz said, "and, Tatiana, he's such a gentle, caring man. So unlike what you might think when you first meet him."

Liz let David's radio voice reassure her as he interviewed his guest about dream interpretation. "I should have said something to you about David earlier, but I wanted to tell you in person. I was afraid ..."

"I guess! With all that creepy stuff happening!"

Liz looked up as Tatiana raised her eyebrows and gave a slight frown. "Yes, Gregg told me all about the kittens and the break-in and the snake. I was waiting for you to call me ... I am your daughter, after all!"

"I'm sorry—I didn't intend to leave you out," Liz said. "I just didn't want to worry you. You were in France and there wasn't anything you could do. We've filed reports with the police—there doesn't seem to be anything anyone can do but wait and hope we've seen the end of it. Besides, there are more important things to worry about now—like the health of my baby girl."

They both rose from their chairs in unison and hugged one another. They pulled apart, Tatiana resting her hands on her mother's shoulders and Liz with her hands on either side of her daughter's waist. Liz smiled up at the beautiful young woman her baby had become.

"We have so much to talk about, but I need to get out to the garden now—I haven't picked anything for two days. It's going to take hours to catch up!"

"I could help … pick beans … or something …"Tatiana said.

"Thanks, dear, but you're not quite dressed for gardening—and your nails would never be the same!"

"I appreciate that—all the hours we spent pulling weeds and picking vegetables and canning and freezing. It just never took with me."

Liz concurred with a smile as Tatiana continued, "However, do you have time to show me your studio before you hit the garden?"

They spent the next hour in the old cob shed as Liz showed her daughter partially finished designs and patterns she planned to construct. Liz demonstrated the various pieces of equipment and Tatiana admired her mother's stock of glass sheets—especially the swirling opalescent ones.

"I can't wait to see what you have for sale at the Country Ladies! I knew you did all the windows in the house, but it never occurred to me to ask why you quit."

Liz hesitated, "I had more important things to do with my time—taking care of my beautiful daughter and, eventually, her brother. I never considered going back to working with glass until Mallory—and then David—suggested it this summer. David's daughter does the art glass for an area company, so she helped me set up my studio."

"I've got to meet this David guy before we head back to New York."

Liz returned a rod of lead came to its holder and turned toward Tatiana, "I don't want to push, but how long are you staying?"

"We have to head home on Friday. I need to be rested for my surgery."

"So soon?" Liz asked. "Funny, I always think of this as your home. Of course you need to get back to New York. I just want to be with you so badly when …" Liz turned away to hide her tears.

When she had worked past the knot in her throat, she said,

"Enough of this. I'm just going to enjoy the time you're here. Now I'd best get some produce picked. If I don't, either the bins at the Country Ladies will be empty—or Meri and Emily will have to fill up my space!"

Liz thought for a few seconds. "Maybe I'll invite the Country Ladies' partners, along with David and his daughter and her children over for a cook-out Wednesday after the shop closes. Would you and André be up to that?"

"Sounds like fun! We can help. Just give us a list of what you need from the store."

Tatiana leaned on the check-out counter talking with Cassie while Liz gave André a tour of the Alvarez farm. They ambled from Cassie's formal herb garden to her wildflower field past the green barn.

"I thought all barns in America were painted red by law," he said, the crinkles in the corner of his eyes conveying his jest.

Liz smiled up at this man who would be her son-in-law, as his easy conversation gradually revealed why her daughter had fallen in love with him.

"Thanks, Mom. Talking to Cassie this afternoon was really a comfort." They sat at the patio table compiling a list of groceries for Wednesday's barbeque. "She's doing so well, and she didn't even have chemo—just radiation treatments. And she said those weren't bad at all. It's all so scary. I still wake up at night saying, 'I have the Big C!'"

"I know." Liz said, "I woke up last night with you beside me, and I just wanted to grab you and hug you. No matter how old you are—or how far away you go, you will always be my little Tatiana. My firstborn—the one who wanted to try anything new. You were the tomboy who climbed to the top of the boxelder."

"But its limbs were so low and inviting …" Tatiana smiled as she rested her hand on her mother's.

"You were the first one your dad taught to drive a tractor …

why we rescued our first horse …"

"Remember when you caught me walking the beams around the top of the barn? That *was* a pretty dumb move on my part!"

Liz smiled, "Don't tell your brother I ratted on him, but he's the one who came and got me that day. He was so scared you would fall!

"You mean the world to that boy. He … we … couldn't bear to …"

"Mom, I'll be okay! I've got a lot of living to do! Now, did you add paper products to the list or do we need to take inventory of what you have on hand?"

Liz kneaded the dough for Tatiana's favorite meal—chicken potpie. She rolled the dough into a thick layer and cut it into square noodles. Tatiana grabbed one, squeezed it into a ball, and dropped it into the simmering chicken broth.

"Your father used to hate it when you did that. You'd make gooey doughballs, and he'd be the one to accidentally spoon them onto his plate. But he'd never be upset with you for long."

"Nah, I had him wrapped around my little finger for as long as I can remember." Tatiana raised her right pinkie finger and waved it in a circling motion then sighed, "It's still so strange coming back and not having him here."

Liz searched her daughter's face over the kettle as they dropped the fat square noodles into the steaming broth. "Is that why you stay away for such long periods of time?"

Tatiana nodded, "If I don't come here I can picture everything as it was—as it's supposed to be. Part of me can understand Gregg's reluctance to see you with another man …"

"It's not just another man—it's David. It's that he's …"

"… everything you warned me against?"

"Yes, I guess. Gregg has his mind set on my dating a fellow he met earlier this summer—an Air Force Lieutenant. They hit it off and Gregg's upset that Brandon—that's his name—Brandon Michaels … anyway, he just does nothing for me, if you know what

I mean."

"No magic?"

"No magic. I'm not looking for a replacement for your father, but ... Oh, why is life so ... unpredictable?"

Tatiana scrunched the last noodle into a ball and lowered it carefully into the broth.

"So what does Grandma McKenna think about your getting back in the dating circuit?"

Liz watched the noodles bubble to the top of the broth and gently pushed them back into the hot liquid with a long-handled wooded spoon. "To be honest, I haven't talked to her about David …"

"Well, I have," Tatiana said.

Liz glanced up, surprise vying with annoyance. "And?"

"She's heard from Gregg *and* Aunt Marian ... so she called me to see what I knew. I told her I would give this David a thorough vetting, but it might be better if you called her."

"Yes, I guess I should. I can't believe that Marian had the chutzpah to call *my* mother in Virginia! I can only imagine what she had to say!"

"What Grandma told me was that Marian was a busybody whose life was so boring she had to live vicariously through everyone around her. Aunt Marian really got Grandma going when she said it was time you, I think the words were, 'Stopped hiding out and moved on with your life—but not with one of those Lower Eastside boys.' Grandma may have put the skids on Aunt Marian's gossip line when she told her you would, 'Move on when you were good and ready and with whomever you chose.'"

"Grandma's reaction to Gregg's description of this guy, however, was another matter …"

"You'll just have to see for yourself tomorrow when you meet …"

They were interrupted by loud voices from the dining room.

"Dang it, Mallory, I don't see why you got so uptight about that little kid last night. You had to swerve to miss him!"

"It wasn't the kid—he scared the life out of me! It's what you called him! Can't a kid just be a kid—does it matter what color his skin is? I really wonder about myself sometimes."

"What's that supposed to mean?"

"I don't know, just when I think there's hope for you, you say something moronic like that!"

"You think you're so open-minded …"

"No, living with you has shown me how dumb I've been. I'm as prejudiced as you … it's just taken me a while to realize it."

Liz and Tatiana waited in the kitchen until they heard one set of footsteps on the dining room stairs and the foyer door slam.

"I thought things were a little tense when they returned with the pizza last night," Tatiana said. "What's going on between those two?"

"I don't know. They've been at it since Mallory moved in last spring. She summed up your brother pretty well. Sometimes he can be such a nice, caring guy—the Gregg I remember. Then other times he's this person I don't know. When I think about it, his dad had a lot of, as Mallory said, prejudices—I just overlooked them at the time. Gregg spent a lot of time with Mack—he thought his dad was the 'be all and end all' and I guess Mack's ideas took root in his son.

"Not that your father was a bad man—don't get me wrong! I loved him for all his goodness … but he did have his faults."

They gathered around the dining room table after the dinner dishes were washed and put away. Tatiana tried to explain the rules of Yahtzee to André as they all took turns shaking the dice.

"Yahtzee—in sixes!" Liz called out.

"It'd be a shame to waste all those sixes, Mom—maybe you should count them as a four-of-a-kind." Gregg suggested.

"You just want to win, my son!" Liz laughed as she scooted the dice to her left. Gregg and Mallory reached for them simultaneously. As their fingers met over the cubes they both pulled their hands back as though they had been zapped by static electricity.

Liz raised her eyebrows as she glanced toward her daughter who flashed her a conspiratorial grin in response.

Tuesday, Tatiana took André on a tour of the area, beginning at the Other Place. Liz planned to go with them just long enough to re-introduce Tatiana to the farm manager, whom she had met only once or twice before.

Liz stayed on as Neil explained how the grain dryer functioned—circulating ambient air, heating it to an optimum temperature to dry the grain, and drawing the warm moist air out.

"What are the long metal cylinders that come to a point above the bins?" André asked.

"Augers to move the grain where we need it," Neil said.

Conversation stopped as Aaron Caine's pickup pulled into the drive. He opened the door and stepped down, nodding at Liz before giving a questioning look toward Tatiana and André. Liz hoped to leave the introductions to Neil, as she excused herself.

"I need to get to the garden, then to my studio," Liz said as she turned toward her Mustang, avoiding looking at Caine.

"Ms. McAlister?"

Liz hesitated, shifting in his direction. He walked toward her, stopping within a few yards of where she stood.

"I bought one of your pieces at that shop down the road."

The steel in his voice never ceased to put her on alert, bringing a hint of amusement to eyes clear as ice. "The monarch on the coneflower."

Liz's eyes widened. She had spent numerous hours fitting just the right colors together to create the stylized butterfly against the deep violet petals of the flower. It was her favorite work so far. It was also her most expensive piece.

He stepped closer, until his fingers could have touched her stilled chin, so that only she could hear what he said next, "I like to think the butterfly's probing the flower—purple, like your eyes— to find all the secrets hidden in its center."

Liz backed away, "I … I'm glad you like the piece, Mr. Caine."

As she hurried toward her car, she called to the others, "I'll see you later, Tatiana. Enjoy your tour, André."

By the time Liz delivered her produce to the Country Ladies and returned home, she had relegated her interaction with Caine to the recesses of her mind. She locked herself in her studio and hit David's cell number on her contact list.

"Hi, it's me. Can you talk?"

For the next hour Liz told David all that had happened since he left Sunday evening. He accepted her invitation to her cookout and offered to call Melody.

After they disconnected their call, Liz hummed along with a song on the radio as she searched through her pattern books for some simple designs. She created several basic suncatchers to restock the Country Ladies, working through lunch and into the afternoon.

She was just about to make a cut on a white flower petal when she was startled by a knock on her studio door. She opened it slightly and saw Gregg standing outside. He pulled on the handle, revealing Brandon Michaels a few steps behind him.

Liz glanced at her son before shifting her attention to the lieutenant.

"Hi Liz," Brandon began, rotating his hat in his hands. "I've missed seeing you. I hope you don't mind, but Gregg invited me to your cookout tomorrow. I thought I should check with you before showing up unannounced."

Liz worried her lower lip, "Thank you, Brandon. Gregg knows we always have room for one more." She tried to keep her annoyance with her son from seeping into her voice.

She hesitated for a few seconds, "I just spoke with David, and he and his family are planning to attend, as well."

Gregg glared at his mother as the lieutenant said, "Perhaps, Gregg, it wouldn't be such a good idea for me to join you. I wouldn't want to cause any trouble. Though I was looking forward to meeting your sister."

ON THE RADIO

Liz sighed, looking toward the west, "What time is it? I've been holed up in my studio all afternoon trying to catch up on my inventory."

Brandon glimpsed at his watch, "5:15."

"Tatiana and André should be home soon." Liz said. She glanced at her son then back at Brandon, "You could stay for dinner this evening. I have a meatloaf thawing that I need to stick in the oven along with some baked potatoes. I'll finish up here and start on a salad."

Gregg and Brandon were deep in a chess game when Tatiana and André arrived, bags of groceries in hand.

"Let me help you with those," the lieutenant offered, jumping up from his chair and taking canvas totes from Tatiana.

"Thank you," she said as they carried the groceries into the kitchen. "You must be the Air Force officer who's befriended my little brother."

Gregg rolled his eyes at her sisterly putdown.

"Yes, Tat, this is Lieutenant Brandon Michaels. Brandon, meet my oh-so-worldly big sister, Tatiana, and her fiancé, André Lefèvre."

"Pleased to meet you both," Brandon extended his hand as they placed their bags on the table.

"May I help you put these away, Liz?" Brandon asked.

"Thanks, but no. I need to organize things as I unpack them. You and Gregg can go back to your game."

"If you're sure …" Brandon said with noticeable reluctance before following the others out of the kitchen.

"Isn't this the chess set Grandma McAlister made for Dad?" Liz heard Tatiana ask from the dining room. "It's good to see it out again!"

By the time she served apple crisp for dessert, Liz's head was throbbing. She wondered if Brandon's obvious attempts to please her and impress Tatiana were as apparent to anyone else. Gregg appeared to hang on the lieutenant's every word as he told of his exploits as an Air Force pilot.

"I thought about applying to be an astronaut, but I was just short of the required number of command pilot hours in a high performance jet when they scaled back the program. Sitting in the Shuttle Training Aircraft at the Johnson Space Center, though—now that was an experience! I tell you, Buzz Aldrin was as down-to-earth as an astronaut could be!" Brandon chuckled.

His vague attempts at modesty grated on Liz more than usual when he told of the places he'd been stationed—perhaps because she had heard it all on their jaunt to Put-In-Bay and other times throughout the summer. Brandon stayed on as they moved from the dining to the living room, dominating conversation that should have been family time together.

When Mallory arrived home after closing the public library, Brandon finally rose from the seat he had taken beside Liz on the red velvet davenport. "I guess I should be leaving." Liz made every effort to keep her exasperation from showing when she replied, "It is getting late …"

He hesitated as though expecting more, then said, "I know the way to the door." After waiting a few seconds longer, he smiled down at Liz, "I trust I'll see you again."

A residual headache sent Liz down the backstairs for coffee earlier than usual Wednesday morning. The sun crept just above the horizon as she passed the east stairway window. She stopped, the blazing predawn sky transplanting her to the previous week-end at Kelleys Island. *I'll see David this afternoon!* She rubbed her neck, her memories mitigating her pain.

By the time she ground the beans, made coffee, and pulled the leftover apple crisp out of the refrigerator, the clock read 6:00. Prin-cess 'Fraidy Cat strolled into the room, hopped up on the counter and to her window shelf. She preened her gray fur, licked her white paw, and summoned her mistress with an impatient meow.

"You are truly a princess and yes, it's time!" Liz smiled as she walked across the room and flipped on the radio.

"I couldn't sleep, either," Tatiana said from the back stairwell door.

Liz turned to see her daughter walking toward her in a floor-length lace-trimmed emerald green silk peignoir set.

"You look so beautiful! I'm so glad you have your father's height. I'd look dumpy in that."

"Mother! You most certainly would not. You don't know how truly beautiful you are, do you?"

Liz just laughed as she poured two mugs of coffee. "Come have breakfast with me before everyone else wakes up."

"Is that him on the radio again?"

"Every morning, six-to-eight."

"I hope he's less of a bore than that guy last night! I think he even had Gregg yawning toward the end of the evening!"

Liz nearly spilled her coffee, "So I'm not the only one who noticed? He isn't usually that bad. I think he was just trying to impress you."

"He's cute enough, with that disarming smile—almost boyish. But the more he talked, the more he sounded like a bag of wind. He couldn't have done all those things and been to all those places!"

David's voice carried across the room as Tatiana nodded toward the radio, "I trust this guy will do a little better!"

The sun shone high in the sky, promising a clear, if warm, afternoon.

"Let's see, we have the five of us plus Cassie and Tina—Jaime's in Toronto and Ben's in Alaska, so that's eight, Meri, Emily and Abigail, Maggie May and Adam and their two boys. Chelsea can't make it. How many is that—fifteen?"

Liz paused as Tatiana said, "I thought you added up the number of guests on Monday!"

"Yes, but that was before I had responses from everyone. I thought about asking the Rowlands and your Uncle Peter and his family, but then I'd have to ask that Aaron Caine and the rest of the McAlisters. Your aunts and uncles will be upset that you were home and I didn't have them over."

Tatiana interrupted with a grin, "That will just give Aunt Marian something *else* to talk about ..."

Liz laughed, raising her eyebrows, "You'll just have to come back when your grandparents are here from Arizona and I can plan a big family reunion. Now, where was I? Fifteen, plus David, Melody, Anacita and Joshua James makes nineteen. We could all fit in the house, but it would be so much nicer out here—especially with the shade from the maple tree. I wonder if Gregg and André could drag a plywood sheet up from the barn and set up a makeshift table using sawhorses? I think Cassie has chairs I could borrow."

By mid-afternoon, the patio and surrounding lawn were crowded with tables covered with checkered cloths of various colors. The gas grill was ready, with Gregg and André in charge of the burgers and hot dogs.

"I have some black bean burgers for Emily and Maggie May. They aren't exactly vegetarians, but they're not big meat-eaters either. The veggie burgers should grill just like hamburgers, but I don't know ..." Liz said as the first of the guests drove across the bridge.

Potato salad, baked beans, taco salad, macaroni and cheese—dish after dish was added to the serving table, either brought out from the house or by arriving guests. Coolers of drinks lined the walk by Liz's studio. As the serving table filled to capacity, an old card table was brought out to hold desserts.

Conversations buzzed as introductions were made, food organized, drinks poured, and children ran off to play under Tina's supervision.

David and Melody arrived last. Liz watched the Jaguar as it joined the line of parked vehicles before she walked toward the driveway. David carried Joshua James in his arms as Melody followed, holding Anacita's hand. David's smile communicated what words could not, as he shifted his grandson to his left arm and took Liz's hand in his. Not to be left out, Anacita ran up to grab Liz's free arm.

"I'll go back and get Grandma's *sopapilla* cheesecakes," Melody said.

"Yum!" Liz said.

"That's not all, *Tía* Juana sent one of her chocolate flan cakes!"

"You told *Tía* Juana you were coming here?" Liz asked David.

"It kind of slipped out, and she wanted to be sure we were well-represented."

"Do thank her for me," Liz said.

"Maybe I'll take you by *Tía's* so you can thank her in person."

As they approached the gathering, Tatiana stepped forward. "Who is this cute little guy?"

"I don't suppose you were talking about me," David jested.

Liz laughed then introduced her daughter to Joshua James and his grandpa. The three-year-old ducked his head on David's shoulder then squirmed to get down.

Anacita swayed back and forth as she wrapped both hands around Liz's arm, waiting her turn to be acknowledged.

Tatiana stooped down to the child's level. "And who are you, little princess?"

"Anacita Maria O'Hanoran and I think you're beautiful!"

"Well, I think you are, too! Would you like me to take you to where the other children are playing?"

"Me too, Gampa?" Joshua James asked.

David nodded just as Abigail arrived with Tina in tow. "I'll take the kids, Uncle David. Abby's been asking when Anacita was going to get here!"

"They're adorable," Tatiana said as Melody walked up carrying the *sopapilla* cheesecakes.

"Melody, I'd like you to meet my daughter, Tatiana. Tatiana, David's daughter, Melody."

David and Liz watched as the shorter, more rounded Latina sized up the tall statuesque stranger.

Tatiana smiled, "Your children are darling!" Then, eyeing the tray in front of her, asked, "May I?"

"Thank you," Melody said, "they can be a handful." She lifted the tray to Tatiana who took a bite-sized cheesecake and slipped it into her mouth, catching crumbs as they fell from her lips.

"Oh … my … gosh—this is *incredible*," she said licking the residue off her fingers. "What is it?"

"Grandma Morales' secret recipe—*sopapilla* cheesecakes." Melody said, grinning. "Just wait until you taste *Tía* Juana's chocolate flan. You'll think you've died and gone to heaven!"

Melody handed the tray of cheesecakes to Tatiana to take to the dessert table and returned to the car to retrieve the flan, as the two parents smiled at one another. "Guess that went well," Liz said.

Plates were being filled and the guests finding seats at the various tables, when Liz glanced around and approached her son, "Have you seen Mallory?"

"She was acting strange and said something about going up to her room a while ago. And before you jump to any conclusions, it wasn't because of anything I said."

"I don't know what I'm going to do about the two of you," Liz said.

"Me neither," Gregg acknowledged as he looked toward the second-story hall window.

Liz found David talking to Maggie May's husband. "Would you excuse us just a moment, Adam?" Liz asked.

"I'm concerned about Mallory—Gregg said she wasn't feeling well and went to her room. It's so unlike her, but when I think about it, she's been a little quiet all day. I'm going to go check on her. Would you take care of things here for a little while?"

David glanced up toward the hall window then said, "She's probably okay. She might just need a little … encouragement to come back down."

That's an odd thing to say, Liz thought as she walked toward the house.

She found Mallory standing to the side of the hall window

looking down on the gathering. The younger woman turned toward Liz as she came up the stairs, then back to the window.

"I'm such a fake," she said as Liz came up beside her.

"No way. You're one of the most honest, straightforward people I know," Liz countered.

"I'm not who you think I am. I'm just trying to work up the courage to be me again. I'm so tired of living a lie."

Completely perplexed, Liz could only put her arm around the girl whom she had come to consider a second daughter. "I'll go down with you. Whatever it is, it can't be as bad as holding it inside."

Mallory nodded, looked at the crowd, and followed Liz down the stairs.

David met them inside the foyer door. "It will be just fine, little Miss Mallory." His gentle smile brought a tentative grin to her face. "Yeah, it will be," she agreed.

They walked to where Melody was stooped down beside Anacita and Joshua James, helping them settle at a table with the other children. As she stood and turned toward Mallory, Gregg came up beside her.

Melody and Mallory took each other's measure. Finally Melody spoke, "Been dancing lately, little sister?"

"Nope, Merry Melody. Been going to school."

Gregg stared at Mallory, "What's the deal here? You two can't be sisters!"

"No, not really." Mallory looked from Gregg to his mother then back to Gregg. "But we used to pretend we were when we danced at festivals. My name is Mallory Martínez. I came here as a child with my family in the summers when they worked the fields." She looked toward the migrant sheds still standing near the barn.

"I think my great aunt and uncle may have worked for your grandfather. They used to tell the story of their last summer in Ohio—when they lived in the upstairs of a house down the road rather than in the farmer's migrant quarters. They called the house the 'Gibson place'—I think that's where Cassie and Jaime live now."

David nodded as Gregg glanced to the west then back toward the sheds, his expression unreadable.

Mallory continued, "The summer when I was five, my grandpa started dropping me off at the library for their reading program. Melody had volunteered to teach the bilingual children. She must have felt sorry for me, because she convinced grandpa to let her take me to her grandparents' house every day after reading. There were so many kids around—they were *los abuelitos,* the grandparents, to the neighborhood!"

Mallory gave a self-conscious laugh and looked toward her old friend, "Melody and I loved to dance, using the rest of the kids for our audience. Over the following summers, we developed more elaborate routines and David paid for us to have lessons so we could dance at festivals. I missed that so much when we stopped coming north.

"I knew you recognized me when we first met," she said as David nodded. "Thank you for not saying anything—for giving me time to learn who I am."

"Why did you ... lie about your name?" Gregg accused.

"It's not that I lied ... exactly. I changed my name legally to 'Martin' before I applied to colleges. And it's not that I was ashamed of my heritage—I truly wasn't. I just wanted to be treated like everyone else. With my hair color and light skin, I always got challenged about being Latina, so I thought college would be my chance to not be ... different."

"Why ... why Bowling Green? Why not go someplace where nobody would know you?"

"In retrospect, I think I wanted to be somewhere different from my home ... but yet familiar. I thought if I stayed in BG, I'd be okay. But things fell apart with my roommate and I saw your mom's ad in the paper.

"When I talked to you, Liz, and you gave me directions, I knew I was coming full circle. And then you showed up, David, and I thought my gig was up."

She looked back at Gregg, "And then when you met David that night, you …"

"… went ballistic," he finished.

"Yeah," she said, "I didn't know what to do. I thought about moving out, but for the first time since coming back to Ohio, I felt like I was where I belonged … where I needed to be."

Gregg looked down at the children chattering as they ate their hot dogs and chips—the round-faced Alvarez girl, the curly-haired blonde with two moms, David's grandchildren, and the two boys who belonged to one of the other Country Ladies' partners—all interacting without regard to their parents' differences.

He took a deep breath and heaved a long sigh. "Guess I can be pretty obtuse when I want to." He laid his hand on Mallory's shoulder, pulling her within the shelter of his arm. "Martin … Martínez … it doesn't matter in the end, does it?"

"Hey, this is a party," Melody said. "I found my little sister again—it's time to celebrate! You have any *sangría* in one of those coolers, Papa?"

They were nearing the midnight hour. Everyone had left but David and Melody. The children had fallen asleep on the living room couch hours before. The food had been stored away and the trash, collected. They sat outside exchanging stories about the evening … their pasts … and futures. Tatiana talked openly about her breast cancer as André gently massaged her shoulders. Melody coerced Mallory to demonstrate a few steps of a favorite dance routine before they burst into schoolgirl giggles.

The wind blew a damp chill across the patio and they moved inside. They had just settled around the dining room table, with Liz standing behind David, resting her hands on his shoulders while looking across at her son and daughter—when the rapid staccato of gunshots and the sound of breaking glass exploded from the front of the house … followed by a child's scream.

CHAPTER THIRTEEN

At the first gun blast, André jerked his hand, splashing merlot from his wine glass onto Tatiana's white top. As a deep red circle spread across the cotton material, the goblet slipped from his fingers, bounced off the side of her chair and shattered on the floor next to Mallory.

She pushed her chair back to avoid the spray of crystal, but the force of the breaking glass cut small gashes on the bare flesh of her calves. Gregg scraped the legs of his chair against the hardwood floorboards at the sight of blood trickling down Mallory's skin. He dropped to the floor between her and the table, stretching the fabric of his cut-off tee shirt to catch the rivulets of red.

Melody braced her arms, locking her hands to the table's edge. "Oh my God, oh my God, oh my God …"

Liz dug her fingers into David's taut shoulders, but as the cries from the living room broke through the chaos, she ran in their direction, stopping abruptly just beyond the archway. Stained glass littered the floor under velvet drapes shredded by flying shards and bullets. Liz could see Anacita's little face peering above the deep red velvet back of the davenport.

"My brother! He's got blood all over!"

Liz rounded the arm of the couch and sank to her knees in front of a panicked Joshua James, trying to calm herself as bright red streams cascaded down his forehead and cheek.

"See! Not see!" he screamed, with his eyelids squeezed tight together.

"Bring a wet washcloth," she called as David, followed closely by Melody, rushed to her side. David drew back the quilt that had been covering the children as they slept.

"It's just his face," he said as Mallory passed a washcloth to Melody who gently cleansed the blood from her frantic child.

"There could be glass in his eyes," Liz said. "It was all over the end of the couch from the door windows. I think we need to keep the wash cloth over them, just in case."

"We need to get him to a hospital!" David said looking up toward the others who surrounded the back of the davenport.

"I called 911," Gregg said as he moved toward the front door.

David nodded and turned to his granddaughter. "Are you okay, sweetheart?" He looked her over as she wiped her face with her little hand, "It just scared me so much, Granpa!" She threw her arms around his neck and buried her head against his cheek when he leaned in to pick her up.

Mallory grabbed Gregg's arm as he scraped opened the bullet-ridden door. "We don't know who's out there—they may be waiting for one of us to step outside! It's so dark, they could be anywhere!"

Gregg looked down at the broken glass. "If they're still out there, this door isn't going to do us any good." However, he pushed it shut and turned toward Mallory. "But you're right," he admitted, "Besides, the sheriff should be here soon."

Within minutes, two patrol cars and an ambulance skidded to a stop in the driveway. With their hands on their gun holsters, Sheriff Moran and three officers escorted the EMT squad up to the house.

A young woman exchanged the bloodied washcloth covering Joshua James eyes with a sterile gauze wrapping while a second EMT checked his vital signs. The boy clung to his mother as Mallory followed them into the ambulance. Liz held a sobbing Anacita close as the truck carrying her brother and mother sped out of the driveway with its lights flashing.

"I'll go with Gregg, Sheriff Moran and his men to scout around the front of the house," David said as his granddaughter buried her head against Liz's shoulder.

"Be careful!" Liz swallowed hard then said, "I'll take her inside."

One of the officers had been interviewing Tatiana and André in the living room. As Liz walked past the dining room table toward their voices, Anacita wrapped her arms tighter around Liz's neck and cried out, "No, no, no, no, no! Don't go in that bad room!"

"Ma'am," the officer said as he emerged through the archway followed by Liz's daughter and her fiancé. "The shells we found in the living room appear to be from an AK 47 semi-automatic pistol. We're fortunate the children weren't severely injured or even killed. One of the bullets lodged in the wooden frame of the armrest. They don't make couches like that anymore—that had to be solid hardwood, five or six inches thick!"

"Thank you, Grandma McAlister," Liz said in a near whisper.

"Can you tell me any more about what happened?"

"Where do I begin?" Liz said as she attempted to pull a chair out from around the table with one hand. André hurried to her side, helping her take a seat while still holding Anacita.

She described the gathering earlier in the evening to the deputy, listing all of the attendees. "Did I remember everyone?" Liz asked Tatiana and André as the officer took notes.

Sheriff Moran came through the foyer door, with Gregg and David following. "Looks like whoever has been trying to scare you has ratcheted up the ante," the sheriff said. "First the cats, then the break-in, and now this." He walked into the living room surveying the damage there. "Those heavy drapes kept more glass from flying in on the kids. It's shards from around the door that shattered onto the …"

The jangle of the phone interrupted the officer. As Gregg picked up the receiver, all conversation stopped. "Hello, Mal?"… "He's okay? Thank God!" …"Yeah, sure. Call when you need a ride home."

Gregg handed the phone to David, "It's Mallory. She said Melody wants to talk to you."

As David carried the phone into the kitchen, Gregg turned toward Liz and the others in the dining room. "Your little brother will be okay," he said to Anacita, then to the adults, "The glass missed his eyes. He has a nasty gash on his forehead and the blood from it is what made his eyes sting." He waited as they breathed a collective sigh of relief. "The doctor wants to keep the boy for a while longer. Mallory will call for a ride home when he's released."

When David returned to the dining room, he was wiping his eyes with a handkerchief. "Grandpa's boy's gonna be okay." He walked over to where Anacita lay against Liz's chest and rested his hand on his granddaughter's head. "Our little Joshua James is going to be fine."

"Is there anyone," Sheriff Moran asked, "any of you can think of who might be targeting Mrs. McAlister?"

Each person at the table looked at the others, shaking their heads, before Liz said, "I know you're going to disagree with me, Gregg, but everything started after Neil hired Aaron Caine. The way he looks at me—he just, I don't know, makes me uncomfortable."

"You never gave him a chance," Gregg countered. "I've worked with him for the last month and a half. He's quiet, keeps to himself, but he's never done anything that would make me think he was capable of killing …" Liz raised her hand to stop him, glancing down at the child in her lap, before he could say anything about the kittens. "… or shooting up the house," he finished.

"Aaron Caine," the sheriff said, jotting the name in his notebook. "Anyone else?"

"How about that creepy ex-cop that crashed your open house, Mom?"

"Crenshaw?" Moran asked. "I didn't know he'd been around."

"We probably should have called you," Liz said. "He was at the open house for the Country Ladies a few weeks ago. He was drunk and scared the children. Jaime … took care of him."

"That would give him a reason to continue his grudge against the Alvarezes. But why you?"

"Maybe just because I'm part of the Country Ladies … and David did help … escort him off the property.

"I've wondered since if he was the guy who tried to kidnap little Abby up in Toledo. Just because he seemed to go toward the children that night." Liz rested her cheek on Anacita's head.

"I hadn't put the two together," David said, glancing down at his granddaughter.

"Poor little thing's fallen asleep,"Tatiana said from across the table. "It's been quite a night for her!"

The phone in the kitchen rang and Gregg jumped up to answer it, saying as he walked back into the dining room, "Okay, I'll be right there." … "Oh, right! Okay, someone will be there."

He held onto the phone as he said, "They're ready to be picked up, but they need the Jaguar with the car seat."

David fished his keys from his pocket and tossed them to Gregg who caught them mid-air with his free hand. "You'd trust me to drive your Jag?"

"It's just a car. It's a five-speed—third gear's a little rough, but you just need to work it a bit."

"Okay, man. I'll be careful!"

Gregg waited at the door for the remaining two officers to enter. The taller one shook his head, "Nothing. Whoever did it could be anywhere by now."

Gregg looked around the darkened yard, then sprinted to the Jaguar.

"I don't think there's anything more we can do tonight," the sheriff said. "We'll be back in the morning to see what we can find in the daylight."

The moon had sunk low in the western sky before David and Melody carried the children to the car and fastened them in their seats. By the time Liz finally trudged up the back stairs to bed, the sun had begun to wash away the night sky.

———

Thursday was a blur. Liz woke after a few hours' sleep, fumbled with her coffee pot, and turned on the radio, comforted at the sound of David's voice as he read the local weather. She called Cassie to give a full report on the late-night attack. By mid-morning, Emily had arrived, offering to harvest what she could from Liz's garden, followed by Cassie with a fresh-baked coffee cake.

"I talked with the sheriff on my way in," Cassie told Liz as she sat the coffee cake on a hot pad on the dining room table.

"They've been combing the yard for an hour, at least," Liz said, heading back to the kitchen for a bowl of fruit. Cassie followed, and together they assembled a continental breakfast for the household. They had just carried in a carafe of coffee and a pitcher of juice when Mallory and Tatiana came down the stairs.

"Are the boys up yet?" Liz asked. "I trust Gregg was able to make André comfortable in the loft."

"Haven't heard anything from the attic," Tatiana said. Cassie greeted the two young women then poked her head into the living room.

"Holy Toledo! This looks like something from those CSI shows Jaime watches on TV!"

"It was too late to clean anything up last night. Besides, the sheriff said not to touch anything until they were through with it. He said they would be in when they were done outside. Sheriff Moran said they could charge whoever did it with attempted murder," Liz said. She heaved a sigh, then sank down onto a chair by the table, "I just want all of this to be done with. I'm so tired of being afraid of my shadow ..."

Liz looked toward Tatiana, "I hate that your last day here is going to be taken up by this ... And I hate that I cannot be with you on Monday ... Most of all, I hate that damn cancer inside you ..." She glanced around the room at the stained glass windows she had crafted so long ago and swallowed hard as tears welled. "And I'm so afraid I had something to do with it."

"Mom, stop it, please!" Tatiana dropped down on one knee beside Liz. "I'll be okay. It's nothing you did—it's a statistic. I'm the one in five women who are diagnosed with breast cancer. Maybe it was the farm chemicals Dad used ... maybe it's just the air we breathe ... the water we drink. Maybe it was caused by living in New York City ... maybe it *was* genetic ..."

"... And maybe it was the lead I used working with glass before I knew I was pregnant with you," Liz finished.

"Mom, don't do this to yourself."

"I miscarried. Three times before you came along. After I lost the third baby, the doctor—and your father—blamed it on my glasswork. I tried to stay away from my studio, but I would get so depressed ... then I'd hide out there for hours and days. When I found out I was expecting you, I gave it up completely. Your dad made sure I wouldn't be tempted to work with glass again. But what if my working with lead when I was first pregnant with you caused this ... this cancer?"

"Wow, you've been carrying that guilt around with you all week?" Tatiana asked. Liz nodded as her daughter diverted her eyes toward the stairwell. Liz turned to see Gregg and André standing on the steps.

"Now you both know your mother's deep dark secret," she said.

"That explains why you and Dad always changed the subject when we asked about the stained glass in the house," Gregg said. He paused to look into the living room on his way to the table, sitting opposite his mother. Tatiana eased into a chair as she, too, looked toward the living room.

"Is that why you kept the panels in the front room covered with Great Grandma's old velvet curtains? I always wondered why you didn't get rid of them and let the sun shine through your stained glass."

Liz shrugged her shoulders, "I always loved the way the velvet and the glass worked together. The living room was my ... I guess I always thought of it as my masterpiece. I loved showing it to newcomers. And now it's gone. The curtains ... the davenport ... the glass panels ... all gone ..."

Tatiana and André left for the airport early Friday morning amidst tears and assurances they would keep in close contact. Liz carried her radio with her to the garden, hoping David would lift her spirits. But even Princess 'Fraidy Cat's antics chasing grasshoppers failed to lighten her mood.

The noon hour found Liz ferrying crates and baskets of produce from her car into the Country Ladies. Cassie emerged from the house and met Liz at the trunk of the Mustang, "I told you I would cover for you this afternoon. You need to rest up after this week!"

"I'm too keyed up to relax. I thought about working in my studio this afternoon, but I'm not up to that yet.

"Truth is, I just don't want to be alone. Gregg's working on machinery with Neil at the Other Place and Mallory was scheduled at one of the libraries. David came over yesterday afternoon and helped us clean up after the sheriff left, but I still can't face walking into the living room. When I think of the children sleeping on the couch, and what could have happened … Joshua James will have a jagged scar on his forehead from the glass.

"According to David, the little guy ran his finger along his grandpa's scar and said now he'd have one, too!" Liz gave her friend a brief smile then worried her lower lip. "When will it end, Cassie? Between all that's happened this summer and Tatiana's cancer, I just don't know how much more I can take."

"We're pretty tough cookies, you and me. You'll get through this and laugh on the other side," Cassie said. "I've never told you about all that happened before Jaime and I finally got back together. If we can make it through, you can, too."

"I'm not so sure, Cas … I'm just not so sure …"

David sat across from Liz at her kitchen table on Monday morning. "Sweet sugar snap, why hasn't he called yet?" she said, stress edging her voice. "Tat should have been out of surgery before this!"

"Don't worry so much, *güerita mía*," David said glancing up at the wall clock. "It's only 11:30. The doctor could have been running late, or they could be waiting for Tatiana to come out from under the anesthesia before they say anything to André. I'm sure everything will be okay."

Though they had been anticipating the sound, they were startled by the jangle of the telephone receiver lying on the table between them. Liz picked it up, "Hello?" … "André? Just a second, David's here. Let me put the phone on speaker. Okay, we're ready."

"Tatiana is doing well … she's in recovery now." Liz and David exchanged sighs of relief. *"Unfortunately, they were not able to get a clear margin around the tumor which means that there will be a second operation when she has had time to heal from this one."*

Liz leaned her head toward the phone, struggling to understand André's accent. "What does that mean—that they couldn't get a 'clear margin'? Does it mean the cancer has spread?"

"Not exactly. It has to do with whether or not the cancer cells have an outlet—the doctor described it as a river or a channel—from the tumor into the rest of the body. Once they get this 'clear margin'—she hopes in the next surgery—they will test what is called the 'sentinel nodes' to see if the cancer has spread to the lymph nodes. I do not understand all of this," André confessed. *"I will ask the doctor more when Tatiana is with me."*

They talked a little longer, with André assuring them he would call as soon as he and Tatiana found out anything new.

"Thank you for being here," Liz said to David. "I should have been out in the garden all morning, but I just couldn't do anything."

"All you have to do is call, Mary McKenna, and I'll be there. Wherever you are … I'll be there." Liz laughed at the name she had first given him so many months ago.

"Thank you, Juan—Moreno or Perez or Smith … How about if I fix us a bite of lunch? I don't know about you, but I didn't have much of an appetite for breakfast."

As they cleared the table, Liz saw the sheriff's car pull up beside David's Jaguar.

"It's the sheriff—maybe they've found out something," Liz said as David walked to the window. "He said he'd call if anything turned up."

They met Sheriff Moran halfway down the walk. His expression was grim as he glanced from one to the other.

"They found Crenshaw's car Saturday night. It appears he tried to camouflage it in a thicket along the Maumee. When the guys went back to investigate yesterday, they spotted an AK-47 along the riverbank. The shells match the casings we found here on Wednesday."

"So it was Crenshaw all along?" David asked.

"I don't know. It doesn't add up. The only prints we could pick up on the car and the gun were Crenshaw's …"

"Wouldn't that mean that he was the one who fired the gun?" Liz interjected.

"Perhaps, but …" the sheriff hesitated and shook his head. "Some fishermen found Crenshaw's body caught in a snag at the dam near dawn this morning. It's at the coroner's now."

"Dear God!" Liz gasped, as David pulled her against his shoulder.

The officer looked from David to Liz, "There wasn't any apparent sign of foul play. It just doesn't figure—why would Crenshaw shoot up your place then jump in the river?"

"Maybe he'd been drinking and fell in. He was tanked the night he showed up at the Country Ladies," David suggested.

"Could be …" the sheriff said with a doubtful shrug. "Anyway, I wanted to let you know before you heard it through the grapevine. Word spreads faster'n jelly on peanut butter around here."

"Thank you," Liz said. "I do appreciate all you've done."

As Sheriff Moran drove across the bridge and headed toward town, Liz said, "I wish I could be convinced it was all Crenshaw …

"It's Monday—Cassie should be at the Country Ladies this afternoon. Let's go down and at least tell her what's happened."

"I'm going to let my apartment go and live at home this year," Gregg informed his mother the next day as he helped her carry a basket of cucumbers from the garden. "I can help Neil with the harvesting and keep an eye on things around here. Aaron thought he could stay through the fall, but he said something's come up."

"Yeah, I'll bet it has," Liz said under her breath, then to her son, "I hate to have you commute every day. Think of the time and the gas you'll be wasting!"

"Mallory does it. Maybe we could ride together part of the time."

"Yes, I guess she does. I thought she might move closer to Bowling Green at the start of fall semester."

"Mom, the first day of classes is a week from Monday."

"Already? I've lost total track of time," Liz said as she opened the trunk of her car. "You do what you think is best." She stepped aside while Gregg put the cucumbers in the trunk and slammed the lid shut.

"Truth be told, I dread being alone … especially now. " Liz said, looking toward the house. "I need to get a contractor out to replace the living room door and windows. I hate having that plywood across the front."

"Dad could do it, if he were here."

"Yes, he could …" Liz wrapped her arm around her son's waist.

With calls to Tatiana, the Country Ladies, and meeting contractors, Liz had little time to spend in her studio the rest of the week. But Saturday morning found her in the cob shed selecting the colors for a coordinating set of windows to replace those broken, while debating whether to fly New York despite her daughter's protests. A sharp rapping on the patio door startled her from her thoughts.

Liz cracked open the door to the studio to see two men in black suits. As she stepped out onto the patio, the man closer to her turned and drew a badge from the breast pocket of his jacket.

"FBI, Ma'am. Are you Elizabeth McAlister?"

Liz gave a hesitant nod, looking with apprehension from the man with the badge to his partner.

The nearer man asked, "Do you have an Aaron Caine employed on the premises?"

"Caine?" she repeated before answering, "Yes ... yes, I do."

Liz pointed to the Other Place as she said, "He should be working at the grain bins down the road." As they turned toward the west, she queried, "May I ask why you want to talk to him?"

The taller agent, who had remained silent, nodded toward the spokesman.

"Insider trading, Ma'am, but that's all we can say right now."

While they watched, Gregg's Ranger pulled out of the drive from between the bins and turned toward them. The men glanced at each other as it drove across the bridge and into Liz's driveway. It coasted to a stop and Gregg stepped out from the driver's side. After several seconds, the passenger door opened and Aaron Caine emerged.

"Is that Caine?" the first agent asked.

Liz nodded, then rushed to clarify, "The passenger, not the driver—he's my son, Gregg!"

Caine looked toward the house then took a few steps away from the truck toward the cornfield behind him.

The agents simultaneously drew pistols and pointed them toward Gregg's pickup. "Don't move!" the taller agent ordered as he steadied his gun with both hands.

"Oh my God! Gregg!" Liz cried as her son stepped into what appeared to be their line of fire.

Caine glanced at the younger man then back toward the towering rows of corn, before lifting his hands into the air.

Liz hurried to her son's side while the agents charged to where Aaron Caine stood, each grabbing an arm as they slipped handcuffs on his wrists.

The sun glinted off Caine's white-blonde crew cut as he

pierced Liz with those unnaturally clear eyes. The steel in his voice cut through her, "We could've been something together, you and I. The first day I saw you, I knew I had to have you. But it's come to this. I'll be thinking of you, Liz McAlister—you wake up in the middle of the night ... know I'll be thinking of you."

"So do you think Caine may have talked Crenshaw into shooting up the house then murdered him?" David asked. He had arrived soon after receiving Liz's phone call. They were alone in the kitchen, as Gregg had not yet returned from the Other Place where he had gone to talk to his Uncle Peter and Neil.

"I don't know what to think," Liz said, sheltered in the circle of David's arms. "I only know what Caine said. That ... that he knew he had to have me since the first day we met! He said *that*! It gives me chills just thinking about the way he looked at me!"

David kissed her hair as she pressed her head against his shoulder. She stepped back just enough to allow her eyes to meet his. "Could this nightmare finally be over?"

As August faded into September, the McAlister household fell into a semblance of normalcy. Mallory and Gregg juggled classes with library jobs and helping with the farm. Their relationship appeared to deepen as they rode to the university together. Liz divided her time between her garden, quiet hours in her studio, the Country Ladies ... and David—always David.

One morning, Gregg and Mallory lingered in the kitchen over toast and coffee. David had just introduced the Beatles' *Here Comes the Sun* on the radio while Princess 'Fraidy Cat bathed her long gray and white coat on the window shelf.

"Your kitten has no shame," Gregg said to his mother as she carried a laundry basket from the back stairwell to the mudroom. "Washing herself in the window!"

As Liz emerged after setting the basket on the dryer she countered, "At least she's not going to be late for class! What are you doing here this time of day?"

"It's Friday. No morning classes."

"You either, Mallory?"

"I've got a reprieve from the library. Someone else took my shift."

Liz glanced at the clock, "7:45. I'll get this load of laundry on while David wraps up the show, then get out to the garden."

"Why don't you slow down a bit and have a cup of coffee with us," Mallory invited.

"I shouldn't, but okay, just until *Davy Jones' Locker* is over."

Liz was pouring coffee into her mug when David's voice caught her attention. "This is a special request for a special lady, Ms. Mary Elizabeth McKenna McAlister, who I trust is listening to the program. They say timing is everything, and if our timing is right, Ms. McAlister will hear a knock on her door right about now."

Mallory had already opened the door for Melody, Anacita and Joshua James. The children ran to Liz as David said, "If all is going well, my little grandchildren will have a gift for Ms. McAlister." Anacita and Joshua James held a small jeweler's box in their extended hands. Liz lifted the box from the children's palms and turned it slowly in her fingers.

"Open the box, *güerita mía*."

Liz opened the lid to find a clear glass pendant in the shape of a teardrop. Within the pendant, the small red piece of North Shore beach glass was suspended in liquid by a golden thread.

As she held it to the light, David said, "It's not a diamond and it's not a ring, but it is my way of saying, 'Will you marry me?' I'll await your response while I play another little-known Beatles' cover song."

The initial cords of *Besame Mucho* floated out from the radio. Liz's fingers shook as she held the pendant in one hand while accepting the cell phone Melody offered with her other.

"I called the station," Melody said. "It's ringing."

After a few seconds, Liz said, "David Morales, I love you and yes … yes I will marry you!"

The size of David's audience amazed Liz. She seemed to get little done but answer phone calls the entire weekend. Most were congratulatory, some were questioning, and then there was the one from Marian McAlister. However, even *her* sharp reprimand failed to tarnish Liz's glow.

Late Saturday afternoon, Liz turned this way and that, observing her reflection in the hallway mirror. The sleeveless black sheath dress she had found at a chic new shop in town fit perfectly. A filmy overlay the color of red wine flowed from her shoulders and swirled around her hips. She touched the oval pendant with its shimmering ruby beach glass that hung from a fine gold chain against her breastbone.

"Wow! Who's that babe and what happened to my mom?" Gregg quipped as he rounded the corner from the attic stairs.

"We've come a long way since last spring," Liz said, smiling at her son, "both of us."

"Yeah, we have," he said. "I'm taking Old Mal to dinner and a movie tonight."

"You think so, *Mister* McAlister?" Mallory said as she stepped out of her room in a burnt orange off-the-shoulder tunic sweater over formfitting brown jeans. Her auburn hair flowed full and free around her bare skin and down her back.

"Whoa! I take back the 'Old Mal' part!" He gave her a lecherous onceover, "Are you sure you're a librarian?"

"Not yet …" she smiled. "I'll practice on the bun and wedge-heeled shoes after I get my degree."

Gregg draped his arm over Mallory's shoulder, "Don't be out too late tonight, Ma … and don't do anything I wouldn't do!"

The two women raised their eyebrows and shook their heads, as Mallory said, "Just remember what I said about first base, Mr. McAlister. Even a surf 'n 'turf at a swanky Toledo restaurant will only get you so far."

"It's going to be a long night …" Gregg said to his mom, glancing back over the top of Mallory's head.

Liz laughed as they disappeared down the stairs, still bantering back and forth.

She surveyed herself in the mirror, wondering if she should change from patterned black nylons to a more neutral pair when she saw David's Jaguar cross the bridge. She grabbed her small sequined red purse and followed Mallory and Gregg down the steps.

She smiled as the two waited to greet David before going on to Gregg's Ranger.

Dressed in tailored black slacks with a muted red shirt open at the neck and a lightweight black jacket, David looked as dashing as he had the first night he had come to pick her up. This time, he carried a dozen red roses with a single purple-hued blossom in the center.

As he handed the tissue wrapped bouquet to Liz, he brushed her lips with the most tender of kisses. "Thank you for saying 'yes,' *güerita mía.*"

Wednesday, already, Liz thought. *So much to get done!* She had spent the entire afternoon in her studio, intent on finishing an intricate circular window featuring a single deep lavender rose as a gift for David. She had fought with the final leaf for over an hour to get a good fit. Her first cut had failed when she tried to run the break. She broke the tip off the second try as she ground a slight bump off of it. Liz smiled with relief as she laid her third attempt against the lead came. *Perfect!* She moved the leaf away from the came, brushed it off, then picked it up and held it toward the light to admire its translucence. As she turned the leaf between her thumb and finger, the studio door opened behind her. Startled, she swung around.

"Sweet sugar ... dammit!" she cried as the delicate leaf slipped from her grasp and shattered on the hard floor.

Brandon Michaels filled the doorway. "Sorry if I surprised you. I tried to call but no one answered the phone. I hadn't seen Gregg in a while, so thought I'd drive on out to the farm." He flashed her his boyish grin, "I understand congratulations are in order. Can't say I didn't give it the old college try."

"Thank you, Brandon," Liz said, stepping over the broken glass as she skirted her worktable and made her way toward the door. "Gregg and Mallory both have Wednesday evening classes, so he rode into Bowling Green with her—which is why his truck is still in the driveway."

"Looks like it's going to be a beautiful evening," Brandon said. He was dressed in khaki pants with a yellow short-sleeved button-down shirt that accented his tan. Liz wondered, not for the first time, why this extraordinarily handsome man would be interested in her—and why she had never been able to reciprocate his interest.

"It sure is. Wish I had time to enjoy it, but I have this project I'm working on ..." Liz hedged.

"Another time, perhaps ..." His smile seemed tinged with regret. "Just tell Gregg to give me a call when he wants to break out the chess set again!"

As Brandon walked toward his Miata, Liz noticed the first hues of sunset across the western horizon. She closed the studio door against his intrusion, released a sigh of annoyance, and grabbed the broom to sweep up the broken glass.

I don't know what I'd do if Gregg wasn't such a big help with the garden, Liz thought, as she arched her back and stretched. She had finished David's window, as well as a half-dozen suncatchers for the Country Ladies. She sighed worrying about Tatiana, then smiled thinking about the weekend ahead.

David and Tatiana had reached a compromise on the phone the night before. As David told Liz when he stopped by earlier in the day, he convinced Tatiana that Liz needed to be with her now *and* Tatiana admitted having her mother visit would be a comfort. Her two caveats were that David accompany Liz to New York *and* they wait until after Tatiana's second surgery, scheduled for Friday morning.

Liz had made a quick call to her daughter to confirm that she expected them the coming weekend, then while David drank a second cup of coffee, she phoned Amtrak. As she had explained to David, after two disastrous flights into John F. Kennedy International Airport, fraught with delays, missed connections, lost luggage, and less-than-helpful airline attendants, she opted for taking Amtrak's Lake Shore Limited to Penn Station on her trips to visit Tatiana. Liz booked the last available roomette on the train leaving Toledo at 3:20 Saturday morning.

Thursday crawled into Friday. Liz fidgeted from one room to another, waiting for news from New York. When André finally called, Tatiana was still in recovery. Though the operation had been delayed, the doctor had assured him it had gone well. She wouldn't, however, discuss the details with him until Tatiana was awake and alert.

David was at the station covering the Friday afternoon program *Ron the Don of Easy Listening* in exchange for Ron Donaldson's deejaying *Davy Jones' Locker* on Monday and Tuesday morning. Cassie had all but forbidden Liz to show up at the Country Ladies for her afternoon shift, so she had procrastinated packing until after André's call.

"I hate this!" she said to Princess 'Fraidy Cat as the gray kitten crawled out from under yet another sweater tossed onto the bed. "I just can't decide what to take! Long sleeves? Short sleeves? Should I dress up or just take casual stuff? What if it rains?"

"Meow ... *me-ow* ..." the furball protested as she shook the sweater off her long tail, took a few steps, and settled herself on a pair of white slacks before preening her ruff.

"Yes, I know," Liz said as she scooted the indignant cat off of her pants, "I shouldn't wear white after Labor Day. But I think that's *passé*. Besides, they're more of an ecru and they go well with my new top!"

Liz picked the kitten up, nuzzled the back of her neck and sighed, "Things will be okay, won't they, little girl?"

Liz carried her luggage down to the foyer, poured a glass of ice tea and took it to the patio to wait for David to finish at the studio. As she watched Peter and Neil working at the Other Place, an aging silver Cadillac slowed in front of the drive. It stopped by the mailbox with the address numbers on its post then turned to cross the bridge. Liz felt an all-too-familiar chill crawl up her spine as she rose to greet the newcomer.

An older woman with hair dyed an unnatural shade of black emerged from the driver's side carrying a brown paper sack. As she approached, Liz reassessed her initial thoughts. The woman was, perhaps more Liz's age, but her over-tanned skin and dark red lipstick gave a hard edge to her appearance.

She stopped, waiting for Liz to come closer.

"Don't know what my brother saw in you," she said. "He never said much, but I knew you were the reason he stayed. He shouldda got when the gettin' was good," she gave a derisive sniff, "but he was under the spell of those purple eyes of yours."

Liz took a step backward. "I'm not sure what this is about, but could I offer you a glass of tea, Ms. …?"

"Adele … Adele Adamson … Adele Caine Adamson …" The woman responded, without extending her hand.

"Aaron Caine's sister?"

She nodded. "He'd still be free if he hadn't tried to help you out. That's how the feds caught up with him. I told him he was a fool, but he wouldn't listen. Didn't talk much, that man. Listened even less."

Taken aback, Liz protested, "What do you mean, I'm the reason the FBI caught up with your brother? I didn't call anyone!"

"You didn't have to." Adele sighed, then looked away. "He got involved in some shady trading—c'moddities market and hedge funds and futures and stuff like that—when he lived in Chicago. Made a good bit of money, but that's why he had to leave and come here. Guess the feds were on to him then and somehow they traced him here when you dumped your corn earlier this summer—'least that's what he told me."

She thrust the bag in her hand forward. "He told me to give you this. Said it was an engagement present." She waited a few seconds before adding, "He also said for you to watch your back since he wasn't there to watch it for you."

Liz took the sack and held it against her chest with crossed arms, visibly shielding herself against Aaron Caine's sister … and his warning.

The woman stood, as though considering what to say next, then looked to the side. Tears unexpectedly rimmed her lower lids, and she wiped them with her hand, smearing black mascara across her cheeks.

"Please, sit down for a moment," Liz said, still holding the sack against her, but Aaron Caine's sister shook her head.

"He's all I have left and you've taken him from me. I told him that I heard you'd gotten engaged—that he needed to forget all about you," she sniffed. "That's when he said to give that to you. Something to remember him by, he said." Adele Adamson finished then turned abruptly and hurried back toward her car.

"But, wait," Liz called after her, "I don't understand! What did he mean when …" The slam of the car door cut off her sentence. She watched as the car backed around then pulled forward toward the bridge. "… when he said to watch my back?"

Liz gently opened the bubble-wrapped contents of the paper sack to find her monarch on the coneflower window—the one she had so carefully crafted. *What if she had misjudged Aaron Caine? What if … ?*

"We're not going to allow this Caine guy's sister or anyone else to cast a shadow on our weekend. In less than twenty-four hours you're going to be in New York City with your daughter. We'll worry about what comes after when we need to." David said on their way to the Amtrak station later that night.

"But, what if …" Liz interjected.

"No 'what if's' tonight … or this weekend. Look—there's a million stars in the sky. It's a perfect night to ride the rails!"

"So this is a roomette?" David asked as he surveyed the,

roughly, six-foot by three-foot enclosure. The Lake Shore Limited sleeper car attendant had made up the bunked beds in advance. Blue blankets enveloped thin mattresses on narrow cots.

"It's … cozy," Liz nodded. "Gregg always takes the upper bed since I'm a bit claustrophobic, but I can do it if you'd like this one," she said, sitting on the lower bunk.

David took a visual measure of the area between the upper mattress and the metal roof of the car. "Nope, if Gregg can handle it, I can. Though I don't see how he could fold himself into that tight of a space!"

They took turns stepping into the hallway while the other changed into nightclothes using the small space in their roomette allotted for standing.

Liz sat cross-legged on her cot as David closed the heavy blue curtains over the aisle windows and secured the lock on the door.

He bent over and grazed her lips, "G'nite, my love." But, as he took the first step up to the top bunk, Liz tugged on the leg of his sweatpants.

"Stay with me a while."

He smiled at her as the light from the hallway filtered in around the curtains. "I would have been disappointed if you hadn't asked."

They sat facing each other as the night sped by their window.

"I guess I'm too apprehensive about tomorrow to be tired," Liz confessed.

"Turn around," he directed.

"What?"

"Turn around."

She shifted awkwardly in the confined space until her back was toward him.

With the balls of his thumbs, he massaged the nape of her neck, gently moving down her spine while spreading this hands so that his fingers barely grazed the edge of her breasts through her modest flannel nightgown.

"Hmmm …" she purred.

He scooted toward her until her back rested against his tee-shirt. His hands roamed from her back to massage her breasts. She turned her head as he nibbled her neck, straining to reach his lips with hers.

She maneuvered around to her original direction, only this time she settled her bottom between his legs, hiking her night-gown up so she could stretch her thighs around his hips.

As they leaned toward each other, the rhythm of the train slowed.

"We must be pulling into Sandusky," David said, looking out the window at the lights beyond the tracks.

Liz captured his lips with hers. She tilted her chin back, but left her forehead against his. "I don't think they can see in—and if they can … well, too bad about them …"

David laughed as he scooted down, pulling her on top of him.

"These bunks aren't as small as they look when you first see them," David said as he cradled Liz against him.

"Oh, but I think they are," Liz said as she rubbed at a kink in her neck.

"Wait, let me get that," David said as he began to massage beneath her hand.

"Oh no … this is where we started last night," Liz said as she carefully turned toward him. "It's a good thing there isn't much floor to fall on, or I think I would have been there!"

"Maybe getting a roomette so you could rest wasn't such a good idea," he chuckled into her hair. "You might have gotten more sleep in coach."

They arrived at Penn Station at 6:25 p.m., slightly ahead of schedule. They retrieved their checked bags and as they left the station, were approached by a man in a frayed jeans jacket offering to help with their luggage.

"Cab?" Liz nodded and the stranger took the larger suitcases to a waiting yellow taxi. As he lifted the luggage into the trunk, Liz pressed a ten-dollar bill into his hand.

"Bless you, ma'am," he said as he opened the back door of the cab.

Liz gave the cabbie the address for the hotel where Tatiana had reserved them a room.

"Okay," David said, grabbing Liz's arm as the cab driver threaded a slot that appeared too small for a bicycle, "this is where I admit I've never been to New York City before. This is insane!" Taxi horns blared as cabs swapped lanes with one another barely dodging fenders.

"It's just like in the movies!" David grinned, "Look, there's Times Square!"

"I've only been down here a few times myself," Liz confessed. "Tat lived in Brooklyn while she was going to school. She and André moved into an apartment on the Upper West Side when they moved back from France."

The cabbie drove up Broadway, stopping in front of a tall gray stone building. David paid the fare and the driver unloaded their bags. As they turned around, André emerged from gilded double doors, pushing a luggage cart.

The lobby of the stately old hotel had been refurbished to an understated elegance. David completed the registration, while Liz and André waited in silence amidst the royal purple velvet and gold-trimmed furnishings. They stashed their bags in their room and freshened up, before walking with André to his and Tatiana's apartment, just a few blocks away.

He led them to a tall, narrow red brick building where a doorman greeted André and welcomed Liz and David to New York, before summoning the elevator.

André opened the door to an airy third-floor apartment. The few walls within were all painted pure white. Woven black and white patterned area rugs graced gleaming hardwood flooring. Sparse, blocky white furniture with midnight black accents gave Liz the sense of having stepped into a painting she had seen in the Museum of Modern Art on her first trip to the city. Tatiana, reclining on black cushions on a white wrought iron chaise lounge in a flowing black and white harlequin-patterned caftan, provided the focal point for the painting.

She smiled at her mother but didn't attempt to get up. "Do you like it?"

Liz glanced around the apartment before answering, "It's a complete 180 from what I am used to, but yes, yes I do—it fits you and André well."

She walked to where her daughter lay, sat down on the black cushion beside her, and gently rubbed the back of her slender hand. "How are you?"

"Well, yesterday's surgery, thank heaven, went much better than the first. The surgeon has assured me they got a clear margin around the tumor. She took fourteen lymph nodes and they were all clean. So, as soon as I heal, they'll put in a port for my chemo. Then radiation, and this will be history!"

Tears welled in Liz's eyes. David had followed her to the chaise, and she leaned back against him as he laid his hand on her shoulder.

"Chemo! I can't bear the thought of your going through all of that! Your beautiful hair!"

"Yep," Tatiana said, almost blithely, "I'll be balder than a bowling ball! My friends are going to throw a chemo kick-off party before I start treatments and all wear wigs! I think it's a gas! And I've already talked to so many women—you wouldn't believe the people I know who have gone through this and beat it years ago!"

Liz smiled at her daughter, "You always were the resilient one. Leave it to you to grab even this and embrace it with open arms." She hugged Tatiana gently.

"Now tell me what's going on with my little brother and the library lady who's got him twisted in knots!"

The sweet corn patch had played out and the pumpkins were

turning from green to orange as summer eased into fall. Leaves skittered about Liz's feet when she carried a basket of large red beets in from the garden. She heard Desert Pro neigh from the barn, reminding her that it had been too long since she had tended to more than his basic needs.

"Sorry, boy," she said, "If I can't fit in more time to work with you, we may have to find you a new home."

She noticed, again, Brandon's Miata parked beside Gregg's pickup. *Hope that boy's not supposed to be helping Neil*, she thought before reminding herself it was not her problem. Gregg and Brandon had fallen into playing chess at odd times of the day or evening over the past few weeks. Liz noticed that Mallory, too, appeared annoyed about the lieutenant's reemergence in Gregg's life. David had also mentioned Brandon's presence when he stopped by earlier in the week. Liz had assured him that Gregg's seeming preoccupation with the man would pass of its own accord.

...And I hope soon, Liz thought as she tucked the beets in the trunk beside the butternut squash and other vegetables she had gathered. She checked the box filled with suncatchers she had laid on the backseat to ensure it would not shift on the short drive to Country Ladies, backed her Mustang around and drove forward past the black sports car.

"I have to admit, I'm not much of a baseball fan," Mallory said, "but these are great seats!"

"There isn't a bad seat in the stadium," Gregg replied. "I like watching the Tigers, but next year I'm taking you to a Toledo Mud Hens game. Of course, with the new Fifth Third Stadium, it's not like it used to be. Dad and I watched the Mud Hens play in the old Skeldon field at least once or twice a year. The teams had to walk from the clubhouse through the crowds to get to the ball field. You wouldn't believe the autographs I got!"

"Mud Hens! Where did Toledo get that name for its baseball team?"

"I think birds called mud hens actually lived in the Great

Black Swamp before all my ancestors drained it." Gregg took Mallory's hand in his. "But, yeah, sitting in the tenth row behind home plate gives you a pretty good view of the game. I can't believe Brandon won tickets to the last Tiger's game of the season, then gave them to us!"

"I guess ..." Mallory nodded as the batter struck out below her vantage point. "What period are we in now? How long does the game last?"

"Inning ... it's inning, not period. It's the top of the sixth, so there's three-and-a-half to go."

Mallory sat quietly for a while longer then said, "There's something I need to tell you."

Gregg turned his attention from the batter to Mallory.

"Things Brandon has said ... just didn't seem right," she said. "So I had an ROTC friend call the Air National Guard in Toledo. She spoke with someone at the 180th Fighter Wing ..." She took a breath and looked at Gregg, "There's no Lt. Brandon Michaels stationed there. They've never heard of him."

"What? Why didn't you say something earlier?"

"We just made the call yesterday ... and I didn't know how you would react. You seem to be so close to him. I was trying to figure out a way to tell you that the man you look up to is a fake."

Gregg shifted in his seat, braced his elbows on his thighs and hung his clasped hands between his knees. He stared ahead then looked back toward Mallory. "That confirms it. I've been trying to add up the stories he's been telling. For one thing, he claims to be an F-16 pilot, but he sure doesn't know much about flying." Mallory leaned forward and looked at Gregg, "Is your mom with David?"

Gregg nodded, "They went to the art museum for the afternoon. Then they were taking advantage of our being gone and Mom was going to fix dinner for David at home—Why?"

"Remember what Aaron Caine's sister said to your mom?" Mallory asked, "You think Brandon may have given us the tickets to get us out of the way?"

Gregg's eyes widened with understanding, "Oh God, No!"

CHAPTER FOURTEEN

Gregg punched the number for the farm into his phone. "C'mom, Mom, pick it up!" he pleaded. When the answering machine message came on, he hit Liz's cell number. It rolled over to the voice mail without ringing. "Great. She's either on her cell or has it turned off. Do you have David's number?"

"Not with me. My cell died after I dropped it in the dishwater yesterday. Do you think we should call the sheriff?"

"I don't know—what do we say? Everything we have is circumstantial. We can talk about what to do on the way home. Let's get out of here!"

He watched the white sports car pull into the driveway and adjusted his binoculars in an attempt to see the people inside. She's probably throwing herself all over him. Well, the bastard had better get his fill of her honey now, because he's not going to have time later. I'll let them get cozy before I make my entrance. He patted the gun in his shoulder holster as he leaned back to wait.

"I didn't think we'd be at the museum so late," Liz said as she unlocked the foyer door. "I need to get dinner on."

The little gray princess met them at the door, begging for food. Liz flipped on the switch for the kitchen light and walked to the mudroom. She measured fish-shaped kibbles into the kitten's bowl and bent to pet her appreciative ward before crossing the room to the sink to wash her hands.

David came up behind her and she turned into the shelter of his arms. His lips met hers as his hands wandered from her rounded bottom to the curvature of her breasts.

"So Gregg and Mallory are off for the evening," he said with a quiet intimacy.

Her smoky velvet eyes answered him as she said, "Thanks to Brandon."

"It may be a short game—perhaps we could … have dinner later?"

"I have a lasagna in the fridge. Let me get it in the oven first or it will be midnight before we eat."

David leaned his back against the counter and folded his arms against his chest, watching the woman he would marry as she busied herself about the kitchen.

"Nice …" he said as she bent over to check the oven before turning it on.

"David Morales, you are incorrigible!" She stood to face him as he closed the distance between them.

"Dare you to do that again," he said, giving a lewd lift to his eyebrows.

"Absolutely incorrigible," she repeated as she took the last step that separated them. Their melding of lips left them gasping for shared air.

"I'll never get this lasagna in if you keep this up," she said with a quiet quiver in her voice.

She placed the Pyrex baking dish in the oven and set it to a low temperature. "Now where were we?" she asked with a coy smile.

As she stepped into David's arms, the phone rang.

"Don't answer it," David said with a soft breath into her ear.

It rang again, and Liz reached for the receiver, but David caught her hand, bringing her fingers to his lips.

It rang a third time and Liz lifted the phone from its cradle just long enough to disconnect the call and lay the receiver on the table.

They eased into the dining room as David began to undo the snaps of the soft lavender sweater that clung to his fiancé's breasts, revealing inch-by-inch the creamy skin underneath.

She stayed his hands, pausing on their way to the stairwell and tugged the tail of his shirt from his jeans. She slowly released its buttons, letting her hands freely roam the thin sleeveless cotton undershirt beneath.

"You are so incredibly sexy, do you know that David Morales?"

"Only if you say so, beautiful woman!"

As he unfastened another snap, he heard an unmistakable click behind him. He turned slowly as Brandon Michaels stepped into the room from the kitchen with a small pistol in his hand.

"Brandon! Oh my God! ... No!" Liz cried out.

He toyed with the gun then pointed it at them. "Not yet ... eventually, but not yet. I was enjoying the little show you were giving me. I wouldn't mind seeing more ... of you, not of your Latin lover."

To David, he said, "Go ahead, finish what you started."

David faced Liz and whispered, "I'm so sorry, *güerita mía*, but we need to buy time." He undid each button at a painstakingly deliberate pace, and when he reached the final enclosure, he turned toward his nemesis.

"Now step aside."

David did as he was told.

"Come here," the gunman ordered Liz.

She walked slowly toward him, her face impassive but for the revulsion that turned her eyes to a dark purple.

He aimed the pistol toward David as he reached behind her to unclasp her bra.

Liz flinched at his touch and instinctively tilted her head back to spit in his face as it loomed above her. He drew his hand back to slap her when David lunged at him from the side. Brandon pushed Liz away and using his pistol as a whip, brought it hard across David's chest. He collapsed, blood seeping against his white undershirt.

Liz dropped to where David lay, cradling him against her.

"Your boyfriend will be fine ... for the time being."

Liz looked up to the face of the man her son had befriended. The deceptively boyish grin had hardened to a malevolent sneer.

"Why don't you pour us a little wine, babycakes, while we have a talk. That is, I'll talk—you listen."

The gunman nudged David with the toe of his black leather loafer as he pointed the pistol at him. "Get up. You can sit over there." He pointed to a chair on the right side of the table.

Wine? Liz thought as she moved slowly around the table. As she focused on the man in the photograph on the buffet, she prayed, *Help us, Mack! Oh God, please help us!* She opened the side compartment of the buffet, moved aside a merlot and a pinot noir, and drew out the last two bottles of a more potent port Mack had kept on hand for special occasions.

She opened the first bottle and poured the burgundy liquid into three glasses, putting the larger brandy snifter in front of Brandon Michaels, who had taken the chair at the head of the table.

"Now, sit there, across from your Latin loverboy."

As Liz lowered herself onto the designated chair, the lieutenant swirled the wine in his glass awkwardly with his right hand, while resting his left on his pistol, then tipped the snifter to his lips, taking a long swallow.

"You called Liz 'babycakes.'" David said, a slow awareness dawning, "That's what Tiffany Crystal's boyfriend called her the night she was killed. Over and over again ... 'babycakes.' She winced each time she heard it."

Brandon Michaels arched one eyebrow as he continued to sip his port.

"He was left-handed, too. Damn, I thought there was something familiar about you. You're Michael Thornton—I'll remember that name until the day I die. But the hair ... the eyes ... you're taller ..."

"Yeah, well, looks like you won't have to remember the name
for long." He caressed the barrel of the gun before shifting his
gaze to Liz. "It's Michael Brandon Thornton, to be precise." Then,
to David, he said, "And it's amazing what can be done with a little
cosmetology and lifts. When you didn't show any signs of recog-
nizing me when her kid," nodding toward Liz, "introduced us I
knew I had pulled it off."

"But why?" Liz asked. "Why me?"

"Because you were screwing him. I'd been watching him for
a few weeks waiting ... just waiting." He lifted his glass, draining
it. Liz rose and refilled the snifter, leaving the near empty bottle
beside their assailant.

"Revenge can be a powerful motivator," Michael Thornton
said, as he looked from the wine to Liz. He smiled as he tipped the
glass to his lips, "I had time ... lots of time. And money, thanks to
my father's, shall we say, untimely passing." He watched the port
as he swirled it around in the snifter, and smirked, "He was the
doctor who gave me my new look. Couldn't let him hang around
afterward, now could I?"

He laughed—a dry, sinister sound—as Liz's hand flew to
her mouth.

"I saw you leave with him," Thornton nodded toward David,
"from that Mexican bar that night. What better way to get back at
the bastard who ruined my life than to stick it to his broad. And
I will, too, before the night's over." He pointed his gun in David's
direction. "Maybe I'll even arrange it so you can watch."

David leaned half out of his seat toward the man at the end
of the table, but quickly sat back down when Thornton shifted his
gun toward Liz.

"What I don't understand," David said, clasping his hands on
the table in front of him, "is why kill Tiffany? She was harmless."

The gunman emptied the bottle of port into his glass and
motioned for Liz to bring him the second.

"She left with you that night. I loved that piece of ass and she chose to go with *you*."

David shook his head, "Unbelievable. You're so stupid you couldn't see that she was just using me to get to you? You treated her like crap. All she wanted was a little attention from you … besides calling her 'babycakes' when you wanted her to fetch something for you."

David clenched his fists on the table, "I walked her to her door—I only went in the room long enough to make sure she made it to her bed, then left."

"You're lying. She said you drilled her good. She told me all about how big …" Michael Thronton gripped the gun handle and pointed the barrel at David. "Tell me you're lying, you bastard!"

David locked eyes with Liz and mouthed, *I love you,* while waiting for the trigger click.

Instead, Thornton laid the gun back on the table, picked up his glass, and again drained it. He slowly opened the remaining bottle of port, filled the snifter to within a half-inch of the top, and brought it to his lips before setting it abruptly down, sloshing the wine onto the crocheted tablecloth.

"What'd you do with my money? You stole fifty grand from me. All the money I had. I had plans for that dough. You musta' walked away with a bundle that night! I knew that other broad took it. I knew I shouldn't have trusted her. Well, she got hers, too." He picked the glass up and tipped it high, letting a trickle of wine drip down his chin.

"Brittanie didn't take my winnings. By the time she came to my place I had wired it back to my sister in Ohio. Same's I did with most of the money I made at the casinos." David gave a slight shake to his head and took his first sip of the port. It burnt going down, feeling good but reminding him of why he gave up drinking that night in Vegas. He pushed the glass back and dropped his hands to his lap. "What did she slip into my drink that night? I don't remember much except her coming on top of me." He glanced up at Liz, "Sorry, love."

"Doesn't matter," Thornton said. "She came back with an

empty wallet."

"So you beat the hell out of her and blamed it on me. Then you planted my billfold in Tiffany's room."

"Easy enough to do," Michael Thornton said, his words slurring slightly. "Just didn't plan on her having a conscience—or the guts to come out with the truth. Wouldn't've happened if you didn't get that hotshot lawyer sniffing around. You must've promised her a good lay …"

David shot him a look of disgust. "Is it so hard for you to believe there are actually some decent people in this world?"

Liz cocked her head and glanced up at David, who gave her a slight nod that he had heard the sound.

"Yeah, well, see where it got her. The cops are still lookin' for me and she's wearing a 'Jane Doe' toe tag." He gave another sinister snort as he tipped his glass to his lips and took a long drink, before sitting the empty snifter back on the table and refilling it.

Princess 'Fraidy Cat poked her head in from the kitchen, paused as she passed by the foyer and looked up. She meowed loudly when she saw the man at the end of the table, started back toward the kitchen then glanced over toward Liz. She looked back toward the man, meowed again, then giving him wide berth, carefully padded her way to her mistress.

As Liz bent to scoop up her kitten, she glared at Michael Thornton, "You slaughtered the kittens! God, you are a sick, perverted man!"

"You don't know the half of it, babycakes. I couldn't count the hours I spent watching you, parked in that place down the road."

A chill traveled Liz's spine, "You chased me in the woods …" She looked across the table at the man who had been her rescuer. "I'm so sorry, David!"

Thornton gave a short laugh, "Could've had you so easily that night. Thought about it, but the timing wasn't right …"

"I almost had me a tasty little morsel with the blond kid that lives with those dykes who work at that shop with you."

"Good Lord, how …?" Liz gasped.

"I'd seen her plenty of times at the *Country Ladies*," he said, giving a sarcastic emphasis to the store's name. "I just happened to be in the shopping center when I saw the tall redhead with the kid. Wouldn't have minded teaching her what it's like to be with a real man, but figured taking the kid would give me some fun."

"And I blamed Crenshaw," Liz said.

"The weaselly little ex-sheriff? He was so full of himself. When I saw him at that party you had down the road and didn't invite me to, I figured he'd come in handy. It was easy to become his friend. Just had to supply him with enough booze. When he showed me his pride and joy—the AK-47 he'd been hiding from the law, it didn't take much to talk him into shooting up your house after your little barbeque."

"Then you killed him."

"He needed a bath—the man had an aversion to water. I just helped him get over it … Guess he'd had a little too much to drink to swim …"

He dripped the port down the edge of his glass as he again filled it to the brim and leaned back against his chair, tipping it slightly. "Now, Lizzie girl, I've waited a long time to see what you're hiding. Spill it out so the boyfriend can get one last look before I blow his brains away."

As Michael Thornton waved the pistol carelessly into the air, Liz and David grabbed the edge of the tablecloth and gave a sharp tug, sending the glass of port tumbling onto the unsuspecting gunman's lap. He knocked his already off-balance chair backward in his haste to avoid the wine, firing the pistol into the air on his way down. Sheriff Moran rushed into the room, dodged the falling chair, and slammed his foot down on the gunman's wrist as he landed on the floor.

"I'll take that," Moran said as he bent down to grab the pistol from Thornton's hand, then to Liz and David, "You two okay?"

"We are now," Liz said. "How did you know?"

"Your son called the station when he saw this guy's car in the drive. He and his girlfriend had started piecing things together. They figured this Michaels guy gave them the game tickets to get them out of the way. With all that's happened out here, we didn't question his story."

Liz was fastening the last snap on her sweater when Mallory and Gregg ran through the door.

"We heard a gunshot!" Gregg looked over to his mother, safely tucked in David's arm then to Michael Thornton as he was being dragged to his feet. "God, I am so sorry. How could I have been so blind? I was so worried about David, and I'm the one who brought this jerk to our house!"

"Don't blame yourself," David said. "I'm the one who endangered your mom. But it's all over now. I trust, with what the sheriff heard and the details we can fill in, this slimeball will be put away for a long time."

EPILOGUE

Four years later...

Liz swayed gently in the porch swing of the house she and David had just built. She shelled peas she had picked that morning from her garden across the road and nudged a rocker on the wooden cradle at her feet with her toe. She smiled as she watched Mallory and Gregg move box after box of their belongings from a U-Haul truck into the McAlister homestead, while Princess 'Fraidy Cat stalked a robin as it hopped across the newly seeded yard in between the porch and the road.

The baby fussed and she lifted her grandson from his nest of blankets. "Gramma's so happy to have her baby moving home. Just think, you'll be right next door where I can spoil you all I want!" The tiny round face that peered back at her cooed and gurgled, waving his skinny little arms about. Liz pulled the newborn tight against her shoulder, covering the baby with a bright yellow receiving blanket adorned with cute brown bunnies.

At one month old, David Mack Miguel McAlister was just discovering the world. He had yet to learn of the legacy that surrounded him. Liz shifted the bowl of shelled peas off her lap, resting it in the old aluminum roaster filled with peapods on the swing beside her, before lowering the babe to her thighs.

She heard her other two grandchildren before she saw them.

"I can read that book to you, Anacita—really, I can!

Joshua James, an impetuous seven-year-old, came running up the porch steps. "Gramma Liz, Anacita doesn't think I can read chapter books yet, and I'm almost through first grade!

"Ohhh … I didn't know little Davy was here! He's so cute!" The boy moved the pan of peapods to the floor and gently slipped onto the swing beside Liz.

"There's room for you on my other side, Anacita," Liz offered.

"I'm so glad Uncle Gregg and Aunt Mallory are going to live in your old house," Anacita said as she let her little step-cousin wrap his hand around her finger. "I was afraid they would stay in C'lumbus."

"Me, too," Liz said. Gregg had moved to the state capital after being accepted into the graduate program in Food, Agricultural, and Biological Engineering at Ohio State University. The following December, he and Mallory, a master's student in Kent State University's Library and Information Sciences program, had driven to Texas to meet her family. They had even chanced crossing the border to meet her father in the outskirts of Nuevo Laredo—the first time Mallory had seen him since his deportation as an illegal fourteen years before. Prior to their return to the states, Greggory McAlister requested and received Miguel Martínez' blessing to marry his daughter.

"And Aunt Tatiana and Uncle André will be home next week! It's going to be such fun," the girl said.

"Yes, yes it is," Liz agreed. "Now, Joshua James, are you going to show me how well you can read?"

As the boy eased over the words, with only a modicum of help from his big sister, Tatiana slipped into Liz's thoughts. She understood how difficult it would be for Tatiana and André to meet their tiny nephew. Liz had gone to New York City after her daughter's second miscarriage in January, just six weeks before Davy's birth. Through genetic testing, they found out both the baby and Tatiana carried a chromosomal deficiency. Liz underwent the same test with the same results—family genetics, and not lead poisoning, had caused her own miscarriages. That she had carried two babies to term was the true miracle. Liz smiled, remembering a phone call with Tatiana a month or so back—rather than dwell on the test results, she was choosing to celebrate her fourth cancer-free year.

"Gramma, are you listening?" Joshua James asked with impatience.

"Yes, Gramma, are you listening?" David repeated his grandson's question as he opened the screen door from the house.

"Granpa, I didn't know you were home!"

"I was taking a nap, but it sounded like you were having too much fun without me!"

As the station manager, David had been up half the night after a transformer blew. Fortunately, the technicians managed to get the station operational before the weekend sports broadcasts.

He stooped down in front of the swing, lifting his newest grandchild from his wife's legs.

"Climb on my lap, Joshua James," Liz said, "then we can make room for your grandpa on the swing, too."

"I have a surprise for you," David whispered into Liz's ear.

"A surprise? What is it?" Anacita asked, as her grandfather settled down between her and her Grandma Liz.

David cradled little Davy in his right arm while resting his left across the back of the swing. Liz leaned her head against the familiar cushion of his shoulder, "Yes, what is it?" she echoed.

"The contractors who did the house have agreed to build a studio to the exact specifications of the old cob shed right outside the back door."

"David! After the house went over-budget, I didn't want to ask about a studio … thank you!" She kissed his cheek, but he shifted his head so that their lips met.

They broke apart to see all three of their grandchildren, as well as plump gray and white furball, watching them.

Liz laughed as she said, "I'll have to call Cassie to ask her to leave room for my suncatchers at the Country Ladies, after all!"

"But first, Gramma, you have to listen to the rest of my story!"

the end

ACKNOWLEDGEMENTS:

Thank you so very much to all of the readers of *Only in the Movies* for your feedback and support. Your letters, e-mails, facebook messages, and in-person praise often came just when I needed them most! I am honored when you say you have shared my book with another.

Words fail to express my gratitude to my initial editor, encourager-in-chief, consultant, and life partner, Chris. You are the best!

To Sascha Instone: Once again, you took my rough idea for a cover and painted a watercolor that was beyond my imagination. Your early support of my manuscript gave me the confidence to go on.

To Andrea Knight and Bigelow Glass, Findlay, OH: I cannot thank you enough for allowing me to shadow you and experience your studio and shop firsthand. You rock!

To Debra Nicholson: My wonderful writing partner! Your suggestions were invaluable, as is your friendship. You are a gifted writer and teacher.

To Kelli Kling: My marketing and technical consultant—without you, I would no longer have hair! You do so ably what I cannot!

To Laura Tolkow: You received a painting and gave me a cover. You received a manuscript and gave me a book. I am, once again, indebted to your book designing skills.

To Ruth Josimovich: I am so fortunate to have you as my editor. Your recommendations are on the mark, and your suggestions encourage me to move beyond what I think is possible.

To Wendy Spencer Geist: Your thorough copyediting was priceless. Thank you so much! (And, thank you, Jude, for keeping the boys occupied!)

In addition, I am indebted to the following readers who gave of their time and expertise, making crucial comments (and/or catching crucial glitches) to improve *Only on the Radio*: Andrea Knight, Anne Tracy, Beth Hofer, Carol Erickson, Jaye Westfall, Jorge Betancourt, Mardi Losoya Rush, and September Kuebler, as well as my proofreader extraordinaire, Kris Eridon.

A special thank you to Denise Feasby for sharing her knowledge of Kelleys Island and for keeping us supplied with lattes and scones at *Rock, Baker, Sippers* during our visits to the Island!

Again, many thanks to Penguin Dave Feldman, author of the *Imponderables* series for your inspiration and to Jack Estes of Pleasure Boat Studio for your endless patience answering questions about publishing.

As always, I owe a huge debt of gratitude to the Doobie Social Club for all the years of friendship and support—from Kelleys to Key West. You are family! And to TNG, Jill Diedrich for your introduction to Bubbies Homemade Ice Cream and other Turkey Day treats.

To my gal pals from PHS—love you!

And last but not least, to my feline inspirations: Alien and Buffy. We miss you, our princess and big guy!

JAG

JAG with Alien AKA Princess 'Fraidy Cat

AUTHOR'S NOTE:

From the peaks of Denali to Florida's Everglades – the skyscrapers of New York City to Utah's red rock canyons – the rugged coast of Oregon to South Carolina's sandy beaches – no matter where the road took us, it always led back to where my heart calls home—the glaciated flatlands of Northwest Ohio.

Inspired by years working with the vast collections at Bowling Green State University's renowned Browne Popular CultureLibrary, three years ago I began another journey – to create a world of characters, plant them in the fertile fields of my homeland, and nurture them into the award-winning novel *Only in the Movies*.

Only on the Radio expands this world, bringing back old friends and introducing new acquaintances with their own stories to tell. I invite you to travel with David and Liz as they trek through the nooks and crannies of Ohio's north coast.

Jean Ann Geist

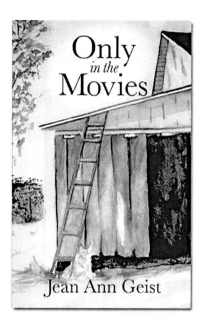

A shattered princess, a reluctant hero, a Machiavellian villain— a story of romantic intrigue woven through the reels of the Silver Screen.

Only in the Movies

First place winner for book-length fiction, 2012 Ohio Professional Writers Communication Contest

Now available on Kindle and Nook
ISBN: 978-0-578-06961-6 (pbk)

JAG with Buffy — the inspiration for Slack-Eyed Joe in *Only in the Movies*

CPSIA information can be obtained at www.ICGtesting.com
Printed in the USA
BVOW040459010713

324527BV00007B/17/P